PRODIGAL DAUGHTER

She must return to face the scandal she caused...

At the end of the war, Sara Boskelly joined thousands of other young women on the long journey to America hoping to be reunited with the handsome GI who had captured her heart. Sadly, the voyage was to end in bitter disappointment and Sara has to return to her native Cornwall and make her peace with Robbie Killaine, but she hasn't reckoned on Miriam Roche, his new love, who is determined to hold on to her man, whatever it takes...

The publishers hope that this book has given you enjoyable reading. Large Print Books are especially designed to be as easy to see and hold as possible. If you wish a complete list of our books please ask at your local library or write directly to:

Magna Large Print Books
Magna House, Long Preston,
Skipton, North Yorkshire.
BD23 4ND

PRODIGAL DAUGHTER

Prodigal Daughter

by

Rachel Moore

Magna Large Print Books
Long Preston, North Yorkshire,
BD23 4ND, England.

British Library Cataloguing in Publication Data.

Moore, Rachel
Prodigal daughter.

A catalogue record of this book is available from the British Library

ISBN 978-0-7505-2734-7

First published in Great Britain by Simon & Schuster 2007

Published in Large Print 2007 by arrangement with Simon & Schuster UK Ltd.

Magna Large Print is an imprint of Library Magna Books Ltd.

Printed and bound in Great Britain by
T.J. (International) Ltd., Cornwall, PL28 8RW

Chapter 1

Sara Boskelly stepped off the late afternoon bus with a huge feeling of apprehension, hardly aware of how deeply she was inhaling the tangy salt air of St Ives. Once she had caught her breath, she took in everything at a glance: the shimmering blue sea in the curving harbour, the colourful fishing boats, the hotch-potch of houses and shops in the maze of irregular narrow streets, the plaintive cries of sea-birds wheeling overhead as they swooped for a taste of the fishermen's catch ... and it was all instantly familiar. She was home.

'Lord help us, it's young Sara, isn't it?' a voice beside her said. 'Sara Boskelly. Heard you was settled in America for good, and you've only been gone little more 'n a year by my reckoning. Summat up, is it, my dear?'

Sara turned with an imperceptible sigh. Of all the people to see her first, one of the town's busybodies was the last person she would have chosen. She gave a forced smile to Mrs Goode, noting the woman's shabby make-do-and-mend coat, a constant reminder of the war years, and felt over-conscious of her own stylish clothes. She may not have had the best time in America – and *that* was an understatement, if anything was – but she had kept herself clean and decent.

'Nothing's up, Mrs Goode. I'm just here to see my mum and dad.'

'Oh, just for a visit, then, is it?' the woman said, her gimlet eyes missing nothing, including the heavy suitcase. "'Tis a long way to come for a coupla days.'

'I'll have to make the most of it then, won't I?' Sara said, telling her nothing.

But the woman wasn't prepared to let her go yet. If there was any gossip to be told, then Bessie Goode was the one to ferret it out. She was known for it.

'I saw your mum in the town the other day. She never said nothing about you coming home. Bit of a surprise for her and your dad, is it?'

Sara's voice was strained, despite her attempt to sound normal. 'I daresay she wanted to keep it a surprise from everyone else. I'd better get on now, or she'll wonder what's happened to me.'

She managed to break away at last, before there were more questions asked about the handsome GI whom Sara had travelled across the Atlantic Ocean to join, along with dozens more excited GI brides, some of whom were already married, some with babies in their arms, and others, like herself, with just a promise.

Her mother wouldn't wonder what had happened to her today, either, since her mother didn't even know she was home, back in Cornwall where she belonged. Sara managed to subdue the small sob in her throat, lifting her head up high the way she had learned to do in this last painful year. What her mum and dad were going to say when they saw her again she wouldn't think. She prayed that the guesthouse the family owned would be busy when she arrived, and then there wouldn't be a scene – at least, not in public.

She was well aware that Mrs Goode was watching her as she walked swiftly along the street and down the steep Tregenna Hill towards the town. It was a long walk, and the suitcase was getting heavier by the minute, but not for a second was she going to admit what an ordeal this was for her. She tossed back her coppery hair, trying not to let her eyes blur as all the well-remembered sights came into view, and braced herself. She hadn't come all this way, by sea and train and bus, to lose her nerve because of a gossipy old woman. Anyway, what had she expected? That people would have forgotten her and the scandal that had surrounded her? No-one had any right to call it a scandal, anyway. When could falling in love ever be considered a scandal?

Only when it was with the wrong man, a voice whispered inside her head, and only when you let down the one who always believed you were his girl.

She gave a small shiver. It was one thing going home to her mum and dad. She was sure they would get over the shock once they had got used to the situation, fingers crossed, and love her as they had always done. It was something else to think about Robbie, and she wasn't going to think about him now. One step at a time. But it wouldn't have made her any more comfortable if she'd heard the conversation between Mrs Goode and one of her cronies a little later.

'She's back with her tail between her legs if you ask me, although she looked pretty flash in her smart American jacket and her smart green frock. There's not much of a utility problem over there by the looks of it,' she added with a sniff.

'She was always a headstrong girl,' the other woman said, nodding sagely. 'I mind very well when she had her head turned by one of them Yanks, and never mind who she trod over in the process.'

'For all that, she were always a nicely-mannered girl,' Mrs Goode said sternly, not prepared to condemn Sara completely. 'Even if she was a bit too nice for her own good when it came to romancing. And she never corrected me when I called her by her maiden name. Any newly-married woman would have done so, and I didn't see no sign of a wedding ring on her finger, so summat's definitely gone wrong there, you mark my words.'

The modest Boskelly guesthouse stood on a small promontory on the edge of town, virtually creating a little island community of its own. It overlooked the sea, which made it such a draw to the upcountry visitors who were coming down to Cornwall in greater numbers now that the long war years were over. Many of them were the evacuees from the cities who had been obliged to stay for five years, and two years after the end of the war they were now eager for their families to explore the places they had known, and to meet the families who had cared for them.

The war had clearly had some benefits if it brought this kind of business to the town. And St Ives, especially, was the most breathtakingly beautiful place. Sara had known it all her life, yet it could still take her by surprise with its hidden corners and beautiful bays, and especially the crystal clear light that drew artists and potters and sculptors like a magnet, and with it a thriving artistic community.

Robbie Killaine was one of those. When they were school children Sara had always teased him that he could do magical things with a paintbrush and a pot of paint. She had stopped teasing when he began to sell his paintings, and eventually opened a little shop and studio right near the harbour. It was a kind of magic to be able to bring something to life on canvas, she thought. He had promised to paint her in oils one day – her with her glorious pre-Raphaelite hair (according to Robbie) and eyes the colour of green jade – but he never had, as far as she knew. There were just the pencil sketches he'd done of her at school, which she had never quite been able to throw away.

His image was so clear in her mind then that she felt as though she could almost reach out and touch him. The short, wavy brown hair that was nearly the same colour as his eyes; the sensual mouth ... and the broad shoulders that so belied his disability. He was a man in every way, to his sensitive, artistic fingertips.

She realised she was doing exactly what she had been determined not to do. Robbie wasn't the reason she had come back. She doubted that he'd want to see her again anyway, after she'd fallen for the charismatic GI who had stormed into her life and promised her the earth. It was too late by the time she had discovered that it was no more than a pie-crust promise ... easily made and easily broken.

There had always been a certain amount of antagonism between the local boys and the GIs in their smart uniforms who had come to the area for their training and been such charmers as far as the girls were concerned. It must have been especially galling for someone like Robbie, knowing he wouldn't be called up on account of being slightly lame in one leg, the legacy of polio when he was a child.

Sara tried to push him out of her mind, but it was near impossible to do so with all the memories crowding back. Perhaps it hadn't been such a wonderful idea to come back without any warning after all, she thought uneasily, no matter how much Cornwall and home had drawn her back.

By the time she reached the promontory her thoughts had become so jumbled that the yapping of a dog startled her, and then the pooch was leaping joyously around her feet. She dropped her suitcase thankfully and knelt down on the soft springy turf, laughing helplessly as the dog smothered her with sloppy kisses.

'Bonzer, you mad old rascal. You must have known I was coming, and you're the best thing I've seen yet. Come on then, let's go and face the music.'

It gave her a reassuring glow to know that at least the family dog was glad to see her back. Maybe it was a good sign – and maybe it wasn't. Her old Aunt Dottie, long deceased, and as batty as her name, would certainly have thought so. But then, Aunt Dottie had seen signs and omens in everything, full moons and new moons, morning mist on the sea or the moors, the old tin mine shafts looming up out of the gloom like monsters, the disappearance of sea-birds, the howling of a dog at night ... or anything else that took her fancy.

Sara gave a wistful smile, remembering her with a surge of affection, and wishing she could listen to more of her nonsense now, with the same rapt attention as she had done as a child. Aunt Dottie had certainly added colour to the guesthouse, and more than one visitor had gone back home with one of her spooky spine-shivering tales to tell.

Sara sighed. Those days could never come again, and people always said you could never go back, even though that was exactly what she was doing. She walked more purposefully towards the guesthouse, its extended glass-fronted conservatory overlooking the sea and forming a sun-drenched lounge area for visitors to sit and watch any activity far below, whether it was fishing-boats returning, or the occasional larger vessel making its stately way up the channel, or simply the crashing of the waves on the cliffs in one of the winter storms that battered the coastline so magnificently.

She paused for a moment, putting down the suitcase again and flexing her fingers. Whatever the season, there was always something magical and mysterious about this place, she conceded, and found herself wondering just why she had ever thought it would be so wonderful to leave it. But of course she knew that, and not for a moment was she going to demean the feelings she had had for Chesney Willand of the US

Marine Corps, nor his for her. They had been real and wonderful ... and ultimately disastrous.

Just ahead of her now she could see the open doorway of the guesthouse. On fine days, especially a day like today in midsummer, her mother always kept it open, welcoming visitors. Inside, Sara could see the large oak desk that had been her grandfather's, behind which stood a familiar figure. She was chatting to some guests, showing the couple a map, and apparently pointing out places of interest in the area. Sara's throat choked for a moment, because nothing had changed here. It was as if the last two years had been swept away in an instant, as if she had never been away at all, and she wanted to hold and capture this last sweet moment – before all hell broke loose.

Bonzer broke away from her and went leaping towards the guesthouse, as if to herald her arrival, and in that moment her mother looked up from dealing with the guests. Her hand froze a little over the map she was holding, and Sara felt the nervousness wash over her again. She should definitely have warned them she was coming, she thought desperately. She should have prepared them for all that she had to tell them. But it was too late now, and she forced her feet to move towards the open door of her old home and went inside.

The couple by the desk thanked Sara's mother for her help, smiled at the newcomer, and went out of the guesthouse. And then there was only one word Sara was capable of saying.

'Mum,' she croaked.

After what seemed like an endless moment,

Ellen Boskelly spoke, her voice as undeniably shaky as her daughter's.

'So you've come home at last. Is he with you?'

Sara bit her lip. 'Chesney's not with me, Mum. I'm on my own.'

It was heartbreakingly true in every sense, and she couldn't bear the way her mother was looking at her now, as if she had let everybody down in the reckless way she had left. She had, of course, but it was obvious that her mother couldn't miss the stark misery in her eyes, because it was only seconds before she gave a smothered exclamation and came around the desk to take Sara in her arms.

'Your father's gone to the market for fresh supplies, so let's go through to the sitting-room and have a cup of tea and then we'll talk. Leah can take over here.'

She called out to her elderly assistant who appeared from nowhere as if on cue, gaping at Sara before taking up her position behind the desk.

'Don't worry, Leah, I'm not a ghost,' Sara said with a weak smile. 'It's just the prodigal daughter returning home.'

'And it's very good to see you back home again, my dear,' the woman said, catching her breath. 'Don't you worry, I'll hold the fort here while you and your Ma chew the fat together.'

And they'd better be sure to shut the sitting-room door firmly behind them, thought Sara, because news of her homecoming would spread through the town quickly enough without Leah's sharp ears, but she needed her family's forgiveness before any eavesdroppers started gossiping about it.

'So let me look at you,' her mother stated, giving nothing away by her voice. As yet, there was no real hint of welcome, nor any censure, nor anything else. Sara felt her heart sink. She was reminded yet again that she shouldn't have turned up like this. It was just as Aunt Dottie had always said, she acted first and thought later. And then she heard a strangled noise from her mother, and Ellen was holding out her arms to her daughter again.

Sara rushed into her embrace, the relief so strong it almost knocked her over. This was what she wanted, what she had missed, what she had longed for during the endless journey home. Her shoulders heaved with the effort not to break down, but it was too much to expect, and then she was sobbing on her mother's shoulder, all her bravado gone.

'I'm so sorry, Mum,' she gasped. 'It was foolish of me to land on you like this, and I know I should have let you know I was coming, but all I wanted was to be home, and I don't care what Dad's going to say.'

Ellen held her daughter fractionally away from her. 'The day your father doesn't feel glad to see his daughter home will be the day the sea freezes, so you can put such thoughts aside,' she said sternly. 'Now sit down and tell me what's happened to bring you all this way. Am I right in thinking the grand romance didn't come up to expectations after all?'

Sara grimaced. So much had gone wrong that she hardly knew where to start. The fact was, she didn't want to have to say the words at all. It was too shaming to admit that she had been such a gullible fool to be taken in by a sweet-talking GI. But he had been so persuasive, so charming ... and she had been so much in love.

Even now, her heart could turn over every time she thought about him and his lies. That was all they had been, she thought bitterly. Nothing but lies and promises, and she had fallen for them so completely, like the idiot she was. She took a deep, shuddering breath.

'Mum, I know I have to tell you everything, but do you think it can wait for a little while? I'm so tired, and I haven't slept in ages. The sea voyage was horribly rough and I was so anxious to know how to face you that I've been in a state of nerves for days.'

'Did you expect us to turn you away?' Ellen said crisply.

'No. Perhaps. I don't know. I can't think properly. All I know is if I don't get some sleep soon I shall collapse from exhaustion.'

'Then you'd better go up to your old room and lie down, and we can talk this evening. It's better that we do so all together when your father's here, and when I've had a chance to warn him too.'

Sara swallowed. She was going to get the third degree, of course, and she deserved it. She was an adult now and yet she felt more like a naughty child who was being sent to her room in disgrace. She had once been her daddy's adored little girl who could do no wrong, but that was before Chesney Willand had come into her life and turned it upside down.

She followed her mother up to the room that had been hers since babyhood. It was as if she was being escorted like a new guest. Did Ellen think she had forgotten the way so soon? Any minute now, Sara thought hysterically, she would have to admire the splendid new bathroom that had been installed in every room and be shown the sea-view from the window – as if she hadn't been able to picture it all so minutely all this time. Thankfully, her mother didn't go that far.

'Get some sleep, Sara, and we'll talk later,' Ellen said abruptly. 'And whatever the reason for it, you're home where you belong now.'

Sara dropped her suitcase on the floor as soon as the door closed behind her, and felt her eyes flood with tears. They didn't know ... and when they did, they would think even more badly of her than when she had run off the minute she was twenty-one, to set sail on the first available ship taking GI brides to America.

Down in the town a young man was setting out some of his paintings in a small display at the front of his shop as he always did in the summer months. He never did it too early in the day. He preferred to wait until the summer visitors were up and about, since they were the ones most likely to stop and look, and if they liked what they saw, they came inside, and hopefully went away armed with some of his work.

By now, his paintings, whether in oils or water-colours, were mostly of the town and the local coastline in all its glories and vagaries. They had proved to be an instant success with the annual visitors who bought them as mementoes of the far south-west. The last couple of years had been good to Robbie Killaine and his name was becoming known, not only here in St Ives, but also in the rest of the county.

Today, however, he didn't feel as optimistic as usual, and he knew he must be imagining things again. There had been far too many times when the glimpse of a stranger's glorious hair, the hue of autumn leaves, and the soft green garments that suited that colouring so well, could turn his stomach upside down. It was never her, of course. How could it be, when she was thousands of miles away in America? But she was still in his heart, Robbie thought savagely, and even now he seemed incapable of getting her out.

He had tried. God knew he had tried. At the time, he should have seen it coming. It didn't take a genius to know that plenty of local girls were dazzled by the Yanks swarming about the town with their money and their smart uniforms and their crew-cut hair and easy talk. Plenty of other girls ... but not his girl. Or so he had foolishly thought. He hadn't even minded when she said she wanted to go dancing on the nights when the local dance halls were raising funds for servicemen's families. It had been a noble thing to do, and Robbie had always gone with her, sitting out because of his lame leg and glad that his girl was having a good time, because he knew he would be the one taking her home.

There was even a song about it... 'Who's Taking You Home Tonight?'

Well, in those days it had always been Robbie,

and for some infuriating reason the words of it were filling his head now, in the middle of a hot summer day, remembering the night that had eventually come when she had said awkwardly that one of the Yanks had asked her out, and would he mind very much if she went to the flicks with him. It wouldn't mean anything, she assured him. It was just being friendly, nothing more, and Robbie had agreed because he knew that she loved him and would always love him.

'Are you star-gazing in the middle of the day, Robbie?' he heard a female voice say now, and he blinked the images away. He hadn't let them intrude for a very long time, yet he knew very well they were still there, just beneath the surface, just as Sara Boskelly was. His one true love.

'It's what artists do,' he said coolly, banishing all other thoughts and smiling back at the girl. 'Don't you know we get our best inspiration that way?'

Miriam Roche laughed out loud. 'I call it going into a trance. You can get locked up for it, you know. People will think you're mad.'

'Let them,' Robbie said with a shrug. 'The mad Cornish artist, that's me. The one with the limp. The cripple, if they're feeling really bitchy about it.'

Miriam's eyes widened. 'What's up? It's not like you to sound so bitter. Is nobody buying today? Perhaps you should change your style and do portraits. If you want somebody to sit for you, you know I'm always available.'

'I don't do portraits,' Robbie said abruptly, knowing he was being ungracious and unfair and that she was only teasing to try and cheer him up.

It wasn't Miriam's fault that he was out of sorts just because he thought he'd seen a ghost. If he said as much, she would really think he was mad. She was a nice girl, a really nice girl, and he was fond of her. They had become closer in the past year ever since her family had finally had the news confirmed that her brother had died in one of the terrible concentration camps in Germany. She had needed somebody to lean on then, and he had been the one she turned to. He enjoyed her company, but he didn't love her in the way a woman deserved to be loved for the rest of her life.

'I'd better leave you to your grumps then,' she said. 'I'm supposed to ask you round for Sunday tea, but perhaps you won't feel like it.'

'Of course I'll feel like it. Thank your mother for me, Miriam.'

'Be in a better mood then, okay?' she said.

Robbie found himself grinning as he watched her swish away. She wasn't all sugar and spice for all her sweet looks, and if she thought he was still pining for somebody else, she'd just as quickly give him the old heave-ho. But he'd never promised her anything. They were walking out together but that didn't mean anything. They weren't engaged and he'd never hinted at such a thing. He knew he was defending himself, because he was pretty sure that in Miriam's eyes that was precisely what the next step was going to be.

He finished what he was doing and went back through the shop to his studio at the back. This was his haven, full of the sights and smells of everything that he loved, oils and turps and glues, canvases and easels, and a scattering of brushes and pencils and charcoals. There too, were all the other accoutrements of his trade, the framing tools, the primers, the drawing inks. Once he had discovered his skills, Robbie had embraced everything about his craft. It was his work and his pleasure. He was like a magpie, Sara Boskelly had once told him laughingly...

At the Boskelly guesthouse, Sara was lying flat on her old bed, gazing at the ceiling and trying to calm her erratic heartbeats. The first hurdle had been overcome, if that was the right way to term her reunion with her mother. But she admitted that it had been an ordeal, and if Ellen had rejected her, she didn't know what she would have done. She had treated them so badly, running off the way she had, leaving only a long and impassioned letter to explain where she was going, and that her whole life was meant to be with Chesney.

She knew they would have stopped her going, and she had begged her parents not to try to bring her back. She was already twenty-one then, and it would have been more than humiliating if her father had come rushing after her. But he hadn't, and the only contact she had had with them since, was the letter she had written when she arrived in America, leaving a post office address where they could write to her. The fact that they hadn't done so still made her heartsore.

Older and considerably wiser now, she knew how much she must have hurt them, especially with their reputation in the town, having to hold their heads up high despite her disappearance.

And Robbie too … the letter she had left him must have broken his heart.

Sara smothered the choking sensation in her throat. But they didn't know. None of them knew how shocked and humiliated she too had been when the wonderful dreams had all turned to dust. The streets of America weren't paved with gold, Sara thought bitterly, and talk was cheap, so tawdry and cheap.

A while later, she heard a smart tap on her door, and then it opened quietly, and she swivelled her head on her pillow. Her father stood there, his expression as uncompromising as her mother's had been, and her heart leapt painfully. She struggled to sit up, not knowing what to say. Her throat seemed to have closed up, and she was once again his naughty little girl awaiting some chastisement.

'We've waited a long time for this day to come,' her father said finally, sounding not quite steady. Whether it was with anger or some other emotion, Sara couldn't tell.

'So that you could say "I told you so"?' she said, her voice a dry husk.

'No. So that I could say thank God you're safely back where you belong,' he said, and then in a few long strides he was across the room and hugging her as if he would never let her go.

The tears streamed down her face, because it was so much more than she deserved. She knew there was still a reckoning to come. There had to be. But for now, for these few sweet, uninhibited, unconditional moments, she could forget everything but the comfort of her father's arms.

Chapter 2

The forgiving moments were soon over, as Sara had known they must be, and then her father held her away from him, his eyes stern.

'You've got a lot of explaining to do, young lady.'

'I know,' Sara said with a gulp. 'And I will, I promise. But first of all please let me get used to being home, Daddy. I'd forgotten just how much I had missed it all, you and Mum and St Ives, and, well, just being here in Cornwall!'

'We could have told you that,' Frank Boskelly said dryly. 'In fact, I seem to remember we tried to tell you a hundred times that this is where you belong.'

'But some things you have to find out for yourself,' Sara said unsteadily. 'You have to learn by your own mistakes, don't you?'

'He didn't hurt you, did he?' Frank said sharply, making her eyes widen with shock, making her gasp. She wasn't stupid and she knew what he was implying.

'Of course he didn't! Chesney was the sweetest, kindest man, even if he wasn't all that he seemed. But I didn't know that then.' She drew a deep breath before she said what had to be told. 'For one thing, I didn't know he was already engaged to somebody else. That was one of the things he'd overlooked telling me when he promised me such a wonderful life in America.'

She couldn't hide the bitterness in her voice now, and reliving the shock of that time was one of the painful things she had deliberately tried to avoid. But her parents had a right to know why she was back and what had gone wrong, and she had always known she would have to tell them. She knew too, with a sense of her Aunt Dottie's foresight, that they would forgive her eventually. Whether Robbie Killaine would, she had no idea, nor whether they could ever recapture the heady feelings of the first love they had both been sure would last a lifetime. But she was going to try, she thought fervently. Oh yes, she was going to try.

Frank was looking at her in a fury. 'So he was already engaged to someone else, which makes him a liar as well as a cheat,' he said angrily. 'To think that we welcomed him into our home the way we did makes me so wild I could wring his handsome bloody neck.'

'Everybody welcomed the GIs into their homes, didn't they?' Sara said, so shocked at hearing her father swear that she unwillingly defended Chesney. 'It was one of the things we were encouraged to do. We were supposed to make them feel less lonely, being so far from home.'

'We weren't expected to turn a blind eye when they courted our daughters, when they were already supposedly attached to someone else,' Frank said curtly.

Sara felt her face grow hot, unsure whether or not her father meant that Chesney was supposedly in love with his fiancée, or whether he meant the childhood sweethearts that she and Robbie had been. Either way, she knew this was dangerous ground now, and even though her parents had thought Chesney a decent, clean-cut fellow at the time, she wasn't going to extol his virtues any more.

Of course he had seemed decent and clean-cut ... and exciting and virile and so different from any man she had ever known before. He had simply swept her off her feet, wanting more than she could give, because she too was a decent, clean-living girl as she had been brought up to be. But she remembered guiltily how hard it had been to be good when he had all the amorous and husky sweet-talk that Robbie never had, as smooth and sleek as a movie-star, softly whispering as he nuzzled into her neck that she was the most beautiful girl in the world, and how much he ached for her and longed to make her totally his...

'You'd best come down for supper,' Frank said abruptly now, jarring into her secret thoughts. 'Once we've eaten, your mother will want to hear what you've just told me, and everything else that you've been doing since you went away. You can't expect to walk back into our lives as if nothing's happened, Sara, and without giving us proper explanations. You owe us that much.'

'I owe you everything,' she said huskily. 'And I'll never do such a thing to you again, I promise.'

She flung her arms around his neck once more, breathing in the faint tobacco scent that came from the old briar pipe he always smoked after supper, and which usually resided in the top pocket of his jacket. The aromatic scent was endearingly familiar, and if she didn't stop getting so emotional over every little memory that was revived, she knew she'd be no good to anyone.

'I'll be down in ten minutes,' she told him. 'Just give me time to wash my face and brush my hair.'

Her father moved to the door, and then he paused and looked back.

'No matter what, it's the best thing in the world to have you home again, girl,' he said, and then she was alone, and fighting back the tears again.

That evening, once he had shut up his shop for the day, Robbie Killaine went back to his studio and began furiously sorting through all the old paintings and pencil sketches that went back to his schooldays. The studio was getting far too cluttered, and it was high time he had a good clear out and got rid of some of the old stuff. Not for a single second was he going to admit to himself that the sketches he was looking for most were the ones he'd done of Sara Boskelly. Nor that the ghost he thought he'd seen today was the main reason for this clear out.

There were so many sketches of her, in folders, in rough note books, on scraps of paper. There were the schoolroom drawings in art class, the cartoon sketches, the adolescent ones when she had begun to blossom into such a beauty, and the later ones, when her eyes had looked back at him with such love that it would have to be a raving idiot who couldn't see what she felt for him, and he for her. Only a true artist could capture the expression in a woman's eyes when he sketched or painted the one he loved and knew he was loved in return.

Robbie had always known that – or thought he had. It was the worst day in his life when he knew how wrong he had been, when he had read the halting, tear-stained letter she had sent him, telling him that she was going out of his life for good. She was leaving him, leaving home and Cornwall and never coming back. She was going to marry someone else, some Yank who had just been one of many in the area as far as Robbie was concerned, but who had obviously meant a great deal more to Sara. His Sara.

He brushed aside the sharp sting of remembering as fresh waves of anger took over. He had felt like murdering somebody then, and he felt the same way now. He still didn't know if what he thought he had seen earlier that day – the glimpse of a swirling green dress and the glossy burnished hair he knew so well, had really been Sara, or no more than an illusion to taunt him. And he didn't want to know. He had made a life without her, and whatever had brought her back, it was nothing to do with him. She didn't want him. She wouldn't have come back for him.

She had made that pretty plain in her letter, clumsily trying to soften the blow that she was madly in love with someone else and had to follow him to the ends of the earth if need be. It was all couched in melodramatic words, almost like a film script, even if Robbie hadn't thought so at the time. It was intended to try to make him understand that her love for this Chesney chap was stronger than anything she had ever felt for Robbie, and that theirs had never been more than a childhood affair. She had broken his heart, but his heart had mended and hardened since then, and he had vowed that no woman would ever break it again. Men were stronger than that.

He began systematically tearing the early sketches of Sara in two and throwing them in his wastepaper bin. But it only took a few minutes before he was putting aside the ones that were too good to discard, and then he was abandoning the whole exercise. He turned in relief when he heard someone calling him, and Miriam Roche came into the studio from the back door which only a few people knew led into his sanctuary. She took in what he was doing at once and her lips tightened.

'You've heard then,' she stated.

'Heard what? I haven't been anywhere to hear anything. I'm just having a sort out, and not before time. There's no sense in keeping all this stuff from years back, and I need the space.'

He didn't know whether he was trying to justify himself, or if he was holding off the moment when she was going to tell him whatever it was she was obviously dying to say. He wasn't sure it was something he wanted to hear. Not if it meant that a certain someone had brought her American husband with her. Her handsome, whole, upright American husband. He felt an ache in his weakened leg, and told himself angrily it was just a stupid psychological reaction, and nothing more.

Miriam picked up one of the ripped sketches from the wastepaper basket, and Sara's clear green eyes gazed back at her.

'She could have been a beauty queen,' she said

jealously. She glared at Robbie. 'You know she's back, don't you?'

'No, I don't know, and if she is, it means nothing to me.'

Miriam said nothing for a moment, and then her shoulders drooped a little.

'If I thought you meant it I'd be over the moon, but you don't, do you? You've never forgotten her all this time, and I was only ever second best.'

For the first time, Robbie realised just how upset she was becoming, and for no reason. How could Sara's return have anything to do with him – with them – after all this time? She was married now, and unattainable as far as he was concerned.

He put his arms around Miriam. 'We've all moved on since then, Miriam, and you should never think of yourself as second to anyone. You're a lovely girl, and we've had some good times, haven't we?'

'You don't have to say it in the past tense,' she muttered.

Robbie forced a laugh. 'And you don't have to look so gloomy. What happened between me and Sara was over a long time ago, you know that.'

'I know you only went out with me on the rebound, and because you were sorry for me after we heard the news about Brian.'

Robbie released her. 'Now you're being silly. Of course I was sorry about your brother. Who wouldn't be, when we got to hear about the terrible things that happened in those camps? Cheer up, for goodness' sake. Even if Sara Boskelly, or whatever her name is now, has come back for a visit, it makes no difference to you and me.'

'According to Mrs Goode her name's still Sara Boskelly.'

That gossipy old fart? For a moment Robbie thought he'd said the words aloud, and Miriam, being a retired vicar's daughter, probably wouldn't appreciate it. So he tempered his words.

'What does that mad old busybody know about it?'

He felt his heartbeat race. He hadn't seen a mirage that afternoon then, just as he had always known in his heart. It was as if he had been waiting for this moment all day, for someone to put into words what he already knew. Sara was back, but he desperately wished it didn't have to be Miriam who was telling him, staring at him so fixedly as if to judge every emotion on his face, and ignoring his insult to Mrs Goode.

'She saw Sara get off the bus with a heavy suitcase and she was by herself. You know what Mrs Goode is like for noticing every little detail, and she told my mum that Sara wasn't wearing a wedding ring, and she didn't correct her when Mrs Goode called her by her maiden name. So what does that tell you?'

'It tells me the woman should be shot for putting two and two together and always getting the wrong answer,' Robbie said angrily.

'Why? Do you know something?'

Robbie saw her lips quiver for a moment. She could be pretty sharp when she wanted to be, but right now he realised how vulnerable she was. And it wasn't fair to make her feel like this, however unintentionally.

He pulled her close. 'All I know is that whatever Sara does with her life, it has nothing to do with us. Forget her, Miriam, and let's get out of here. I'll buy you fish and chips if you promise to stop scowling at me.'

He tipped up her chin, seeing the smile that she forced back. She was a sweet girl, and for a long time now, he knew she had considered herself his girl. He breathed in her subtle perfume and kissed her lightly on the cheek, hating himself all the while for the thoughts hammering through his head that she wasn't Sara, and no matter what she did, there was still only room for Sara in his heart.

Frank Boskelly looked at the dark smudges beneath his daughter's eyes, and knew he could only push her so far. The time had long gone when she would rush to him and tell him all her childish troubles, knowing her daddy could always put them right. She was no longer a child, and whatever had happened between her and Chesney Willand was something she had had to deal with herself.

'I think we've done enough talking for one night,' he decided, after a nod from his wife. 'You're tired, and so are we. You've only told us the bare bones of what's happened since you left us, and don't think we don't know that, my dear, but I daresay it'll all come out in your own good time. Some things have to get settled in your own mind before you feel like sharing them with other folk.'

'I will tell you and Mum everything, I promise.

But it makes me feel like such a failure, Daddy, and the more I talk about it, the worse I feel. I wanted to come home so badly, but I've still got to face other people and – and old friends – and I'm not brave enough for that yet. You do understand, don't you?'

Her mother spoke swiftly, before Frank could reply. 'Of course we do, darling, and I'm sure it was an ordeal for you to walk through the town today with your head held high, but you did it.'

'Only just. I think I'll go to bed then,' Sara muttered, seeing the glances that passed between her parents. She knew her father would still press to hear everything if he had his way, but her mother was more perceptive, knowing that right now Sara would be feeling like a wounded animal, needing to hide away from everyone until she had recovered. Frank watched her go, and turned to his wife.

'Whatever happened over there, she'll have more problems to face here if I know anything about it,' he said meaningfully.

Ellen and he both knew that one of the first people Sara would have to face was Robbie Killaine. She knew how badly she had behaved towards him and she would want to make her peace and beg his forgiveness for the way she had run out on him. Everyone who knew him was thankful that Robbie had eventually got over his bitterness at Sara's betrayal, and that he was now courting that nice Miriam Roche. Everyone knew it but Sara.

She lay on her bed, eyes open wide, staring at the

ceiling, unable to sleep. She had thought long and hard before coming back here, but in the end, it was the only place she could be. She wanted to be where she belonged, comforted by the familiarity of people like herself, the way they spoke and the way they lived, Cornish folk who were steeped in the lie of the land and the smell of the sea.

And yet everything felt so strange. The town was the same, throbbing with visitors now, the way it was every summer, and this house was the same. Her bedroom was just as she had left it, and nothing had been altered at all. The pictures on the walls were the ones she had chosen, the flowery curtains and bedspread were the ones she had wanted. On the chest of drawers was the collection of teddy bears and soft toys she hadn't been too old to throw away when she fell in love. In pride of place was the one that Robbie had given her, won at a fairground for a few pence.

She moved restlessly, remembering that special day when they had cycled all the way over to the outskirts of Penzance to that fair. She had been thirteen and he was two years older, and she was already on the brink of first love. Or perhaps love had always been there, just waiting for her to be old enough to recognise the feelings. She remembered that day so well. She remembered everything as if it was yesterday, and now that she was back where she belonged, the memories seemed even more crystal clear than usual.

'You can't throw darts for toffee,' she had yelled at him, when he had missed the dartboard a few times. 'Can't dance, can't run, can't throw!'

Was it cruel, referring to his lame leg in that way? She had never thought so, and neither did he. It was simply a fact of life that never bothered either of them.

'Yes, I can! I'll win you a teddy bear, and you can name it after me,' he'd yelled back above the noise of the crowd.

'No, I won't. I'll call it Darling, after the people in that book we're reading at school. The one about the crocodile and the boy who never grew up.'

'You mean *Peter Pan,'* he said, in case she thought his lack of schooling while he recovered from polio a few years ago had made him illiterate.

Instead, those weeks of inactivity in hospital had allowed him to read and to draw as much as he liked. He had given more than one of the nurses a pencil sketch of themselves that had astonished them at his young, raw talent. Polio had never been a total waste of his time, Robbie had thought then, because it had told him exactly what he wanted to do with his life.

'So is it all right if I call my teddy bear Darling?' Sara had asked daringly, not knowing why it should be so significant, but important that he agreed.

Robbie had started to scoff, and then he had looked at her blazing green eyes and the flyaway coppery hair that framed her face, and his throat had closed up for a moment. The artist in him recognised her immature beauty, but something else in him recognised far more. She was too young to know the effect those stunning eyes could have, and he was still a boy, but with all of a fifteen-year-old's turbulent awareness of the opposite sex. At that moment, Robbie wanted her with a passion that startled him, and he vowed that one day she would be his.

'What's up with you? Your face has gone all funny,' she'd said, poking him in the ribs. 'And you haven't answered my question.'

'I've got to win the flipping thing first,' he'd ground out, conscious of all kinds of weird things going on inside him. 'When I do, you can call him any darned thing you like.'

Sara laughed, dancing up and down and clapping her hands like an idiot child until her hair swung around her face even more, brushing against his arm and forcing him to yell at her to stop it or he'd never keep his arm steady enough to throw the darts at all. It wasn't the only thing making him feel weak and he knew it, but somehow the last dart hit the target and the stall holder handed him the teddy bear with a wink and told him to give it to his girl to keep her quiet before she frightened all his customers away.

'I'm not his girl,' Sara shrieked, her face going red.

But you will be, Robbie promised silently, handing her the bear.

Without knowing what he intended to do he leaned forward and kissed her cheek, and said mockingly: 'Here you are, *Darling!* Meet your new owner.'

He was referring to the teddy bear, but he knew that his lips were tasting the first time he had called her, or anyone, darling. She was giggling stupidly, the way thirteen-year-old girls did, hugging the bear and skipping away from him and into the crowd and yelling that she was going to get some candyfloss. By the time he caught her up she had already bought it and was standing there with pink goo all around her mouth, and he had never felt more like kissing it.

Sara remembered it all so vividly, as if she was watching a moving picture of her past, including that moment when the sweet sticky stuff was all over her lips and she had caught Robbie gazing at them as if he was mesmerised, as if he had never seen them before. It had almost knocked her off balance, that look. It had made her catch her breath, and then the candyfloss had tickled her throat and she was coughing and spluttering and he was thumping her back and laughing and making her cough all the more until she begged him to stop.

Was that the moment when they first fell in love? That crazy, madcap, uninhibited moment when the world had seemed to stop turning for a few seconds and then came whirling towards her, full of noise and colour and people, and above all, the one person she knew she was destined to be with for the rest of her life.

Perhaps that was it. Or perhaps there was no single moment when it happened. Perhaps it had been happening so subtly that there was never any doubt in either of their minds that they were meant to be together. Aunt Dottie always said that when you found your soul mate there was no force on earth that could separate you. But Aunt Dottie had reckoned without Chesney Willand of the US Marines.

Sara got out of bed, abruptly willing all the images away. What was the use of going over things that couldn't be changed? She prowled around the bedroom, touching and caressing familiar things, and avoiding the teddy bears, looking back at her with dead, accusing button eyes. She went to the window, threw back the curtains and gazed down at the calm, indigo sea. From here, it seemed to stretch out to infinity to touch the sky at some distant point and to simply merge into it.

But Sara knew it wasn't like that. Somewhere out there, beyond the horizon, was another land, one that had drawn foolish young girls like herself as if by a magnet to all that was exciting and new and full of hope. In America, anything was possible. In America, the poorest person could become President. It was the land of opportunity, and foolish young girls were easily seduced by handsome young men in smart uniforms who promised them the earth and stars, and a life beyond their wildest dreams. Promises and lies.

She caught her breath as her eyes blurred. She didn't think she had been any more gullible than the next girl, and Chesney had been so very persuasive, so sincere in all that he said, and she had believed every word. Why shouldn't she, when he had shown her the photos of his parents and the lovely rambling farm on which they lived in the state of New Jersey, south of New York, where they grew juicy red apples in vast orchards.

'In summer,' Chesney had told her enthusiastically, 'the whole farm smells so wonderful that you could almost be intoxicated by it.'

He had painted a picture of such glorious beauty that Sara was already almost transported there by his words. She didn't know, then, that the farm didn't belong to his family at all, and that he was merely an itinerant fruit picker. The smiling older couple weren't his parents, but the farm managers, and as for the girl who was supposedly his sister – they were all lies, to add to all the other promises he'd made.

Sara felt the sobs rising again. She was home, she reminded herself. Safe at home with the people she loved, and who loved her, and no lying rat was ever going to ruin her life again. She would make sure of that. She was stronger now ... and she hated herself for not being able to completely dispel the memories of how charming Chesney had been, and how she had so nearly succumbed to his sweet seduction. She had thought herself truly in love, but she thanked God and her upbringing that at least she had been strong enough and sane enough not to give in to him until she had a wedding ring on her finger. The ring that she discovered would never be hers, because it was already promised to someone else.

He had never expected her to turn up, of course. He had never really believed she would follow him, sailing all that way to America along with dozens of other girls, all dizzy with excitement at the new life awaiting them. He had never expected her to make the journey out of New York down to New Jersey, and present herself at the farm that she knew so well from the pictures he had shown her.

And oh God, the memory of knocking on the

door of that farmhouse, her head full of dreams and her heart pounding with the anticipation of being swept up in Chesney's arms.

'Yes?' said the ample-bosomed woman whose photo she had seen.

'Mrs Willand?' Sara had said eagerly. 'I'm Sara. Sara Boskelly from Cornwall in England. Chesney will have told you all about me, I'm sure.'

She saw the blank look on the woman's face, followed by a hurried consultation with someone inside the farmhouse, and the first stabs of doubt entered Sara's mind. Then came the invitation to come inside, where the grey-haired man she thought was Chesney's father was getting up from his armchair.

'You'll be another one, then,' was all he said, and in that instant, Sara knew. She didn't know all of it, though. That was to come later when she had sobbed her heart out on the woman's sympathetic shoulder, and learned the truth.

Chapter 3

At least St Ives never changed. It was the one permanent thing in Sara's world. Well, St Ives, her parents, and old Leah, who was a family friend as well as an assistant at the guesthouse. She was as permanent a fixture as Sara's grandfather's desk, as close to the family as Aunt Dottie had once been, and just as ready to speak her mind. Once everyone else was busy the next morning and she and Sara were alone for a while, she came out with what had obviously been simmering.

'You'll be wanting to get off and make your peace with young Robbie as soon as possible, I daresay,' she said, when Sara had been wandering about the guest-house like a lost soul.

She flinched at Leah's words. 'I suppose so.'

She didn't really know what she was wanting to do. It felt as if she had been away for an eternity. Here at the guesthouse a young girl came in every day to help her mother in the kitchen and to make the beds. They were managing very well without her. In any case, that wasn't what Sara wanted to do. Before she went away she had worked for a firm of family solicitors, but her job there would have been filled long ago. Why would they want her back, anyway, when she had run out on them as well? The enormity of what she had done seemed to keep leaping up at her all the time.

'It'll do you no good to put it off,' Leah went on, as blunt as ever. 'You treated him badly, and you owe him an explanation.'

'I've already explained! He knew where I was going, and why!'

'But not until after you'd gone. It was a shabby way to treat him and everybody else, and you should be ashamed of yourself.'

Sara looked at her in astonishment. Leah had always been her champion, but right now she looked hot and flustered, and something in the way she busied herself with a bit of unnecessary dusting told Sara there was more to come.

'I expect he's got over it by now,' she said uneasily, even though part of her didn't want Robbie to have got over it. Part of her wanted him to have been pining away all this time, but she knew that wouldn't have been Robbie's style at all. He may have been ineligible to go and fight during the war because of his leg, but it didn't make him less of a man. He was a proud man, and he was *all* man, as far as Sara was concerned, and despite her anxiety at how he would react when he saw her, she couldn't deny the wild thrill that they would be together again.

'Oh, ah,' Leah said without expression. 'You couldn't expect a healthy young man like Robbie Killaine to do otherwise. A lame leg don't stop a man from being a normal man in other ways. And there are plenty of other pretty maids in the town ready to catch his eye.'

'So is there one pretty maid in particular?' Sara said mockingly, wondering if Leah was just out to tease her today or if she was really trying to tell her something.

'Might be. It's none of my business, anyway.'

Sara spoke impatiently. 'You can be so maddening sometimes, Leah. You're just like Aunt Dottie, giving me half a story and making me ferret out the rest of it.'

'Your Aunt Dottie was a wise old bird, and I miss her something terrible at times,' Leah said, her old eyes misting for a moment. 'It was good to have somebody of my own age to yarn with, instead of all you young 'uns who can't wait to hear the end of a good tale.'

'Are you going to tell me about Robbie or not!' Sara snapped, not wanting to get into too many reminiscences of Aunt Dottie, or they'd both be wallowing.

'Well, I know he's been seen about with that nice Miriam Roche quite a few times. Her family was that cut up when they heard young Brian had died in one of them wicked concentration camps. I daresay Robbie felt sorry for her at first.'

Her last words seemed to hang in the air, full of meaning, whether she meant them to or not.

'So he's been seen about with her since then, has he?' Sara said woodenly. 'Are you trying to tell me he's courting? Proper courting?'

'Why shouldn't he be? Did you expect him to turn into a monk just because you didn't want him any more?' Leah said, more acidly than before.

'No, of course not. Well, perhaps I did. I don't know. I didn't think about it.'

'That was always your trouble, my lamb. You never did think before you rushed into things, and now I suppose you're going to rush down to his studio and declare your undying love.'

Sara glared at her. 'You were the one who told me not to waste time in seeing him, Leah, so why are you being so unkind to me?'

Her mouth shook, because although she was used to Leah's bluntness, just now it was more than she could bear. She deserved all the censure she got, but Leah had always been like an echo of Aunt Dottie, always on Sara's side, no matter what the circumstances. When Sara was a child, the two older women thought so much alike they had often seemed to her to be two halves of the same person, and she wouldn't have been surprised if Aunt Dottie's ghost came to Leah in the night now and then to give her a bit of her whacky advice. And she must be getting as mad as these two old biddies to be thinking such things.

'I'm not being unkind,' Leah said more gently. 'But I don't want you to spoil things for Robbie if he's found someone else.'

'He wouldn't have done! I was always his girl and I'm still his girl!'

She listened to her own words in horror, knowing she was sounding unbearably selfish and that it was stupid and unrealistic to think that Robbie would have been sitting around all this time waiting for her to come back. The hell of it was, though, deep down it was exactly what she had thought.

She felt Leah's arms go around her, and then the touch of a papery cheek against hers. 'Just go gently, my dear. Things have a habit of turning out right in the end. You came home, didn't you?'

Sara supposed those words were supposed to be mysterious and enigmatic. It only made her more anxious to get out of here. Even in America there had been reports of the last terrible winter this country had had, but now the summer seemed to be making up for it by being blisteringly hot. She needed to breathe the stimulating sea air, and she announced that she was going out and would be back later.

But Leah was right. There was one place she was desperate to be. She had to hear it from Robbie himself that the impossible had happened and he had forgotten her and was courting somebody else. Even so, her footsteps faltered as she left the comparative haven of the guesthouse and went down into the town.

It was already bustling. The harbour was alive with colourful pleasure boats and fishing-boats and the excitement of holiday-makers. The smell of fish was on the air, mingling with the pungent scent of sun cream, and the mouth-watering smells of Cornish pasties and ice-cream. It was a world away from the wartime years, when the hordes of Americans had swarmed into the area from their training camps in preparation for D-Day, some declaring it was like the back of beyond, and others loving the quaintness of it all and grateful to the families who made them welcome.

Sara ignored those thoughts, not wanting to be reminded for a moment of the first time she had seen Chesney Willand, gazing out into the harbour and looking a bit lost. Then he had turned around and seen her and she was lost too. He was tall and fair-haired and amazingly like the newspaper photographs of the handsome Greek prince that Princess Elizabeth was going to marry. She hadn't known about the similarity then, but she had realised it since.

Chesney wasn't Greek, of course, although he had all the looks of a Greek god. He had spoken with an engaging American accent as he asked her what there was to do around here. Everyone was keen to do what they could for the War Effort, and in particular to make their American Allies welcome, and when Sara offered to show him the way to the best beaches, it had been the beginning. It hadn't meant anything, just a brief friendship that would be over as soon as the Yanks moved on, but it had grown and developed, and eventually taken over her life – and ruined Robbie's. As it turned out, it had also ruined hers.

She was halfway around the curve of the harbour, still intent on reaching Robbie's shop, no matter what it took her to do so. She had been greeted by several old school-friends and managed to avoid any long conversations that would mean too much awkward questioning. Ahead of her now was Robbie's shop and studio. Her heart thudded, knowing she was so near.

She could see the framed paintings propped up outside on the small pavement, and she could imagine how these holiday-makers who had taken the place of the Yanks would want to buy his pictures of the local area to take home. He had such an artistic eye for a scene, whether a seascape or landscape in whatever mood, and he was especially good at depicting sunrise or sunset. Those had always been the colours Sara loved the best, the delicate pinks and glorious golds and blues of morning and evening.

'So it *is* you,' she heard a voice say nearby. An accusing voice.

She turned around to see Miriam Roche glaring at her. She remembered her from schooldays, a rather large, pasty-looking girl, always bragging about her father, the retired vicar, who was years older than anyone else's father in the school, and her brother Brian who was keen to be a soldier. The war hadn't even started then, but Brian had achieved his ambition, and died for it.

Miriam wasn't pasty-looking now, Sara noted. Her long hair was decidedly lighter than Sara remembered, as if she had been at the bleach bottle. She was well-rounded and very flushed and she had a furious glint in her eyes.

'Well, it was me the last time I looked,' Sara said in answer to her comment, trying to sound amused even though her heart was jumping. Miriam thrust her face close to hers and almost hissed the words.

'Don't think you're going to come back here and make trouble for Robbie and me, because you're not. He doesn't want second-hand goods. He's mine now, and after the dirty way you treated him, he doesn't want anything more to do with you, so you just keep away from him.'

Sara was stunned by such vehemence. The second world war may have ended, but this one had clearly just begun. She snapped back at the girl.

'Are you his puppet now then? Since when did he need anybody pulling his strings, and since when did you think you could tell me what to do?'

'Since you went chasing after your Yank!' Miriam spat out. 'And anybody with any sense could guess why that was. What have you done with the kid, or have you palmed it off on the poor unsuspecting father?'

The implication made Sara speechless with shock for a moment, but only for a moment.

'You bitch! How dare you say such things to me. For a vicar's daughter you've got a filthy mouth. Have you been spreading these lies about me?'

Miriam mocked her. 'Why? Are you telling me it's not true? I'm only saying what everybody else thought. Why else would you go off like that with some cock and bull story if it wasn't because you were in the family way?'

It was too much. One minute they were standing and shrieking at one another, unaware that a small crowd was gathering around them, and the next minute Sara had lunged at Miriam, grabbing her blonde hair and yanking it for all she was worth. Then Sara felt her own hair being pulled almost out of its roots, and the two of them were kicking and screeching like banshees, until someone began pulling them apart and yelling at them to stop showing themselves up.

Sara's eyes smarted with the pain of the tugging on her hair, registering that Miriam Roche was no longer the simpering child she had been in the classroom but a real tigress. And then her eyes cleared and she found herself looking into Robbie's furious face, and to her incredulous rage she saw that Miriam had now dissolved into little-girl tears as she clung to him.

'She just flew at me,' Miriam sobbed. 'Now that you can see just how hateful she's become, you're well rid of her, Robbie.'

'It wasn't like that at all!' Sara yelled. 'She was the one who started it, saying such terrible things about me.'

She became suddenly dumb at the swift realisation that if Miriam Roche was saying these things about her, it was likely that other people had been saying them too. Whispering about her and calling her a bad girl who had fled the town because of her shame. And it hadn't been like that at all. It had never been like that. Surely Robbie hadn't thought it of her? Surely not her parents, still waiting for a proper explanation, or old Leah, who had seemed so odd that morning?

Her throat was choked with the shame and humiliation she didn't deserve. The small crowd around them had drifted away out of disinterest, and there were only the three of them now, plus a few curious small boys and a dog busily sniffing at a discarded paper bag that had been wrapped around somebody's pasty.

'Robbie, I need to talk to you,' she said huskily. 'I need to explain.'

'You explained everything a year ago in your letter.'

'But things have changed. I've come home, and I want to tell you everything that's happened while I've been away. It's not what you think.' She spoke desperately to his uncompromising face, angry that Miriam was clinging to him so pathetically now. She had never expected her to be such a clever little actress.

But she saw the flash of something in his eyes that gave her a small feeling of hope. 'Please, Robbie, it's not what you think,' she repeated.

'Come back tonight,' he said curtly. 'I can't stand here discussing things when I've got a business to run, and I hardly think either of us is in the mood for talking sensibly now. We'll talk then.'

Sara saw Miriam's mouth open and then close again, so if she was going to object to this meeting tonight she obviously thought better of it.

'I'll be there,' Sara said shakily. She turned and walked away with her head high, but her nerves were in tatters. Surely other people in the town didn't think the way Miriam Roche did. Her parents couldn't have thought that the reason she had gone away was to hide such shame, she thought with a shudder, and she couldn't imagine what it would have been like for them if such evil whispering had begun about her.

She tried to regain her composure as she walked quickly away, hardly knowing where she was going, telling herself they would surely have said something to her last night. They couldn't have ignored such a monumental worry. Sara prayed that all the things Miriam had hurled at her were only the ravings of a jealous woman, but she was a vicious one too, if she was putting such ideas into Robbie's mind. And suddenly Sara realised what she was up against.

‘What the hell did you say to her?’ Robbie said angrily, finally shaking Miriam off as they went back to his shop. ‘I know she has a fiery temper, and so do you, but I thought you’d both be above brawling in the street.’

‘It was her,’ Miriam said, quivering. ‘She thinks she can just come back here and everything will be the same as before she left.’

‘You must have said something,’ Robbie persisted. ‘Sara was never that friendly with you in the past, and she couldn’t have known we’d been seeing one another unless you opened your big mouth and started it. So what was it?’

In Miriam’s eyes, this was all so unfair. That she was jealous of the girl who was so much prettier than she was with the dramatic colouring that obviously appealed to Robbie’s artistic nature, was one thing. But to accuse her of starting something when she was only defending her own position with him was really mean. And she didn’t have a big mouth, either.

‘I only said what plenty of other people probably thought,’ she said sullenly. ‘You’d have thought it yourself if you didn’t think the sun shone out of Sara Boskelly’s you-know-what!’

Despite himself, Robbie’s mouth twitched because she looked so indignant, standing there with her hands on her hips like some old washerwoman.

She saw the look and her face flamed even more, thinking he was laughing at her. ‘Well, don’t tell me you never thought it!’ she screamed.

‘For pity’s sake, Miriam, come through to the

studio or you'll be frightening all my customers away and people will think I'm murdering you.'

'What customers?' she said rudely. 'I don't see anybody rushing to buy your stuff, do you?'

'My stuff, as you call it, is my livelihood, and I thought you understood how much it means to me.'

She probably didn't, of course, since she didn't have an artistic bone in her body, and her classroom drawings had been the cause of much guffawing and cat-calling among the other pupils. She could never have posed for the occasional real-life class, either, the way the more graceful Sara Boskelly had, because she was big-boned and clumsier in her movements. It had never endeared Miriam to Sara to be fully aware of the difference between them.

She faced Robbie in his studio now, her heart beating rapidly She didn't want to fight with him. It was the last thing she wanted to do, and she wasn't always as bitchy as she had been today. Her father would kill her – if it wasn't against his Bible-reading principles – if he knew how she had behaved, and what she was going to do now.

'So come on, let's have it,' Robbie said, folding his arms. 'What exactly is it that you think you know?'

'I don't know it,' she said nervously. 'It's only what I heard, that's all. Well, it was common knowledge that she went away chasing that Yank of hers, wasn't it? But why did she do it? Why didn't she wait until he came back for her, like any decent girl would? Why didn't she want to get married in white in her own town with her family around her, if there wasn't some hole-and-corner reason for running off the way she did and getting hitched so quickly? Ask yourself that, Robbie.'

His face was thunderous now, and she hoped she hadn't gone too far. To be honest, she hadn't really heard that kind of gossip at all, but Miriam was a girl who found that by repeating something often enough in her mind it was easy to make it believable. Even so, Robbie's stricken expression was scaring her now, and she really wasn't a wicked girl, she thought tremulously. It wasn't lies, just speculation, but such a likely piece of speculation that it could easily have been the truth. And why shouldn't he speculate about it too?

They both heard voices from the shop, and she turned away with relief, preparing to slip out of the back door of the studio.

'I'm sorry, Robbie, but you did ask.'

She was gone before he could reply, even if he had any idea what to say to her. His nerves were jangling, because he had honestly never considered any sinister reason for Sara fleeing the way she did. Nor had he ever believed she had the kind of loose morals attributed to a few local girls who had seen the Yanks as fair game and didn't care what they did for a pair of nylons or a few bars of chocolate.

But he forced a smiling and professional face when he saw that the elderly couple in the shop had brought one of his paintings inside from the pavement and were enquiring about the price. He couldn't afford to be grouchy with customers just because his personal life was in danger of being turned upside down, even though the thought of asking Sara for the truth about that lost year when he saw her that evening was churning his gut.

Sara's nerves were also jangling far too much for her to think of going straight home. Miriam's words had shocked her deeply, but her accusations had started all kinds of questions in her mind. Did people really think she had run off because she was expecting a baby? It was so grossly unfair she could almost laugh at the idea if it wasn't so deadly serious and totally untrue. It couldn't be true because she had never let Chesney go all the way, nor anyone else. Oh, he had wanted to, of course, and there had been a time when she'd been very tempted. She wasn't made of stone, but she wasn't a brainless idiot either, and she was aware of the consequences.

She wasn't aware quite how far she had walked until she realised she was by now striking out across the heathland along the cliffs above the coast. There were old tin mine chimneys up here, and a smattering of small isolated farms in the area, including Pennywell Farm where her one-time Best Friend lived. She glanced back, seeing St Ives miniaturised by distance as if in a child's picture book, the sun glinting on the picturesque houses and chaotic jumble of little streets, the colourful boats bobbing about in the harbour appearing as toy boats, and Smeaton's Pier reaching out to the sea. She felt a rush of affection for the town, and at the same time, a feeling of anger for the people in it who could think such ill of her.

Guiltily, she knew she deserved their gossip, even though she had been through a hellish time that they knew nothing about. She had probably scandalised them all when she had left in the way she had. The fact that her parents had never replied to any of her letters, despite her pleas, told her how much she had hurt them. The shame of it had almost decided her never to come back at all, but the tug of home was too strong, coupled with her longing to see them again, and to try to make her peace with Robbie.

She sank down on the springy turf, drawing in her breath as she thought of him. Of all the foolish things she had ever done, one of the worst was surely expecting everything to be the same when she returned. Expecting time to have stood still, instead of moving on – and taking Robbie with it.

What she had never expected was that he would have found someone else, betraying her, as she had betrayed him. The honest part of her asked why on earth he shouldn't have found a new love when she had abandoned him. But to find it with lumpy Miriam Roche, of all people! At that moment, she felt exactly the way she had at school, when some other girl had got higher marks than she had, or more praise from a favourite teacher, and she told herself out loud to stop feeling so damn sorry for herself.

Out of the corner of her eye she could see somebody approaching her, and she wished she'd had the sense to keep walking, because she desperately wanted to avoid company, especially someone she knew, and she had once known this girl very well indeed. Best Friends was how they had always thought of themselves at school. Closer than limpets, according to their respective parents, but there was nothing friendly in the accusing way Hilary Weeks was looking at her now.

'I heard you talking to yourself. First sign of going mad, that is,' she said, flopping down beside Sara. 'Didn't think to let me know you were coming back, did you? Nor anybody else, I bet.'

'Don't you start on me, Hilly,' Sara said. 'I'm finding it hard enough with people looking at me as if I've committed a mortal sin. For God's sake, I didn't kill anybody!'

'You just about killed Robbie. Do you have any idea what you did to the people who loved you, Sara?'

'I'm beginning to,' she muttered.

'And you didn't even tell me. I know we weren't as close as when we were kids, but I'd have thought you'd want somebody to confide in. We shared all our secrets in the past, and there was a time when I'd have been the first person you wanted to tell.'

'I couldn't. How could I? My parents would have gone straight to you to find out what you knew.'

'They did,' Hilly said dryly.

Sara rushed on, hardly noticing what she said. 'I knew what I was doing was wrong, but you know how madly I fell for Chesney, Hilly. He wanted me to follow him as soon as I felt able to, and when the opportunity came, I just went.'

It sounded lame and pathetic, and so it was. Sara felt waves of misery wash over her, knowing how it had gone so badly wrong.

'So where is he then, the love of your life? I heard he wasn't with you when you got here. Old Mrs Goode has already seen to that. My mother saw her at their Bible-reading meeting last night.'

Sara looked at her mutely She had lived with the shock of Chesney's lies for so long now it seemed impossible that nobody else seemed to realise why she had come crawling home like the prodigal daughter. She had more or less got over the shame of it all ... but in retelling it, she was reliving it all over again.

'He's not with me. I never even saw him again. We never got married, because he was already engaged to somebody else. It was all lies. Everything he told me about himself, it was all lies, Hilly, even about the fruit farm and his family. So now you know, and you needn't bother calling me the biggest fool in creation, because I know I am!'

She hadn't meant to cry. She had told herself for so long that he wasn't worth it. But somehow she was sobbing on Hilly's shoulders, and blubbing out the rest of the hurt before she could stop herself.

'And you know what that bitch Miriam Roche said? She said people thought I'd gone away because I was in the family way. Can you believe it?'

When Hilly said nothing, Sara jerked away

from her, her eyes wide with shock. This was her friend, her one-time Best Friend, who was looking decidedly uncomfortable now. Who was looking downright shifty, in fact!

'My God, you thought it too. How could you, Hilly?'

Chapter 4

She scrambled to her feet, rushing back the way she had come, and hardly able to breathe from the sobs tearing at her throat.

'Sara, come back. I never thought such a thing.'

But by then, Hilly's voice had been carried out to sea on the breeze.

She should never have come back at all. She should have written a sensible letter to her parents, telling them the truth and that she had decided to make a new life for herself in America after all. If she hadn't felt so wretched and disorientated there, she would have seen that it was the only solution. People said you could never go back, and she had certainly proved that.

All the same ... Sara told herself she had more backbone than to scuttle back through the town with her head held low. She had done wrong, but it wasn't as terrible as Hilly was implying, and she wasn't going to be accused of being something she was not.

She slowed down, feeling her heartbeats slow down as well. This was where she belonged, and no-one had the right to make her feel like an outcast. As she reached the curve of the bay beyond Smeaton's Pier she stuck her head in the air and marched along the edge of the promenade without a single glance towards Robbie Killaine's shop and studio.

Holiday-makers jostled her on all sides, and without realising where she was going she turned into one of the many twisting alleyways leading away from the shore. The higgledy-piggledy old buildings shut out some of the sunlight and the cobblestones were cool beneath her feet until she turned into one of the larger streets leading off the alleyway. It wasn't the main thoroughfare, and there were mostly discreet businesses here, including the dark windows with the gilt lettering on them announcing the firm of Potter and Grebe, Family Solicitors.

Sara hadn't meant to come here, and she hardly knew why she was tormenting herself like this. The last thing she wanted was to linger here, and it would be far too embarrassing for one of the partners to see her and have to make stilted conversation. Especially if they too had heard the false rumours about why she had gone chasing after Chesney Willand. Her eyes were blurred as she turned back quickly, and she blundered straight into someone coming up the hill from the other direction.

'Crikey, Sara, mind me buns!' she heard a laughing voice say, and she blinked away the salty tears to see a girl a few years older than herself clutching a bag of currant buns, which the partners and secretary always had for their mid-morning break. 'I heard on the grapevine that you were back. How did it go?'

The non-censorious cheeriness in her voice was too much. Before she knew it, Sara had burst into tears, and the other girl had taken her arm and was steering her back into the elegant confines of the front office of Messrs Potter and Grebe.

'You sit right here while I take these to his nibs, before I make us all a nice cup of tea,' Sara was told.

'I can't stay,' she began weakly, but she was talking to the air as the other girl disappeared out of the office and went clattering up the stairs to the solicitors' rooms.

She should make her escape, she thought desperately. She couldn't bear facing her old employers, sure that they wouldn't be as forgiving as Angie Reid. Yet she seemed to be rooted to the spot, knowing she wasn't helping herself by running away. She had already done that once, and now she should have enough backbone to face everyone, however painful. In any case, she had already faced the worst, in her parents and Robbie, even if things were far from being resolved. They hadn't even begun...

The next moment the white-haired and portly Lionel Potter came down the stairs, holding out both hands to her.

'My dear girl, it's a real pleasure to see you back in St Ives,' he said, at which the tears began again.

'I didn't expect you'd want to see me ever again,' she wept, 'and in a crazy way I don't think I want people being kind to me when I've come back to face the music!'

He gave a gentle laugh. 'Well, in my line of work, I see enough people who don't have that kind of courage, as you very well know, so dry those tears and come up to my rooms. I'm sure Angie bought more buns than are good for us and I'm sure there'll be one for you.'

Sara followed him upstairs meekly, leaving Angie giving her the thumbs up behind his back. The smells of old leather and oak furniture rushed into her nostrils as she entered the office that looked as if it hadn't changed in years. She had often felt as if one of Charles Dickens' characters could easily come scuttling into the room with a quill pen in one hand and an ancient scroll in the other. Or maybe she was mixing up the centuries...

She sat on the other side of Mr Potter's desk, feeling the way a client must feel, coming to unload her problems and hoping to find solutions. Not that he would have any for her. She felt the tears welling up again, and swallowed hard as Angie brought in a tray of tea and buns and left them to it.

'Now then, my dear girl, let's have our tea and buns, and then you can tell me whether you want to unburden yourself, or if this is just a social call. I don't have to tell you that whatever you say in this room will be confidential, do I?'

Sara knew the truth of that. There were only three types of people you could fully trust to keep things totally confidential – priests, doctors and solicitors. And she would trust this man above everybody. She gulped her tea and felt her nerves begin to relax. She hadn't intended coming here, but now that she was, she was comforted by the concern she saw in her old employer's eyes.

'I know you must have thought badly of me for the way I behaved, Mr Potter, just like everyone else in the town did,' she mumbled.

'Let's say I was disappointed in you, but few things surprise me about human nature any more. People always think they're doing the right thing at the time, even if in their hearts they know it's really the wrong thing, and there's always a reckoning, Sara. You've discovered that now.'

'I did love Chesney,' she said defensively.

'Of course you did. I can't imagine you would have thrown away the love of a good Cornish man and upset your family and friends without having the deepest feelings for this other man, my dear. But you say it in the past tense. Does that have any significance?'

She recognised the experienced professional in him now. He was drawing her out, making her examine her own feelings, offering her choices in her answers. Her voice choked in her throat.

'I think I will always have feelings for Chesney, otherwise it will all have been for nothing. But my feelings now are nothing like the wild craziness I felt when he first came into my life. He was like a drug.'

She blushed furiously, never having said anything like this to anyone before, and it was only to this man that she could reveal exactly how she had felt at that euphoric time when falling in love with someone so different and so exciting, had blinded her to all else, even the love of a good Cornish man...

'And now?' she heard the solicitor say.

'Now I despise him. I loathe him for what he put me through,' she said, her voice shaking. 'I was completely taken in and besotted by him, and yet to my shame I know I will always wonder how I would feel if he came striding into the room right now and told me it had all been a mistake, and that it was me he loved and wanted to marry.'

'But that wasn't the truth of it, was it?' he prompted gently.

Sara flinched. He didn't know the truth of it, and she felt doubly humiliated at having to tell it. She hadn't even told her parents all of it yet, nor Robbie. Her breath was coming so fast it was strangling her, but somewhere in the back of her mind she found herself remembering one of Potter and Grebe's maxims – that the healing of any problem began with the telling.

'You have work to do and I'm being a nuisance,' she muttered.

He became brisker. 'If I didn't want to know, I wouldn't have asked. Now, dry your eyes and pretend this is a regular consultation – waiving the fee, of course.'

She gave a shaky smile at that, but the barrier was broken. She found herself spilling out all of it: the thrill of sailing to America with all the other excited young girls anticipating a better life after the austerity of the war years; the shared stories on the ship that made sisters of them all; the subsequent journey to New Jersey and the first sight of the lovely white-painted farmhouse and the intoxicating scent of apples; and then the total disillusionment of Chesney's lies and deceit.

'The people I thought were his parents were very kind to me. There had been other girls coming to look for Chesney, though no-one as stupid as I was, to come all the way from England on a promise,' she added bitterly. 'Their names were Mr and Mrs Irish, and when they realised I had nowhere else to go, they simply took me in and I worked for them until I had saved up enough money for my passage home again.'

'And you never contacted your parents in all that time?'

'Oh, but I did! I wrote to them to try to explain, but they never answered. I was too ashamed to tell them what had really happened, but I begged them to forgive me and to keep in touch. I even sent them a post office address – just as if I thought my dad might come rushing over to America to drag me back and find out how badly things had turned out! But of course that never happened. They just cut me out of their lives.'

'I think you did that yourself, Sara.'

Her anger flared up for a moment, and as quickly subsided. He spoke no more than the truth. She fiddled with her gloves, thanked him for listening, and said it was time she left.

'Not so fast, young lady. First of all, I'd like to know how long you're planning to stay in St Ives this time.'

'This time? Why, I'm here for good, of course. I'm home. This is where I've always belonged.'

'So are you looking for a job, or are you going to work for your parents?'

She was startled by the question, but half an hour later, Sara walked home in a daze. She hadn't expected this, even though it had occurred to her that Angie Reid had been flashing a tiny engagement ring under her nose at every opportunity, even if she was being too tactful to actually tell Sara that she was engaged to be married. But not only that. She was getting married in two months' time, and moving away to Penzance, where her husband-to-be was a bookbinder. Potter and Grebe were shortly to advertise for a reliable and discreet new receptionist cum typist to join them as soon as possible, so that Angie could show them the ropes before she left.

'And then you walked in, like a gift from heaven,' Angie had told her excitedly, when she was informed that it had all been settled. 'Mr Grebe's away on a case right now, but I know he'll be as pleased as Mr Potter that they won't have to train somebody who's totally green about the job. When can you start?'

At last there was something positive to tell her parents, Sara thought, walking home. Something they would surely approve of, because it was a job she knew and loved, and one that would enable her to hold up her head in the town again, and prove to certain people that she wasn't shunned by everyone.

As if to reinforce her sense of relief, the family dog came bounding towards her as she neared the guesthouse again, and she hugged him to her, registering his warmth and unconditional love. She nestled her face into his thick coat and whispered into his receptive ears.

'We'll get through this, won't we, boy? Everything will turn out all right in the end, you'll see.'

Showing his approval, Bonzer barked excitedly. Sara laughed, exhilarated by these brief happy moments in what was still a traumatic ordeal for her. Out of the corner of her eye she saw someone approaching from the direction of the guesthouse, and she straightened up.

'Hello, Leah,' she said brightly as the colourfully-dressed woman came near, and then she saw that Leah looked unusually flushed. Sara sighed, wondering what the problem was. It wasn't unusual for her father to bark out his orders when he wanted something done, but Leah usually gave as good as she got. Today, she looked anything but ready for a verbal battle.

'What's wrong?'

Leah scowled, her eyebrows drawn together in a straight line of annoyance.

'Nothing that a drop of brandy wouldn't cure. 'Tis a poor day when a body ain't allowed to work off a cold. Lot of namby-pamby nonsense sending me home for fear of spreading germs to them upcountry folk. 'Tis more likely them that's bringing the germs down to we!'

As she finished speaking she gave an enormous sneeze, deftly swiping the sleeve of her jacket across her nose and glowering at Sara for the expected comment. She wouldn't have done that in her father's presence, thought Sara keenly. He was a stickler for hygiene in the guesthouse, so of course Leah couldn't be seen sniffling and snuffling when they had paying guests.

'Let me walk you home and make you some tea, Leah,' she said encouragingly.

'Ah, providing 'tis well laced with brandy,' she was told. 'You're a good girl in many ways, Sara, but you'd best not stay long at my cottage. Your Ma and Pa have told me to stay home for a day or two, so you'll be expected to help out.'

Sara was aghast. 'But I can't! Well, I suppose I can if it's only for a day or two. You'll be well by then, won't you?'

Leah looked at her suspiciously as they strode back the way Sara had come and then turned into one of the narrow alleyways where the roofs of the opposite cottages almost met and daylight was in short supply.

'What's so important about that? You're not thinking of going off again so soon, and breaking your folks' hearts all over again, are you?'

'No, I'm not,' Sara said crossly, as Leah fumbled with the latch on her cottage door. She followed her inside, trying not to wrinkle her nose at the stale smell of old furniture and ancient furnishings in a confined space. 'Sit down and I'll make you that tea and then I'd better show my face at home.'

'What's all this about, then?' Leah persisted, sneezing again as she sank into an armchair that had lost its springs long ago.

Sara filled the kettle from the kitchen sink and then told Leah her news.

'I've got my old job back with Potter and Grebe, and I can start any time. Next week, if I like. Angie Reid is getting married in a couple of months' time and she'll be moving to Penzance.'

'Penzance!' Leah snorted, as if it was akin to Hades. 'What would anybody want to go and live there for? In any case, your plans will have to wait a while, because your Ma and Pa will be wanting you to help them until I'm better.'

'But that won't be long, will it? You're never ill,

Leah. Not really ill.'

She didn't know why she said it so anxiously, unless it was because for all the years she had known her, Leah had very rarely taken a day off. She scorned illness the same way other people scorned changes in fashion. It was just a lot of fuss and bother.

Leah was looking at Sara strangely now. 'Do you think I'm immortal or summat, girl? The day will come when my Maker needs me more than your Ma and Pa do, and when that day comes I'll be ready.'

Sara banged the milk jug down, uncaring that the splashes flew. 'Well, now you're scaring me, and if you're going to talk like that I'm going home.'

Leah chuckled. 'Gullible as ever, I see. I'm glad to know them Americans haven't knocked all your Cornish ways out of you. I'm not thinking of turning up my toes just yet, you silly maid, so stop looking so dippy and make me that tea. You'll find the brandy bottle in the sideboard.'

Sara felt relieved. Her dad used to say that old Leah was as tough and wiry as couch grass, and would probably outlive all of them. Right now she was prepared to touch every weathered bit of wood in this old cottage to believe it.

After half an hour, though, Sara was more than glad to leave the stuffy atmosphere of the cottage and breathe some good clean air again. She didn't think her parents had ever been to Leah's cottage, and she wondered just how horrified they might be if they knew how their trusted assistant lived. It wasn't rat-infested or particularly dirty, Sara thought, it was just old and cluttered with the peculiar smell attributed to old things – and people.

Anyway, things had taken a different turn now, she thought, her heart sinking. Her parents would expect her to do Leah's work and there would be no getting out of it until Leah's cold was better. She imagined there would be a good few trips to the brandy bottle before that happened, but hopefully it wouldn't be more than a couple of days.

When she got home and explained what had happened, it was just as she feared. She was expected to take over Leah's duties at the guest-house, and she accepted the knowledge without demur. She had stirred up too much anger in the past to argue about it. She could still inform her parents of her job offer, though, and as she did so, she suddenly realised just what a boost it had given her to know that at least Lionel Potter didn't censure her for her actions.

'It's good news,' her mother agreed. 'But since there's no hurry on it, it'll have to wait until Leah is well again, and for all that she blusters and says she doesn't believe in illness, she's not a young woman, and she should take things more slowly.'

'It's only a cold, though,' Sara protested, unwilling to believe it could be anything more. She knew she was burying her head in the sand, because people didn't live for ever, and who knew how old Leah was. She had been around for so long and never looked any different, but inevitably the day had to come...

'You're shivering. I hope you haven't caught it,' her mother said sharply. 'How long did you stay with her, Sara?'

'Not that long, and I'm sure I haven't caught anything. You know what Leah's like. She didn't want any fussing.'

Besides, it wasn't the cold that had made her shiver, but a premonition that she didn't want and couldn't quite shake off, no matter how much she tried to ignore it. It was old Leah and her Aunt Dottie who believed in omens and superstitions and such things, not a level-headed modern girl who had crossed the Atlantic Ocean twice, and seen wider horizons in her lifetime than either of them. But without the wisdom of their experience, she acknowledged.

She didn't feel very level-headed when her mother insisted that she spent the evening helping with the guests' evening meals, then she was to do the washing-up and set the tables ready for the following day's breakfasts. Their young girl helper only came in during the day to make beds and clean the bedrooms.

'Then I'll go through the weekly rotas with you,' Ellen went on. 'Leah knew them well enough, but you won't.'

'Oh, but I can't! I have to go out this evening, Mum! It's really important, or I wouldn't insist.'

Ellen spoke sharply. 'You'll do as I ask, Sara, and I don't think you're in any position to insist on anything. Whatever it is that's so important, it's taken you a year to think about it, so it can certainly wait a bit longer.'

'But I have to see Robbie,' Sara almost wept. 'I

promised I'd see him tonight to try to explain everything, and if I don't turn up I don't know what he'll think.'

'Well, perhaps he'll think you've changed your mind again. He'll be getting used to it by now, won't he?'

Sara looked aghast. Ellen never used to be so – so cruel – but she would have had to put up with plenty of gossip and speculation over this last awful year as well, and it was only now dawning on Sara how many people she had upset. It was like skimming a pebble across the water and watching the ripples begin to spread out. Once they began, there was no stopping them.

'It wouldn't take long, Mum.'

'It won't take any time at all, because I need you here,' Ellen said crisply. 'We have a duty to our guests, Sara, and you know this is a busy time of the year for us. You can see Robbie tomorrow once the morning chores have been done. I'll give you a list of groceries to buy, and you can combine the two.'

She was implacable, thought Sara. She had never been like this before, or at least, not in any way that Sara remembered. It seemed to underline just how hurt her mother must have been at the scandalous way Sara had behaved, and she knew she was a long way from being totally forgiven – if she ever would be.

But she had been hurt too. Hurt and humiliated, and feeling as if her life had come to an end the day she found out just how much Chesney Willand had deceived her. She had given him all her love, and he had repaid her with lies. She also knew what a fool she had been, to travel thousands of miles on no more than a promise. If she hadn't been so besotted with him, she would have waited for him to come back for her and put a ring on her finger ... but that would never have happened, because it was some other girl who already wore it.

'Sara, my dear, I don't mean to be hard on you, but I need you now.' She heard Ellen's voice as if through a fog. 'Robbie will still be there tomorrow, and you've plenty of time to make your peace with him. He's not going to go away.'

Whether or not she was unconsciously twisting the knife with those last words, Sara wasn't sure. But she could see her father's car approaching the guesthouse, and knew she would get no sympathy from him if she didn't do as her mother wanted. She swallowed her disappointment. She had been building up her courage all day towards seeing Robbie, and now it would have to wait. She could only pray that he would wait too, and accept her explanation tomorrow morning.

By late afternoon Robbie had shut the shop and gone upstairs to his flat for a quick snack. He didn't feel much like eating at all. His thoughts were in a turmoil over Sara Boskelly. Part of him wished she had never come back, that she had left him with his memories, whether good or bad, and his bitterness. While the bitterness remained, he told himself he could get over her, even though he knew damn well he could never forget her.

But now she was here, and there was another,

more passionate part of himself that gloried in the fact that she hadn't been a dream, that she was real and back in his life. He reminded himself that she wasn't, of course, and nor did he know why she was here at all. All he knew was that she had left him and everything she loved for this American chap. Someone's feelings had to be pretty powerful to do that. She hadn't thought enough of him to stay where she belonged, and he was still sick to the stomach whenever he thought about it.

They had always considered themselves soul mates, and had been ever since they were children, but it had only taken one glamorous GI to make her forget all that. He knew there were plenty of other girls who had had their heads turned by the Yanks' slick, easy talk, but he had never thought it would happen to Sara. Not his beautiful Sara. Even when she had asked if he minded her going to a dance or two with the GI, he hadn't objected. It was being kind to someone far from home, that was all. But those nights had obviously developed into something else, something deeper that excluded Robbie, taking something he thought was his. He should hate her for it, he thought savagely. The hell of it was, he didn't, and never could.

His upstairs window looked out on the sweeping bay. He didn't put on any lights, and as the sun got lower in the sky, the sea was a golden sheen now, reddening by the minute, or so it seemed. The artist in him would normally itch to transfer every changing nuance of the scene onto canvas, but not tonight. Tonight Robbie's gaze was fixed somewhere beyond the bay to the promontory where the Boskelly guesthouse stood. He knew he couldn't see her leave it from this distance, but he might glimpse her bright hair among the holiday-makers still thronging the shoreline to watch the fishing-boats bringing in their catch.

He couldn't believe that she wouldn't come. She had been so adamant in wanting to explain what had been happening this past year, and he desperately wanted to hear it, and to hope there was a rational explanation. Not that he could think of one. There still had to be a reckoning between them ... but his anxiety slowly turned to anger as the time went on and there was no sign of her.

It seemed a long while later when he heard the sound of someone at the back door leading into the studio, which he had left open for her. By then his stomach was in knots, and he didn't know whether to be furious with her for tormenting him like this, or relieved that she was here at last. He went down the stairs as quickly as he could, cursing his lame leg that slowed his progress, and went into the dimness of the studio.

'I thought you weren't here,' said a complaining voice. 'Why is the place all in darkness? You're not ill, are you?'

His disappointment was searing, and he raged at her.

'Miriam! What the hell are you doing here?'

Chapter 5

Robbie flipped on the light, finding it difficult to control his feelings.

'Well, that's a nice way to greet me, I must say,' she said, affronted.

'I'm sorry, but you gave me a bit of a shock,' Robbie snapped, and then saw how her face flushed. 'I wasn't expecting you, Miriam.'

'I could see that. So who were you expecting?'

He didn't answer, hoping desperately now that Sara wouldn't choose this moment to turn up. It would be farcical if she did, with Miriam so full of rage, and himself still in a turmoil of emotions, and he didn't fancy being caught in the middle of another catfight.

'It was her, wasn't it?' Miriam screeched. 'You'd made arrangements to see her again behind my back. I knew this would happen. She was always the one for you, and I was only ever second best, wasn't I?'

'Don't be so melodramatic, Miriam,' Robbie snapped. 'You heard me arrange to meet Sara tonight.'

She was practically wailing now, and Robbie moved to where she stood with her arms hugging herself tightly. When he pulled her into his arms, she barely moved, and it was like holding a statue. He knew she was hurt, but he'd never expected her to react like a banshee, not now, or that other time. There had never been any indication that she had an uncontrollable temper in all the time he had known her, and he was alarmed at such a violent reaction. But she had never been threatened before, in the way she imagined she was being threatened now that Sara Boskelly had come home. He gave her a little shake, trying to calm her down and spoke more carefully.

'Miriam, you know very well that Sara and I have some unfinished business between us. I have to talk to her, and this is a small town. None of us will be able to avoid her now that she's come back. It's far better that we get things sorted out from the beginning and then everybody knows where they stand.'

'I thought I already knew where we stood,' she returned, her eyes brimming now. 'I thought I was your girl. I've never looked at anybody else since you, Robbie, and I never would. You know that, don't you? I'm the kind of girl you can trust, not like some.'

She didn't need to make it any plainer, and her attitude had miraculously changed. She was soft and pliant in his arms now, her voice wheedling. She was like a chameleon, thought Robbie, and this was the girl he usually saw, not the one who had torn at Sara's hair in public, and who seemed intent on keeping what was hers. But he wasn't hers, and never had been. He wasn't anybody's, and he was man enough to be damned sure he wasn't going to be manipulated by any female.

'Robbie?' he heard her whisper. 'You know I'll always be here whenever you need me, don't you? I'm not going anywhere.'

It was like a line from a Hollywood picture, and she had probably been watching too many of them lately, he thought savagely. He was beginning to feel trapped. This evening had gone all wrong, but the first disappointment was giving way to the old bitterness he'd felt when he'd realised that Sara had left him for the Yank. The feeling had been horrendous then, and it was the same now.

He extricated Miriam's clinging arms from around his neck.

'Look, Miriam, we've had some good times together, and you're a great girl, and a good friend.'

She pushed him away. 'I know what that's supposed to mean! But that's not all I am to you and you know it. If you let this little tramp come back in your life and ruin what we've got, I shall never forgive you, and if you let her walk all over you, Robbie, I'll let everyone in this town know what kind of a man you are.'

'Really? And what kind of man is that?' he said. His voice was steely, and she should have been warned. But subtlety was never one of Miriam's attributes.

'A wimp, that's what. That's what the Yanks call it, don't they? A spineless wimp who can't wait to go running whenever an old girlfriend raises her little finger.'

'If that's what you think, then I don't know why you even bother with me. You know where the door is, Miriam.'

'Are you throwing me out?' she said, outraged.

'Not at all. I don't think a wimp is capable of such a thing.'

She glared at him. 'You were always clever with words, weren't you, Robbie? You and Sara Boskelly. Even at school, you were both too darned clever for your own good, giggling over things the rest of us didn't understand. Well, you're welcome to the little bitch. If you're satisfied to take another man's leavings, I'm well rid of you. Until I choose otherwise, anyway.'

She turned and flounced out of the studio, banging the door behind her. Robbie locked it swiftly, knowing that Sara wouldn't be coming now. It was too late – too late in every respect, he thought. He hadn't meant to upset Miriam this way, and the argument had grown out of nothing. Though not in her eyes, of course. In Miriam's suspicious eyes, he was the kind of rat who played with people's feelings.

He realised he was breathing too heavily for comfort and he turned abruptly and went back upstairs to cool off, wishing the whole human race, and bloody contrary females in particular, to Kingdom Come.

It was the most frustrating night Sara had ever spent. The chores that were normally Leah's seemed to take for ever, and she was obliged to smile and be pleasant to the guests, knowing that her mother would be furious with her if she wasn't. All the time she was imagining Robbie's reaction when she didn't turn up as they had arranged. He would think she was too cowardly after all, to face up to him and admit that what she had done was terrible. It was, and she knew that it was, but she so desperately wanted to make amends with him. He must know that.

She so desperately wanted to know if they could still salvage anything of the love they had always known – or if he had so easily turned to another girl. But Miriam Roche! Despite herself, Sara couldn't stop her lips tightening whenever she thought of it. Miriam dumb-bell Roche, of all people... How could he possibly love her, hold her close, whisper tender things in her ear, kiss her...?

Her throat caught. If only Leah hadn't caught that rotten cold, this would all have been in the past by now. Robbie would know the truth. He would know how much she regretted her impulsive actions and just how foolish she had been – and how wickedly she had been let down by Chesney's lies. She would make him see that it had been no more than a mad aberration that had made her go running after Chesney, and once begun, there had been no turning back. The letters had been written to Robbie and her parents, the passage on the ship had been booked, and she had been carried along by the excitement of it all.

She had planned to tell him all of it, however painful it would have been, begging him to understand, and to forgive her. She would still have to try, but it would be more difficult in daylight, instead of in the soft evening light in his flat, where they had spent so many blissful hours together looking out at the bay and all its beauty.

She got ready for bed that night, brushing her gleaming hair the obligatory hundred times the way the movie stars did, practising her soulful look in the mirror. But she felt shame wash over her. This was all wrong. If she had been betrayed by Chesney, how much more had Robbie been betrayed by her, and if he truly loved Miriam dumb-bell Roche now, did she really have the right to try to break them up, breaking another girl's heart? Was she wicked enough for that?

She turned away from the mirror and dived into bed, pulling the covers right up to her neck. Staring blindly at the patterns made by the moonlight on the ceiling, she knew that she was. Except that it wasn't wicked at all. It was merely reclaiming Robbie's love, which had always been hers. Uneasily trying to console herself with that thought, she tried to sleep.

The next day she did as she was told and put on a bright face for the paying guests. None of them knew the circumstances of her being there, and they seemed to appreciate the change from Leah's colourful appearance. By mid-morning most of them had left the guesthouse to look around the town or the surrounding countryside. Sara finished plumping up cushions and straightening newspapers in the conservatory before going to the shops for her mother, still wondering just what she was going to say to Robbie, when she heard footsteps behind her.

'You've got a visitor,' Ellen said.

Sara whirled round, her heart leaping in her chest. He hadn't waited. He had come to her. He still wanted her.

'I had to come and see you after we quarrelled yesterday, Sara,' Hilly said when Ellen had discreetly left them alone. 'I couldn't bear to fall out with you after all this time.'

Sara gulped. The realisation that it wasn't Robbie after all made her eyes sting. But why would it have been? He had too much pride for that, and he also had a business of his own, like everyone else in St Ives. Time didn't stop just because Sara Boskelly had done the stupid thing and gone chasing a dream.

Seeing the distress in her eyes, Hilly rushed across and hugged her. 'I'm sorry for what I said, Sara, or rather, what I didn't say. I didn't mean any of it.'

'I think you did,' Sara muttered. 'And I know I can rely on you to tell me honestly if it's what everyone else was thinking when I left. Did they really think I'd got myself in the family way?'

'Well, I suppose some probably did. It wasn't the best way to leave town, was it?'

'But I couldn't have been. I never would have – and I never did – oh, you know what I mean, without my having to spell it out.'

'No, I don't. Do you mean you never went all the way with your Yank?'

'For goodness' sake, keep your voice down,' Sara hissed. 'I don't want my mother to hear what we're saying.'

'Perhaps she should. So tell me the truth, Sara. Did you or didn't you?'

She was like an interrogator, thought Sara crossly. Right from their schooldays they had always been able to talk about anything, laughing nervously over intimate things, such as when their mothers had tried to explain about their monthlies, and keeping themselves nice, and not letting boys get too familiar, and not staying out too late, and always staying in a group ... while skirting all around the basic things they were dying to know. Now Sara faced her friend squarely, her green eyes blazing.

'For your information, no I didn't. I'm not saying he didn't want me to, and I'm not saying I wasn't tempted. But that's the thing about temptation, isn't it? You either give in to it and regret it afterwards, or you don't.'

'So there was no real reason for you chasing after him then.'

Hilly had gone too far now, and Sara snapped at her. 'Only the fact that I loved him. Don't you think that's reason enough to want to be with somebody?'

Her voice choked, because Hilly didn't know the half of it. She didn't know just how madly she had fallen for Chesney, blinding her to everything that was right and sensible, and sending her halfway around the world to be with him. Only to have it all thrown back in her face so cruelly.

'Let's go for a walk,' Hilly said. 'It's hot and stuffy in here, and we've always been able to talk more freely out on the cliffs.'

'I'm supposed to be grocery shopping,' Sara muttered. 'But it can wait.'

They slipped out of the open French windows of the conservatory and were met by the warm air of the promontory. The breeze blew softly in from the sea far below. It was as smooth as a millpond today, with no indication of the raging winter storms that could batter these coasts.

They sat together on the sweet summer grass, hugging their knees.

'It's almost hard to believe there's any land out there,' Sara murmured, suddenly awkward. 'It looks as if the sea goes on for ever.'

'What was America like?' Hilly said, glad to change the conversation.

'Noisy, full of people jabbering away too fast, great tall skyscrapers that took your breath away, oh, and the Statue of Liberty, of course, which we passed as the ship neared New York harbour.'

'It must have been quite an adventure, Sara. You shouldn't forget that you've seen far more than many girls our age have seen – well, apart from those old enough to join up in the war, of course, but you wouldn't have called their experiences an adventure, would you? We had Land Girls on the farm, but they grumbled most of the time at being sent to the back of beyond.'

It occurred to Sara that Hilly was talking too fast now. She was obviously nervous, and it was also obvious that you couldn't describe a year's events in a day, especially when she was unwilling to share most of those events. But perversely, she wanted to talk about it now.

'Don't you want to know what happened when I got to New York?'

'Of course I do, if you want to tell me.'

'Well, it's what everyone's dying to know, isn't it? Even old Ma Goode who saw me arrive back, and wasn't getting anything out of me! All right, then. I knew the address of Chesney's farm in New Jersey – except that it wasn't his, but I didn't know that then. I had to find my way there, and it was a bit of a nightmare with buses and trains, and finally hitching a lift on somebody's truck. And before you say anything, I know my mother wouldn't have approved, but I had to get there somehow, didn't I?'

She swallowed, thinking how pathetic it all sounded – a love-struck girl crossing an ocean and turning up unannounced by whatever means she could find.

'I was really tired by then, but excited at the thought of seeing Chesney again and joining him on his family's fruit farm. When I got there, the scent of apples in the orchards was wonderful after that long journey. But then it all began to go wrong. As soon as I knocked on the door I was met with blank faces, and when they told me the truth I wanted to die with shame.'

She was crying softly now, and Hilly's arms were around her, hugging her tight. 'He's the one who should be ashamed,' Hilly said fiercely. 'He was a liar and a cheat, and it's a pity you didn't see through him right from the beginning.'

'Did you? You met him a few times, Hilly, and you knew what a charmer he could be.'

'I think you fancied yourself as the heroine in a Hollywood picture, and that it was all going to have a happy ending. Except for Robbie Killaine, of course. Did you never think what this was going to do to him?'

'Of course I did. Do you think I didn't agonise over what I should do? But I wanted Chesney so much, Hilly, and even when I learned the truth from Mr and Mrs Irish I still wanted him. I still loved him. I suppose I always will, in a weird kind of a way.'

Hilly released her, staring at her.

'My God, you're the one who's weird, if you can still say such things. How are you going to explain all that to Robbie? Or don't you intend to tell him that he's second best, and that you'll settle for him now?'

Sara flinched. 'You can be so cruel! Robbie was never second best in the way you mean. He was my first love, my real love, and when I say I suppose I'll always love Chesney a little, it's only because the feelings I had for him then were so strong. I certainly don't want him now!'

'Because you can't have him, you mean. What makes you think you can have Robbie, either, now that he's been seeing Miriam Roche all this time?'

'I don't,' Sara said miserably, her shoulders drooping. 'I just know I have to try to explain.'

'Well, good luck,' Hilly said, scrambling to her feet. 'I don't fancy being a fly on the wall when you do.'

Sara hadn't moved. 'I guess there's no point in us seeing each other again if we're only going to argue all the time, is there?'

'Don't be so soft. We always argued, didn't we? It's what keeps us going. So how about the flicks on Saturday night? I'll see you outside the fleapit at seven o'clock, okay?'

'Okay,' Sara said, her eyes starting to water again. 'Providing Mum doesn't keep me tied to her apron strings.'

'She won't,' Hilly said cheerfully, turning to go. 'Not if you've got the kind of gumption that sent you all that way across the Atlantic on your own. It was a pretty brave thing to do, and I know I couldn't have done it!'

By the time Sara had composed herself again, she decided she had come a long way that morning too. She had told Hilly everything, more than she had told her parents, but that must come soon. She owed them the truth, and if they too had had suspicions that she had fled Cornwall because she was in the family way, she had to put them right, however embarrassing it would be. But not as embarrassing as turning up with a child in her arms, she thought keenly.

'I'll go and get those groceries now, Mum,' she said, going back inside the guesthouse. Her eyes were bright and her cheeks flushed, but Ellen knew when to keep her thoughts to herself. She just hoped the no-nonsense Hilary Weeks had been able to get Sara to talk.

'Are you going to see Robbie as well?' she asked casually.

Sara shook her head. 'Not yet. I'll go this evening after I've finished the chores. I don't think this would be a good time, with people going in and out of the shop. By the way, Hilly wants me to go to the flicks with her on Saturday night. Is that all right?'

'Why wouldn't it be? You're not a prisoner here, my dear.'

Sometimes she felt as if she should be. Didn't the prodigal daughter have certain obligations to her family before she could totally redeem herself?

'Oh, and by the way, you might take a flask of chicken soup to Leah while you're out. I doubt that she'll be bothering to eat very much, and it's always good for a cold.'

'I'll do that,' Sara said, thankful that at least she and her mother were talking reasonably to one another again. Her father still seemed to be keeping out of her way as much as possible, and it grieved her to realise it. She had always been Daddy's little girl, but no more, it seemed, and who could blame him?

It was almost midsummer now, and the day was going to be hot. Down in the bay the waves rippled in gently, and the sunlight on the water glittered like diamonds. Sara felt her heart begin to lift. She and Hilly were all right again, and that was one gigantic hurdle to have overcome. As she went down into the town she could see plenty of people near Robbie's shop, and his paintings were stacked outside now, but she meant to do as she had said, and not go near him until the evening. This wasn't the time for soul-searching and begging for forgiveness.

She turned into the cobbled alley where Leah lived, carrying the flask of chicken soup her mother had prepared. Old Mrs Goode lived in the same stretch of cottages, and Sara prayed she wouldn't meet her again today. She didn't want to stay too long, just long enough to make sure Leah was all right, and to find out how soon she would be able to come back to work, so that Sara could think about her own job again. Mr Potter had said there was no hurry, but she was eager to return to as much normality as possible. The sooner she did, the sooner people would forget, she thought hopefully.

Like most older people, Leah never locked her door. She always said there was nothing to steal in her cottage, and if folk were so dippy as to think there was, they must have something wrong in the head. So Sara lifted the latch and went inside, trying not to wrinkle her nose as she did so. If anything, she thought the smell was more pronounced today. It smelled stale and bad, as if the windows had never been opened in all the years Leah had lived here. She hadn't pulled back the curtains that morning, and after the strong sunlight outside, the room was very dim, and it took a moment or two for Sara to accustom her eyes to it.

She went to the window first of all and pulled back the curtains, gasping as the dust flew out from them.

'Wakey, wakey, Leah,' she called out as she did so.

She turned back, and gave a small scream as she did so. She had assumed that Leah would be upstairs in bed, but she was sitting in her old armchair in the same position as when Sara had left her yesterday. She looked as if she had hardly moved at all.

'Mum's sent you some of her chicken soup, Leah. It'll make you feel better.'

She put the flask on the table, pushing aside some of the clutter as she did so, and preparing to pour the hot soup into the cup on top of the flask. Only then did she turn to look at the old woman properly.

'Leah?' she whispered uneasily. 'Leah, are you all right?'

Her eyes were half open but she looked as if she was asleep. She had to be, thought Sara. Some people seemed to be able to do that, to look half awake when they were really asleep. Leah had to be one of them.

Her thoughts were jumbling about in her head, and when she called Leah's name again, her voice was hoarse and afraid. She couldn't think which was going to be worse: to be startled out of her wits if Leah suddenly moved and opened those gimlet eyes of hers; or if she stayed exactly where she was, and never moved again. But of course that would be worse. If that happened, it would mean that Leah was dead – and hadn't her dad always said she was as tough as couch grass? But even couch grass had to die eventually.

Sara felt the sobs rise in her throat and made herself go nearer to the old woman in the chair. Leah's arm lay along the arm of the chair and Sara touched it gingerly. As if it had been finely balanced, it immediately dropped lifelessly over the edge, and Sara jumped back with a louder scream. There was no reaction at all from Leah, and with her heart beating so fast it felt as if it would burst, Sara turned and ran out of the cottage. She had to get help. She had to get away. She had to get the image of Leah's slumped body out of her mind ... and then, her eyes almost blinded by panic, she blundered straight into somebody.

'Here now, where are you going so fast? Where's the fire, young Sara?'

‘Mrs Goode,’ Sara gasped. Of all people ... but it wouldn’t have mattered if it was Old Nick himself, providing it was someone warm and breathing to cling on to.

‘Whatever’s the matter, my dear?’ the woman said, her voice more concerned.

‘It’s Leah,’ Sara stuttered. ‘I think – I’m sure – she’s dead!’

‘Dead? Of course she’s not dead. I saw her just a few days ago, and she was as right as ninepence then.’

Sara felt a childish urge to stamp her feet. ‘She’s dead, I tell you,’ she said shrilly. ‘She’s had a cold and my mother sent her some chicken soup, but she’s sitting in her armchair exactly where I left her yesterday, and she won’t wake up,’ she finished on a sob.

Mrs Goode tucked Sara’s arm firmly in the crook of her own.

‘Let’s go and sort this out, my dear.’

Sara pulled back. ‘I don’t want to go in there again. I can’t.’

‘Yes, you can, and you must. If what you say is true, then she can’t be left there alone. Wake up your ideas, girl. Do you think our poor soldiers in France were too feeble to take care of their comrades when they were shot and killed during the war? I’m sure even those Yanks didn’t leave their own to rot.’

Sara flinched, not sure if this was a snide reference to her own association with a Yank. But this wasn’t the time to be examining what the old woman said or why she said it. The bizarre fact was that gossipy old Ma Goode was practically holding her up and steering her back into Leah's cottage. She was the one with all the strength, and Sara was the one who felt near to fainting with shock.

She still hung back a little once they were inside, while Mrs Goode walked right over to Leah's chair. After a minute or two she straightened up.

'She's not stiff any more, so she's probably been dead all night, and she'll not be needing chicken soup, nor anything else. I'll stay here with her while you run and fetch the doctor, Sara. He'll need to check her over and start making arrangements. She's got no family, that I do know, but I daresay your Ma and Pa will want to be involved, her being with them for so long.'

Sara's eyes were becoming glazed as Mrs Goode went on talking so calmly, as if death was an everyday occurrence, as much as waking and sleeping. It was, of course, but not to people she knew, Sara thought in confusion. People as close as Leah, who had always been her champion.

'Go, girl,' Mrs Goode said more sharply. 'There's work to be done here, and this one's not going to be doing it!'

Sara turned and fled. The doctor's house was a good half a mile away, and she ran all the way, until the breath was so tight in her chest it felt as if it was strangling her. The saner part of her knew she was being completely irrational. Leah was old, and she had to die someday, just as everybody did. It was simply the shock of finding her like that, and when she rushed into the doctor's surgery and past the small group of startled patients waiting to be seen, he ordered her to sit down and thrust her head between her knees before she spoke a word.

'Now then,' he said, after a couple of minutes. 'What's all this about? Is someone ill at the guesthouse?'

If there had been, her mother would have telephoned him ... the inane thought skidded out of her mind.

'It's Leah,' she croaked. 'I took her some chicken soup this morning, and I found her sitting in her armchair, the same as I left her yesterday. Mrs Goode said she would stay with her while I came to fetch you, because Leah's completely and absolutely dead,' she gasped dramatically.

Doctor Melrose stood up. 'Then we'd better go. We'll take my car as far as the harbour.'

'I don't want to go back there!'

'I think you should. There's nothing to be afraid of.'

Oh, but there was! It was all right for him. He'd probably seen dozens of dead bodies, but she hadn't, not a single one – until now. He looked at her more kindly.

'She was fond of you, Sara. You're not going to let her down, are you?'

If only she didn't see an undercurrent of censure for the way she had let everyone down in the simplest thing anybody said to her now. She had sensed it in Mrs Goode's words, and she sensed it now. She lifted her chin.

'Of course not,' she mumbled.

It was strange how something like Leah's death could change someone's opinion of a person.

Mrs Goode became something of a good Samaritan, following the doctor's instructions and organising things in a quiet way. But it worked both ways. Sara was told to make tea for them all, hot, sweet and strong, and a long while later, when the undertakers had come to take Leah away, and the doctor had left the cottage, Mrs Goode told her she had done well, and there was nothing to be ashamed of in facing the death of a friend in the way she had.

She hadn't died from a cold, the doctor had told Sara gently. Her heart had simply given out, the way old hearts did when they'd done their lifetime's work. It had sounded noble enough, but it didn't change anything. Leah was still dead.

'I wasn't exactly brave, was I?' she muttered to Mrs Goode, when they were out in the fresh air again, and Sara was about to go home with the news.

Mrs Goode pressed her hand. 'If you'd been my daughter, I'd have been proud of the way you coped with the shock and then got on with things. You've got nothing to reproach yourself with today, Sara.'

Well, maybe if she was seeing things that weren't there in what other people said, she could take a crumb of comfort in those words too, thought Sara. She walked home quickly, her head down, not wanting to see anybody or talk to anybody. Not until her mother knew ... and when Ellen asked her crossly where were the groceries she'd been sent to buy all that time ago, she was unable to answer at all, and simply collapsed in tears.

Chapter 6

'My mother was magnificent,' Sara told Hilly on Saturday evening when they were walking back from the fleapit cinema.

She hadn't wanted to go to the flicks at all, sure that it wasn't right to sit there enjoying the antics of the comedy on the screen when Leah wasn't even buried yet. But Ellen had been very firm, telling her that although they were all sad at Leah's passing, she had been old and it had been her time, which was more or less what the doctor had said. Leah would have been the first to agree with that. She'd be somewhere up there in her own heaven now, looking down on them and approving that they were all getting on with their lives, she told Hilly.

'Do you believe in all that? About heaven, I mean.'

'Of course! At least I think I do. Don't you? We had it drummed into us enough at Sunday School. Anyway, I'd far rather believe that Leah's soul has gone to some pleasant place now than being nowhere at all,' she said, almost fiercely.

'Oh well, that's all right then. It's just that when you live on a farm you see a lot of things dying, and you get more used to it, I suppose. I don't imagine there's an animal heaven. We rear them to send to the slaughterhouse for the meat we eat. And when we want a chicken for our dinner, my dad just wrings its neck.'

Sara stopped walking abruptly. 'My God, you can be so callous, Hilly, and I think it's a horrible thing to say when Leah's just died.'

Hilly laughed uneasily. 'Come on, I wasn't meaning anything personal. I wasn't suggesting that people should be dealt with in the same way that animals are. You shouldn't be so sensitive about it, Sara.'

'I am sensitive about it. Leah was my friend, and I shall miss her.'

'Have you and Robbie made up yet?' Hilly said, changing the subject quickly, as they neared the moonlit sweep of the bay where they would part company.

'I haven't seen him. I couldn't go there on the night I was supposed to, and too much has happened since. He must have heard the news about Leah, and he knew how much she always meant to me, so if I mean anything at all to him you'd think he could have sent me a note or something.'

Perhaps it had been too much to expect, but she had expected it, and she was hurt and resentful that he hadn't even bothered. She could see the light in his upstairs window now, and it was so tempting to go rushing over there and pour out everything. But this wasn't the time. She had had a first-hand experience of death, and she was too vulnerable. She knew he would be sympathetic over Leah, but it wasn't his sympathy that she wanted.

'Anyway,' she went on, 'at least I've told Mum and Dad everything now, and it's cleared the air a little. Dad is still a bit frosty towards me, but he knew how upset I was over Leah, and I have to admit that I cashed in on it a bit.'

'Nobody could blame you for that. Will you go to the funeral?'

'I'll have to. It will be expected. I'm not looking forward to it, but we were the only excuse for a family that she had. She was quite a character in the town, though, and I think a lot of neighbours and other people will turn out for it. I hope so. It would be awful if was just us, wouldn't it? It would be so sad for her.'

'If she's looking down from her cloud, you mean.'

'Hilly!'

'Well, for goodness' sake, you can't go on being gloomy for ever, and you're taking this sudden religious fervour a bit far, if you ask me.'

'I didn't, actually.'

They were the ones getting frosty towards each other now, and Sara didn't want it. She gave Hilly's arm a squeeze.

'Sorry. My nerves are still a bit on edge. I'm sure I'll feel better once the funeral's over.'

'You don't have to clear out her cottage, do you?' Hilly said, as the thought occurred to her.

'Good God, no! That would definitely be above and beyond the call of duty! The local church and charity workers are seeing to everything. There's nothing there that anybody would want, anyway, poor old dab.'

She was in danger of remembering that stifling little room all too clearly again, and every time she did so, it was with the memory of that cold, dead arm dropping by the side of Leah's armchair, and those half-closed, half-open eyes that had so alarmed her. She shivered in the cool night air.

'Come on, I'm walking you home,' Hilly said firmly.

'You can't! It'll take you for ever to get back and there's no need!'

'I'm a farmer's daughter, remember? I'm used to tramping the fields and the moors. Stop arguing for once, and do as you're told.'

The funeral was arranged for the middle of the following week. Although it was an unseasonably damp day, as expected the small church was filled to capacity with friends, neighbours, well-wishers and curiosity-seekers. That old Leah had been a town character was undeniable. The Boskelly family were the nearest to a family she had, and when she had finally been laid to rest in the churchyard, Sara breathed a shaky sigh that they had done all they could for Leah, and now they could leave this place to its ghosts.

The life of the Boskelly guesthouse had to go on, and there were visitors to cater for. The death of an old lady they didn't know wouldn't affect them, and they would expect to see cheerful faces. For the first time in her life, Sara welcomed the fact, but there was also an important matter to discuss with her parents. So far, all of them had avoided mentioning it, but Sara couldn't go on pretending that she wanted to take Leah's place for ever.

There had been no sign of Robbie, and no word

from him, and she guessed that he had assumed she hadn't been able to face him after all, even though he must have heard the news about Leah. It seemed clear to Sara that he hadn't cared enough to contact her, and she'd been living in a fool's paradise to think she could simply come back and be welcomed into his arms again. It was a bitter realisation, and one she found hard to accept.

Had she known it, on the night she and Hilly had paused for so long at the harbour after they'd been to the pictures, Robbie had seen the two of them from his window, while keeping well out of sight. It seemed to him that Sara had become well-adjusted very quickly after coming home, even after the death of the old woman who used to work for her parents. The two girls seemed to be enjoying a friendly evening together, probably sharing secrets the way he remembered they used to do, their heads close together, until they finally walked away in the direction of the promontory with their arms linked.

'You see, Robbie?' Miriam's soft voice said beside him. 'I told you she'd only been trying it on when she came back. It didn't take her long to get over you, and she never bothered to come and give you a proper explanation, did she? Too ashamed, I daresay.'

He heard the clink of glasses as she held out his glass of lemonade to him. They had been playing draughts and listening to a favourite programme on the wireless together. It was tacitly accepted that there was nothing wrong in her being here in his flat, especially when he could be relied on to be such a gentleman. With her father being a retired vicar, she had the strange idea that this made her immune from any gossip, a comment that always made Robbie smile.

If she only knew it, she was perfectly safe with him. It wasn't that he wasn't fond of her, but he didn't love her in the way she wanted to be loved, and he had no intention of compromising himself or her, by doing anything to ruin that fact. He had a good reputation in the town, and a rakish artist wasn't the way he wanted to be seen. Unfortunately, if he made any kind of move, he wasn't at all sure that Miriam would protest.

It made him extra cautious when she was around, and he knew it frustrated her. She had been quick enough to encourage the rumours about Sara, but Robbie was damned sure she wouldn't want to be put in that position herself. Her father would probably disown her. There had been more than one instance in the town when a girl had got a man to marry her after he'd got her in trouble, and he wasn't going to be put in that situation himself and face the shame of a shotgun wedding.

Miriam was a tease, and she was quite capable of leading him on, and sometimes he felt as though he was walking on eggshells as far as she was concerned. It was completely different from the easy relationship he had always had with Sara. He turned away from the window, irritable with himself for letting his thoughts stray to her so much. But who was he kidding? She was never out of his thoughts.

'Let's forget her,' he said abruptly. 'Do you want another game of draughts?' he asked next, knowing he sounded more like an old man than a lover.

Miriam laughed softly, and put her arms around his neck. She smelled fresh with the flowery scent she always wore that tickled his nostrils, and he knew he was doing her an injustice by letting her think there could be any future for them. But for a few minutes he let himself be seduced by her nearness and the sinuous feel of her in his arms. Considering he was a cripple, which was how he harshly regarded himself, at least he knew someone wanted him, even if she wasn't the right one.

Her lips were eager on his, and they were sweet with the taste of lemonade, and he held her close to him and kissed her back. She was the kind of girl of whom a man could never have a moment's doubt. But he had never had a moment's doubt about Sara, either, which made the disbelief and shock of what she had done all the harder to bear. After a moment, Miriam pulled away with a sigh.

'All right, one more game of draughts and then I'm going home. I can see your mind isn't on much else tonight. It's late, and I don't want Dad sending out search parties for me, thinking I've been abducted by the wicked artist.'

'There's nothing wicked about me,' Robbie said with a harsh laugh.

'No, I'm afraid there isn't, darling,' Miriam said lightly.

A few days later, Sara knew this situation couldn't

go on. She had to talk to Robbie and she had to do it soon. Whatever he thought about her now, she wanted him to know that she had never stopped loving him. She wasn't sure how she could make him believe it when she had run off so callously, but it was true. Loving Chesney had been a kind of madness, the kind of Hollywood madness that was dramatic and heart-wrenching, but her love for Robbie was real. Even when she was on the ship taking her to America, she had spent more nights worrying over him than anticipating Chesney's face when he saw her again. It was Robbie's tortured face as she thought of him opening the letter she had left him that filled her dreams.

By now her mother had advertised for an assistant to replace Leah, since it was clear that there would probably be friction between Sara and her parents if she continued doing Leah's job. She had never wanted to work at the family guesthouse, and her job at the solicitor's would only be held open until Angie Reid left to get married in September, so in Sara's mind it was imperative that someone applied to take Leah's place quickly.

That morning she cycled down to the town to queue up for whatever meat was available at the butcher's. Their visitors had to hand over their ration books on arrival, and through necessity during the war years, Ellen had become adept at producing interesting and nourishing meals. But even though Britain and her Allies had won the war, there were still many privations, and coming back from America, Sara was ever conscious of them. The Americans had suffered huge losses in manpower, but they hadn't had the physical bombardment of their cities or the terrible blitz in London and other big cities. They didn't understand in the same way ... but one thing that visitors to Boskelly's guesthouse could be sure of, was the succulent fish that Ellen served up on a regular basis. Guests from the cities were always entranced by the sight of the gleaming catch being brought into the harbour each evening, knowing that the fish on their dinner plates was fresh and plentiful from Cornish waters.

'Here, take your turn, miss,' she heard someone say as she was jostled in the butcher's queue. 'We all want our bit of scrag end and a couple of sausages.'

Sara smiled weakly, caught up for a moment in the memory of how different it had been on the Irishes' New Jersey farm – once the shock of Chesney's betrayal was over. The couple had been extremely kind to her, and the fact that the area was surrounded by other farms meant that they never went short of meat or other produce. It had seemed wonderful to Sara at first, but later on, she had begun to wonder how her mother would have reacted to all this luxury, and felt guilty for knowing they were still being severely rationed at home.

She edged forward in the queue, aware that people were muttering behind her, and she knew it would be a long while before people stopped talking about her. It was a daily ordeal to go into the town, but she had no intention of hiding away. Her bright hair was too distinctive for her to disguise who she was. But for all her resolve the occasional whispers that reached her ears felt as if they were written and shouted in sky-high letters. The comments were always the same.

'...no better than she should be...'

'...her mother must be so ashamed...'

'...and where's the husband, I'd like to know? If there is one...'

By now, Sara had discovered the best way to deal with the gossip-mongers was to try to embarrass them so she turned around in the queue and spoke sweetly to the two women with their heads nodding closely together.

'Good morning, ladies. I'll try not to take up too much time with Mum's order when I get to the front of the queue.'

Sometimes her affrontery was greeted with indignant sniffs, and sometimes by smothered giggles by others in the queue. She didn't care. If she had done something wrong, she had certainly paid for it and if her parents were prepared to forgive her and welcome her back like the prodigal daughter that she was, she didn't care what these old biddies thought.

The bravado soon faded, depending on however long she had to wait to reach a shop counter. At least here, the butcher always had a kind word for her, especially since it was his young daughter Peggy who worked at doing the bedrooms at the guesthouse, and he probably knew all there was to know by now.

'Now then, young Sara, what can I do for you today?' he said cheerfully, sharpening his lethal-looking butcher's knife on his sharpening stone as he always did to impress his customers, just as if he had vast quantities of joints to carve.

'I've got Mum's list,' Sara said, 'but I've got another errand to do, Mr Tully, so if I can leave the list with you, I'll collect the meat in about half an hour if you don't mind, so you can serve these other ladies first.'

'Right you are, my dear,' he said, and as she slipped back through the women crowding into the shop, she caught his words to the next customers.

'A real nice girl, that one, and I'll not hear a word against her. Now then, what can I do for you, ladies?'

It was nice to know she had a champion of sorts, thought Sara, as she left the shop and breathed deeply again. She would leave her bicycle where it was until she collected her mum's meat order. It was sensible to leave it until she was ready to go home, she didn't want to risk the blood from the meat seeping out of the brown paper bags and dripping all the way home. People might think she had murdered somebody to add to all the rest of her crimes.

She wandered around the bay, steeling herself for what she knew she had to do. There seemed to be more summer visitors than ever in the town today, and she had seen several go in and out of Robbie's shop. But she couldn't wait for ever. His door was open to invite customers, and fighting down her nerves, she went inside.

Robbie looked up with a ready smile, which froze when he saw Sara.

'So you haven't disappeared again,' he stated.

It wasn't the best way to start, and she flushed angrily.

'You must have heard that old Leah died, and I've been taking over her duties for Mum. It's been difficult to get away, but I'm sorry I didn't come and see you when I said I would.'

'You found time to see Hilly, though.'

She groaned, knowing he must have seen her when she and Hilly lingered for so long at the harbour after the pictures. For two pins she'd march right back out, but that would be childish and would achieve nothing. She spoke stiffly.

'Robbie, I'm sorry, but I do need to talk to you. I have to explain things properly. You do see that, don't you? I know this isn't the time or the place, but just tell me where and when, and I'll be there, I promise.'

She was practically begging, and it wasn't her style at all, but when did anyone ever stop to think of pride at a time like this?

Outside his shop window now, several people were examining the paintings stacked there, and at any minute they would be interrupted.

'Please, Robbie,' she said, more urgently. 'Don't shut me out completely.'

His gaze flickered. 'Sunday afternoon, two o'clock,' he said abruptly. 'Come to the rear of the studio. We'll go for a short drive out of the town where we'll be out of range of busybodies.'

'You have a car now?' Sara said in surprise.

'You're not the only one to have made a lot of changes in your life.'

'Including Miriam. Won't she expect to see you on Sunday afternoon?'

'Miriam will be teaching Sunday School for an hour or so as usual. With her father still in charge, despite his so-called retirement, she never misses a class.'

So she was going to be slotted in to the one hour when Miriam would be safely out of the way and needn't ever know that Sara Boskelly was going for a drive in Robbie Killaine's car. Unless somebody told her.

'I'll see you then,' she said quickly, before the unworthy idea took hold.

She went out of the shop with her heart thudding, but a flicker of hope in her heart. No matter what the reason or the circumstances, the fact remained that she and Robbie would be spending an hour together on Sunday afternoon, and if she couldn't make him see then that she had made a hideous mistake in going after Chesney, and that Robbie would always be her one true love, then she wasn't the girl she knew she was.

She hurried back to Tully's butcher's shop and collected the parcel of meat to put in the basket at the front of her bicycle, and raced back to the guesthouse with it, knowing she had been away too long.

'Where have you been all this time, Sara?' her mother complained. 'I was almost ready to send out search parties for you.'

It was just an innocent remark, and one that Sara would have laughed off if she wasn't so sensitive to such remarks now. She felt her face flush again.

'I'm sorry. There was such a long queue at Tully's, and you know how he likes to talk to his customers.'

She hadn't realised how defensive she sounded

until Ellen put her hand on her daughter's arm.

'It's all right, dear. I know this is still a difficult time for you, but you do well to hold your head up high. Time is very forgiving.'

'It's a pity that doesn't always apply to people, then,' Sara muttered.

'Well, I'm glad you're back now, because I've got some news for you,' Ellen said, determinedly asking no questions. 'I've had an enquiry about Leah's job before even advertising it, and I'm seeing the person this afternoon. So you probably won't have to be tied here for much longer.'

Sara was relieved at her words, but at the same time she was surprised to realise that she felt nervous. She was thrilled to know she could go back to her old job for Potter and Grebe, and she needed to feel independent again, but the guesthouse had also been like a security blanket. It was familiar and it was home, and the weekly visitors who came from different parts of the country didn't know anything of her background. They merely saw the smiling owners' daughter, not the girl who had brought shame to her family and heartache to the man she loved.

'I'm seeing Robbie on Sunday afternoon, Mum,' she said quickly. 'He has a car now, and we're going for a drive so that I can try to explain things to him.'

She avoided her mother's eyes as she spoke, but there was no missing the concern in Ellen's voice.

'It's your business, Sara, but you shouldn't try to come between him and the life he's made for himself now.'

'I know that. But we were always meant to be

together, Mum.'

'You didn't think that when you left him for someone else, did you? It's well known that he's been seeing another girl for a while now. Are you going to ruin her life as well?'

Ellen rarely spoke frankly about personal things and it made Sara feel uncomfortable. She didn't know how much Ellen knew about Miriam Roche, and she prayed she had never got to hear about the undignified brawling between them when they had confronted one another at the harbour. That hope was dashed in a moment.

'You know I always try to pay no attention to gossip, Sara. But arguing with a vicar's daughter in the middle of the town is no way to behave.'

'I know, and I'm sorry! But she was the one who provoked me. You wouldn't have had me just stand there and let her attack me, would you? Anyway, our guests come from out of town, so they wouldn't have been affected by it, would they? Anybody who witnessed it probably thought it added a bit of spice to their lives at seeing two wild Cornish girls having a go at each other.'

She knew she was sounding petty, but she was upset and needed to lash out in any way she could. The anticipation of being with Robbie on the following Sunday afternoon was fading away, and she was already wondering if he would tell Miriam about it. If he did, it would indicate that this drive in the car meant nothing to him other than indulging Sara and getting things over between them once and for all.

'I think you're acting like a child now,' her mother said coldly. 'If you can't talk more sensibly, then I suggest you go and find something useful to do. Your father's in his shed, so go and tell him I'll be making some coffee in ten minutes.'

Sara turned away with her eyes smarting, wondering why it was so darned easy to upset people when it was the last thing she wanted to do. It only proved how fragile her nerves still were at coming back here at all. If it hadn't been for the pull of home, which was stronger than anything else, she would have done better to stay in America and never come back.

She went to the shed at the rear of the property alongside the guesthouse and found her father inside. He was a keen amateur carpenter who liked to do many of the domestic repair jobs himself. Sara watched as he planed a length of wood, breathing in the fragrant scent of the wood shavings. Knowing what a perfectionist he was, she said nothing to disturb him for a minute or two. Then he caught sight of her shadow and looked up. She wished desperately that he would smile at her the way he used to, but although she could talk to her mother, her father was still angry at her behaviour and found it difficult to come to terms with what she had done. She forced a smile to her own lips.

'Mum says she's making coffee in ten minutes,' she told him. 'What are you doing out here, Dad?'

There was a time when she was small, when she would sit on the little wooden stool he had made for her, marvelling as he whittled a piece of driftwood into a recognisable shape, then stained it and polished it until it became something wonderful, at least to a child's eyes.

'I'm making a few ornaments for the church bazaar,' he said. 'I could be doing something more useful, but your mother thinks we should make an effort, so she'll be baking some cakes for it as well.'

He was so uncompromising. He spoke to her, but there was no warmth in his voice, and Sara ached for their old relationship to return.

'Maybe I could do something as well. I could buy some plain handkerchiefs and embroider something in a corner of each. Do you remember one Christmas when I was quite small, and I gave you a tie as a present? Mum bought the tie but I embroidered a fish on it.'

'It was quite a nice tie, and not a bad fish, considering your age at the time,' he acknowledged.

'It was embroidered with love, and you wore it all that Christmas, and told everybody I had done it for you. I was always good at sewing, and I'd mend your heart if I could, Dad.'

The words were out before she could stop them, and her mouth was trembling now. She hadn't meant to mention the tie at all. It had been somewhere in the back of her mind, along with all the other idyllic childhood memories, and she had certainly never meant to say anything so stupid as a wish to mend his heart.

Her father didn't speak for a moment, and then to her utter joy he dropped the piece of wood he was working on and held out his arms to her, and she was weeping in his embrace.

'Oh Daddy, I'm so sorry for everything, you do know that, don't you? If I could change it all I would, and I've regretted bringing all this shame to you and Mum so much. I longed to come home and for everything to be the way it was, but I know now that it can never be. We can't ever go back, can we? Not completely.'

Frank Boskelly stroked her hair, holding her close, his own voice not quite steady. 'You did something very wrong, Sara, but you came home where you've always been loved, and I've been a fool for not realising how much you needed us. It's true that we can't ever go back to the way we were before, but we can always go forward, can't we? Starting now.'

She hugged him back, feeling as if they had come a very long way together in so short a time, and if they could come this far, then it had to bode well for the future. She had always been an optimist, and her heart felt as though it was bursting now. It was as though she had somehow absorbed something of old Leah's and her Aunt Dottie's wisdom, all their omens and superstitions and portents for the future. And for her, that meant Robbie.

Chapter 7

Sara knew better than to try to rush things with Robbie, and she didn't go anywhere near his shop for the next few days. She and Hilly were going to the flicks again on Saturday evening, and once the usherette had shown them to their seats, she couldn't wait to tell her of her date with Robbie the next day.

'You can hardly call it a date,' Hilly pointed out prosaically. 'You shouldn't get your hopes up too much about this, Sara. Miriam Roche has still got her claws in him, and she's not going to give him up easily.'

Sara dismissed any such thoughts. 'Robbie's got a mind of his own, and once we're alone together I'm sure I can make him see how sorry I am that I made such a fool of myself. I know he'll forgive me.'

Hilly was her usual pithy self. 'You did more than make an absolute fool of yourself! You went halfway around the world chasing a Yank, and when it all went wrong you came back expecting everything to be the same. You thought he'd wait for you to come to your senses, and he didn't, Sara. That's what you've got to get into your thick head. He found somebody else, just as you did.'

Sara flinched. Nobody could put it quite so bluntly as Hilly, she thought crossly, and even if what she said was true, she didn't want to hear it.

She didn't want her fragile confidence undermined until she had had the all-important talk with Robbie. It had waited too long already.

Thankfully, the lights in the cinema dimmed, putting an end to any more of this uncomfortable conversation. All the same, Hilly's words stuck in her mind, and Sara found it hard to concentrate on the romance being played out on the screen. Afterwards, she couldn't have told anyone what the film was about. She was almost glad when they parted company that evening, before she had to listen to any more warnings about taking things slowly. But Hilly couldn't resist a final comment that it wasn't fair to queer Miriam's pitch now that she was Robbie's girl.

'Queer Miriam's pitch?' Sara mocked, even though the words made her heart quail for a moment. 'What kind of language is that, for God's sake? You wouldn't have got very far in an English test with that sort of phrase.'

'Probably not, but it's a long time since we were at school, and you know damn well what I'm talking about. Did it never occur to you that Robbie might be in love with Miriam?'

'What utter rot!' Sara said, starting to laugh. 'How could anyone imagine him being in love with that frump! By all accounts, he only went out with her because he was sorry for her after her brother died.'

'Maybe that's how it started, but maybe they both needed somebody, and haven't you ever heard of finding love on the rebound?'

'I'm not listening to any more of this,' Sara said. 'I'll see you next week and let you know how things went, and I'm sure it will be good news!'

She flounced off in the direction of the guesthouse, but her heart was thumping, because she wasn't at all sure it was going to be good news. She wasn't completely heartless, and if what Hilly said was true ... if Robbie and Miriam were truly in love ... but she couldn't believe it, and she wouldn't believe it. Not unless she heard him say the words himself, and she prayed that she never would.

She spent a restless night fretting over what she was going to say to him, going over and over in her mind the things they would say to one another. When she finally slept, in her dreams she acted out the best scenes of all, where Robbie would swear his undying love for her and tell her that nothing else mattered ... and then the sweetest dreams were interrupted by the impossible scene where he said there was no future for them any more, and that he was in love with Miriam Roche and intended to marry her...

'You're looking pale today, Sara,' her father told her the next morning when she had finished her chores in the dining-room. 'Your mother told me where you're going this afternoon, and I can only advise you to go slowly. If you try to rush headlong into things, you'll get nowhere with that young man.'

'I do have to talk to him, though, don't I? I have to make him understand that it was all a kind of madness. You understand now, don't you, Dad?'

'I'm trying to, but it's a different situation for Robbie. His pride will have been hurt in a different way. I can only advise you to be yourself, my dear, to be the girl he used to know.'

If the town gossips, and plenty of others, were to be believed, she was anything but that girl now, Sara thought dispiritedly. She was a shameless hussy who had turned her back on one of their local boys – one with a lame leg as well and gone chasing after one of the flash Yanks with their chocolates and nylons. Sara could imagine what they had all been saying of her when the news got out, and right now, with her nerves so jittery, she could imagine it more vividly than ever.

That Sunday morning seemed to drag interminably, but at last the hours passed, and after pecking at her dinner, Sara changed into a pink flowered summer dress, white shoes and white crochet gloves. However nervous she felt inside, she wanted to look her confident best for this afternoon, which she was now thinking of as the most important afternoon of her life. Which it was. She wanted her sweetheart back.

The sun was a brilliant orb in a clear blue sky today, and she made herself believe that at least that was a good omen. It was the kind of day that brought people out into the open air and lifted their spirits. Sara cycled down into the town, weaving in and out of the holiday-makers, waving to several of their own visitors who recognised her, and saying hello to the local people she knew. She could almost pretend it was like any other Sunday, one of hundreds that she and Robbie had spent together ever since they were children. There had been no war clouds on the horizon then.

If only the war hadn't happened ... if only the Americans hadn't sent their boys over here in droves... Life was full of 'if onlys' and it had been a great and glorious day when the Americans had added their weight to the Allied cause. Without them who knew what the outcome might have been? Their expertise on the battlefields was unquestionable, but it was here in the towns and villages where they had stormed into people's lives and hearts. Dashing and handsome in their smart uniforms, so good with the children, so polite to the adults, and so alluring to young, weak-willed girls like herself...

'For God's sake, stop it,' Sara muttered to herself. The last thing she wanted to do was to think about Chesney in such terms, and yet she was almost compelled to do so, to try to explain to Robbie just why she had fallen for him. She wanted to forget Chesney and his betrayal, but because of what she had to do today, he was as real in her mind as on the day she met him.

She propped up her bicycle on the wall outside Robbie's studio, noting the modest little car parked in the narrow street outside. Without thinking, she found herself comparing it to the flashy cars she had seen in America, long and sleek and brash, and she willed the images away. She didn't know whether or not to go inside the studio, but Robbie must have seen her coming, because he came out before she got the chance.

'Let's go,' he said abruptly.

'Why are you doing this? I wouldn't have thought you'd want to be seen taking me out in your car,' she retaliated before she could stop herself.

'I think it's best if we go somewhere on neutral

ground. We'll drive out to the cliffs on the way to Zennor and park where we won't be disturbed. And then you can tell me what you've got to say.'

God, he was a cold fish today! He was as unlike the warm, loving sweetheart she had once known as it was possible to be. He was holding her so much at arms' length she might as well still have been on the other side of the Atlantic. But as he held the car door open for her she caught the slight nervous twitch at the side of his mouth, and she knew instantly why he hadn't wanted her in his studio. It was too full of their past, all the memories, the laughter and the love they had shared, and he was obviously determined to keep it all in the past where it belonged. The very thought that he couldn't bear for this meeting to take place in his studio after all gave her a glimmer of hope that he must still care for her a little.

He should have thought twice then, Sara thought, obliged to sit close to him in the small interior of the car. It was as intimate as sharing a sofa.

'Don't say anything until we park the car up by Clodgy Point,' Robbie continued grimly. 'I haven't had this car long and it's a bit temperamental so I need to concentrate on my driving.'

'All right,' Sara said, more meekly than she felt.

She knew this wasn't a good idea. The car's engine stuttered a little as it climbed up the steep hill out of St Ives, and she could hear Robbie cursing under his breath. It would be pretty awful if they broke down at some stage. Maybe they would be stranded up on the cliffs, and would have to walk all the way back to St Ives. How would he explain all that to Miriam...? It was perfectly bitchy to wish for such a thing to happen, but even so...

Once away from the town and heading for the open moors, the car settled down, and Sara gazed out at the well-remembered countryside, the ancient chimneys of long-abandoned tin mines that had once flourished here, and the gorse and wild flowers in full midsummer profusion. Long ago when they were on the brink of adolescence, and gauche in the extreme, Robbie told her that whenever the gorse was in bloom, it was supposed to be kissing time. And that sometime, somewhere, there was always gorse in bloom...

She remembered his words vividly now, seeing the bright yellow fronds of gorse against the dark green foliage, wondering if he too remembered that first adolescent kiss they had shared that day. From the set look of his face, it was hard to believe he was remembering anything, and that this outing was no more than a necessary duty to get out of the way. It was strange and sad to be so close to him, and yet feel he was as unreachable as if there was still an ocean between them.

And whose fault is that? asked a voice inside her head.

Clodgy Point was only a few miles outside St Ives, but from here right around to Land's End the cliffs soared and rock-climbers risked their lives scaling them in a sport Sara had never been able to understand. To reach Clodgy Point, with its marvellous views back to St Ives and beyond, it was necessary to walk from the main road. If this was what Robbie had in mind, Sara hoped her fine white American shoes would stand up to it, but she didn't dare bring his attention to them while he seemed to be in such a foul mood. To her relief, he eventually stopped the car when the road widened out a little, and turned to her.

'Right. I don't imagine you'll want to go cliff-walking, so we can sit on the grass overlooking the cliffs. It's not exactly isolated, but it'll do.'

She had already realised they were far from being alone. Sunday afternoon was a popular time for visitors to explore the surrounding countryside, and locals too took advantage of all that nature had to offer. At sea level, there was fine fishing to be had for amateur anglers, and she could see other cars parked at intervals on the road ahead. At least if they broke down, they could probably hitch a ride back to town, which would save dear Miriam worrying too much, she thought dryly. She tried to stay cynical about her and the impossible thought that Robbie might really love Miriam Roche, to try to offset the uncomfortable way her heart seemed to be leaping about in her chest with nerves.

'I've never seen so many people here before,' she said quickly as she got out of the car and felt the welcome heat of the sun on her face. 'Do you remember the horror we felt at school when we were told that Clodgy was Cornish for leper? It sent shivers down our spines, didn't it?'

Robbie didn't answer. He merely strode ahead of her until they reached a grassy patch of land on the seaward side of the road. She sat down abruptly, refusing to go any further, and wondering just what she had to do to break down the barriers between them. Right now it seemed like a hopeless task, and one that was slowly breaking her heart.

Robbie sat beside her. 'So now talk.'

She had wanted to explain things to him so desperately, and yet she was suddenly tongue-tied. How was she ever going to explain what she had done? She had broken his heart and behaved in a shameful way, and now she was back and expecting him to take her into his arms and back into his life ... how could she be so foolish as to think it could ever happen?

She swallowed the huge lump in her throat and continued looking out to sea while she fought for the right things to say. There was a clutch of small white yachts sailing gracefully out from St Ives, and they looked so peaceful and idyllic, so very different from the way she was feeling.

'Do you still wish you were out there?' she heard Robbie say.

'Of course I don't! If I'd wanted to stay in America, I'd never have come back, would I?'

'So why did you? You disrupted everybody's life once, so why do it all over again? Or do you enjoy twisting the knife?'

She gaped at him, shocked by the harshness in his voice. 'How can you say such a thing? It's not like you to be so cruel.'

'Isn't it? What do you know about the way I am? And what gives you the monopoly on being cruel?'

She was really starting to get upset now. This wasn't going well at all, and although she knew she couldn't expect him to be instantly forgiving, he wasn't giving her a chance. Her voice was tremulous.

'I know I deserved that, but we've come here for a purpose, haven't we, Robbie? If you're not going to listen to me, there was no point in coming, was there?'

She made to scramble to her feet, but he put out his hand and stopped her. His hand was warm and strong. It was the first real contact between them, and a sad little shiver ran through her, because it was so much less than the contact she wanted. So much less than love...

'All right, so try to explain, if you can, why you did what you did, why you hurt me and your parents so much, and scandalised so many people. There must have been something very powerful between you and this Yank to make you do such a thing.'

Sara clenched her hands for a moment, her body so tense it felt brittle. She had said it all so many times now, but never to the one who meant so much to her. She had tried to tell him why she was going away in the letter she left him, but this was so much harder. This was doing penance – and trying to save his pride too.

'You met Chesney a few times, Robbie, and you know how charming he could be,' she said in a low voice.

'I don't need to hear a character study of the chap. Just tell me how it happened, and why.'

'I wasn't pregnant, if that's what you thought!' she burst out. 'Anyone with any common sense would have worked that out from the timing involved. But of course, once I was branded as a good-time girl, that's what everyone would have assumed, isn't it?'

'Not everyone. I never thought that.'

'Didn't you?'

The glimmer of hope faded as he went on. 'I just thought you were a silly little girl, seduced by the glamour of America and what the Yanks could offer. Far better than being tied to a Cornish cripple. So did he marry you?'

Sara stared at him. 'No, he didn't marry me. He wasn't even where he said he would be, and he wasn't who he said he was, either. I'll tell you all of it, if you'll only shut up and listen! And don't call yourself a Cornish cripple, either. You're anything but that, and you know how it annoys me!'

She saw the hint of a smile on his face as she reverted to her old quick-fire replies. He leaned back on the grass on his elbows and let her talk.

It started slowly, and then it all came out like a flood, all the initial excitement coupled with the dread at knowing what she was doing to him and her family ... then the shock and the hurt at knowing how Chesney had deceived her.

'But I was never as close to him as people seemed to think, Robbie. You do understand what I mean, don't you? I didn't have carnal knowledge of him, as the Bible puts it.' She didn't know how else to say it without being crude and putting pictures into his mind that she didn't want.

He didn't look at her, his eyes on the distant horizon, as if he would see right into those faraway places that had taken her away from him.

'Maybe not, but you wanted to be swept off

your feet like some idiotic film star. Did you expect the streets of America to be paved with gold and that this Yank of yours was going to be the hero of every picture you ever saw? If so, you were more gullible than I ever believed, Sara.'

'Don't you think I don't know that?' she flashed at him angrily. 'Don't you think I told myself a thousand times what a fool I was to throw away everything that I loved the most, to go chasing a dream?'

She listened to the passionate words she was saying, and hated herself for talking to him like this. It felt so artificial, as if they were the ones acting out a stupid scene from a stupid Hollywood film. It wasn't the way they had always been with one another. It wasn't the way they were, but somehow they had lost the art of being natural with one another.

She stood up too fast, swaying slightly, her head dizzy with the knowledge that this wasn't going right at all – if she had ever thought that it could.

'This was another mistake, wasn't it?' she said bitterly. 'Leah always said you could never go back but I didn't believe her. I thought I could come back and that you'd want me again, as much as I want you. I never stopped loving you, Robbie, but I must have been mad to think your feelings would have stayed the same, because they haven't, have they?'

She ached for him to sweep her into his arms and tell her that of course he still felt the same about her, but she could hardly expect him to do that now that Miriam Roche was well and truly on the scene. He had too much integrity to let

Miriam down the way Chesney had let Sara down. She smothered a sob in her throat and turned to rush back across the road to where the car was parked, unable to look at him any longer.

The couple who were out for a Sunday afternoon jaunt on their motor-bike were a blur to her. She didn't even register the sound of their chugging machine until she heard them shout out a warning, and then she felt Robbie's arms grabbing her back from the certain collision. The motor-bike wobbled as the driver avoided her, still yelling back cuss-words as the couple rode on in the direction of Zennor, leaving her shaken.

'That was a crazy thing to do,' Robbie yelled, just as angrily. 'Those people could have been badly injured because of you, and so could you.'

She didn't want his censure. She didn't want him thinking she was a crazy idiot on top of everything else he thought about her. She didn't want anything but the realisation that she was being held tight in his arms, and even if he didn't want her there, she couldn't miss the chance of this moment. She twisted round and clung to him, her hair in his face, her mouth upturned to his, and everything was the right way up again. Sara and Robbie ... Robbie and Sara. The next minute he was kissing her, kissing her, kissing her ... and just as quickly he pushed her away, his eyes dark and furious.

'That wasn't meant to happen, and you'd better forget it.'

'I will if you will,' Sara said, challenging him with a voice that wasn't quite steady. 'Will you, Robbie? The next time you see Miriam Roche, will you really be able to forget that kiss? Because as sure as eggs are eggs, I won't.'

'It's time we went back,' he said curtly. 'I think we've said all we had to say and it doesn't alter anything. You still went running after that Yank and when it didn't turn out the way you'd planned, you decided to come home and take second best. Except that that didn't turn out the way you planned either, did it?'

'You were never second best! How could you ever think such a thing? I always loved you, Robbie, and I always will.'

'But not enough to stay.'

He had strode ahead of her across the road to the car now, and she followed him, feeling more distressed than ever. He had said some heartless things to her, and she didn't deserve them – well, not all of them. She caught at his hand as he opened the car door for her.

'You don't really think I planned everything that happened, do you? You can't really believe I'd be as calculating as that, Robbie.'

'I don't know what you planned. I don't even know you any more. Now, get in the car, will you?'

She sat beside him silently all the way back to St Ives, more miserable than ever. Even this stretch of road was full of memories. For they had walked or cycled along it so many times in the past, running down to the little coves and kicking off their shoes and racing, screaming with laughter, into the surf and ending up lying exhausted on the sand, squinting at the sun and happily planning a future that had never come true. There were memories everywhere they turned, because they had once been so much a part of each other's lives that neither of them could have imagined a time when it would change.

Despite the awful way this afternoon had ended, Sara felt that small sliver of warmth steal into her heart again, because no matter what he said, he could never forget the memories, any more than she could. They were too closely entwined with one another. For now, she had done all she could to try to make him understand that she loved him, always had and always would, and that this other madness was just that and no more. But she knew his pride had been deeply hurt, and because of that, she could forgive him anything, even the cruel words he flung at her.

From now on, though, she resolved not to hide away from him. She would do things differently. Everywhere he looked, she would be there. Not in a brash way that would make him furious with her, but enough to rile Miriam Roche to distraction. It was a plan that would be wrong in Miriam's pious eyes, but everything was supposed to be fair in love and war. And this was war.

Finally they reached the quiet road behind Robbie's studio, neither of them having said a word on the way back. Then Sara stepped out of the car and gaped. Her bicycle was still propped up against the wall, but both tyres had been slashed to ribbons.

'Oh God, who the hell has done this?' Robbie groaned. 'It seems you've still got a few enemies in the town.'

'Or just one,' Sara retorted. But in a strange

way, she felt almost relieved. So she wasn't the only one to think that a state of war existed between them, to use old Chamberlain's famous phrase. She took a deep breath.

'I'll leave it there if you don't mind, and ask my dad to collect it in his van later. I can easily walk home. I need some fresh air, anyway.'

'I'm sorry about this, Sara,' he said awkwardly, and she guessed that he had reluctantly reached the same conclusion as she had.

Sara shrugged. 'Never mind. It just shows how vindictive some people can be. Don't let it bother you. It's only a couple of tyres. It's not a broken heart, and both of them can be mended, can't they?' she said enigmatically.

Before Robbie knew what she was about to do, she touched his face with her finger and then pressed a swift kiss on his cheek. Then she walked off with her head held high, wondering as she did so, just how near or far Miriam Roche was at that moment. Was she watching to see the effect her vandalism would have had on Sara, expecting her to throw a tantrum or burst into tears? If so, she was out of luck. Sara hadn't gone through the shock of Chesney's betrayal and the trauma of coming back to St Ives to face the music, to fall apart at the sight of two slashed bicycle tyres.

Robbie let himself into his studio and stood perfectly still for long moments before going upstairs to his flat, his head throbbing with all the tension of the afternoon. When he wasn't working, he kept his studio curtains closed during the brightness of the day so that the sunlight wouldn't affect his paintings, and today it was cool and dark after the brilliance of that Sunday afternoon.

Sara was right about one thing, of course. He wouldn't forget that kiss, any more than he had ever forgotten any of the thousands of kisses they had shared over the years. Tremulous childhood kisses that were little more than shy pecks on the cheeks ... the kisses of growing awareness of one another as young adults ... and later, the passionate kisses of sweethearts with all the promise of a future that was destined to be spent together.

She had been just as passionate and eloquent in her explanations of all that had gone on in this past year, holding nothing back, trying to make him believe that she had never felt anything for this Yank that could compare with what she felt for him. But she must have loved the Yank. She had loved him. With searing honesty, she had admitted that too. Even if it wasn't the love that grew from years of knowing one another, she had loved another man and felt strongly enough about him to cross an ocean for him. He couldn't forget that, either.

His thoughts shifted to the moment she had got out of his car and stared at the ruined tyres on her bicycle. Her heart must have been pounding, and he had expected her to fly into a rage, but there had been a quiet dignity about the way she accepted it that he had found touching, and grudgingly admired. As to who could have done it – he gave a smothered curse, and went up to his flat, pushing the uneasy suspicions out of his mind.

Chapter 8

Sara's father collected her bike from Robbie's studio on Sunday evening and fitted it with two new tyres, heeding Sara's plea that it was probably just stupid kids who had vandalised them and she didn't want any fuss. She knew Frank would have preferred to find the culprits, and hadn't wanted to ignore it, but he gave in to her wishes in the end.

She hadn't intended seeing Hilly until the following Saturday, but several things happened to change her mind. Firstly, the prospective new replacement for Leah was eager to start work at the guesthouse on Monday morning, so Sara was relieved of her duties. She went to Potter and Grebe that morning and was told she could start in a week's time if she wished, as Angie was forever wanting time off now to get everything ready for her wedding in September. So that left Sara with time on her hands, and the ideal opportunity to cycle over to Pennywell Farm to see Hilly and tell her how it all went on Sunday.

'You've come at a good time, my dear,' Hilly's mother told her. 'We're in the middle of haymaking and Hilly's gone out to the fields with bread and cider for the men. She forgot the jar of pickled onions, so you can take it for me, if you've a mind. You'll find her in one of the far fields.'

It was the best day to be out in the country. The

air was as sweet as wine, and the scent of new-mown hay tantalised Sara's nostrils as she went across the fields to where she could see the farm-hands working alongside Hilly's jovial father, and hear them shouting to one another above the roar of the tractors. She could see Hilly too, looking every bit the part in green dungarees and work boots, her hair scraped back into a practical pony-tail.

'I thought you were one of the men for a minute,' Sara said with a grin.

'It's best to dress this way,' Hilly said airily. 'It's the way the Land Girls used to dress, and it stops the men from getting any lecherous ideas about me.'

Since most of them were nearer her father's age or already spoken for, Sara didn't think she'd be in much danger of that, but she laughed dutifully.

'So,' Hilly went on, 'you didn't come here just to deliver pickled onions, did you? I suppose you're dying to tell me what happened yesterday.'

'I am, but not here. You know how voices carry in the fields, and I don't want any more gossip passed on about me.'

'I've finished here now, anyway. I've got to deliver eggs and butter to some of the neighbouring cottages today, so you can wait until I've changed out of this clown's outfit and come with me.'

They linked arms and walked back to the farm, and Sara thanked her stars to have a friend like Hilly, one who could be relied on to listen to her and give her no-nonsense opinions, no matter what. It may have been a bit tricky when she first came home, but true friendship never died, and she had never appreciated it more.

At the farm, they went upstairs to Hilly's bedroom with its patchwork quilt and rag rugs that seemed almost from another age, and yet which suited the farmhouse so well. There was a sense of timelessness here that was never found in towns, the same kind of comfortable unworldliness as in a New Jersey fruit farm.

'So how did you and Robbie get on yesterday?' Hilly said, deftly exchanging the unflattering dungarees for a skirt and blouse and pulling her hair out of its pony-tail to shake it free. 'Is he going to ditch the delectable Miriam for you?'

Sara scowled. 'I never expected it to happen just like that!'

'But you do expect it to happen, don't you? Did anyone ever tell you you can be very arrogant, Sara?'

She said it teasingly, but Sara felt herself flush. Being candid was one thing. Being a little too near to the mark, was another.

'It's not arrogant to want what's mine.'

'He's a person, not an object, and thinking like that is what makes your attitude arrogant, Sara. I hope you didn't go in with all guns blazing.'

'For pity's sake, stop talking as if you're in a cowboy picture! I did not go in with all guns blazing. If you must know, I was practically humble.'

She realised that Hilly was laughing now, and her mouth relaxed into a smile. It did sound pretty unlikely for Sara Boskelly to be humble, but she had certainly not spared herself in telling Robbie how foolish she had been.

‘And has he forgiven you?’

Sara shook her head. ‘Not yet, but he will.’ She caught Hilly’s arch glance and laughed with her. ‘Oh all right, that’s being arrogant! But I know he will. We were always meant to be together and I’ve got a sixth sense about it.’

‘So all you have to do is dispose of the lovely Miriam.’

‘With any luck, she might just dispose of herself,’ Sara said mysteriously as they went downstairs to collect the boxes of eggs and pots of butter Hilly had to deliver.

As Mrs Weeks fussed around them, asking after Sara’s mother, and declaring how upset they must have been over old Leah’s death, and wanting to know all the details, they didn’t get a chance to say any more until they were cycling through the lanes towards the scattered cottages on the moors.

‘What did you mean by saying Miriam might just dispose of herself?’ Hilly burst out. ‘I hope you’re not thinking of putting the evil eye on her, Sara. It’s dangerous to wish somebody ill, and Leah didn’t leave you a book of spells in that fusty old cottage of hers, did she?’

‘Of course not, and if she did, I wouldn’t have looked at it. That sort of thing gives me the creeps.’

‘Yes, well, it still happens in isolated rural areas,’ Hilly retorted. ‘I just wouldn’t want you to get involved with anything so spooky, that’s all.’

‘Well, I’m not. All I meant was that Miriam might have done something to make Robbie think she isn’t quite the shining saint he thinks she is.'

They paused for breath at the top of a rise on the moors, gazing at the cottages ahead of them, in a small, isolated community where a person with a vivid imagination could picture anything happening. Black magic ... incantations ... witch-craft ... ritual killings... Sara shivered, wondering why she was letting such weird thoughts enter her head at all. They wouldn't have done so if Hilly hadn't put them there. She told her quickly of the incident with her bicycle.

Hilly hooted. 'You surely don't think a vicar's daughter would stoop to such a thing, do you?'

'Why not? It's her father who was the vicar, not her. She was never particularly churchified, ex-cept for running the Sunday School now, and I daresay that's only because of her father's say-so. He always ruled their household with a rod of iron, and that's putting it mildly.'

'I think you're getting it all out of proportion, Sara,' Hilly said flatly. 'And if you don't mind me saying so, there could be quite a few other people who might have a grudge against you and think it a lark to slash your tyres.'

'Why would anybody have a grudge against me? The only person I hurt by my actions was Robbie.'

'And your parents and your friends! But Robbie has friends too, and perhaps they don't care for the fact that you've come back to disrupt his life all over again.'

'Oh, I wish I'd never come and told you anything now. Let's get on with these deliveries. I have to get back sometime today.'

She didn't, actually. Her time was her own for the rest of the week, although she would feel obliged to help out at the guesthouse for a couple of hours each day, if only to show the ropes to Doris, the new assistant. But she was becoming upset by Hilly's words. She had known she would face opposition and anger when she returned home, but she didn't want to think that Robbie could be influenced by other people. This was between the two of them, and they were the only ones whose feelings mattered. Or perhaps she had been so blinded by what she had to do, she had simply stuck her head in the sand and ignored the fact that those other friends would have been supporting him all this time, telling him he was better off without her, and were probably still doing so. She had never thought of it as being a battleground, but that was exactly what she was thinking now.

'Don't let's quarrel, Sara,' Hilly said. 'It's far too nice a day to get on one another's nerves, and you could be right about Miriam and the tyres. It's anybody's guess who did it, really, though.'

'If you say so.' She might as well give in, although nothing would change her own mind. There was nobody else who would hate her quite as much as Miriam, or who had quite as much cause.

'Anyway,' she went on more brightly, 'it's Robbie's birthday next week, and I'm going to send him a card, same as always – well, except for last year.'

'Do you think that's a good idea?'

'Oh, for goodness' sake, Hilly, stop analysing

everything I say. I've had enough advice from people to last me a lifetime. I actually bought him a card last year too, but I didn't send it.'

She remembered that day last year very clearly. They had always spent both their birthday evenings together, and there she was, as far away from him as it was possible to be, in every sense. She had tried to picture what he would be doing – but the one thing she had never pictured, was that he would have been celebrating his birthday with Miriam Roche.

'Let's get on with delivering the eggs,' Hilly said abruptly, before she said anything else to rile her friend.

The cottages were well away from St Ives, and the people in them were unlikely to know anything about a silly girl who had gone to America chasing a dream, leaving her sweetheart behind. If they did, they probably wouldn't connect the scandal with Hilary Weeks's friend, so it was a cheerful way to spend the rest of the morning, chatting with the countryfolk in these outlying areas.

But Sara was still determined to do as she said, and send Robbie a birthday card. She still had the one she had bought last year, but that wouldn't do, since it had been printed in America, and it would be like rubbing salt in the wound if he noticed it – as he surely would. Before she went home, she purchased a card that wasn't too obviously romantic, but merely stated that it was from one friend to another. Miriam would be sure to see it – but if Robbie didn't show it to her, that would mean something completely different.

There was one other thing she intended to do. Long ago, ever since they had discovered that their feelings for one another went deeper than those of mere friendship, they had used a secret code whenever they sent birthday cards to one another. On the back of the card in tiny letters there would be some initials.

'It would hardly take a scientist to work it out,' Robbie had grinned, hugging her tight the first time he had used the code on the back of her birthday card. 'I mean, what else could ILY mean, except I love you?'

'And do you?' Sara had asked provocatively.

He had replied in a very satisfactory way without any need for words, but ever since then they had added a few more initials, learned from their basic French lessons. Jt'A also meant I love you, and Sara had no intention of leaving out the code they had always used. She loved him and always would, and if she couldn't show him any other way, at least he would know that she still remembered, and that some things would never change. It made her heart thrill as she wrote the message inside the card, 'To Robbie, from Sara', and then added the little initials on the back of it.

'What on earth are you doing up there, Sara?' her mother called, when she had been in her bedroom for a long while.

'Nothing. I'm coming now,' she gulped, putting all the birthday cards Robbie had ever sent her back into the box where they belonged. Whether she would be getting one from him in November when her own birthday came around, she didn't know – but she hoped desperately that she would.

True to her plan, she spent as much time as she decently could near the bay, hoping that every time Robbie glanced out from his shop, or came outside to talk to the customers admiring his paintings, he would see her. She offered to do all the shopping her mother needed, just so she could spend the time in the town, and she knew it was pathetic and probably childish, but short of hovering outside Robbie's door every moment, it was the best she could do.

She had forgotten that Miriam also worked in a small hairdressing salon near the harbour, and on Friday morning, she was accosted by the other girl, standing squarely in front of her, her eyes flashing furiously.

'I know what you're doing,' Miriam snapped.

Sara spoke innocently. 'I'm just doing some shopping for my mother. Do you have any objections, or are you going to start pulling my hair out again?'

'You don't fool me,' Miriam hissed, 'and it won't work. Robbie's with me now, and he's not interested in second-hand goods. You can flaunt yourself all you like, it won't make any difference.'

'Am I flaunting myself? I thought I was buying groceries. Do you want to see what I've got in my bicycle basket, or should I check first that you don't have a pair of scissors with you?'

'You can't pin that on me. I never touched your tyres.'

'Did I say you did? You obviously know all about it, though.'

Miriam went a dull red. 'Of course I know

about it. Robbie told me. We don't have any secrets from one another.'

Sara gave her a smile that would have done justice to the Mona Lisa, and cycled away with a wave of her hand, knowing that her refusal to retaliate would infuriate Miriam even more.

She wished she was as calm as she looked, but her heart was thumping now. What she was doing was mean and petty, and if she once paused to put herself in the other girl's shoes, she knew it was shameful too. She had no right to spoil things for Miriam, if Robbie really loved her ... but she was convinced that nobody could have kissed her the way Robbie had kissed her last Sunday if he was truly in love with another girl. They had belonged to one another for far too long, and she had to keep believing that this past year was nothing more than a hiccup.

As she neared the guesthouse, Bonzer came rushing out to meet her, barking joyously and coming perilously near to knocking her off her bike. It was so blessedly normal, so like the way everything had been before she went away, that she found herself laughing at his frantic greeting with tears in her eyes. She knelt down and nuzzled her face into his thick coat.

'You'll always be glad to see me, won't you, boy?' she whispered.

She felt more cheerful as she entered the guesthouse and took the groceries into the kitchen. Doris and her mother were deep in conversation, enjoying a mid-morning cup of tea and a bit of gossip, the way Ellen and Leah used to do. For a moment it made Sara's eyes prickle, but then her mother poured her a cup of tea and told her Doris's news.

'Now that Leah's cottage is empty, some new people from upcountry are interested in renting it.'

Doris put in: 'I daresay the place needed to be fumigated before anybody could look at it. Old Leah wasn't dirty but she never got rid of anything, so there was plenty of work to be done there.'

'Well, I know she liked to keep all her things around her,' Sara murmured, not wanting to hear a thing against Leah.

'There was no family, so the landlord has put everything that was of any consequence into boxes,' Doris went on. 'They're sending the best bits to the church jumble sale and the rest for burning. I know you were fond of the old girl, Sara, so if you fancy anything, you'd best get down there quick.'

'Go back to the cottage, you mean?' Sara was horrified to hear all this. 'I couldn't bear to go inside the place again, and nor can I bear to think of people sorting through Leah's precious possessions.'

It was upsetting her far more than she had expected. It was so ghoulish ... but her mother spoke gently.

'It might be a good idea, Sara. You'd know the things that Leah treasured most. If she wanted anyone to have them, I'm sure it would be you.'

'I can't. I couldn't go in there alone, either.'

'Then we'll go together,' Ellen said quietly. 'It's better than having strangers going through her things. I'll arrange it with the landlord before he gets rid of it all.'

Sara didn't want to do this, but she knew Leah would have felt easier knowing her few precious things were going to a good home. Nothing she had was precious in the material sense, only to her, such as old books and baubles and ornaments – and all the Christmas cards Sara and her parents had ever sent her. She had been such a magpie, and looking through those cardboard boxes would be like prying into her life. But there was a lot of sense in her mother's words. Better to have the people who had loved her doing it, than strangers.

Ellen arranged with the landlord of the cottage that she and Sara would go there on Thursday evening, and when the appointment time arrived it was with a trembling heart that Sara stepped inside, remembering so well the last time she had been there, and fearful that Leah's ghost would be resentful of this intrusion, however kindly it was meant. But the cleaners had done their work well. The place was free of clutter, save for the dozen or so boxes stacked on the table. It had lost its air of decay, now smelling mostly of disinfectant and polish, and Sara breathed a little steadier. And the chair where Leah had been sitting when Sara found her, was just a chair…

'Let's be businesslike,' Ellen said briskly. 'If you see anything you'd like, put it on one side, and the rest can stay in the boxes for the church jumble sale.'

It was obvious that much of it would simply be sent for burning. Old newspapers that Leah hadn't bothered to throw away would be of no use to anyone, and many of the baubles were nothing but trinkets. Except one. Sara's eyes blurred as she picked up the little turquoise brooch in a cheap setting. It was as worthless as all the rest, but it was something that Sara had bought for Leah the very first Christmas she had earned her own money. And Leah had kept it all this time, wrapped in tissue paper. Sara remembered the words she had said then, as clearly as if Leah was saying them to her now.

''Tis far too fine for the likes of me, Sara love, but I'll keep it for ever, and I'll wear it every Christmas Day, special-like, to remind me of my special maid.'

The words were so vivid in her mind that Sara involuntarily turned her head to where Leah's old chair stood like a silent sentinel. Her eyes were damp with tears, and she had to turn away again before she conjured up an image that would send her screaming out of there. Her mother was calmly going through the boxes, setting aside a few things, unaware of how Sara was affected at that moment. It was better so. She didn't want to show her fear, remembering that in Leah's old eyes, there would be nothing to fear. Death had never scared her; she always said it was nothing more than going through a door into the next room. Everybody had to do it, and she had been as curious as the next person to know what was on the other side.

Like a lot of old people, Leah was philosophical about dying. But Sara had had quite enough of remembering such things for today, preferring to be in the realm of the living, rather than thinking of anything remotely supernatural.

'I think we've done enough, my dear,' Ellen said, noting Sara's sudden shudder. 'I've got a few things to remember Leah by, and if you've found all you want, it's time we left the place to its memories.'

Sara was thankful she had used that word, and not said that they should leave the place to its ghosts. Leah's would be a kindly ghost, but by now Sara had had quite enough of the pungent atmosphere of the place, and was anxious to get outside and into the daylight again.

'I think I'll take a walk before going back home, Mum,' she said quickly, more upset than she'd thought she would be at being back in Leah's cottage. 'I'd like to be on my own for a while.'

Ellen didn't object, so they parted company at the waterfront, where the smells of fish and sun cream mingled on the air, reminding them this was summer, ordinary life went on, and people came to St Ives to relax and enjoy the pleasure of the Cornish seaside. Sara kept her head down low as she hurried around the bay and out on to Smeaton's Pier, breathing in the ozone and blinking away the threat of tears. They seemed to come all too easily these days, even when there was no reason. But of course, there was always a reason.

She had been a fool to throw away everything that she loved the most, and then to come back here, expecting everything to be the same. Leah would have told her she was thinking with her heart, and not her head. But was that such a bad thing? And then there was the shock of finding Leah the way she had. Leah, who had always been there, as immovable as a rock, but people weren't immortal, not even those as tough as old Leah. And if she couldn't weep a few tears for an old friend, then what kind of person was she, anyway?

The muddled thoughts went round and round in Sara's head, making her oblivious to the holiday-makers looking curiously at the beautiful girl with the glorious red hair who seemed so lost in thought.

'Are you all right, love?' she heard someone say. 'You're not thinking of throwing yourself in the drink for fish-bait, are you?'

She gave a start and focused on the couple with two small boys standing awkwardly behind her. She forced a smile to her lips.

'I'm not likely to do anything like that. I was just thinking about a friend who died, that's all.'

'That's all right then.'

The little family seemed to melt away, as if this was too personal a statement to share on a lovely summer evening. They were strangers who wouldn't want to be involved in something that had nothing to do with them, especially something that had happened so recently. As if anyone could choose the date when they died, Sara found herself thinking indignantly. She was sure Leah hadn't.

As the thought entered her head, Sara shook herself, wondering if she was going completely mad. It was definitely time to go home, to immerse herself in some ordinary, everyday task that took her thoughts away from the sad little contents of those boxes that were all that was left of Leah. She walked quickly back from Smeaton's Pier the way she had come and headed for home.

Inside his shop, Robbie Killaine had seen her walking around the bay and out to the pier. He had seen how her shoulders drooped and how the sun glinted on her hair as she had stood motionless for so long gazing out to sea. She had the rare ability to be still for long periods of time that appealed to his artistic soul. He had seen the strangers approach her and the way she had straightened and recovered from whatever ailed her. He had no way of knowing what it was, but he knew her well enough to know when she was troubled. He knew her as well as he knew himself – or he had always thought he did.

He was no mind-reader, and nor did he have the gift of second sight that some of the old biddies claimed to possess. But if ever he wished he had it, it was now, when he would have seen into Sara's mind if he could. She had told him everything so frankly on that Sunday afternoon, not sparing herself, and he had so wanted to believe that she thought no more of the chap who had let her down. He had wanted so much to forget all that had happened, and to wipe out everything in that past year, but it wasn't that easy.

He was courting Miriam now, and he wasn't the kind of sewer-rat that the Yank had been. One thing hadn't changed, though. He still loved Sara and always would, but it brought him no comfort to know it. He wished he could forget her, but it had been impossible to do while she was away, and it was even more impossible now that she was back. And seeing her looking so dejected on Smeaton's Pier had made his heart turn over. He wasn't a great churchgoer, but there had been a time when he might have gone to the vicar for some calm advice, and tried to come to terms with the way his life had changed. It would hardly be the sane thing to do now, though, since he didn't know the new vicar too well, and the old one was Miriam's father.

He turned away from his window and tried to push the whole lot of them out of his mind: Sara, the Yank, Miriam and her pious father. If only her brother hadn't died during the war, he thought savagely, and if only she hadn't seemed so sad and lonely, the way he'd been feeling too. He loved her in a protective way, but it wasn't the passionate love he still felt for Sara, and he knew it. The hell of it was, Miriam didn't know it, and he didn't know how he could tell her without breaking her heart. At the same time, his conscience constantly nagged away at him, asking if it was right to let her go on hoping, when he was so in love with someone else.

Chapter 9

Sara discovered that returning to work was the best way to cope with problems. They didn't go away, but they had to be submerged in the everyday business of Potter and Grebe, Family Solicitors. There were enough problems coming in and out of the offices, anyway, handling domestic tiffs and more serious affairs such as separations and the occasional divorce. She wasn't personally involved with the real business, of course, but the anxious faces of the couples coming into the reception area for their appointments were enough to make her heart jump with sympathy.

She could almost picture herself being one half of any of those couples coming here for advice ... striving to keep a marriage together ... or intent on tearing it apart ... and she knew very well that putting herself into their position was one of the worst things she could do. It was one of the first things she had been told when she first came here to work. She had to be objective, in the same way a doctor or nurse was supposed to be objective – though how they could ever do that with some of the ghastly things they had to do for their patients, Sara couldn't imagine, either.

But working was definitely a panacea of a sort. It stopped her thinking about Robbie every minute of every day, except on his birthday. All that day, she kept wondering if he had received her card yet, and what his reaction would be. It must mean something to him. It must let him know that she never forgot for a single moment all that they had meant to one another – and what he still meant to her. She was increasingly jittery about it, and her wretched imagination was in full flow, wondering if she was going to get it posted back to her in shreds in a couple of days' time. If that happened, it would be a bitter blow to her pride.

However, the days passed, and then the weeks, and summer drifted into autumn, and there had been no reaction about the birthday card from either Robbie or Miriam. No thanks, no rages, no spite, nothing.

'What did you expect?' Hilary Weeks asked her as they walked back from the cinema one Saturday evening. 'He probably took one look at it and then put it in the wastepaper basket.'

'You're a great comfort, aren't you?'

'You've got to face it, Sara. If it meant anything to him, he'd have let you know. He'd have sent you a note, or met you accidentally-on-purpose, if you see what I mean, just to say thank you. And if Miriam had seen it, I'm darned sure she wouldn't have let it go.'

'So the fact that I've heard nothing at all means that he didn't care.'

'I reckon that's what silence means,' Hilly agreed.

Sara wouldn't believe it. In her blunt and sometimes mysterious way, Leah used to say she had been born an optimist and that it was both a blessing and a curse. She hadn't understood what Leah meant by that at the time, but she was beginning to understand it now. It was a blessing in that she could always hope, but it was also a curse, because how long was a person condemned to go on hoping for a miracle when all hope had died? Robbie couldn't love her as much as he had always said he did, or he must surely realise how much he was hurting her now. But maybe this was her punishment. She had hurt him so badly, and now he was paying her back.

Two weeks later she was cycling home from work in a heavy storm that had sprung up from nowhere, whipping up the sea and sand into a frenzy, stinging the eyes and legs of those unfortunate enough to be still on the beach – although most of the holiday-makers were scuttling away to find shelter in cafés and shops. Sara had only worn a thin jacket over her dress to work that day, and she was soaked by the time she reached the guesthouse. Below the promontory, the sea was now a grey heaving mass, the horizon merging into a greyer sky, and she dumped her bicycle in the garage beside her father's car and raced indoors to dry off.

'What a day!' she gasped. 'My hair's like rats' tails and I'm wet through. I'm going upstairs to dry off and change my clothes.'

She was suddenly aware of her mother's anxious face behind the big oak reception desk, and she paused.

'What's wrong, Mum?'

'Mr and Mrs Elliott and the children had planned to go out in a pleasure boat this afternoon and they should have been back by now. I'm worried about them. Your father's going down to the harbour to check that all the boats returned before this storm began.'

'I'll go with him,' Sara said quickly. 'I'll just change my dress and put on my mac, so don't let him go without me.'

'There's no need, my dear.'

She was talking to herself by now as Sara raced upstairs to her room and struggled out of her damp dress. The Elliotts were a sweet couple from Dorset, and their two small boys were adorable. Sara had taken to them at once, and they responded to her as if she was a big sister. She couldn't bear to think of them out on the sea on such a day. The children would be terrified. The coastline around here was benign on a good day, but its benevolence could change in an instant if the weather deteriorated. The treacherous rocks all around the Cornish coast had sunk the strongest vessel, and even nearer inland there were whirlpools and eddies to trap unwary swimmers who went out too far.

She was downstairs again in five minutes, and rushing out to the garage where her father had already started up the car's engine. She slid in beside him.

'What do you think, Dad?'

'I'm thinking that I hope the family might have changed their minds when the sky got darker,' he said grimly.

Sara hoped so too, but she remembered how excited the small boys had been at the thought of going out in a pleasure boat. Generally she didn't get too involved with their guests, but this family had been different. The parents were young, and she could almost identify with them ... with herself as a young married woman, with two small boys ... and a husband looking very like Robbie...

'I'm sure you're right,' she said nervously.

Her father grunted. 'I gather those two boys were jumping about with excitement at breakfast and telling the other guests what they were going to do. I doubt that their parents would have the heart to disappoint them. Unless, of course, they went out earlier and were back before the storm began. But if they did that, why haven't they returned?'

Sara glanced at her father. 'I know we take pride in the general care of the guests, Dad, but you seem to be thinking of them almost as if they're our family.'

'Your mother always says that's exactly what they are while they're in our care,' he said shortly. 'And we know well enough how distressing it can be when someone we care about is missing, and we don't know what's happened to them or if they're ever coming back. You wouldn't know that feeling.'

Sara felt her eyes sting. It was a direct reference to the way she had gone missing, of course, even though she had left a letter telling them exactly where she was going, and why. But she had learned long ago that no letter could ever explain the emotional turmoil she too had gone through at the time; and nor could she have any idea of just how hurt her parents must have been when they discovered what she had done. It wasn't only Robbie she had let down.

'Dad, you know how sorry I am for everything

that's happened,' she said in a small voice as the car veered crazily down to the harbour, avoiding pot-holes and puddles. 'If I could undo the past, don't you know that I would?'

'That's something none of us can ever do, Sara, but let's just hope that today things are going to turn out well, and that the Elliott family have come to no harm.'

She wondered if he was comparing the two events in his mind. Sara had finally come home where she belonged, and pray to God that these four people who felt almost like family would return unscathed as well.

The scenes at the harbour were chaotic. People still gathered in little knots, despite the rain, some busily going about their work, others gawping at the sudden turn in the weather. The small rowing-boats for hire had already been pulled up on the beach as high as possible; fishing-boats and other craft jostled and bumped against one another in the swell. On the harbour itself, the placards announcing trips around the bay and deep-sea fishing trips were being battered. And then, as so often happened, the wind eased as swiftly as it had begun, and the pelting rain became an intermittent shower. Through the scudding clouds, a hint of blue sky came and went, and the chill of the rain made her mac become clammy on her skin.

'Did your boat go out today, man?' Sara heard her father shout to one of the pleasure boat owners trying to right his placard again.

'She was due to go,' the man growled, 'but she was holed last night, so she's gone in for repairs.

Cost me a packet, paying back the folk who'd booked her.'

'Do you remember their names?' Sara stuttered.

The man shrugged, clearly still put out at losing money on the aborted trip, and impatient with a slip of a girl asking damn fool questions.

'I don't keep no records, miss. Folk pay their money and get their tickets, and if they turn up, they get on the boat. If not, they don't.'

Sara and her father turned away in frustration. This wasn't the only pleasure boat in service, but none of the others were in evidence. They must be still at sea somewhere, hopefully having been aware of the storm and put in to a safer shore, or ... she shuddered, not wanting to think of the alternative.

The rain was still falling enough to make for a steady soaking. Her hair was still hanging damply from earlier, and looked even worse now, but none of it seemed to matter very much.

'We're doing no good at all,' Frank said decisively. 'Most holiday-makers would have taken refuge in one of the cafés around here. We'll take a quick look, and then we might as well go home. If there's any news, we'll be sure to hear it.'

It wasn't exactly giving up. Sara accepted that it was the only thing to do, in the hope that the bedraggled little group would turn up at the guesthouse sooner or later. But a quick tour of the little cafés around the harbour produced nothing, and when Frank said it was time to go, Sara told him she would wait a bit longer, just in case. She took off her clammy mac and gave it to her father to put in the car.

When he had driven away, she stood for ages alongside the advertising placards again, oblivious to the rain, straining her eyes out to sea in the hope that one of the brightly-coloured pleasure boats would soon appear through the mist.

'Are you trying to catch your death of cold?'

She turned swiftly at the sound of the rough voice, the heavy wet strands of her hair flapping uncomfortably against her cold cheeks.

'Would you care?' she whipped out.

Robbie frowned. 'Stop being an idiot and come into the studio and dry your hair. I don't know what you're doing out here on a day like this, but it's not doing you any good.'

Her heart was thudding now, and she could hardly believe that he was offering her some shelter out of the rain, but she wasn't foolish enough to refuse it. She followed him quickly across the road and into his shop. He shut the door behind them and turned the Closed sign before they went through to the studio. The ambience that she remembered so well almost took her breath away.

'Here,' Robbie said, tossing her a towel. 'So what were you doing out there?'

She sat down abruptly on a stool, hearing the uncompromising tone of his voice. This was definitely not meant to be a social visit, and she scrubbed harshly at her hair, uncaring that it would end up in a million knots by the time she finished.

She told him briefly why she and her father had come down to the harbour.

'I couldn't bear to think of those two little boys out in such a rough sea. I had a bit of experience of that myself, and that was in a large ship so what they're going through must be even worse.'

She bit her lip, knowing it was the wrong thing to say to remind Robbie of the time she too had been at sea, and she scrubbed even harder at her hair.

'For God's sake, let me do that, or you'll end up looking like the wicked witch of the west,' he snapped, taking the towel from her hands.

'I thought that was what I already was.'

She bowed her head, feeling his hands on her hair, feeling the emotions rushing over her at this most intimate of care. He had done this before, on so many occasions, but then it had always ended with kisses, on her nape, on her forehead, on her cheeks, on her lips.

'I'm sorry,' she mumbled, so softly that she was sure he didn't hear it. She wasn't even sure if she wanted him to hear it. But his hands paused briefly. Then, as if the words were forced out of him, he said something to make her heart jump.

'I was watching you for quite a while. And the craziest thing that came into my head was how much I wanted to paint you exactly like that, standing by the harbour with your back to the town, looking out to sea with your arms held tightly around yourself and your hair darkened like sodden ropes on your shoulders. You were the only splash of colour against the greyness of the sea and sky, and you looked as immovable as a statue.'

She couldn't bear this. She twisted around so

that his hands involuntarily slid to her face instead of her hair.

'I'm not a statue, Robbie. I'm not a cold thing, made of stone, and I can't bear for us to be so distant from one another.'

'It was you who put the distance between us.'

'But I'm here now. I'm back where I belong, and you know it as well as I do. You got the birthday card I sent you, didn't you? You know what it meant.'

He dropped his hands, handed her the towel and moved away from her.

'You shouldn't have sent it, Sara. We can't change what's happened.'

'Why shouldn't I have sent it? Because it reminded you that it's still me that you want, the way you've always wanted me? You can't forget a lifetime of loving, Robbie. You can't forget all the special times we had, any more than I can.'

Someone was knocking on the studio door. They might have been knocking for some time, but neither of them had heeded it. Robbie swore beneath his breath and he called through the door that he was closed for the rest of the day.

'You'd better let me in, Robbie,' came Miriam's shrill voice. 'I know she's in there with you.'

'Oh God, now look what you've done,' he muttered.

Sara snapped back. 'I didn't do anything. You invited me in, remember?'

'Well, I can't leave Miriam outside in the rain, so don't let's have a repeat performance of what's happened between you before.'

'You can't blame me for the fact that she's such

a harridan,' Sara hissed as he went to the door and opened it.

The next minute it was as if a whirlwind had blown in. Miriam practically hurled herself across the room and thrust her face close to Sara's.

'I saw you posing by the harbour, hoping that Robbie would see you.'

Sara began to laugh. The whole thing was becoming ludicrous and the weight of her hair was still so revoltingly damp on her shoulders that all she wanted was to get out of there and leave them to it. If this was what Robbie had to put up with all the time, he was welcome to it. She was starting to realise she could afford to think like that because she was damned sure he wouldn't put up with it for ever. He always said jealousy was one of the most unattractive traits in anybody, and Miriam was constantly demonstrating it.

'What's so funny?' Miriam shrieked.

'You are,' Sara answered calmly. 'You're being ridiculous. Robbie just did me a good turn and offered to lend me a towel to dry my hair, that's all. And I wasn't posing, as you put it. I was waiting to see if one of the pleasure boats brought back some of our guests safely.'

'So you say.'

'Yes, I do say! What's wrong with you, Miriam? Are you so unsure of Robbie that you've got to watch him every minute of the day? That sounds more like hounding somebody.'

Robbie came between them. 'All right, Sara, that's enough. The rain's nearly stopped now, and if you want to borrow the towel you can bring it back some other time.'

'That means she'll have to come back,' Miriam said at once.

Sara smiled. 'So it does. Thanks, Robbie.'

She draped the towel beneath her hair and around her shoulders, and brushed past Miriam to go out of the studio door. Her heart was thudding again, because this definitely meant she would have to come back. It meant Robbie wanted to see her again. It probably meant nothing ... or it could mean everything.

Outside, she walked around the back street to the harbour, where there were flurries of activity now. Advertising placards were being restored, and any damage to boats and deck chairs was being assessed. People were appearing from shops and cafés. Holiday-makers who had previously been strangers were now chatting together over how quickly the storm had come and gone. And Sara heard her name being called by two shrill voices.

The next minute the two small Elliott boys came racing towards her from one of the cafés, followed by their parents.

'Thank goodness you're all right,' she gasped. 'We were worried about you, knowing you'd booked to go out in one of the pleasure boats.'

'We cried off at the last minute,' Godfrey Elliott said. 'The boys wanted to explore farther along the coast, so we've been to Hayle, and we've just had a cream tea in one of the little cafés here.'

'It was sweet of you to be worried,' his wife added. 'But we're all fine, and Godfrey's going to fetch the car now, so we can give you a lift back, if you like, Sara. You do look rather damp, if I may say so.'

She shook her head. 'Thank you, but I think I'll walk. I've had quite an afternoon, one way and another.'

Besides, she wanted to think, and she didn't feel like having two small boys climbing all over her in the back seat of their small car and wanting to know why she was so wet. She was relieved that they were all right, and that was enough. Above all, she wanted to remember and relish the fact that Robbie obviously wanted to see her again, otherwise he would never have loaned her the towel. She began the walk back home with a lighter heart than when she had started out. By the time she got there, the Elliotts would have arrived, and they could make their own explanations to her parents.

She decided to leave it a few days before she returned Robbie's towel, when it would be washed and ironed. She needed to wash her hair first of all, to get the stickiness and the smell of the rain out of it, and to restore it to its normal glossy condition. It wouldn't hurt Robbie to wait for his towel, and it wouldn't hurt Miriam to be fretting over just how long it was going to be.

September was usually the most glorious month in St Ives, and the holiday-makers still came and went for their annual week in the sun, and showed no signs of abandoning the far south-west just yet. It had been a good season, Ellen Boskelly said with satisfaction, and even more welcome after the terrible winter in the earlier part of the year. Not even Cornwall had escaped the snow and ice of that hard winter. But it was all behind them now, and give or take the occasional storm that no-one could foresee, the autumn was an exceptionally balmy one. It put everybody in a good mood, and Sara began to think the gods were looking kindly on her at last, especially when local folk like the gossipy Mrs Goode now stopped to pass the time of day, and didn't seem to see her as quite the scarlet woman they once had.

The church jumble sale was to take place the following Saturday afternoon, and Ellen said she would go, if only to see how Leah's things were disposed of.

'Do you want to come?' she asked Sara.

'No thanks,' Sara said, shaking her head vigorously. 'I don't fancy seeing Miriam Roche behind one of the stalls, nor her father lording over everything in his pompous manner.'

'You can't avoid people for ever, Sara, and you've been doing well lately.'

'I don't have to go out of my way to see people I don't like, though,' she replied stubbornly, 'and you know I don't like jumble sales. They're always so depressing, full of old, smelly stuff that people don't want any more, all hoping to pass them on to somebody else.'

Ellen laughed. 'Well, that's a fine assessment, I must say. But since it's done in aid of the church funds, we all have to do our bit, don't we?'

'I'm still not going!'

Ellen gave up. She hadn't really expected Sara

to go with her. For herself, it was good to get away from the guesthouse for a couple of hours, and to meet other people. Sara never minded manning the reception desk on Saturday afternoons. New guests rarely arrived until late in the afternoon or early evening, and she and her father were perfectly capable of seeing to their luggage and showing them to their rooms. It was like old times, Sara thought, more relaxed than of late, greeting newcomers who didn't know anything about her, and who were simply excited to be here, and charmed by their first sight of the quaint little town and its colourful harbour. It was always a relief when they arrived on a sparkling sunny day when the whole town was looking its best. It was easy to forget how quickly and unexpectedly storms could break up the idyllic scene.

About four o'clock Sara was preparing trays of tea for the few guests who had already arrived, when her mother arrived back, red-faced and flustered.

'Are you all right, Mum?' Sara said at once.

Why did people always say that, when it was obvious her mother was far from all right? It was the same when you went to see the doctor and he asked how you were, and you always answered that you were fine, before you reeled off a string of ailments ... the inconsequential thought was in her head as her mother sat down heavily to catch her breath.

'That vicar could do with a few lessons in human kindness,' Ellen said.

'Vicar Roche?' Sara echoed, although who else

could it be? He may have given up preaching in the church, but he was still full of his own importance, and hung on to every other thing he could, including organising the church jumble sales.

'Of course Vicar Roche,' Ellen snapped. 'He really is the most objectionable man, and I can't imagine him ever giving comfort to the bereaved. No wonder his poor wife is so insignificant and his daughter is turning into a shrew.'

'Good Lord, Mum, what happened down there today?' Sara said, startled. It was unlike her mild-mannered mother to be vindictive about people; she was normally the most tolerant of women.

Ellen accepted the cup of tea Sara handed her and took a few sips before she answered. And then her mouth twisted.

'It wasn't so much what they said, as what they were implying, and I'm afraid I took it far too personally, and told them just what I thought of so-called church folk who preached one thing and acted something else.'

'You mean they were implying things about me?'

Sara was more distressed by the second. Her mother shouldn't have to go through all this on her account, especially now, when everyone should be used to seeing Sara Boskelly back where she belonged, and the shameful way she had behaved was so far in the past.

'I left them in no doubt about what I thought about their nasty little comments, and from the murmurs around me, there were plenty of folk who approved of what I said to them.'

'Good Lord, Mum!' Sara didn't dare smile, but it really was unlike Ellen to stand up in public and say what she thought. She was no shrinking violet, but she was careful never to make a show of herself as she was always protective of the unblemished reputation of the guesthouse. Today, her daughter's reputation had been clearly worth more than that, and Sara felt touched by her concern. She was a mother hen protecting her chick today.

It was Ellen whose face broke into a smile at that moment.

'I don't think they'll tussle with me again,' she said with an astonishing amount of satisfaction.

'But what did you actually say to them?'

Ellen tapped her finger to her nose. 'Ask no questions and you'll be told no lies,' she said infuriatingly, in a way that was worthy of old Leah. 'Now, let's just forget these irritating people and get down to the more important business of running the guesthouse.'

She was marvellous, thought Sara admiringly. Whatever she felt inside, on the surface she would dismiss what had happened as easily as swatting a fly. She had such strength of character, and she had never needed it more than when she'd had to face the town after her daughter had run off to America. Impulsively, Sara threw her arms around her and hugged her.

'I do love you, Mum.'

Ellen went pink. It wasn't something they normally said to one another. In fact, Sara couldn't ever remember saying it before, which suddenly seemed sad. Ellen hugged her back, told her not to be so daft and that they had better get on and deliver the trays of teas to the early guests, and so the moment passed.

Being one of her father's prime helpers, Miriam was obliged to wait impatiently for the jumble sale to end, and then she left the final disposal of what was left to the other church ladies, while she tore down to the harbour.

On Saturday afternoons, Robbie closed his shop and spent the time in his studio, doing what he loved best, and his hand jerked over his canvas as he heard someone hammering on the studio door.

'I'm closed,' he shouted, annoyed at being disturbed.

'Robbie, let me in,' Miriam screeched. 'You'll never believe what's happened.'

He gave an angry sigh. She was making a habit of this, and whatever it was, he didn't want to know. And nor did he want Miriam here right now, while he was relying on memory and his mind's eye to create the painting he was working on. He strode across to the door and opened it a chink.

'Whatever it is, it'll have to wait until this evening. Come back when I've finished in here and cleaned up.'

'It won't wait.' Miriam pushed past him and came inside, almost catching him off balance on his weakened leg, which did nothing to endear her to him.

'For God's sake, Miriam, you know I don't like being disturbed when I'm working.'

Too late, he tried to stand between her and the canvas he was working on. She stared in disbelief, her face going a dull, furious red.

'It's her, isn't it? It's that day she was standing by the harbour and I said she was posing. She *was* posing, and I bet you asked her to stand there like that.'

'Don't be ridiculous. Even if I asked her, Sara's got more sense than to stand in the rain just so I could paint her! It's just a picture, Miriam.'

They were both looking at it now. Miriam's face was blotchy with rage, and Robbie drew in his breath. Despite himself, he knew he was seeing his creation through her eyes as well as his own. The background of the painting was a turmoil of grey mist, with sea and sky merging into almost anonymity, while in the foreground was a motionless girl in a green dress, the fabric clinging seductively to her shape, her glorious red hair like darkened ropes hanging down her back. There was a compelling stillness about her, compared with the fury of the sea, and there was no need to see her face to know that she was beautiful in the eyes of the artist.

Chapter 10

Robbie knew there were two options open to him. He could discard the painting altogether, as Miriam was screaming at him to do, or he could continue with it, knowing it was destined to be one of the best things he had ever done.

The contrast of the silent, motionless girl and the implication of the dangerous, raging sea, stirred an excitement inside him he hadn't found in a painting for a very long time. It was almost nothing to do with Sara – and yet it was everything to do with her. She was the only one who could have stood like that on such a day, innocently capturing a moment in time that went straight to his artistic soul.

'I won't destroy it,' he said flatly.

'That means you're still in love with her, doesn't it?' Miriam's voice was filled with rage. 'You want her more than you want me. After all she did, I don't how you could be so pathetic.'

His eyes flashed with anger.

'If you think I'm so pathetic, I don't know why you bother to come around here, Miriam. I'm sure you could find another chap who's more worthy of you.'

She didn't say anything for a moment, and then her shoulders slumped as she moved across the room and put her arms around him. Her voice became wheedling.

'I couldn't bear it if you didn't want to see me any more, Robbie. You've been through some bad times, the same as I have. You know I'm still trying to get over what happened to my brother in that dreadful POW camp.'

What he knew damn well was that this was a kind of emotional blackmail, because her brother had died several years ago now, and Robbie wasn't aware that the two of them had ever been particularly close. But she still used him in a way that was pretty distasteful if Robbie ever thought about it too deeply. Right now, all he wanted was to get her out of here, and to recover the mood he'd been in before she arrived, the mood where all that existed was himself and his painting, and the girl who was the pivotal part of it.

He spoke briskly. 'All right, let's forget it, and if you like, we'll go out for a drive this evening. I'll pick you up at your house around seven o'clock.'

In other words, get the hell out of here, and let me get on with my work.

After a moment, Miriam nodded and pressed a kiss to his cheek. Seconds later she was gone, and he breathed a sigh of relief. She could be a sweet girl when she chose, and she had been around when he needed somebody most. She had been prepared to listen, even though he was never going to unburden himself completely to her or anyone about how raw his feelings had been when Sara left. But he was gradually learning the truth of what Sara had called her. She might be a vicar's daughter but that didn't turn her into a saint; for the fact was that she could also be a harridan, and he found himself wondering uneasily which was her true personality.

He applied himself again to his painting, ignoring the issue that neither he nor Miriam had commented on the fact that he never denied her taunt that he was still in love with Sara, and that it was Sara he wanted.

The elderly postman was cycling laboriously up the slope towards the guesthouse and met Sara cycling down on her way to work. More than ready for a breather, he waved out to her to stop, and she paused to say hello.

'There's one here for you, my dear, if you want to take it along with you. Looks pretty important with that fancy stamp on it too. The rest are for your Ma and Pa, so I'll take 'em on up.'

She didn't have the inkling of a premonition. Her head wasn't full of omens and signs the way her Aunt Dottie and Leah's had been. She didn't know who could be writing to her, but sometimes one or other of the guests wrote back to say how much they had enjoyed their stay at the Boskelly guesthouse, and sometimes the letters were addressed directly to her. She took the envelope from the postman with a word of thanks and a cheery enquiry about his rheumatism, and only when he had gone on his way did she take a proper look at it, and felt her heart jolt. The fancy stamp was American, and she prayed with all her heart that it was the kindly Mrs Irish at the fruit farm who was writing to her, and not somebody she would far rather forget. She hoped it wasn't bad news about Mr Irish, whose health had been ailing before she left. A million thoughts whirled around in her head, putting off the moment ... but she couldn't put it off for ever.

She knew she was going to be late for work, but this was far more important than sitting behind a desk and waiting for clients to arrive. She threw down her bicycle and tore open the letter with shaking fingers, and then her breath became ragged in her throat as she saw the familiar signature at the foot of the letter. That was enough.

She couldn't read it now, and she wouldn't read it now. She stuffed it back in the envelope and thrust it in the pocket of her jacket as she went on her way

Angie Reid's wedding day had come and gone, and she had left work now, so the front desk belonged solely to Sara. She tried to act as normally as possible, knowing that the letter from Chesney was virtually burning a hole in her jacket pocket, but there was work to be done, and much as she dreaded seeing what Chesney had written, she needed to give the letter her full attention when she eventually came to read it.

'You don't look quite yourself today, Sara,' Lionel Potter remarked when she had taken him his morning coffee. 'Is there anything you want to discuss with Grebe or myself? You know that anything you have to say will be completely confidential – and free of charge!' he added, attempting to make a joke in his dry way.

'I'm fine, really, Mr Potter. It's a bit hot, that's all.'

'We don't have any more clients this morning, so why don't you go out for a breath of air? Just turn the Closed sign on the door and come back in half an hour.' Sara knew he was used to summing up people quickly, and he probably saw more than she gave him credit for. But she wasn't going to miss this chance to be by herself. She did as she was told and walked down to the harbour and out to the end of Smeaton's Pier. Then she took Chesney's crumpled letter out of her pocket and opened it.

'My dearest Sara,' it began.

The words made her mouth tighten, because she wasn't his dearest Sara and never had been. He was a liar and a cheat, and her eyes blurred at remembering how gullible she had been, and how nearly she had forgotten her decent upbringing and abandoned herself to his seductive and persuasive tongue. She swallowed, hardening her heart and blinking away the tears as she began to read the letter properly.

'I had one boomer of a shock when I went to the fruit farm this summer for the annual apple-picking and found you had been there for all those months. I don't know what you must have thought of me when you discovered the truth about me, honey, and I can only apologise a thousand times for deceiving you the way I did. It's hard for a guy to be so far from home, and to find a lovely young girl like yourself so willing to be a friend must have turned my brain in more ways than one.

I know we made impossible plans that I should never have done, but I honestly never expected you to follow me to the States. I was touched that you did so, but horrified at the same time. It was never meant to happen this way, and I can tell you I had my ear bashed pretty much by Mrs Irish when she saw me again. I did love you, Sara honey, and I still do, and I'm writing to tell you I'm free now, and that's the God's honest truth.'

There was a lot of his so-called honesty in this letter, Sara thought bitterly, and how much of it was she supposed to believe this time!

'Some of my buddies are coming over to England later this year and I'm coming too. They're bringing their wives and kids to see some of the places we stayed, and the wives are keen to be there for the royal wedding of your Princess Elizabeth to the Greek prince. We'll be visiting Cornwall, and I hope you'll agree to see me again to remember the good times. If you feel like writing to let me know if I'll be welcome, it will be great, but if I don't hear from you, don't be surprised if you see me sometime at the beginning of November anyway.'

Sara screwed up the letter, her eyes smarting. The gall of him, thinking she would ever make him welcome again, after what he had done to her. He had all but ruined her life. He had made her leave the family she loved and brought them shame and heartache. Even worse, he had made her turn her back on her one true love.

But she was the one thinking honestly now, because Chesney Willand had actually made her do none of those things. She had been the one who chose to do them all. She had abandoned everything that she loved the most to go chasing a dream, and she was as much to blame that it had all gone sour.

Not for one second would she let herself think that if everything Chesney had told her was real ... if he really was the owner of the fruit farm and really wanted to marry her, then things might have been so different. She didn't want to think it, and she didn't want to see him again. She shivered, not wanting to imagine how she might feel if she did. Not wanting to wonder if what he said now was true, and that he really was free. In any case, what difference would it make to her?

There were other people wandering about on Smeaton's Pier now, and she was no longer alone. She turned away and hurried back to the offices of Potter and Grebe, Family Solicitors, resisting a single glance to where she knew the paintings of Robbie Killaine would be propped up outside the frontage of his shop and attracting the attention of holiday-makers.

Once inside the sanctuary of her workplace she lost her composure and burst into tears, and the next moment she felt Lionel Potter's fatherly arms around her.

'I think we'd better have a brief consultation, don't you, my dear? You're hardly an advertisement for the clients today, are you?'

By the time she left work at the end of the day, Sara was pale and shaken. It had been slightly easier to talk to her boss than to talk to her parents, but this new development had left her nerves in shreds. She didn't want to see Chesney ever again, even though Leah always said it was wise to lay to rest the ghosts of the past by facing them. She wished Leah's old sayings didn't keep entering her mind, for Leah wasn't here to advise her any more, and the first thing she had to do now was to show the letter to her mother. From now on, there were going to be no secrets between them.

Ellen's face was as pale as her daughter's when she read what Chesney had written. 'What do you feel about this, Sara? You must remember how he let you down before, and he's quite capable of doing so again. A man who cheats once is just as likely to cheat again. I'm sure that with all his experience of family problems Mr Potter would have told you the same thing.'

'He did, and I know it. Of course I don't want to see Chesney, Mum, but he says he's coming here anyway, so how can I stop him?'

'You can write to tell him exactly how you feel. I know your father would do it for you if you ask him.'

Sara shook her head vigorously. She could just imagine the things her father would say, and anyway, it wasn't right to ask him to do it. It was her problem, her mess, and she was the one to clear it up.

'I'll write and tell him I don't want him here, and then it's up to him, isn't it? But if some of the others come here looking up old haunts, I'm sure he'll do the same, whatever I say. And we did make him welcome once.'

'Do you believe that he's free now?'

'I don't know. If he is, what happened to the

other girl? Did he let her down too? Whichever way you look at it, it's not pretty, is it?'

Ellen gave her a hug. 'At least you're able to be objective about it, Sara, and that's a good thing.'

Actually, she wasn't feeling objective at all, just thoroughly churned up.

'Don't worry about your dad,' Ellen went on. 'I'll let him know what's happened, and I'm sure he'll give Mr Willand his marching orders pretty quickly.'

They discovered that Frank Boskelly had become aware of the GIs returning to Cornwall with their wives and families before either of them had a chance to tell him about the letter. He came home that evening with the news that the town was putting on a special welcome for the group in the way of a social evening to thank them for their support during the difficult days of the war.

'It's official then,' Ellen said, without thinking, and then had to tell him what she knew.

'The damned blaggard,' Frank said, his face darkening. 'When they mentioned wives and families I hadn't thought of him. It would have been bad enough if he'd brought a wife with him, but contacting Sara again and trying to get back in her good books is beyond belief. You'll refuse to see him of course, Sara.'

Her parents were both looking at her now. She was of an age when she could please herself who she saw, but good manners and a sense of obligation were ingrained in her, and she knew how embarrassing and humiliating it would be if she defied her parents' wishes and agreed to see

Chesney here. They definitely wouldn't welcome him as they had once done, and they wouldn't want to see him again. But did she...?

'Sara?' her father said sharply. 'Don't tell me you're thinking of forgiving the fellow for the lies he told you. If so, you're not the daughter I thought you were.'

'I never said I was thinking of forgiving him. I'll never forgive him,' she said passionately. 'I'm as upset as you that he's written to me again, and I don't know what I'm going to do about it yet. If I ignore the letter he'll turn up anyway, and if I write back, as I feel I must, he may think I'm softening towards him.'

'That depends on what you say, my girl.'

Frank was uncompromising now, his jaw set, his eyes angry, and Sara felt like a little girl again, being reprimanded for some small misdemeanour. But this was so much more than that. This was bringing back into their lives the man who had caused all of them so much heartache. Her nerves prickled, because no matter how much her parents had suffered, she was the one who had had all her hopes dashed beyond repair. She was the one who had expected to be married with a child of her own by now.

'I'll have to make up my own mind about what to do,' she muttered. 'In any case, I can't stop him coming to England, can I?'

She could just imagine Chesney's reaction if she tried. He had been given a medal for gallantry after the war and he was a proud and, in many ways, a brash man. He was hardly going to tell his buddies and their wives why it was he couldn't go to England after all. He was hardly going to say that some little Cornish chick didn't want him there. Her eyes smarted, almost hearing him saying the words in her head, and not liking the sound of them at all. She was under no illusions over what Chesney had done, but she knew him well enough to know he wouldn't risk losing face on this occasion.

'I'm sure you'll do the right thing, Sara love,' she heard her mother say gently. 'This whole visit is unfortunate, but we'll just have to deal with it.'

Sara found it impossible to stay indoors that evening. She cycled over to the Weeks's farm to see Hilly, taking the letter with her. The instinct to tear it up into minute pieces was very strong, but as yet she couldn't do that. In any case, it had an address on it where she could send a reply.

'Well, I know what I'd do,' Hilly said flatly. 'I'd burn it with the rest of the rubbish! He's got a hell of a nerve, expecting you to see him again.'

'I know, but he's coming here, anyway. If I don't write and say something, he'll just turn up at the guesthouse, and how am I supposed to greet him then?'

'By throwing something at him, if you've got any sense.'

'You're not helping, Hilly.'

They were sitting on Hilly's bed, with the offending letter between them.

'Well, what do you want me to say? He must know he won't be welcome, not by you, or your parents, or anybody else who's aware of what happened. I'm amazed he thinks he can dare to show his face in St Ives at all, if you really want to know what I think. But he was always so damned arrogant it'll be like water off a duck's back to him.'

'Did you think he was arrogant?' Sara said, her thoughts diverted for a moment by the word.

Hilly snorted. 'Oh come on, Sara, everybody thought it but you, but then, he wasn't whispering sweet nothings to everybody else, was he?'

'You never said so at the time!'

'Would you have listened? You were so besotted by the chap it would have been like talking to the wall. Even Robbie saw it in the end, although he chose to ignore it, sure that you'd come to your senses eventually.'

This was enough to take Sara's breath away. 'What do you mean "Robbie saw it in the end"? How do you know that?'

Hilly looked uncomfortable. 'Well, he said something to me once. He was getting anxious about the amount of time you were spending with the Yank. I told him he needn't worry, and that he was the only one for you, but it just goes to show how wrong people can be, doesn't it? Even the two people who thought they knew you the best.'

Her voice was accusing and angry now, and Sara gasped. She jumped off the bed, snatching up the letter and stuffing it back in her pocket.

'I don't have to stay here and listen to this. I came for some sympathy and advice, and all I've had is abuse.'

Hilly was on her feet as well now 'No, you haven't. You've just had some plain speaking, and it's about time too. You were as arrogant as the

Yank, in thinking you could just come home as if nothing had happened, and that it would all go back to the way it was before. You hurt people, Sara, and you can't turn the clock back. I wonder just what you'll say if this Chesney chap turns up and asks you to go back to America with him.'

'Don't be ridiculous. He won't do that, and if he did, I'd never go.'

'Why not? You did it once.'

'Because I don't love him, that's why not! Robbie's the one I love, and he always has been.'

'Well, I hope he sees it that way when the Yanks come marching in.'

Sara turned away from her. 'There's no talking to you tonight, and I wish I'd never come.'

'So do I. See you on Saturday for the flicks, then, if you're speaking to me by then,' Hilly called out as Sara clattered down the stairs.

I might be, Sara thought furiously, knowing very well that she would be there. It would all have blown over by then – the row between them, anyway. The other thing would be far from over.

Cycling back to the town, a stormy expression on her face, she knew there was one more place she had to go. She had to see Robbie, to tell him what had happened. She wouldn't show him the letter, of course, that would really be rubbing salt in the wound. But she wanted to let him know she had received it, that it meant nothing to her, and above all, she had to let him know that the Yanks were coming back. She couldn't seem to stop thinking of it in those terms now.

She rapped on his studio door, sure that he'd be

working there, and when he called out that it was open she went inside.

'Well, this is a surprise,' he said coolly. 'Have you brought back my towel?'

She stared at him, gulping, as she saw how unfriendly he looked. The borrowed towel was the last thing on her mind, but perhaps he had already heard of the mass influx of overseas visitors ... for a moment her heart stopped, because presumably some of them would be looking for places to stay while they were here. It wasn't something she had considered before, but now she hoped desperately that none of them would be contacting the Boskelly guesthouse. But of course they might well do, since it was on the official St Ives list of hospitality accommodation. The implications of this visit started to reach nightmare proportions in Sara's mind.

'You'd better sit down before you fall down,' Robbie continued, seeing how she suddenly seemed to sway. 'What do you want?'

'Nothing,' she said, backing away. 'It was a mistake. I meant to bring the towel and I forgot it,' she added, grasping at anything for an explanation. Her foot kicked the corner of a canvas that was propped against the wall, and involuntarily she went to steady it. As she did so, her eyes widened in shock.

She was looking at herself. At least, at the back view of herself, wearing the slim green dress she had been wearing on the day of the storm. Her hair was a terrible mess, and yet it was somehow extraordinarily beautiful too, hanging down in sodden ropes on her shoulders. In the background was the greyness of sea and sky, in total contrast to the figure who dominated the scene. Her mouth trembled as she spoke.

'You painted me from memory on that awful day.'

'Yes, well, I think I have enough memories of you not to need a sitter,' he said shortly, 'and that day was bad enough to stick in anybody's mind.'

She turned swiftly. He was moving forward to cover the painting and she was right in his way, and before either of them knew what was happening, she had put her arms around him and pulled him to her, holding him fiercely.

'You don't need me to sit for you because I'm in your head and your heart, just the way you're in mine. It will never go away, and we both know it, Robbie.'

She thought he was going to push her away, but the next moment his mouth was on hers. He was kissing her as if it was with his last breath, and she was kissing him back, recklessly and passionately, wanting him so much that she would have done anything for him. Hardly realising they were moving, they stumbled across to the little couch at the side of his studio, useful for when his leg ached and he needed to rest it for a while. Somehow they were falling down on it together, and his hands were everywhere on her.

'God, I've missed you so much and wanted you so much,' he groaned. 'I don't think I really knew how much I loved you until–'

Sara put her fingers over his mouth, not wanting him to say anything to spoil these perfect moments.

'I'm here now, Robbie. I'm here now, for always, and I'm never going to go away again,' she whispered.

She felt his hands moving upwards towards her thighs, and she did nothing to stop him. If he wanted her, how much more did she want him, to know that this was the ultimate forgiveness. She was sure it would be the first time for both of them, and that was the way it should be for two people who were always meant to be together. Nothing else mattered, only these moments when Robbie became totally hers, and she became part of him at last.

The night was dark by the time she cycled home from his studio, her legs feeling like water, her mind full of the shocking words he had said after they had made love. It should have been the most beautiful time of their lives, sealing their love for ever, but there had been nothing but bitterness, as unexpected as it was hateful.

'That should never have happened,' he rasped, moving away from her and straightening his clothes, leaving her to tidy hers. 'You shouldn't have come here, and I shouldn't have given in to temptation.'

'Temptation? You can't pretend that was all it meant to you! You love me, Robbie, just as I love you, and what we did was natural and wonderful,' she cried, but her voice was already faltering.

'Natural, is it? If that's what your Yanks taught you, then apparently they think nothing of the sanctity of marriage.'

Sara gasped. 'Don't be so bloody priggish,

Robbie. You know very well what I mean. In any case, I always believed we would be married one day. I thought you believed that too.'

'I did, once. So how often have you done this natural thing before?'

She gasped again, but with fury this time. 'Never, of course! Couldn't you tell? You must have realised! It was the first time, Robbie, truly it was.'

'And you must think I'm the most gullible chap in the world.'

It was the most horrible and humiliating conversation she had ever had with him, having to protest her innocence, when he should never have doubted it. But clearly, he must have assumed that she had done this with Chesney, that she had been easy.

His girl, easy with a Yank ... maybe even more than one ... she wanted to sob at the injustice of it all, but she wouldn't sob in front of him. If he couldn't believe her now, after the exquisite time they had just experienced, then it was truly all over between them.

She went straight to bed when she got home and cried her heart out. This evening had turned out so very differently from the way she had meant it to be. She had gone to Hilly for help, to ask what she thought she should do about Chesney, and ended up alienating her best friend. She had gone to Robbie, meaning to forewarn him that Chesney and the other GI families would be coming here and to tell him that it meant nothing to her. Instead of which, she had seen the painting of herself on the day of the storm, and knowing instantly that it had been painted with love, it had sent everything else out of her mind.

And then the rest ... the incredibly tender moments when she had lain in his arms and he had become everything she ever wanted ... only to have the accusations hurled at her that she had done this before. That she was no longer the innocent girl he had always known, but easy with the Yanks. How could he have thought such a thing? But obviously, it was what everybody in the town had thought when she went chasing after Chesney. It was what she deserved, and now that she had heard the truth from Robbie's own lips, she had never felt so low in her life.

Chapter 11

When Sara met Hilly at the cinema on Saturday evening, she was still unsure what to do about Chesney's letter. By then, it seemed that everyone was tacitly agreeing to say nothing about it until she did. Hilly was the same as ever, and Sara's parents judiciously avoided any mention of the Americans' visit to the town at all. There was no question of Sara going to see Robbie again, and she kept the borrowed towel as a kind of trophy, just to remind her where reckless behaviour could lead. At least there was going to be no permanent reminder of what had happened between them. Three days later her monthly arrived as usual. If she let herself think about it too much, she could almost be sad, but mainly she was mightily relieved, because one more scandal would have been one too many for her parents to bear. Even so, she had tasted the sweetness of intimacy with Robbie now, and she knew there could be nothing sweeter than having a child between two people who truly loved each other. Maybe that day would never come ... and maybe it would, she thought, with stubborn optimism.

But she knew she couldn't put off replying to Chesney for ever, and on Sunday evening she composed her letter as best she could, discarding a dozen sheets of writing paper before she was satisfied that she had made it as impersonal as

possible. She read over the words she had written.
'Dear Chesney,' she had written, even though he certainly wasn't her dear Chesney, and she'd been tempted to just put his name starkly at the top of the letter.

'Your letter gave me a shock as I never expected to hear from you again. If you have any sense of decency you should know that you won't be welcome in my home. I can't stop you coming to St Ives if that's the intention of your group, but I don't want to see you. I don't know what happened between you and the girl you were engaged to, or if there even was such a girl, and I don't want to know. If she exists, then I feel sorry for her, being engaged to such a rotter. Or perhaps she had her eyes opened and wasn't as gullible as I was, in believing all your lies.'

Sara paused. That was something else that had occurred to her. Did he even have a fiancée, or was that something else he'd invented for the benefit of Mr and Mrs Irish? She signed her name at the end of the letter, folded it in half and sealed it in an envelope. Tomorrow she would take it to the post office with the usual correspondence from Messrs Potter and Grebe, Family Solicitors, in the hope that no-one would think anything odd about a letter to America being sent from their offices. As far as she was concerned she had done everything she could.

On Monday morning Miriam Roche raced along the road to Robbie's shop from the hairdressing salon where she worked. He had just negotiated a very satisfactory sale of one of his paintings and felt more buoyant than of late.

'You'll never guess what's happening,' Miriam burst out excitedly.

'You'd better tell me then,' he said with a grin.

'The Yanks are coming back at the beginning of November, loads of them with wives and children. My dad's on the committee that's organising a social evening for them at the church hall for the few days that they'll be in St Ives. Then they're doing a tour of some other places they knew during the war, and going to London in time to see the royal wedding. All right for some, isn't it? Fancy coming all this way for that. My dad always said they had more money than sense, and that was why half the local girls fell for them.'

She stopped for breath without realising what she had said until she saw the stony look on Robbie's face. She had been quite animated with the news, but his reaction was as plain as her normally plain face.

'Well, not that all of them were after their money, of course. I'm sure there were other attractions,' she babbled on, making things worse.

'I don't know why you thought I'd be in the least interested,' Robbie said. 'Haven't you got enough work to do without spreading pointless gossip?'

Miriam flushed. 'Well, I thought you might be a little bit interested, especially if *he's* coming back to stir things up again. I'd like to be a fly on the wall at that particular meeting!' she added spitefully.

She didn't need to mention any names. She was so wrapped up in the prospect of Sara Boskelly meeting her old flame again that she hardly noticed how vindictive she sounded. If she did notice, she didn't care.

'You are a prize bitch, aren't you, Miriam?' she heard Robbie say coldly.

'Why do you say that? Just because I know how much she's hurt you and that I don't want her to do it all over again? That's not being a bitch, that's being a friend – and I thought we were far more than friends.'

She didn't wait for a reply. She turned and flounced out of the shop, knowing she was leaving him with plenty to think about. Her dearest wish would be for Sara and this Yank of hers to get together and clear off back to America, leaving the way clear for herself and Robbie. They'd been getting on so well before Sara returned home, but Miriam had never lost the fear that in his heart Robbie still loved Sara, and would always do so, no matter what she did. But if this Yank of hers could be persuasive enough to take her back with him, that would surely be the end of it.

Her spirits rose again, despite Robbie's reaction. Let nature take its course, she thought gleefully. Then he would see just how fickle his one-time girl could be.

Despite himself, it was all Robbie could think about too. Miriam's words had left his gut churning. After the other night, when he and Sara had been everything in the world to one another for that brief, blissful time, could she seriously fall for the Yank for a second time? Was it going to happen all over again? And if it did, said a cold little voice inside his head, it would be all his fault, since he had driven her away with his accusations. He should have known – he did know – that she had never made love before. His own common sense told him so. He had been the one to spoil it, to wreck something that had begun so long ago, a love that was as inevitable as breathing. It was as though there had been some devil inside him at that moment that had wanted to hurt her the way she had hurt him.

He had never made any promises to Miriam, and she knew it. They had needed one another at a time when they were both vulnerable, and although, as far as he was concerned, their relationship had never developed into anything closer than mere friendship, he was beginning to realise that she was tenacious enough to cling on to him by whatever means she had. She was showing her true colours more and more since Sara had shown up again, and he pitied the man who married such a shrew, knowing it would never be him.

To say he had been knocked sideways by what she had just told him would be an understatement. The war was long past, and everyone was slowly returning to normality again, despite the continuing shortages and rationing, yet now these rich Americans would arrive, to show up their shabbiness by their flashy clothes and pampered kids and the almighty dollar that could buy anything.

Across the harbour he caught a glimpse of

someone with bright coppery hair. She was doing her daily business chores, and his heart leapt as always. He hadn't been able to fight physically during the war, but he would fight for Sara's honour to the death if need be, he thought in a sudden fit of rage, and if this Chesney bastard thought he could woo her again, he'd have Robbie Killaine to answer to.

He saw Sara glance his way, and on an impulse he waved at her. He saw her hesitate, as if unsure what the gesture meant, and then she started walking towards him.

They hadn't met since that memorable night, and neither of them knew what to say for a moment, until he told her curtly she had better come inside. Sara realised he was as jittery as herself and she knew instantly the reason why.

'You've heard the news, haven't you?' she said directly.

'It depends which news you mean.'

'Oh, come on, Robbie, don't play games. You know as well as I do that the town is going to get some American visitors at the beginning of November, and you're wondering just how I feel about it.'

'So how do you feel about it?'

She fumed at being interrogated like this, when what she wanted to know was how he felt about it, but she answered carefully.

'For the sake of the town I suppose everyone should be pleased that they want to come back and visit their old haunts, bringing their families with them. Personally, I'm angry and upset that Chesney Willand will be one of them, since I've no wish to see him ever again. Is that what you want to hear?'

'And how do you know that?'

He was doing it again, asking all the questions, and Sara felt her heart sink. She had intended to tell him about the letter she had received, but now she could either lie and say she just assumed Chesney would be among the group, or tell him the truth – and there had already been too many lies.

'He wrote to me, telling me about the visit. It was the first time I'd heard from him since he left England, and I was furious to hear from him at all. If you must know, I've just posted back a reply, saying I don't want to see him. But I can't stop him if he's crass enough to come to the guesthouse, can I?'

She was shaking now, waiting for Robbie's reaction. But why should he care if she saw Chesney or not? He'd made it plain that he was courting Miriam now, and even after they had shared those ecstatic moments together in his studio, he had still snapped those humiliating insults at her.

After dealing with Miriam's gleeful arrival earlier, and the spiteful way she had discussed the Americans' visit, Robbie was feeling less than tolerant.

'I've no doubt you'll be glad enough to see your lover when he turns up.'

She gasped angrily. 'There's just no talking to you when you're in this mood, but he was never my lover, and you know that, Robbie, so I'll leave you to remember it. You, of all people, and you alone, know it!'

Her face was burning when she left his shop. She could hardly make it any clearer, and it was even more humiliating to have to try to explain. What had happened between them should have been a beautiful memory to cherish, but he had completely ruined it by intimating that it hadn't been her first time. That he hadn't been her first, when he had always been destined to be her only one.

'Sara, come back!'

She heard him call out, but she was beyond talking to him any more, and she rushed back to work, her eyes smarting. It was obvious now that he didn't want her any more. He had succumbed to their love-making in a moment of weakness, and she had been so willing, so full of love ... so damned easy...

She couldn't get the hated word out of her head now, and she was glad there were clients at the solicitors' that day, keeping her busy, keeping her mind on the troubled marital and family problems of other people, rather than on her own aborted dreams.

It was noticeable that her parents pointedly said nothing more about the letter from Chesney. It was as though, by totally ignoring it, they could pretend it had never happened. It wasn't so easy for Sara. She should have got rid of it, but somehow she couldn't. Even if she never read it again and kept it underneath her underwear and stockings in her dressing-table drawer, it was as if she had to keep it as a reminder of just how foolish she had been. She also allowed herself a few moments of rare satisfaction, imagining the shock on Chesney's face when he had turned up at the fruit farm that year, and faced the wrath of Mr and Mrs Irish. It must have shaken him to the core to know that Sara had been mad enough to follow him to America. That's what it was, of course. Sheer madness. She hadn't even had a ring on her finger like those other girls on the ship, and thankfully, no baby to present him with, either.

By early October the town was already planning the welcome for the Americans' visit in a month's time. The local newspaper was full of it, making a point of printing the occasional letter that had arrived from one or other of the GIs who had been stationed in the area, all saying how thrilled they were for the chance to show their families around this quaint little Cornish town, and to meet the folks who had been so kind to them during those dark days.

You couldn't escape it, thought Sara desperately. By now they all knew that the trip had been especially arranged to coincide with the royal wedding in November, two days after Sara's birthday on the 18th. The Americans seemed obsessed with British royalty, and had seen this as a good opportunity to combine excitement and pageantry, with a short nostalgic visit to each locality where they had been stationed during the war.

Sara had frequent panic attacks about the visit of one particular American. She didn't want to see him. She wanted to hibernate and bury her head in the sand until the St Ives visit had come and gone. In a weak moment she had even told her father as much, hoping for his understanding. Instead, she had received a stern talking-to.

'In my day, such an action would be called lily-livered, Sara,' he'd said. 'If this man has the audacity to show his face here, then you should face him and tell him just what you think of him. You have to face your demons, my dear. You can't pretend it never happened, and we were all taken in by his charm.'

'Do you want to face him then?' Sara demanded.

'I do not, but if I have to, I will. But I'm afraid this is one time when you are on your own, Sara. It was your mistake, and hard as it may seem, it will probably do a great deal towards settling your feelings if you face up to the man in person, and with as much dignity as you can muster.'

'Well, I don't have any lingering romantic feelings for him, Dad, if that's what you're thinking. The only feeling I have for him is contempt.'

He had leaned over and kissed her on the cheek then, and the scent of his old briar pipe wafted into her nostrils, safe and familiar.

'Then we're in complete agreement, my dear,' Frank said quietly.

She knew he was right, but it was one thing to resolve that she would be calm and dignified if she had to meet Chesney. It was another to imagine exactly how she would really feel if and when the time came. And whether she confided in Hilly or her father or anyone else, in the end she was the one who had to deal with it. Of one thing she was certain, however. She wouldn't be attending the social evening the town was arranging for the GIs and their families. She could just imagine the sly glances and snide remarks that would be coming her way if she did. But to her horror she discovered that her mother had other ideas about that.

'We will all go, Sara, and we'll show our goodwill to the visitors, the same as we have always done. We have a position in this town, and how would it look if we all stay away?'

'But Mum, people will be staring at me. Everybody knows what happened, and they'll all be speculating over what I'm feeling.'

'Let them stare. If they don't have it in their hearts to be tolerant towards you, then it's their problem, not ours. You rode the storm when you came home, my love, and you'll do it again.'

It would be an ordeal for her too, Sara realised, seeing the heightened colour in her mother's cheeks. Ellen was so much stronger than she was. Right now she felt so vulnerable, and she wished she still had the luxury of being a child, who would be able to hide behind her mother's skirts. But next month she would be twenty-two years old, and she could never do that again. She nodded slowly, trying to ignore the lump in her throat and the futile longing to return to those idyllic days of childhood.

She had got into the habit of taking Bonzer for a walk on Sunday mornings, sometimes along the cliffs, and sometimes down to the town to watch the comings and goings of the pleasure boats and general harbour activity. On the following Sunday morning she chose the town, and as soon she reached the harbour Bonzer raced away from her, barking joyously at a familiar figure who was chatting to an old seaman. As Robbie leaned down to ruffle the dog's thick coat, Sara walked right up to him, and the old seaman drifted away.

'I've got something to tell you, and I want you to know it before you find out for yourself,' she said.

He shrugged. 'I thought you'd already told me what you wanted me to know.'

'I haven't told you that my parents intend to go to this social evening for the American visitors, and that they think I should go as well.'

'And you think this would be of any interest to me?'

She almost stamped her foot in frustration.

'Oh, for goodness' sake, Robbie, I'm trying to save you from any embarrassment, that's all. If you turn up there as well, people will be sure to notice and make comments.'

'I doubt that people will be in the least interested. So what are you suggesting? That I stay away? Do you expect me to stay away from every street in St Ives, just in case we bump into one another and cause gossip or embarrassment?'

He was so cool and so clever. He was treating her as a babbling idiot, Sara thought, when all she had intended was to warn him that she would be at the social evening too.

'Oh well,' she said, trying to be as cool as he was, 'if you're there with Miriam, I guess that will set any gossiping straight, won't it?'

'I guess it will,' he said, and he strolled away

from her as if he hadn't a care in the world.

Sara bit her lip in annoyance, her eyes smarting. She had only said what she had on the spur of the moment. It had been an excuse for talking to him and making him listen. And she had wanted him to be upset. She had wanted him to say that he wouldn't be going to the church hall that night, and that wild horses wouldn't catch him near any event involving the ex-GIs. But he hadn't said anything of the sort. He hadn't denied that he and Miriam would be there, either, because she would be full of importance with her daddy on the organising team, of course.

She watched as Bonzer raced about on the sand, wild and exhilarated and enjoying the freedom of it all, and she wished she could be as free and uninhibited. Coming home from her year in self-imposed exile had been nerve-racking enough. But although she had made her peace with her friends and family, nothing had turned out in the way she had hoped it would.

In particular, she had never expected to find Robbie courting somebody else, and she knew how naive she had been in thinking nothing would have changed. Life had moved on, and so had he. The trouble was, she hadn't, not as far as he was concerned.

'Come on, boy,' she called out to Bonzer when she thought he had had enough rolling about. There was never a truer saying than the enjoyment of a dog's life, she thought wryly as he came bounding up to her, shaking himself free of sand.

She walked back the way she had come, but she wasn't ready to go indoors yet. Such a brief meeting with Robbie had set her nerves jangling again, and she was beginning to wonder how wise it had been to come back here after all. If he continued seeing Miriam Roche and eventually married her, how could she bear it? She knew she would never do anything as reckless as leaving the country again, but there were other towns in Cornwall, other jobs, another life. She could move away from St Ives, where she wouldn't have the daily humiliation of seeing Miriam Roche clinging to Robbie like a leech. It was a thought to keep tucked away in her mind, should she ever need to do something about it.

She walked past the guesthouse and struck out along the top of the cliffs with Bonzer busily ferreting out anything he could find in the furze and bracken. There were often holiday-makers up here, who had discovered the delights of cliff walks away from the town itself, and enjoyed the spectacular views far below, but there was no-one else in the vicinity on this Sunday morning. All Sara could see was a small red kite flying high in the sky over the sea, well adrift from its owner. She watched it, fascinated, as it made crazy patterns in the blustery wind.

As Bonzer began barking she went nearer to the edge of the cliffs to see what he had found, hoping it wasn't a dead bird that he'd want to bring back to the guesthouse as a gift for her mother.

Among the bracken there was a child's sandal. Sara stared at it for a moment, her heart pounding. It was quite a small sandal and it looked fairly new. It might have been there for days, but Sara didn't think so. To her inexperienced eyes it didn't look as if it had been lying there for very long. But what child would have lost a sandal and not tried to retrieve it? What parent would not have scolded such a child and sent him or her back to look for it? Wild thoughts of kidnapping and abduction, and even worse, flew through her fertile mind. The wind was blowing quite strongly now, and the sea was being churned up, and because of Bonzer's excited barking she didn't immediately hear the cries for help.

She moved nearer to the edge of the cliffs, where she could see a youngish man balancing precariously on a small ledge of sandy ground before the cliffs plunged down to the sea. He was holding on tightly to a small boy with his leg bent beneath him. The boy wore only one sandal and he seemed to be unconscious. The man almost sobbed with relief when he saw Sara.

'Thank God somebody's come. My son was chasing his kite and lost his footing and went over the cliff. I think he may have broken his leg, and if this ledge hadn't been here, I dread to think–'

He was too choked to finish, and Sara spoke quickly.

'Hang on, and I'll go and get help. My father will know what to do, and he'll send for an ambulance for the boy, so try not to panic.'

'Please be quick, miss. If Jamie comes round I think he'll be the one to panic, and then we could both go over.'

'I'll be as fast as I can,' Sara said, trying not to imagine the truth of what he was saying.

She raced back to the guesthouse and gasped

out what had happened. Emergencies like this happened occasionally with holiday-makers, and Frank immediately telephoned for an ambulance and the voluntary cliff rescue team who would be there as soon as they could muster their members.

Sara's mother also moved quickly. 'You're the only one who knows exactly where they are, Sara, so you go back and talk to the man to calm him down. Take a blanket from one of the cots to cover the child, and make sure you're visible on the cliff top for when the rescuers arrive.'

It was a relief to have her mother's sound advice, thought Sara, her own teeth chattering with shock by now. She did as she was told and took the cot blanket back to where the child seemed to be stirring slightly and whimpering a little. She prayed that he would remain semi-conscious, because once he woke up fully and discovered where he was and how much pain he was in, she knew he would begin to panic.

'They'll be here soon,' Sara told the man. 'Cover your son with the blanket and just hold on tight, and don't look down. What's your name and where are you from? I know he's Jamie.'

Instinct told her to keep him talking, and she learned that he had brought his son to fly his kite on the last morning of their holiday while his wife packed their belongings prior to going home to Somerset. They lived in a rural, flat part of the county and Jamie had been so desperate to fly his kite here, where it could soar so high in the wind currents. Then this had happened.

Sara couldn't have said how long she kept him

talking, about anything and everything, but at last the rescuers arrived, bringing the father and son to safety with the expertise of a team who had made many previous cliff rescues far more difficult than this one. The boy was taken off to hospital to have his leg checked over, with the reassurance that it didn't seem to be broken, and was probably just badly bruised and sprained. By now he was fully awake, in obvious pain, but more concerned with the loss of his kite than his injury, with his frantic father already promising to buy him another, providing they didn't use it near the edge of any cliffs.

'You've been a real heroine, miss,' the man told her. 'I'd like to have your name and address, because I know my wife will want to write and thank you for what you did today.'

'Bonzer was the real hero, finding Jamie's sandal,' she said shakily.

'We'll pass on the information he wants, Sara,' the ambulanceman said. 'Right now it's more important to get this little lad off to hospital.'

She was limp with relief as she watched them all go, and when she turned to go home, she felt in dire need of a good cry now that the trauma of it was all over.

Chapter 12

Sara would have preferred it if the incident was kept quiet, having had enough unwanted publicity and gossip about her movements. But she might have known that the news would permeate through the town as quickly as any other news did. In her eyes, she wasn't a heroine. She just happened to be in the right place at the right time. In her opinion it was Bonzer who was the real hero. But others didn't see it that way. The rescue team had already praised her common sense in keeping the boy's father talking to calm him, and the incident appeared in the local newspaper, naming Sara as the instigator of the rescue.

Mrs Goode stopped her on the way to work on the morning after the newspaper report appeared.

'Well, young lady, you're to be congratulated, I hear. I always say there's good and bad in everyone, and you did a real good turn that day, my dear.'

Considering the woman's main aim in life seemed more inclined to find the bad in people, Sara couldn't resist a smile.

'I only did what anybody else would have done, Mrs Goode.'

'Now Sara, don't sell yourself short, as the saying goes. You were a good Samaritan on that Sunday morning, and the Lord don't forget His messengers.'

Any minute now, and she'd be calling her a saint, thought Sara, barely able to conceal her laughter until she saw that the woman meant it in all sincerity and she swallowed back any smart remark she might have made.

'It's very kind of you to say so, Mrs Goode,' she told her instead.

'Yes, well, anybody who does God's work is deserving of a bit of praise, in my opinion, and if I'm asked, I shall say so.'

There were still people who looked at Sara a bit askance, wondering what exactly had gone on during her year in America, and it was weird to think she now had a kind of ally in Mrs Goode, yet oddly comforting too.

The letter duly arrived from the rescued man's wife, thanking Sara for what she had done, and informing her that she had written a similar one to be published in the newspaper.

'It's too much,' Sara protested, when her father read the newspaper article out to her the next day. 'I wish they had just let it go.'

'Wouldn't you be grateful to anyone who had done what you did? If you hadn't heard the man's shouts, Sara, they could have both gone over the cliff. He might have crawled back to the cliff top if he'd been on his own, but he wouldn't have dared leave his son. The child would certainly have panicked, so don't belittle your part in all this.'

'Your father's right, Sara,' her mother added. 'A lot of people in the town have told me how lucky it was that you were able to help, and admired what you did, so enjoy your bit of fame, my dear.'

Ellen didn't need to add that it wouldn't do Sara's tarnished reputation any harm, either. It was good that people thought better of her now, but the most important person was Robbie, and she couldn't help wondering what he made of it all. She had left him in a huff on that Sunday morning, and if she hadn't still been angry and upset over the fact that he was probably never going to forgive her, she would have taken Bonzer straight home, and never gone on the cliff walk at all. She shivered, thinking how precarious life could be, and how such small coincidences could change what happened to that life.

She was also wondering what Miriam thought of it all. She would hate to think her rival was being feted now, instead of being the black sheep of the town. Sara gave a wry smile at the derogatory phrase, preferring to think that perhaps the prodigal daughter finally deserved her title.

'Well, I must say, she knows how to get in people's good books,' Miriam said with a scowl, after reading the newspaper report and the accompanying letter. 'Everyone will think she's marvellous now!'

Over the breakfast table, her father frowned at her. 'That's very uncharitable of you, Miriam, and I won't have it. I know you don't like the girl, but what she did for those people was a Christian act.'

'Your father's right, Miriam,' her mother put in gently. 'And you've no reason to be resentful of Sara. She might have been Robbie's sweetheart once, but he's fond of you now.'

Fond? Was there ever a more insipid word! Miriam wanted more than fondness from him, and she had been confident that she was going to get it, until Sara Boskelly came back. She didn't want to hear Sara referred to as Robbie's one-time sweetheart, either, and resentful was hardly the word to describe how she felt about her, but it would be the best that Miriam's ineffectual mother could find.

It wasn't her mother's fault that she was so feeble. She had been dominated all her married life by her overbearing husband, and when Miriam's brother Brian had died in that awful prisoner of war camp, it had all but finished her.

On an impulse, Miriam put her arm around her mother's thin shoulders and hugged her.

'You're right,' she said with an effort, 'and I'm with Robbie now, aren't I?'

Privately, she was wondering savagely how Sara would feel when her Yank came back to St Ives if some other girl fawned all over him. No matter what Robbie said, Miriam was quite sure Sara had never forgotten him, and she too remembered very well the good-looking, fair-haired bloke with a slight resemblance to Prince Philip. At that moment she felt a tiny, unexpected thrill at picturing Chesney Willand, and her thoughts raced on. How would Sara feel?

'I'm going out for a while, Mum,' she said hastily, before her thoughts ran on to impossible situations.

But somehow she couldn't stop them. How would Sara feel at the social evening, if some other girl flirted with her Yank? More soberly, she wondered how Robbie would feel if Miriam was that girl. Would he see history repeating itself? But would it matter if it was all in a good cause? the little demon inside her whispered. He was still against going to the event at all, which would make things a little more comfortable for her in the circumstances. Of course, it wouldn't be a serious flirtation, she thought quickly, perhaps just a few friendly smiles and maybe a dance. As the vicar's daughter helping to organise the event, it would be her duty to show the hand of friendship, wouldn't it?

She wasn't even sure what she would be trying to achieve, or if her nerve would fail when the time came. The sweetest result would be if Sara decided the Yank was the man for her after all, and decided to go back to America with him.

In Miriam's mind there was also the sneaking longing to prove that she too could attract a good-looking American, which had never been the case in the war years. It was always the beautiful, happy-go-lucky girls they preferred, and she was too plain, too lumpy, too restricted by her upbringing. But all that was changed now that she was officially an adult – well, almost.

Her parents hadn't objected when Robbie had asked her out, since he had been a friend of her brother's, and it had been no more than kindness when he came to the house to offer his condolences after hearing the news about Brian. Everyone knew he had his own sadness to bear, although for very different reasons. His sweetheart hadn't died. She had just gone chasing another man and humiliated him.

Miriam could vividly remember the evening he had come to the house to talk to her parents about Brian. Robbie had finally left that sad little threesome to go home, and she had told her parents she was stifled by all the memories and photographs in the house and needed some fresh air. She had caught up with him at the harbour, and they had naturally fallen into step together to share their own memories about Brian, and when she hadn't been able to hold back her tears, he had asked her into his studio for some tea and sympathy. And so it had begun.

Oh yes, she thought, more positively. It wouldn't hurt Sara Boskelly's ego one little bit if she thought her precious Yank was attracted to another girl, especially the one who had already taken one man from her. It would serve her right for stirring up Robbie's emotions all over again, just when he was starting to forget how she had treated him so shabbily.

'I definitely won't be going,' he told her shortly that evening, when she had tentatively got around to the subject of the social. 'I've no interest in Americans.'

Miriam made a small protest about his civic duty, but she was secretly relieved. It would make her own plan much easier to put into operation.

'I bet Sara will be going,' she added, to test his reaction.

'Oh, I've no doubt all the local girls will be there, eyeing up the Yanks, and quite a few of them will probably be disappointed to find their blue-eyed boys were married all the time. It will rather take the edge off the glamour when they turn up out of uniform and touting around their wives and kids,' he said cynically.

At the same time, he couldn't help remembering how passionately Sara had related all that had happened to her when she went to the New Jersey fruit farm, expecting a welcome from Chesney Willand, only to learn the truth from two middle-aged strangers. If it was the truth, she must have been devastated, in the same way he had been devastated when he read the letter she had left him. They had both suffered, and maybe the two things should have cancelled each other out by now. They might even have had a chance to do so, but for the fact that he was now with Miriam, and Chesney Willand was coming back on the scene.

Every time he thought about that, his heart hardened, and he had no wish to see the chap. He had told Sara nobody would be interested in them at the social, but he knew that wouldn't be the case. A scandal might go away for a time, but in a small town like this where they were both well known, it didn't take much to revive it, and all eyes would be on them, wondering how they were going to react.

'Let's talk about something else,' he told Miriam now. 'I'm fed up with hearing about this social. Do you want to go for a drive before the evenings start drawing in?'

She knew when to agree and leave things alone, and they drove down to Land's End to watch the waves thundering on the cliffs and spraying them with spume. It was exhilarating enough to put the colour in her cheeks, and for Robbie to pull out his sketch book and do some rough drawings. He was so absorbed in what he was doing, she might not have been there at all, she thought, and as she stepped nearer to the edge and looked down into the foaming sea, she knew how terrifying it must have been for the small boy and his father, stranded on a ledge ten feet below safety.

What would Robbie do if she pretended to slip and cried out for him? Would he be the one to rush to her side then and clasp her in his arms, vowing his undying love? Would this be the moment she craved for?

'Don't go too near the edge,' Robbie called out absently. 'It would take a crazier man than me to dive in after you in that water.'

She laughed and turned back, knowing her thoughts had been no more than a moment's madness. That was all it took sometimes, but she had no intention of falling into that churning water and certain drowning, when she had everything to live for. She had Robbie, she thought, her spirits lifting. When all was said and done, he was hers now, and once this visit from the Americans was over, they could go back to the way everything was before. She wasn't a natural optimist, but this time she had to be.

'You were a star, Sara,' Hilly told her, as they walked along the cliffs, where Sara had pointed out where the accident had happened, and the narrow ledge below that had thankfully broken the child's fall.

'No, I wasn't,' Sara said crossly. 'Why does

everyone keep talking about it? I only did what you would have done. I didn't actually pull the boy and his dad up from the ledge, did I? I just got things started.'

'If you hadn't, it might have ended up very differently. I bet a certain person was proud of you, and another certain person is chewing her lips in annoyance.'

Sara gave an impatient sigh. 'You can be so coy sometimes, Hilly, and it's not your style! If you mean Robbie and Miriam, why not say so?'

'I didn't want to annoy you.'

'Well, you are annoying me. Everybody's annoying me. I wish people wouldn't keep smiling at me now when most of the time they've been giving me black looks. I wish I could just go and hibernate and that I didn't have to come out of it until winter.'

Hilly laughed. 'You've got that all wrong, dummy. Animals hibernate in winter, and come out of it in the spring, and it's not what you really mean at all, is it? What you really mean is that you wish you could put your head beneath the blankets and not come out of them until the Yanks have come and gone, and then you wouldn't have to see *him*.'

'You're doing it again. If you mean Chesney, why don't you say Chesney?'

'I thought the fewer times you heard his name, the better you'd like it. Or have I got that wrong too?'

Her voice was too innocent, and Sara glowered at her.

'You can't think for one minute that I'll be glad

to see him after what he did to me, leading me on the way he did.'

'The trouble was, sweetie, you were just too gullible, and he called your bluff. He never expected you to follow him to America, and it must have been a hell of a shock to him when he found out.'

'So I'm the bad guy, am I? I'm the one who's at fault, not that toe-rag!'

Too late, Hilly realised what a state her friend was getting in, and she put her arm around her shoulders and gave them a squeeze.

'Of course you're not the one at fault, and maybe if I'd had a handsome GI swearing undying love to me, I'd have believed him too. I just happened to keep my distance and didn't get too involved with any of them. But I don't blame you for falling for him, Sara.'

'Robbie does, and he has every right to,' Sara said unhappily. 'Oh, if I could undo it all, don't you think I would? If I hadn't been so bloody self-righteous and thought I should do my bit for these Yanks so far from home, like everybody was telling us, and if I hadn't danced with him – with Robbie's full approval, I might say – and got to like him more and more–'

'Well, you might as well say that if the war hadn't happened, the Yanks wouldn't have come over here in the first place. So really, you can blame it all on the war. Blame it on Hitler, or Mr Chamberlain. Take your pick.'

'Or both,' said Sara.

Or she could just blame the whole damn fiasco on her own stupidity, and no matter how long she thought about it, or how much she tried to justify her actions, it always came down to that. She had been utterly stupid to fall for Chesney in the way she had, and even more stupid to get on that ship and follow him. And she could go on thinking about 'if onlys' for ever more, and it didn't change anything. If only Robbie hadn't got polio as a child that curtailed his movements a little. It wasn't impossible for him to dance, and he had danced with her on a few occasions in the past, but she knew he hadn't wanted to look foolish in front of those slick Americans who seemed to know every damn dance step in creation.

'I don't want to talk about any of it any longer,' she declared now. 'What are we going to see at the flicks on Saturday night?'

Hilly didn't answer for a moment, and Sara glanced at her, to see that she had gone bright pink. She stopped walking, making Hilly do the same.

'Look, I was going to tell you before, Sara, but so much has been happening lately that I never seemed able to get around to it.'

'Around to what?'

'I shan't be able to go to the flicks with you on Saturday night.'

'Why not? We always go there! It's practically a ritual!'

Hilly looked decidedly uncomfortable now. 'I know, but it's just – well, it's just that somebody else has asked me to go, and I've said yes.'

'What "somebody else"? Who is she?' Sara said, mimicking her, but more angry than she showed. She couldn't believe that some other girl was muscling in on their friendship, and that Hilly was letting it happen.

Hilly blushed more furiously now. 'It's not a she. Why must you assume that it is? Do you think you've got the monopoly on chaps?'

Sara felt her mouth drop open. Hilly was such a tomboy, it had never occurred to Sara that there was a young man in the wings.

'Have you been holding out on me?' she demanded, her disappointment over the cinema fading for the moment.

'No! It's all been a bit sudden, if you must know. Dave was one of the farmhands from a neighbouring farm helping us out with haymaking when you came over that day. Since then he seemed to be always at our farm for something or other, and in the end my dad asked him jokingly if there wasn't some ulterior motive for him always hanging around, and he went all colours of the rainbow and said he'd wanted to ask me out for ages but didn't know how.'

'And you were there at the time?'

'I was in the scullery, helping Mum with the washing up and I could see him through the open door. He looked so nice and so awkward, like a big puppy dog really, and I felt sorry for him. So I went right back inside and said if he wanted to ask me out, why didn't he just come on and do it?'

Sara was laughing now, imagining the scene all too well. Hilly was never one to hold back if something needed to be said, and this Dave never stood a chance.

'So he's asked you to the flicks on Saturday

night,' she stated.

Hilly looked anxious. 'Yes, he did, and I had to say yes, didn't I? If I hadn't, I know he'd have taken fright and never got around to asking me out again. And I do like him, Sara. I know I called him a puppy dog just now, but really, he's very nice. I'm sorry, but I couldn't miss this chance.'

'Well, of course you couldn't, you idiot,' Sara said quickly. 'But you'll have to tell me everything, mind – well, perhaps not everything, but as much as you think I should know!'

It was quite odd to think of Hilly with a young man. She'd never bothered too much about them in the past, and Hilly's mother had once commented to Sara that it would take a man of iron to tame that girl. To Sara it was even more weird that a young man whom Hilly had likened to a puppy dog should be the one to attract her. But that was the thing about love. There was no rhyme or reason to it when it struck, and nobody knew that better than Sara.

There was also no truer song than the one Frank Sinatra sang ... 'Saturday night is the loneliest night of the week' ... Saturday night had always been special, and in the past, she and Robbie had always spent it together, sometimes at the pictures, and sometimes just sitting and talking or walking on the cliffs, just exhilarated at being in one another's company, and thinking that it would never end.

She had spoiled all that, but when she and Hilly had picked up their friendship again, Hilly had been her constant companion on Saturday nights, and now that had gone. It was only their first date, but Sara had no doubt that now she and this Dave had found one another, there would be no turning back for Hilly. She wished them all the luck in the world, while bemoaning her own bad luck at finding herself out in the cold again. Robbie had Miriam; Hilly had Dave; and she had no-one. Angie Reid had married her pasty-faced fiancé, and brought the wedding photos into the office to show everyone. Sara was determined not to feel jealous and depressed, but it was very hard not to.

'What's wrong with you this evening, Sara?' her mother asked her on that particular Saturday night. 'Aren't you meeting Hilly for the pictures?'

'I decided to give it a miss this week, Mum,' she said with an effort. 'We were getting too predictable, like an old married couple!'

It was meant to be a joke, but she couldn't help the catch in her throat as she said it. One half of an old married couple was something she would dearly love to be, and the other half could never be anyone but Robbie Killaine.

Ellen nodded, not understanding where her daughter's thoughts were going, but she did her best to cheer her up.

'We'll all feel a sight better when these blessed American visitors have come and gone, my dear, and we can all settle back into normality again.'

'I'm sure you're right, Mum,' Sara said, wondering what was ever going to be normal about her life again.

'So if you're free tonight, why don't we start clearing out the old box room now that we don't have many guests in this week? I could do with your help now that we're planning to turn it into an extra bathroom for next summer's intake.'

'All right,' Sara said listlessly. She had nothing else to do, so why not?

Her father was always full of plans to extend and improve the guesthouse as much as possible. Every year there was something new, and the big conservatory overlooking the sea at the back of the property had been a huge success. Until now the box room had been used as a store room for all the unwanted junk and memorabilia that people generally accumulated, and never quite knew what to do with. There were boxes and boxes in the aptly-named box room, and they all had to be inspected before Ellen was prepared to be ruthless about their disposal.

'You didn't keep all my old school reports, did you?' Sara exclaimed, when she found the dusty old pile of reports tied together with string.

'It's one of the things that mothers do,' Ellen replied. 'Whether they're good or not so good, they're a record of your childhood.'

Sara wasn't sure that she wanted to read them, but in the end it was irresistible. Not so many years had passed since her schooldays, yet it was like looking at the past of someone else to see the comments made in the spidery handwriting of her old teachers – some more tactfully written than others.

'Sara's work suffered this term because of the unfortunate time she spent away from classes with the chicken-pox.'

She remembered that term so well, and the

misery of the spots that itched so abominably, and the way she had to be kept confined from the guesthouse visitors, which made her feel even more like a leper. A clodgy, she reminded herself.

'Sara should pay more attention to her work than to outside influences.'

She smiled at that, knowing it was the history teacher's arch comment on the fact that the opposite sex was becoming far more interesting to an adolescent girl than dry old dates and learning boring facts about the kings and queens of past centuries.

There was one particular comment that made her heart twist.

'It's gratifying to see that Sara has developed a sudden interest in art classes, and it is to be hoped that it will continue, whatever the reason.'

The pithy teacher probably knew very well why there was a great attraction for her in art classes. It was Robbie Killaine, whose skills were the envy of the other students, but who mattered far more to Sara than the magic of his drawings. She remembered vividly the day when the students all had to draw somebody in the class, and she had been chosen to be the model because of her striking hair. Some of the drawings were little more than caricatures, but Robbie's had been breathtaking, even reducing the art master to silence for a few moments.

Sara's green eyes had looked out from the drawing as if they were alive, looking straight at the artist, and her hair was a riotous cascade about her shoulders. Any acute observer could see that the sitter was somebody special to

Robbie, and either he hadn't tried to disguise it, or he hadn't been able to do so. Love was in every pencil stroke, as tangible as if you could reach out and touch it. Maybe at the time, neither Robbie, nor Sara, nor the rest of the class could see it, but the art teacher certainly had, and she was never asked to be the class model again.

As if it had made any difference, she thought scornfully now. As if trying to keep them apart in any way could have made any difference to the way they had felt about each other...

'Are you going to sit there dreaming all day, Sara?' Ellen said sharply.

She shut the report books with a bang.

'Do you want to keep these or shall we throw them out?' she asked.

'That's up to you, my dear.'

'I suppose we may as well keep them,' Sara said, tossing them into the keep-box. It might be foolish and pointless, but throwing them away would be like throwing away moments in her life that could never come again. She had never imagined, until now, that something as mundane as a teacher's comment in an old report book, could evoke such poignant memories.

The rest of the day was spent more prosaically, laughing together over some of the old clothes that should have gone to jumble sales years ago, but just might be worn again. In any case, during the war years it had been a crime to throw anything away that could be cut up and made into something else. There was even a short jacket that Sara remembered her mother making for her from an old blanket. It had been made with love, and she had worn it with pride, thinking herself very smart to have something fresh to wear, even if it had been made with reference to one of the government's urgings to 'make do and mend', and to save precious clothing coupons for something more essential.

Even wedding dresses had been made out of parachute silk – although Sara had never been sure how it had become available, whether legally or through the Black Market. There was a rumour too that French knickers had also been made out of the delicate silk, a rumour that had caused much sniggering and speculation among the older girls of her class who were all about to leave school and become young ladies. Some of them had already been eyeing up the American soldiers when they came flooding into Cornwall, thankful that the school years were behind them, and excited at the prospect of romance.

Sara pushed such thoughts out of her mind. There was only a certain amount of time that could be spent in nostalgia before some things either became too unbearable to remember or were definitely cloying. It was a relief when Ellen decided they had done enough, and they could both go down from the dusty box room to the everyday world of today and have a welcome cup of tea and a piece of Ellen's homemade lemon cake.

Chapter 13

As November came nearer, the more jittery Sara became. She hadn't heard from Chesney again, and she hoped vainly that perhaps he would decide not to come to Cornwall with the rest of the group after all, and she need never see him again. Perhaps he would have the gumption to realise how awkward it would be for everybody and do the decent thing. But of course he wouldn't. He was a brash American, who wouldn't take no for an answer. Sara shivered at the thought, remembering how near she had come to giving him the answer he wanted on those nights when passion had been uppermost in both their minds, and her heart had been in danger of ruling her head.

Why did people say that? she wondered, giving a brutal examination of the facts. It wasn't her heart that had been in danger of ruling anything. It had been something much lower down. It was lust, not so pure and not so simple. Of course it had been love as well, she reminded herself hastily, because she had truly loved him, even though she should have recognised that it wasn't a love that was ever destined to last. Perhaps if she had given in to him, just once, he would have tired of her, and she would have seen him for what he really was.

And perhaps if she had, she told herself even more brutally, she would have been left with more than memories. She would have become exactly what the town had assumed her to be when she ran off to America – a fallen angel, a scarlet woman, a slut left holding the baby ... and God only knew why she was torturing herself in this way, because it had never happened, and Robbie knew that. He must have realised when they made love that one, beautiful time, that it had been the first time. He wasn't an idiot and her bitterness overflowed, because how could he not have believed her then?

As the days passed, it seemed as if the whole town was looking forward to renewing its acquaintance with the Americans they had known, and meeting their families. Sara sometimes found it hard to concentrate on work, and on dealing with the applications of other people's problems that came and went at the offices of Messrs Potter and Grebe, and it was noticed by Lionel Potter and even the more reserved Arthur Grebe who asked if she was feeling peaky.

'I'm a little out of sorts today, that's all,' she replied, at which he quickly retired, and she smiled ruefully.

Arthur Grebe could deal magnificently with strangers' problems, which made him an excellent counsellor, but when it came to the personal problems of someone he knew well, he floundered. She could understand why he had never married. It was always Mr Potter, the family man, who was more perceptive to Sara's unease. But she knew she mustn't let it interfere with her job, or she'd be looking for another one. What the firm required from her was to be an efficient receptionist with a pleasant and sympathetic manner, and she tried to remember that.

In a close-knit town like St Ives it was unavoidable for her not to see Robbie quite often, and also to see Miriam and him together. It was never the most comfortable of occasions when they turned up at the same place at the same time. As it was the middle of October and nearing the end of the long summer season for visitors, there was to be a beach carnival, one of the purposes of which was to raise money for the firework display planned for the end of the social evening with the visiting Americans in November.

Sara had volunteered to take around one of the buckets to collect money from willing onlookers at the carnival. Although it was a Saturday night and many people would be going to the cinema as usual, a carnival would still guarantee a good turn-out. The sea was silvery calm in the harbour, and the carnival was in full swing as the evening darkened, the fishing-boats bobbing gently on the swell, lit by colourful lights along the shore as the decorated floats and individual entrants paraded round the harbourside. Sara swung her bucket to encourage people to put in their pennies, and hopefully more, and suddenly felt her bucket clanging against someone else's with a similar idea. She laughed, starting to apologise, and looked up straight into Robbie's eyes.

'Is this where we say "Snap" and go our separate ways before the competition gets too great?' he said jokingly.

Sara caught her breath. 'We could do that, or

we could join forces and see how well we could do. We always made a good team in the past,' she said, before she could stop herself.

For a moment she thought he was going to agree. It probably wasn't the best idea, but it would have been the sweetest thing to combine forces and spend the rest of the evening laughing and joking with strangers and locals alike, while cajoling them into parting with their money for a good cause. Then he shrugged, and she knew she had lost.

'Maybe not. We'll do better separately.'

'Why are you doing this, anyway? I'd have thought it was the last thing you'd want to do.'

'Miriam taunted me about it, and you know I could never resist a challenge, nor seem to be small-minded,' he retorted.

'Where is she tonight then?' she couldn't resist saying. 'Didn't she want to hang on to your coat-tails?'

Robbie's voice went a couple of degrees colder, and Sara cursed herself for being so sarky. 'Miriam stubbed her toe at work and couldn't face walking around all evening.'

He moved on before Sara could say any more. But what could she say? That she was sorry Miriam had stubbed her toe, when she wasn't? That she was sorry Miriam wasn't here to enjoy the carnival, which she wasn't? She might be a lot of things, Sara thought keenly, but she was no hypocrite, and she was glad Miriam wasn't around, giving her those half-jealous, half-triumphant looks as she clung as close to Robbie as she could. Besides, when the carnival was finished, it had been arranged that the bucket collectors were going to meet with the organisers at a local hostelry to see how much they had collected for the fireworks, and it promised to be a jolly end to the evening. It promised even more than that now, thought Sara with a sliver of excitement. Miriam wasn't going to be there, but Robbie was.

Being a Saturday night, the pub was quite full, and the collecting party was obliged to squeeze into a small area, with extra chairs and stools filling the space. Knees rubbed against knees with many laughing apologies from the gentlemen to the ladies, and plenty of under-the-breath ribald comments. The organisers bought everyone a well-deserved glass of cider, golden and frothy and refreshingly strong.

'Sorry about this,' Robbie said to Sara, as the atmosphere in the pub grew hotter and they seemed to be as close as limpets.

'You don't need to be. We've been closer than this before.'

She didn't mean it in a provocative way, nor did she mean to murmur it so that only Robbie could hear, and maybe it was the cider that was going to her head. Or maybe it was being so close to him like this, the way they had been on a thousand other occasions, sharing a glass of cider at the end of a lovely evening together. She felt happy and relaxed, and there had been so few times since her return home when she really had felt like this. It felt so normal to be here with him, with the company of people she had known all their lives around them, chatting and joshing together. She couldn't help smiling into his eyes, simply for the joy of feeling accepted at last.

'Don't, Sara,' he said in a low voice.

'Don't what? I'm not doing anything, am I?'

She had to lean towards him to hear him, because the others were laughing loudly over somebody else's joke. She was a little dizzy with the cider, and with his nearness, and she automatically put her hand on his knee to steady herself. His hand immediately covered hers, warm and intimate, and it stayed there for a moment before he removed it. It was almost as though they were somehow isolated from the rest of the world in that brief moment of time, and they were the only two people looking into one another's eyes.

'You know what, and don't pretend that you don't,' he said, and then the world crowded in on them as the organisers decided the time for jollity was over, and the counting had to begin properly.

Sara felt momentarily bewildered. She wasn't a tease, and besides, she had never needed to be with Robbie. He knew her as well as she knew herself ... or he always thought he did, until she went off and left him. The shock of that must have made him wonder if he had ever really known her at all.

The business of the evening was finally over, and they were well pleased with the amount they had collected, which would provide a good fireworks display on the beach to round off the social evening next month. The Americans were tentatively arranging to arrive on November the 4th and would stay in the town for three days, so the social was fixed for November the 5th, which fitted in nicely with Guy Fawkes' Night, a British tradition which would undoubtedly charm them.

Sara stepped out of the pub and felt her head swim. She knew how strong cider could be, but she hadn't balked at drinking a large glass of it, if only to ward off her feelings at the way she had been rebuffed by Robbie. She swayed for a moment, and then she felt someone holding her arm firmly.

'Come on, I'll walk you home,' Robbie said.

'There's no need. It's too far.'

'I might have a gammy leg, but I'm perfectly capable of walking a girl home when she's under the influence,' he said shortly.

It was such a daft remark to make, and so unlike him to be so bloody formal, that Sara started to giggle.

'I'm no more under the influence than you are.'

'That's a matter of opinion, but I'd rather not stand here all night arguing about it and drawing attention to ourselves.'

'No, we wouldn't want to do that, would we? All right then, take me home!'

He may have meant he didn't want them to draw attention to themselves by arguing outside a pub, but Sara took it to mean that he wouldn't want too many people to see them walking out together. Somebody might tell Miriam that he had been spending time in the company of his old girlfriend, and Miriam might not like it... Miriam definitely wouldn't like it...

Defiantly, she tucked her arm more firmly inside Robbie's, and leaned her head against his arm. If he thought she needed help, then she might as well make the most of it. It was a blissfully balmy night for mid-October, the way that only Cornish nights could be. It was a night meant for lovers, and it was exactly what she and Robbie should be right now, what they were always meant to be.

'Damn,' she heard him say beneath his breath.

She had closed her eyes for a moment, knowing she could rely on him to steer in the right direction, but now she opened them quickly, to see a stream of people walking their way. Instantly, she realised it was time for the cinema to throw out its customers, and there was no chance, now, of not being seen together.

'Sorry about this,' she mumbled. 'If you'd rather leave me here, I'll be perfectly all right, Robbie. I know the way blindfold!'

'I said I'd see you home, and I will,' he said. 'Just try not to hold on to me quite so tightly, Sara.'

She wasn't having this. She wasn't prepared to make people think they had happened to meet by chance and were going the same way, when anybody who knew them knew they lived in opposite directions. Perversely, she clung on tighter.

'I don't fancy tripping up, if you don't mind. You don't want two girls with bashed toes, do you?'

'I don't want two girls at all,' he retorted, but before she could think of a furious response to that, she was confronted by a startled Hilly, walking alongside a brawny farmhand she took to be Dave.

'Well, this is a surprise,' Hilly said at once. 'Is there something I should know, Sara?'

'You should know how to mind your own business,' Robbie snapped.

Hilly glared at him. 'I never liked you much, Robbie, and there's no need to get shirty with me. Sara's my friend, and I was talking to her, not you.'

Sara giggled again. As far as she was concerned, this entire evening was taking on a slightly bizarre quality.

'Robbie's just walking me home before I fall down. We've been drinking cider in the pub.'

'We had one glass each, and we were there to count the collecting money for the social evening,' he corrected her. 'It wasn't a date.'

Sara giggled again. She couldn't seem to stop it, and the night air was making her feel reckless. 'Oh, stop being so defensive, Robbie. We all know you and Miriam Roche are besotted about one another, so you don't need to go on making excuses for being in my company.'

'You see how she is,' he suddenly appealed to Hilly. 'The sooner I get her home and into bed, the better.'

Both girls were laughing uproariously now, and he realised what he'd said as the unfortunate Dave tried to stop them. People were looking; people who knew them all; people who knew Miriam, and Robbie dragged Sara away as quickly as he could and marched her up the hill towards the guesthouse before any of them said anything even more indiscreet. By the time they reached the top, they were both out of breath, and the cooler air was starting to make Sara come to her senses.

‘I’m really sorry if I’ve done or said anything I shouldn’t this evening, Robbie. You know I would never hurt you intentionally.’

Her voice shook a little, knowing she had already done that. She had hurt him as badly as any woman could hurt a man she supposedly loved, and probably compounded that hurt by coming back here at all. The small breeze lifted her hair, and the sweet scent of cider was on her trembling lips, and with a smothered oath he pulled her into his arms and he was kissing her lips and her face and her eyes, and then he was letting her go, leaving her stunned as he turned and went rapidly down the hill the way he had come. Leaving her wondering if she had simply imagined those last moments, or if they had been a dream. She stumbled into the guesthouse, thankful that it was all quiet and that her parents were asleep. She crept upstairs as quietly as she could, undressed, leaving her clothes where they fell, climbed into bed and continued the dream.

Hilly caught up with her as she was walking Bonzer on the clifftop the next morning. She hadn’t wanted to take him out at all, but she thought the exercise might clear her head, which felt as though a dozen sledgehammers were doing their worst inside it.

‘Tell me to mind my own business if you like, but you have to admit it was a hell of a shock to see you and Robbie looking so cosy last night,’ she started.

Sara sighed. She wasn’t in any mood for an argument, and she’d rather not have company at all. But she knew Hilly would hang on like a leech until she got the information she wanted so she might as well tell her. She did so as concisely as she could, avoiding the last moments when he had kissed her so passionately. That was private, even from Hilly.

'So you see, it was all perfectly innocent. Robbie was just doing a friend a good turn.'

'That's not the way it looked, and it's not the way other people must have seen it as well. It's going to get around to Miriam sooner or later, Sara.'

'I know,' she said with a groan. 'But that's for Robbie to sort out, not me.'

She found out differently the next day when Miriam stormed into her workplace, regardless of any stubbed toe. She banged the door shut, making Sara jump, and her eyes were blazing.

'What do you think you're playing at?'

Sara hissed back at her. 'You can't come in here like this. There are clients upstairs and my boss won't thank me for letting a crazy woman into the office. If you've got something to say to me, it will have to wait and it will have to be somewhere else.'

'I've got something to say to you all right, and it won't wait. I'm fed up with people telling me they saw you out with Robbie the other night, and that you were drunk. Nice habits you learned from your fancy Yank, I don't think!'

Sara felt her face flush with fury. The thought that the clients upstairs might be hearing any of this was bad enough, but if either of her bosses was hearing it too, it was going to spell disaster.

'Don't be more stupid than you already are, Miriam,' she snapped. 'I was certainly not drunk, and I was not out with Robbie. He merely offered to walk me home after the carnival collecting business as it was getting late.'

'And I'm supposed to believe that, am I?'

Her voice was less certain now, and Sara guessed at once that she had already had it out with Robbie, and had come here to see if their stories tallied – as they obviously did.

'I think you already know it's true if you've spoken to Robbie about it. I don't know why you should mistrust him unless you're so unsure of how he feels about you.'

'I'm not unsure of him at all.'

'Then if you want my advice you need to be a bit more careful in what you say to him. He never did like jealous females and it's a sure way of losing him.'

She stared at Miriam coolly, as various emotions flickered over the girl's face.

'You're the last person I want any advice from,' she said finally. 'You had your chance with him, so just keep away from him in future.'

She flounced out of the office, and Sara wilted, finding it hard to concentrate on anything else after the vindictiveness in Miriam's face. She couldn't honestly blame her, though. In her place, she would have done exactly the same.

'Good Lord, I never thought she'd turn up like that,' Hilly said, when they next met. 'I wonder how Robbie puts up with her at all.'

'Well, I don't suppose she'll be like that when

she's with him, will she?' Sara said with a shrug. 'She'll be all sweet and docile.'

Hilly sniffed. 'I can't see her ever being sweet and docile. When we were at school I always thought there was a pig inside her trying to get out.'

Sara laughed. 'And I thought you liked pigs.'

'I do, providing they're the farmyard kind. But never mind all that. Have you seen Robbie since that night?'

'No. He's probably avoiding me like Miriam told him to.'

It was a depressing thought, but she couldn't blame him for that, either. Not if he and Miriam were definitely together now ... but there had been that long, unforgettable, passionate kiss that nobody else knew about, and the thought of that changed everything. How could he be in love with somebody else if he could kiss her like that? She had lapsed into silence now, and Hilly knew her too well.

'Something else happened that night, didn't it? You and he didn't – you know what – did you? You didn't give in to temptation and all that rot?'

Hilly didn't really believe it for a second, and she said it jokingly, hoping to provoke a juicy response about just what did happen between them. Something like a fleeting kiss, perhaps, for old times' sake ... so she was totally unprepared for what she was actually about to hear.

'We'd already done that a few weeks ago,' Sara said all in a rush as if the words had been bursting to come out.

Hilly's mouth fell open. 'What? You don't

mean... Sara, you don't mean that since you came home … since Robbie's been with Miriam, that you and he … that you've actually–'

'Yes, that's exactly what I mean,' Sara said agitatedly.

It didn't sound quite so wonderful to have it said out loud in such an underhand way, and she could have bitten out her tongue for being so reckless as to tell Hilly. Not that she thought it would go any further. Hilly could be as close as a clam when she chose, but now it was a secret shared between three instead of two.

That evening Sara had cycled over to Pennywell Farm, and they had been trying on shades of lipstick in Hilly's old-fashioned bedroom, but now Hilly pulled her down on the bed and gripped her hands in excitement.

'You've got to tell me everything now. When did it happen? And how the heck did it happen, considering the trouble between you? And – what was it like?' she couldn't resist adding.

Sara gave a small, nervous laugh. What was it like? How could she ever explain what it was like to be as intimate as two people could be without going into raptures and sounding stupid and ridiculously sentimental, like a swooning heroine in a soppy novel? Besides, it wasn't something you wanted to talk about. It was too personal, too private, too precious … and if it never happened again, something to keep guarded as her dearest, most perfect memory.

'Well?' Hilly said.

Sara flinched. 'It happened by accident, and of course we never meant it to. It was in his studio one evening, and we were arguing, and somehow, well, it just happened, and that's all I'm going to say, so don't ask me any more.'

'Well, there's one thing I've got to ask you, and you can shout my head off if you like. But was this the first time – with anybody?'

Sara shook her off. 'Oh, for God's sake, Hilly, haven't you been listening to anything I've been saying ever since I came home? I never let Chesney Willand touch me, and although I was mad enough to think that I loved him for a time and that he loved me, it was nothing like the feelings I always had for Robbie, and still do. Robbie knows that. The moment we made love, he knew I had never been with anyone else. I told you all that before, and I thought you believed me. What kind of a friend are you, anyway?'

Before she could stop herself, she burst into tears, which maddened her even more. All this time she had been so strong. It had been an ordeal to return home and to face everybody, but once she had been reassured of Hilly's friendship it had seemed like a good omen. The terrible twins were back together again, and everything would be all right. Now, she wondered if Hilly had ever believed in her at all.

She suddenly found herself almost smothered by a bear hug, and she realised Hilly was crying too. A fine pair they were, she couldn't help thinking, and if Hilly's mother came upstairs to see what was going on, she'd think they had gone completely crazy.

'Of course I bloody well believe you,' Hilly said fiercely in her ear, 'and I'm the best friend you ever had because I'm not afraid to come out and say what I think, instead of going behind your back. Which would you prefer?'

'You of course, you dimwit, and you'd better not let your mother hear you swear or she'll think I'm an even worse influence,' Sara said with a weak grin, and moments later they were laughing and crying together.

Cycling home later that evening, Sara realised that in the midst of all that emotion, there had been a sobering moment. There had been so many people who would have been whispering and speculating behind her back over all that had gone on in the year she was away. There were those who believed in what she had told them, and those who never asked, but came to their own conclusions, and none of them would have been complimentary. Her parents, Robbie and Hilly would have been among the people most affected, both by what she had done, and by the rumours and ugly innuendoes in the town. St Ives was a small town, and she had done something unforgivable. The most amazing thing was that some people had forgiven her: her parents, Hilly, dear old Leah, even Mrs Goode ... and, at last, Robbie.

His forgiveness was the one she needed the most of all, and even if forgiveness wasn't quite the right word to use, there was no doubt in her mind that despite everything, he still loved her as much as she loved him. The hell of it was, there was nothing they could do about it, since she knew he would never let Miriam down now. It would be too cruel. So in the end, Sara had no option but to wait and see whatever the future held for them.

And really, what had she achieved? They had made glorious love on that one beautiful evening. He had kissed her more passionately than she could have dreamed about on the evening of the carnival – in fact, sometimes she wondered if it really had all been a dream – but basically, nothing had changed.

He was still with Miriam, and Miriam had made it plain that she wasn't letting him go. But could even a girl like Miriam, who had once been so pasty and lumpy and never attracted any other boyfriends, be satisfied with a man who was still in love with someone else? Sara almost wished she could see into her mind and fathom her out. She wished she had old Leah's professed second sight and could see what the future really held for them all. But perhaps it was better not, she thought with a shiver, remembering how both Leah and her Aunt Dottie had once warned her that you didn't always like what you saw.

She cycled on home, keeping her head down low as she passed some revellers down by the harbour, catcalling out to her, whether they knew who she was or not. It didn't matter. There was a light on in Robbie's window, and she would have given the world to be the one who was able to be there with him, openly and freely.

But she wasn't the one, and she had forfeited that right. At that moment, she felt as if she was truly lost, and she had no-one to blame but herself.

Chapter 14

There had been a bit of confusion as to the actual date of the town's welcoming social for the American visitors, but now there had been an official confirmation of travelling dates from their group organiser.

They would now arrive in two special charabancs on Tuesday the 4th, and the social evening would be on Wednesday the 5th and they would depart for London the following day. They would be escorted to the various hotels and guesthouses which would be their hosts for the visit, and once it was finally announced in the local newspaper, everybody knew where they were.

At least it wasn't to be a long-drawn-out visit, for which Sara was fervently thankful.

'I really wish I could disappear for those few days,' she told her mother when she had read out the information over breakfast. 'Do you think anybody would miss me if I slipped away to somewhere in the country until the visit was over?'

She had spoken lightly and she hadn't meant to be taken seriously, but she might have known her mother wouldn't see it that way. She put down the teapot with a bang.

'I hope you won't do anything so foolish. It will just compound your guilty feelings over what happened, and I would like to think my daughter was capable of holding her head up high in any circumstances.'

Sara flushed. 'I didn't mean it, Mum, and of course I'll be here! I just don't think it will be a very comfortable few days for me, that's all.'

'I know, love,' Ellen said more kindly. 'But try to remember that it's not just one man who's coming here. There will be many others who have fond memories of the welcome they had in St Ives during the war and many people who'll be eager to renew their acquaintance with them. We all got to know and like them, and it's not all about you and Mr Willand.'

'I know. It feels like it to me, though,' Sara muttered.

And if ever there was a time to be self-obsessed about something, surely this was it. How could she help it, when she knew she would have to face Chesney again, and there was nothing she could do to stop it?

The 2nd of November was a Sunday, and Sara took Bonzer for his usual run on the cliffs, laughing at his madcap antics as he chased about like a mad thing. It wasn't a very warm day, and Sara had the place to herself for once, which was the way she liked it, enjoying the frothing of the sea foam far below as it crashed against the cliffs.

She loved all of Cornwall's changing seasons. Each one had its own particular charm, including the wonderful light reflected from sea and sky that was so beloved by artists in the area, and attracted an ever-increasing bohemian community in the summer months. Artists, sculptors, photographers, writers, whether they were professional or just dabblers, seemed to have found their way to this corner of the country as if drawn by a magnet.

Bonzer suddenly stopped in his tracks, his head lifting, his great ears perking up. Seconds later he was barking joyously and bounding away from Sara as someone he recognised came striding towards them from the direction of the town.

Her breath caught in her throat, ragged and tight. The man was tall with an easy, confident stride that was almost arrogant. His hair was fair, blown by the breeze, and no longer as short-cropped as the military had once dictated. He no longer wore the sleek, well-fitting uniform of the US marines that so often put the British soldiers' uniforms in the shade by comparison with their rough material. He wore a check sports coat and easy fitting beige slacks, and even from a distance, he was unmistakable.

'Chesney,' Sara whispered.

His name on her lips was taken away by a flurry of the breeze. And then she panicked. Oh God, what was he doing here? He wasn't due here for two more days. She had more or less prepared herself for the sight of him being cushioned for her because she would be with her parents at the social event. He would be in the company of his peers, of the American families, of local people excitedly welcoming old wartime friends, and she had never expected – never wanted – to see him alone.

And now he was here, just yards away from her, with Bonzer showing that at least one member of the Boskelly family was pleased to see him. The only member...

'What are you doing here?' she stammered, when she could get her breath back. She didn't know what else to say. Her heart was thumping so fast she thought she might keel over at any minute, and she tried to remind herself frantically of all he had done, and that she should keep her dignity at all costs. Which wasn't so damn easy when she found it just as hard to forget how very close they had once been, and that he was smiling the same smile as before, the same, charismatic, film-star smile that used to make her go weak at the knees just thinking about him.

'Sara, honey,' he said, in the same way she remembered as he came near and caught hold of her limp hands in his.

It was that name that did it. Honey ... it was the easy word they all used, all the dynamic Yanks who had come storming into their lives at a time when the country so desperately needed them, and were so grateful to them, even if they did turn up a bit late, some said sarcastically, but that wasn't their fault. That was their government's fault.

It wasn't the fault of the handsome young men with their nylons and their chocolate and the extra rations they were so pleased and eager to share with their Cornish hosts, and who were so lovely and friendly with the children, practically like Pied Pipers, and so charming to the girls...

Sara snatched her hands away. 'Don't call me that,' she said tightly. 'I'm not your honey and I never was, was I? And you still haven't said what you're doing here, two days too early.'

She couldn't think of anything else to say. She couldn't think properly at all. She didn't want him here. She wished she had never met him, disrupting her life, disrupting Robbie's life the way he had. Although she had been the one to strike the final blow on hers and Robbie's relationship, she reminded herself brutally. Chesney had merely been the bait, and she had taken it, so stupidly and recklessly.

'I came ahead of my buddies because I wanted to talk to you,' he said, his voice as low and beautiful as ever in that so-seductive accent. 'I called in to see your parents earlier, hoping to see you, of course, and I had a long talk with them.'

Sara gasped furiously. 'You had no right to do that! I made my own mess, and we've finally got on with our lives since then, and it's not fair to involve them in it. I never wanted it all stirred up again.'

She was close to tears now, but she was damned if she was going to let him see it. She blinked them back hard.

'Would you rather I had just showed up at this social that's been arranged and that we made small talk with the rest of the town listening in? I know I've been a bastard to you, Sara, and I apologise for the word, but there's no other word for it, but I thought if we could just get together before that evening, we could perhaps smooth things out between us. I can just imagine how your old Leah would come marching over to me to give me a piece of her mind if I had not tried to make my peace before then. I quite look forward to doing battle with the old girl,' he added as an afterthought.

Sara looked at him mutely. He didn't know How could he know? He was as far removed from her real life as it was possible to be, and she wished to heaven he had stayed that way.

'Leah's dead,' she said starkly.

'Gee, I'm sorry, kid. I know how much store you set by her.'

Was he laughing inside now? He'd been tolerant enough towards Leah, even teasing, but Sara always knew he thought her a mad woman, and she'd often suspected he went back to his buddies at camp and made them laugh at some of her crazy stories. It incensed her even more to remember it, and she didn't want his sympathy, either.

'There's nothing I want from you, Chesney. I made that clear in the letter I sent you, and if you'd had any decency at all, you wouldn't even have come back for this reunion or whatever you call it.'

'Why should I stay away? I made some good friends in St Ives, and shared a good few pints of beer in the local pubs. I know that what happened between you and me ended up in an unfortunate way, but hell, honey, I never expected you to jump on a ship and come follow me, did I? I always thought you were a bit of a wild one, and I loved you for it, but I never expected that!'

He was unbelievable. Sara stared at him, wondering how anybody could be so arrogant and not know it. He was blaming her for chasing him and finding out the truth about him, and she couldn't let this pass.

'Would you rather I'd stayed here and grieved for ever about the love I'd lost like some pathetic little Victorian heroine? I had more backbone than that, Chesney, and I had to go through a lot of soul-searching before I did what I did, because I believed everything you said. I believed you loved me, and what a fool I was to believe such a liar!'

Somehow he had caught hold of her hands again, and he was gripping them too tightly for her to pull away.

'I know I deserve everything I get, Sara, but I was kind of thinking maybe you'd give me a second chance. You were always my girl, you know.'

'I was *never* your girl. Not your only one, anyway. Mr and Mrs Irish made sure to tell me that. How many more of them have you got tucked away, I'd like to know? Do they all think they're your girl?'

'There's nobody, and that's the God's honest truth. That's why I was so determined to come back here early before the other guys. I wanted you to know I really do feel deeply about you, Sara, and I want to make amends.'

She wrenched away from him, shouting for Bonzer to follow her as she tore back the way she had come. She couldn't bear to listen to another word of this. She had no idea what he was suggesting. Was he telling her he loved her after all? Was he going to propose they got engaged or married, or that she went back to America with him? He must be out of his mind if he could think she would accept any of those things. Totally and utterly out of his mind if he thought she would believe such a liar and a cheat ever again.

She was near to sobbing as she reached the guest-house, thankful that at least he hadn't followed her. Her mother was in the kitchen where everything was warm and homely and normal, and with one look at Sara's distraught face, Ellen opened her arms to her daughter.

'How could he come here like this?' she wept. 'It was an awful shock to see him, Mum.'

'It was a shock for us too, love, but your father made sure to tell him that we knew what had happened and what we thought of his nasty little games.'

Sara gave a weak smile. She could imagine the scene when her father got into his stride. Eloquent wasn't the word for it, and Chesney would soon have discovered that Frank wasn't always the amiable *mine* host the holiday visitors knew. There were none in the guesthouse now, but the Boskellys had been firm in saying that they preferred not to have any of the Americans staying with them for their brief visit, and the reason for it was tacitly – and sometimes not so tacitly – understood by the town organisers.

'I doubt if we'll see him again, Sara,' Ellen said. 'I'm sure he wouldn't be so brash as to turn up at the social now.'

'Oh, he'll turn up all right,' Sara said. 'It would be like getting through the hide of a rhinoceros to make him see how distasteful that would be.'

Although, just how true was that? People in the town had heard so many rumours, and she had been the one to scandalise the town, not him. Now that she was back, they only had her word for it – those she had chosen to tell – that Chesney had had plenty of other girls at his beck and call, and had never expected a silly little Cornish girl to follow him to his make-believe home. She shivered, knowing that all eyes would be on her, whether Chesney was at the social or not, and she wondered wildly if she could invent some fatal illness that would strike on the very eve of the social.

Ellen looked at her daughter with suspicious eyes. 'Whatever you're thinking, Sara, you will come to the social with your father and me, and you'll hold your head up high.'

'Are you a mind-reader now?' Sara muttered.

'No, my love, but I know desperation when I see it, and there's no need. We'll be there, and so will plenty of others who know you well, including Hilary. I presume she's planning to attend?'

'I certainly hope so, even though she hates that sort of thing, and dances like a carthorse.'

Ellen laughed. 'Oh well, what with Hilary dancing like a carthorse and that man having a hide like a rhinoceros, it should be quite an evening. Now let's all try to forget what happened this morning.'

It was easier said than done, but since they had no guests, Sara decided to have a long soak in a hot bath that afternoon, and she was feeling a mite calmer by the time the family sat down for their evening meal. As the light began to fade, she said she was going to take a book into the conservatory. It was her favourite place when they had the guesthouse to themselves. It would still be warm enough from the day, and she could look out at the changing patterns of the sea far below, or to the left of her, down to the twinkling lights of the town and the harbour.

How could anybody ever want to leave such a place, she thought, with a rush of affection. During the war, the Yanks might have thought them quaint with their old-fashioned bathtubs and antiquated plumbing, but whatever new-fangled things the fast-paced Americans had, they were welcome to it. This was home.

'Somebody to see you, Sara,' she heard her mother say a long while later, when she had become so totally immersed in the book she was reading that she hadn't even heard her approach.

The book on her lap dropped to the floor, and she bent to retrieve it with her heart thumping while she tried to gather her thoughts. How dare he come back again! The next moment her heart jumped.

'I had a visitor this afternoon,' Robbie said.

Oh God, this was awful. She didn't have to ask who it was, but this was even more crass of Chesney than she would have believed.

'I'm sorry,' she stammered.

He closed the conservatory door behind him and strode across to where she sat on one of the comfortable loungers, her hands clasped tightly together now, not knowing what to expect of him. He sat down very close beside her.

'You don't need to be sorry. It wasn't your fault the bastard decided he ought to see me.'

Sara drew in her breath, ignoring the ugly word

he used – the same word Chesney had used about himself.

'What did he want?'

'He came to apologise, if you please, and to hope there were no hard feelings, and to say, of course, he had never expected you to follow him to America the way you did. I told the bugger just what I thought of him.'

Sara drew in her breath again. It was so unlike him to resort to swearing unless he was really provoked, and she hoped her parents weren't within hearing range.

'I'm sorry, Robbie,' she said, her voice full of misery. 'It seems to go on and on, doesn't it? If only the group hadn't planned to come back here to stir things up all over again, we could all have got on with our lives.'

'Do you think it's that easy?' he said, in no mood to be pacified.

Sara bridled at once. 'No, I don't think it's that easy. None of it has been easy for me, and every day I risk facing somebody with doubts and condemnation in their eyes. I know I did a terrible thing to you, but what he did was wicked and wrong, leading me on the way he did.'

'He never asked you to go chasing after him, did he?'

It was the stark question that she never wanted Robbie to ask. Chesney had never put the question to her, and of course the answer was that it had been all her own doing, and she had been the one to learn the truth and to deal with the consequences, the shame and humiliation of it all. She didn't answer Robbie now, and she turned her head away, so that he couldn't see the stinging tears in her eyes. But he knew.

'Sara, don't,' he said in a low voice. 'I only came here tonight to let you know that he's here already, so you'd be prepared if you saw him.'

'I already know,' her voice was jerky now. 'He came here too, and when Mum told him I was taking Bonzer for a walk, he found me. It gave me an awful shock to see him, and I told him a few home truths and that I never wanted to see him again.'

Robbie didn't answer for a few moments and any fragile rapport she thought they had had seemed to be disappearing fast. But she had misread his reaction.

'Oh God, Sara,' he muttered, and then, quite how it happened she didn't know, but she was being held tight in his arms and her face was muffled in his shoulder. 'Between us, we've made a hell of a mess of things, haven't we?'

'I have, you mean,' she mumbled, her voice almost lost in the fabric of his jacket. 'Whatever's happened, it's all my fault, and you can't take any of the blame.'

'Well, that's not quite true,' he said, angry at both of them now. 'If I hadn't been so willing to let you dance with that Yank and been so trusting, and so sure there was nothing in it, things might never have got so out of hand. If I hadn't got polio as a child and been so bloody self-conscious of my leg, and the fact that all the other chaps were in uniform, showing me up, I'd have said to hell with them, and never let you out of my sight.'

'Well, that's just daft talk,' Sara said, wriggling away from him. 'You might as well say if we'd never been born we'd never have fallen in love in the first place. But we did – didn't we, Robbie?'

'Of course we did. And you could also say that if you hadn't gone off the way you did, I'd never have felt sorry for Miriam after her brother died, and started taking her out. Not that it could ever compare with what we had, never would, nor ever will, but there's nothing I can do about it without breaking her heart the way you broke mine,' he added almost savagely.

'I suppose not,' Sara said, feeling sick at the thought. He was too honest, too upright to do anything of the sort even though her jealous little heart was tempting her to rush to Miriam and demand to know how she could bear to be courted by a man who was in love with somebody else.

'I'd like to know what the old biddies you set such store by would have had to say about all this,' Robbie said suddenly, holding her hands tightly now and changing his mood so quickly it startled her.

'Do you mean my Aunt Dottie and old Leah?'

'Well, they're the ones who used to get their heads together and sort out the world, didn't they? I'd like a bit of their second sight or whatever it was, to see what the future holds for us.'

Sara leaned towards him, her voice passionate, her long hair brushing his cheek, sending a fragrance of the moors into his nostrils, a piquant mixture of wild heather and the sweet grass of summer.

'I don't need them to tell you what it won't hold for me. I'll never go back to America again; the place I most want to be is right here.'

She couldn't have made it more plain, and he folded her to him until their heartbeats merged as close and fast as if they were one.

A sound from elsewhere in the guesthouse made them pull apart, and Robbie said roughly that he should go. She held his hand for a moment more.

'You will go to the social evening, won't you, Robbie? Don't let anybody think you can't face it.'

'You can be sure of it,' he said grimly.

Long after he had gone, she remained in the conservatory with her own thoughts until it was cold and dark. She didn't know what was going to happen, but what she did know was that love never truly died. He might have hated her for what she had done, but there had been too much between them for it to be ruined for ever. Knowing that he was still seeing Miriam and wouldn't think of letting her down, the knowledge that he still loved her wasn't a great deal of comfort, but for now, it had to be enough.

Thankfully, Chesney never came near the guesthouse again. She didn't know where he was staying, and she didn't care. On the allotted day, the gaily-decorated charabancs came into town, their horns hooting to announce their arrival. They brought the visitors as far down the narrow streets as it was possible to come, before depositing the large group of Americans and their families. From there, unless they were to stay within walking distance, local cars with willing drivers and helping hands would take them to their hotels and guesthouses for their brief stay in St Ives.

It was hardly possible to miss them. It seemed as if half the town had turned out to greet the charabancs and to renew acquaintance with the GIs they had got to know during the war. Many of them had seemed no more than boys then, but those who returned resembled prosperous businessmen now. Their wives were smartly dressed, their children noisy and excited and constantly chattering about the cute little streets and the cute boats, and the cute way that people talked. Everything was cute, it seemed.

But if they were excited, so were the people of St Ives who had turned out to greet them. There was no ignoring the fact that it was like a mini-invasion. It was almost comparable to the excitement of VE Day when everybody had poured out on to the streets, as if their houses were far too small to contain them on such a memorable and historic occasion. On such a joyous day, you had wanted people around you, singing and laughing, sharing in the emotions and tears of joy ... and the silent tears too, for those who wouldn't return.

Today was like that. Sara had begged to be allowed to leave her office to join in the general melee, and was given ready permission from her bosses, knowing there wouldn't be much work out of her that day. It wasn't that she had any special friends to greet, but she had known more than the one who had let her down so badly. There were others who had been far from home, and had been glad of a friendly smile at the dances and the local shops. Some of them recognised her, and drew her in to their family circles.

'You're a sight for sore eyes, honey,' one said, while his curious little daughter hung back, staring at this vision with the glowing coppery hair and sparkling green eyes whose hand her father was shaking vigorously now.

'Is she a film star, daddy?' the girl whispered.

The American laughed. 'No, she's not, sweetie, but she could be one, couldn't she? Come and meet the wife, Sara honey.'

They were all so nice, so generous in their warmth, but wasn't that what had attracted her to Chesney in the first place? She hadn't seen him anywhere among the crowds, much to her relief, but this man, whose name she now recalled as Kyle, was introducing her to a smiling woman called Gloria. To Sara they sounded more like film stars themselves.

'Hi there,' she heard somebody else say, and she turned with a ready smile, to look straight into Chesney Willand's eyes, arriving from wherever he was staying to join his buddies. Her smile froze immediately, and she simply couldn't answer. Heart thudding, she turned back to where Kyle was explaining to his daughter about the small town and how much he had enjoyed being here during the war.

'Were you in the war?' the young girl asked Sara.

She smiled at the innocent question. 'I was a bit

too young to do anything important like the soldiers did, love.'

No, what she did was disgrace her family and let down the man she loved, she thought, and all because of the one hovering far too near to her now. She broke away, saying swiftly that she had to get back to work, but that she hoped she would see them all at the social event the town was arranging for them.

'You surely will,' Kyle said. 'We're looking forward to it, aren't we, Gloria? She wanted to check out all you good-looking Cornish gals I've been telling her about.'

Gloria laughed. 'He's kidding, Sara. I think I can trust this old buffer by now! Better than some, I daresay!'

Sara kept the smile tight on her lips as she escaped among the crowds to go back to the office, telling herself she shouldn't read a double meaning into everything any of these friendly people said.

Across the harbour she could see Robbie standing in the doorway of his shop. She would have been surprised if he'd bothered to come out and mingle, even though he had known many of these servicemen, and there had been a time when he too had been a friend to those who were far from home, only to have that friendship thrown back in his face in the most despicable way.

She kept her head down until she reached her office, hardly realising how she had been holding in her breath. She had felt compelled to go down and greet the charabancs, forcing herself to smile at the faces she remembered and to be as welcoming as everybody else. Why should she let one bad apple ruin the affection the whole town had for these Americans?

But once inside her office, she wilted, feeling as though she had come a very long way mentally, just by making the effort.

'Well done, girl,' she heard Lionel Potter say as he came heavily down the stairs from his office.

She gave him a watery smile, knowing exactly what he meant.

And then he added gently: 'In words of the vernacular, we can't let the buggers get us down, can we?'

It sounded so incongruous in his impeccably correct accent that it started her laughing at once, even if it was shaky laughter laced with tears.

Chapter 15

Hilly turned up at the guesthouse about an hour before the Boskellys were ready to go to the social evening. Sara turned in relief as her friend knocked on the door of her bedroom where she was getting ready, and then sat down on the bed. Sara had already been all fingers and thumbs deciding how much make-up to wear this evening. Too much would make her look defiant, resembling the proverbial scarlet woman half the town still thought her; too little would be like apologising ... so in the end she had just applied enough to suit herself.

'I thought you could do with some moral support,' Hilly greeted her.

'You're darn right I do, but where's Dave tonight? You haven't ditched him already, have you?' she said with a nervous laugh.

'He's still working on the farm, so he'll be along later. Have you seen you-know-who yet, Sara? Sorry, I mean Chesney.'

'I've seen him all right, and the sooner tonight's over and he goes away with the rest of the group, the better I shall like it.'

Hilly's eyes opened wider. 'Why? What happened?'

Sara told her briefly. Then she told her how Robbie had come here later that same evening, and how awkward it all was. What she didn't tell her was how close she and Robbie had become for those few achingly sweet moments.

'Well, at least it's all out in the open,' Hilly said, ever practical. 'You all know where you stand now, don't you?'

'You could say that.'

Sara stared gloomily at her reflection. She had been tempted to wear black tonight, to show the town that this was a bad night for her, but her parents would never have approved of that! Instead, she had worn a soft green dress that showed off her hair and eyes so dramatically, and would hopefully show these smart American wives that not all Cornish girls looked like hayseeds.

Actually, Hilly looked pretty good too, she noticed for the first time. Hilly didn't care for dresses, and except when they went to the flicks, she slopped about far too much in her farm overalls and wellies, in Sara's opinion. But that was before Dave. Tonight Hilly wore a flowered dress and reasonable sandals, and she wore make-up too. Sara wondered fleetingly what Dave would wear. He wasn't the most elegant of chaps, but she found herself hoping he would make an effort for Hilly's sake.

'You look smashing,' Sara told her. 'I'm glad to see that this Dave is having some influence on you, farm girl!'

Hilly laughed, her face unusually pink. 'I was nagged by my mother into wearing something girly tonight. Dave hasn't seen the new me yet. He might run a mile when he does.'

'Not if he's got any sense,' Sara retorted, thinking that no matter what Hilly said, she was already half smitten with Dave, even if she didn't know it herself. Lucky Hilly, who had never looked at another boy, and might have found the right one straight off. Just like herself and Robbie, she reminded herself painfully, and turned around quickly before the uneasy memories came crowding in again.

'Right. So since we both look the part, let's go down and face my parents and see if we'll do,' she said brightly.

Hilly caught her hand as they reached the door of the bedroom.

'Sara, me and Dave intend to stick close to you tonight, is that all right? We'll feel a bit out of it with all these townies.'

'That's more than all right,' Sara said, knowing full well why she said it and loving her for it.

Her parents thoroughly approved of their appearance, and Frank drove them all down to the church hall where people were already gathering. It was even more reminiscent of the end of the war now, with banners and balloons adorning the inside and outside of the hall, and music already blaring out from the trio of musicians who would be providing the music for the dancing later in the evening. Before that, there would be speeches of welcome, poetry readings, traditional solos by local singers and a church choir to give gravitas to the proceedings. Some of the older local children were putting on a small tableau to explain who Guy Fawkes was to the visitors and why his name was so important in British history on this day.

There was also going to be a short play put on by the smaller Sunday School children called

Hands across the ocean, referring to the successful alliance of Britain and America during the war. No single rendition was going to be too long, as the organisers were keen to make the evening go with a swing, as one ageing bigwig was heard to say in an attempt to sound transatlantic.

Friends and families greeted each other as ecstatically as if they hadn't met for months, many of them introducing the American guests they had brought with them, and many more renewing old acquaintances with screams of delight. Children raced about the hall, paying no heed to their elders, all caught up in the excitement of the event, even if they didn't fully understand the reason for it.

Vicar Roche was in overall charge of the evening, full of importance, and puffed up like a bull frog, Hilly whispered to Sara, making her giggle sufficiently to hide her nervousness at being here at all. He rushed about the room, his face becoming ruddier and ruddier as he tried to do everything himself, to the annoyance of the committee who considered it as much their affair as his.

'Just look at him. He'll blow a fuse soon,' Hilly went on. 'His poor wife won't be much good at calming him down, and Miriam's already being roped in to help, by the looks of it.'

Sara hadn't noticed Miriam or her mother at the other end of the hall, but now she followed Hilly's gaze. Mrs Roche looked as meek as ever, dressed in the habitual beige that drained her of most of the colour in her face, and Miriam was looking decidedly cross at having to be her father's helper. No doubt she'd have much preferred to be swanning about with Robbie, but when Vicar Roche barked, everybody jumped, even his daughter.

Sara constantly looked around for Robbie, but she couldn't see him anywhere. She was sure he wouldn't have backed down from coming tonight, but perhaps, like the unsophisticated Dave, he intended to slip in later. Sara caught sight of Miriam glaring at her in between staring around the hall, also presumably looking for Robbie. There was no sign of Chesney yet either, she thought thankfully.

In any case people were taking their seats and shortly afterwards there was a drum roll of sorts from the musicians and Vicar Roche took the stand. He had a droning, onerous voice, and no matter what he said, it always sounded like a heavy sermon. He could even make the welcome to the visitors seem like a chore, and it was hard to miss the occasional giggle from the high-spirited children and the shushings from their elders. But at last the speeches were over, one of the committee members announced the order of the evening's programme, and it got under way with no more fuss.

Once the more formal events were over, the chairs were pushed back to the sides of the room ready for dancing, and light refreshments were served as there was no licence for alcohol. The trio of musicians then took over for the final part of the evening, and that was when Sara finally caught sight of Chesney across the far side of the room. Her heart jolted. Like most of the Americans, he wore his uniform for tonight's occasion, and she would have been blind not to remember that this was the way he had looked when she first saw him. Dashing and handsome, with that easy way of talking and paying compliments, so different from anyone else she knew.

'Keep cool, Sara,' she heard Hilly whisper, accompanied by Dave now, who was looking fairly dapper and well-scrubbed for such a large chap.

They seemed to close in around her, protecting her, shielding her, and it was sweet and generous of them, but she didn't need it. She had known it the moment she saw Chesney smiling and chatting and putting on the sweet-talk to several local girls who had caught his eye, and even from a distance she could see the way they responded to him. He had instant charm, and she knew that, but it was completely shallow.

'Don't worry. I was over him a long time ago,' she told Hilly. 'If you and Dave want to dance, don't let me stop you.'

Hilly laughed. 'Dave doesn't dance, and I'm not prepared to go clod-hopping around with his big feet trampling all over me!'

The remark could have been hurtful, but from the way Dave laughed, and the shine in Hilly's eyes whenever she looked at him, it was obvious that they knew one another too well for him to take offence. Lucky Hilly, Sara thought again. She felt her friend nudge her as the trio began playing a waltz and people began dancing.

'What's Miriam up to, do you think? She seems to be more agitated than usual.'

'She's waiting for Robbie, of course. What else?' Sara muttered.

'Yes, but don't you think she's behaving oddly? What with her mother apparently nagging her and pulling at her skirt, and her father looking as if he's past his best now, she looks as if she'd rather be anywhere but here.'

'That makes two of us then.'

Although, she admitted that so far it hadn't been so bad. The first part of the evening had been surprisingly entertaining, and the Americans had certainly seemed to enjoy it without finding it all too quaint and rustic... It was now that the dancing had started that she felt uncomfortable, echoing as it did, those other nights when the Yanks had been here during the war and she had fallen under the spell of Chesney Willand.

'Robbie's here,' Dave said, and this time he was the one who got a dig in the ribs from Hilly.

Sara felt as if she was watching from the sidelines now, waiting for Miriam to leave her parents' sides and go marching over to Robbie and claim him as if he was the pot of gold at the end of the rainbow. He had seen her, and it was obvious that she had seen him, but then, to Sara's complete disbelief, she saw Miriam walk across to Chesney and stand straight in front of him.

The next moment he had given her an exaggerated little bow and was leading her on to the dance floor.

'Well! What do you make of that?' Hilly hissed to Sara. 'What's she trying to do, for goodness' sake? It's not a Ladies' Excuse-Me, is it?'

'It doesn't seem to make any difference whether it is or not,' Sara said, bemused. 'She's not the only girl to ask one of the Yanks to dance, and nobody seems to mind.'

She couldn't think what Miriam was trying to do, either. If it was to make Robbie jealous, the stupid girl couldn't have done anything worse. She could have danced with anybody else in the hall, but not him. Not the arrogant Yank who had already taken one girl away from Robbie. She was unbelievably thick-skinned if she thought this was a clever thing to do.

As if her feet had a will of their own, she found herself leaving Hilly and Dave, and weaving her way through the crowded hall to where Robbie was standing with his back to the wall, his face dark with an emotion she couldn't judge. She stood as close to him as she dared, and spoke so that nobody else could hear. It was doubtful that they could, with the noise of the music and excited chatter going on all around them.

'Will you dance with me, Robbie? Please.'

She thought he was going to refuse. He didn't care to dance, but this was a gentle waltz, and Sara was looking up at him with a mixture of love and pleading in her eyes, and her hand was on his arm now, almost burning into his skin.

'Why not?' he said roughly.

She drew in her breath. It was so much more than she had hoped for, but it was happening, and if it was Miriam's stupidity in dancing with Chesney that had made Robbie agree, then she didn't care. It was enough to be in his arms. There was too much of a crush on the floor to dance properly, and it was little more than a slow shuffle for most people, but this was what she wanted, what she desired so much, just be embraced like this, and to breathe him close to her.

She was vaguely aware of the astonished glances of people around them: her parents; Hilly and Dave; certain gossips in the town who would be chewing it all over tomorrow. She was also aware of Miriam's furious glares as she realised what was happening. She didn't care. She felt exhilarated and alive again, knowing this was truly where she belonged. She knew Miriam was unlikely to make a scene here, with her father still blustering and bragging over the success of the evening, as if it had been his personal idea to bring the Americans here, when they themselves had made the first move. Miriam would have to hold her fury in check for now, but whatever happened as the result of this waltz, whose melody would stay in her mind for ever now, thought Sara, it was worth it.

The music came to an end, and they stood perfectly still for a moment, as if loath to leave one another's arms. Then, as if to add to the unreality of this evening, Robbie bent his head and brushed her cheek with his lips.

'Thank you,' he said simply.

Seconds later he was gone from her side, and as the crowd seemed to swallow him up, she didn't see him again. Dave thought he had left the hall, and Hilly said she'd done a great thing in showing up that bitch Miriam, and Sara knew she had to get out of the over-heated hall and find him.

He was exactly where she thought he would be, leaning over some railings and gazing down towards the harbour where a great bonfire was waiting to be lit at the end of the evening, accompanied by the organised firework display. She hesitated, then moved towards him and slid her arm through his, hugging him to her.

'We can't ignore our feelings, Robbie,' she said quietly.

He didn't speak for a few moments and then his voice was steady. 'I think we do, at least for the time being. Until the time is right.'

Sara took her arm away. 'Right for what? For telling Miriam you don't love her and it's me you want to be with? When is the time ever going to be right for that?'

'When I feel it will hurt her least.'

'And what about me? Do I have to stand by until you've made up your mind when to break it off with that little madam?'

'You don't have any choice, do you?' Robbie was cool now. 'If it wasn't for you, none of us would be in this position, and I won't be so cruel as to rub Miriam's nose in it now.'

'So you didn't mind her dancing with Chesney out of spite? You didn't see history repeating itself?'

'Hardly. Could you see Miriam leaving her parents and behaving like a camp follower to go three thousand miles across the Atlantic Ocean?'

Sara gasped. It was like a vicious blow to her stomach to hear him say the words in that clipped tone.

'Is that what you really thought of me, Robbie?' she said passionately.

'That was the way it looked, sweetheart,' he said.

He used the endearment but there was no affection in it. It was like the Americans' easy 'honey' or 'babe'. It meant nothing. She turned away from him, her eyes brimming. There was movement on the beach below now and the bonfire was lit, indicating that the social was over, and soon people would come spilling out of the church hall to watch the last of the entertainment. Once the bonfire threw its orange flames high into the night sky the whole place would be alive with shrieks of pleasure and excitement. And suddenly Sara couldn't bear to be sharing it all with Robbie, who didn't really want her any more, despite everything he had said and done to the contrary. In any case, as soon as Miriam came out of the hall to find him, Sara knew she would be redundant.

She moved away from him and ran down the hill towards the beach, knowing he wouldn't follow. He would be looking for Miriam. People were already appearing from the hall to find a good position on the beach and around the harbour, and pretty soon they would both be swallowed up in the crowds. Sara felt a sob in her throat, but if he didn't want her any more, then she wouldn't want him. And that was about as stupid and childish a statement as saying the sun wouldn't rise every morning.

'We wondered where you'd got to,' Hilly said, when she eventually caught up with Sara, leaving Dave gassing with some of his mates.

By now the bonfire was fully alight, the flames lighting the sky and illuminating the excited faces of everyone around it. The organisers were in their allotted places to light the fireworks, ensuring that the onlookers were kept at a safe distance, and within minutes of the crowds appearing, it seemed as if the sky was ablaze with the spectacular effects. It was accompanied by much applause and excitement, and many people reflected on how different it was from a few years ago, when nothing of the sort could take place. In those days, blackout curtains in every building stopped any chink of light being shown to alert enemy aircraft that here was a target to bomb. A bonfire and fireworks would have spelled certain disaster and were strictly banned. But happily, no such restrictions applied now.

'I'd had enough of being social, and I needed some fresh air,' Sara told her friend when she could make herself heard.

'I saw what happened,' Hilly whispered in her ear, 'and so did Miriam. It was worth it to see her face when you and Robbie were dancing.'

Sara shrugged her shoulders. It all seemed like such a hollow victory now Miriam had clearly been trying to point out that she too could attract a dashing chap like Chesney Willand, if only for a dance, and she never would have expected Sara to ask Robbie to dance – or for him to accept. But what did any of it matter, Sara thought wearily, if nothing was changed? She was still the bad girl of the town, and Miriam was still Robbie's girl.

'It doesn't make any difference,' she said listlessly.

'You know what I think?' Hilly persisted. 'Robbie's a prize drip if he can't ditch her. Anybody can see you two are meant to be together, the way you always were.'

'He's not a drip. He's a decent and honourable chap and after what I did, you can't really expect him to just drop Miriam, can you? She doesn't deserve that.'

'Oh God, I give up!' Hilly said. 'The two of you are being so bloody noble it makes me want to throw up sometimes, Sara.'

She marched off to catch up with Dave, and Sara gave a wry smile. Hilly was so defensive on her behalf, but no matter how she hated the thought, the more she had to agree that if Robbie was truly waiting for the right time to tell Miriam they were finished, then they should try to ignore their feelings, and stay as far apart as possible. She had to trust him on that.

The next minute she felt her arm being tugged, and manicured fingers were digging deep into her arm so hard that she gave a yell of pain.

'What the hell did you think you were doing?' Miriam hissed.

Sara pushed her away, knowing there were going to be vicious red marks on her arm by tomorrow.

'What did you think you were doing, you cow? If you thought it was going to make Robbie jealous, it didn't work.'

'What about you? Did it make you jealous?' Miriam said triumphantly.

Sara stared at her. She wasn't as pasty as she had once been, but right then, with all the spite showing on her face, she looked like a wizened witch. What the hell did Robbie ever see in her?

'You're mad. Chesney means nothing to me any more and you didn't see me falling over myself to dance with him, did you?'

Miriam ignored that. 'Well, just keep away from Robbie in future. He doesn't want you any more, and who could blame him?'

Before Sara could think of an apt response, Miriam's mother was calling plaintively to her, and with a sigh of annoyance, Miriam flounced off to see what she wanted. The three members of the Roche family were suddenly clustered together, and then they seemed to move as one unit away from the bonfire and the fireworks. Vicar Roche had clearly had enough for one day, Sara thought grimly, but she had to admit they were a formidable group, even with the ineffectual mother. Miriam had got her claws dug very firmly into Robbie; her father would be glad to get a troublesome daughter off his hands; while Mrs Roche would probably just be thankful that her plain and irritating daughter had found a young man at all.

But she couldn't waste her energy on any of them any more. Robbie seemed to have disappeared, and Hilly obviously couldn't be bothered to talk to her now that she had Dave. She looked around for her parents, and finally found them, chatting to the American couple she had spoken to earlier, Kyle and Gloria, and their daughter.

'This little town has put on a great show for us, honey, and we won't forget it,' Kyle greeted her.

'Well, you put on a pretty good show for us during the war, so we were happy to do it,' she said as lightly as she could.

'I wish we could stay longer, but we have a tight schedule to keep up, and some of the guys are keen to see as much of England as we can before we go home.'

'We understand that,' Sara said.

Ellen was perceptive of her daughter's feelings. 'I think we're all feeling exhausted by now, so whenever you want to go, Sara, just say the word.'

Gloria spoke quickly. 'We're exhausted too, and I think we should get this little lady off to bed. We've got a long journey tomorrow, and we're going to visit Stonehenge and then Stratford-upon-Avon next. We don't have anything like that in America.'

The child protested about going to bed, but the mother was adamant. Thank God for mothers, Sara thought. She liked this little family, but just hearing the mixture of different American accents all evening was taking its toll on her nerves. She still kept expecting Chesney to turn up alongside her, and the sooner she got away from the proceedings now, the better she would like it. Even so, it seemed to take ages before they could wend their way through the crowds, stopping to say goodbye to so many people on the way back to their car, friends and visitors alike. But at last it was over, and everything could go back to the way it was before...

Until she was inside the car and on the way back to the guesthouse, with the glow of the bonfire behind them, and the last of the fireworks still shooting their amazing patterns high into the sky to shouts of delight, Sara hadn't realised what an ordeal this had all been for her. The effort to keep smiling and put on a welcoming face had taken more out of her than she had expected, but she was sure, now, that she had said goodbye to Chesney for good.

When she got home from work the next afternoon, she found a card and a small bouquet of flowers waiting for her. Her face flamed as she read the words he had written on the card.

'For old times' sake, and no regrets, honey. Chesney.'

She flung the flowers into the wastepaper bin and tore the card into shreds.

'That seems like a waste of a good bunch of flowers,' her mother said mildly. 'Why don't you take them to the churchyard and put them on Leah's grave? She'd have chuckled to think Chesney was wasting money on her. She was always grumbling that the GIs had money to burn so I'm sure it would tickle her.'

'She won't know,' Sara said sullenly.

'Oh, she'll know,' Ellen said, exactly as Leah herself might have said it.

Sara knew she would get no peace unless she did as her mother suggested, so she cycled down to the churchyard with the flowers in her bicycle basket. She didn't care for churchyards, especially when it was getting dark. It was odd, but the older people got, the less fear they seemed to have of them, even though, logically, they would be ending up there the soonest. Although, during the last few years, there had been many young men – and women – even younger than herself, who had ended their days prematurely in places like this. Some hadn't even had the dignity of being buried by their loved ones. Sara shivered, trying not to linger on the far too graphic thought.

Among the headstones of the once-wealthier occupants of the churchyard, Leah's modest grave was no more than a mound of earth with a single vase that Ellen had placed on it. Sara fetched some water from the tap at the corner of the churchyard and arranged the flowers in the vase. It seemed churlish to simply turn and leave, and she stood by the graveside for a few minutes, remembering Leah's funny and mysterious little ways, and wishing with all her heart that she was still here. Almost against her will, she found herself muttering.

'Chesney bought these flowers, so you'll like the irony of this, Leah. I know you never cared for him and you were right all along. You thought all the Yanks were rowdy and flashed their money about, but we owed them a lot, and the town did them all proud last night. I wish you could have seen it.'

She felt a sudden lump in her throat. If what her mother implied was true, and if what Leah herself always vowed was the case, then she probably had been there to see it. It was a lovely sentiment to think that those who were loved never really died – but anybody with any sense knew that of course they did. Yet somehow, in this quiet place, with the dusk folding all around her now, birds gone to roost and stars appearing in the sky, it was too easy to start to imagine things, and it was all getting too creepy for comfort. Gravestones seemed to loom up like crouching monsters; trees and shrubs rustled in the sea breeze, and once the imagination took hold, you could imagine there were shadows and movements everywhere. Sara turned and walked swiftly back to where she had left her bike, and cycled home as fast as she could with her head down and her heart thumping, preferring not to know whether angels or demons were following her.

Chapter 16

After the hectic few days when the Americans were there, life in St Ives quickly settled back to normal. At the weekend, there was an enthusiastic piece in the local newspaper about the social event, together with a letter of thanks to all concerned from the leader of the group, and that would seem to be that.

'Did he contact you again?' Hilly asked Sara a week later.

Sara was tempted to be difficult and ask who she meant, and she was also tempted to say no, but what was the point? Hilly had a knack of ferreting out the things she wanted to know.

'He sent me a card and some flowers. I tore up the card and put the flowers on Leah's grave, and that's all I'm going to say about it,' she said flatly.

'I suppose he was trying to make amends in his own peculiar way. I wonder if he'll send you a card on your birthday.'

Sara shrugged. 'If he does I won't open it.'

There was only one card she was hoping against hope to receive, and that was from Robbie. She hadn't seen him since the night at the social when she had asked him to dance, but she couldn't forget how sweet it had been, nor how furious Miriam Roche had looked. Not that she had anything to talk about, being whisked around the dance floor by Chesney Willand. Sara still couldn't imagine why she had done it. If she'd hoped to make Sara jealous, she had certainly failed, and if it was all in aid of trying to make Robbie jealous ... well, she didn't think that had had the desired effect either. He might have been angry and outraged at her tactlessness, but he wasn't jealous. She could almost feel sorry for Miriam's efforts. Almost.

'Have you heard about Vicar Roche?' Hilly said next.

'What about him?'

For somebody who lived on a farm so far out of town, Hilly had an uncanny nose for news.

'He's been ill ever since the social. My mum says he brought it on himself, trying to organise everything and being the big I-Am as usual.'

'What's wrong with him?' Not that Sara was in the least interested in Vicar Roche's health, for he had never been particularly charitable towards her.

'I don't know any details, but Dave heard that it's something to do with his heart. My mum didn't like his colour the last time she saw him, and that was quite a while ago. I thought he'd been born that beetroot shade, didn't you?'

'He's never been any different as far as I know,' Sara agreed.

She didn't think any more about Vicar Roche's health until her mother came back from the market the following Saturday with the news that there had apparently been an ambulance outside the vicar's house at two o'clock in the morning and that the lights had been on in the house all night.

'Something's up, that's for sure,' Ellen said. 'Leah always used to say it was anybody's guess whether he'd be the one to go first what with his temper and all, or whether he'd drive his wife to death by boredom.'

'Mum, that's awful!' Sara said, laughing. 'Did Leah really say that?'

'She did. Now, help me unload these groceries, my dear. We've got these late holiday-makers coming in this evening, and Doris will be here this afternoon and all next week, to help with the rooms.'

There were always last-minute stragglers coming to Cornwall to take advantage of the far south-west's milder weather. Ellen was always pleased when they were folk who had been there before who appreciated the relaxed atmosphere the Boskelly guesthouse provided. They could be assured of comfortable accommodation, good nourishing food and beautiful scenery. Why anybody would want to go abroad, Ellen was often heard to say, she simply couldn't imagine, when Cornwall had everything anybody could ever want.

Doris toiled up the hill to the guesthouse early that afternoon, puffed up with exertion as well as excitement and importance. It couldn't be because of the chance to do an extra week's work here, Sara thought, so it must be something else. She slipped out to the conservatory to rearrange the chairs and put small vases of autumn flowers on the little tables, knowing she would hear all the gossip later. But Doris's voice carried.

'He's dead,' she announced as soon as she

could get her breath back.

'Who's dead?' Ellen asked, knowing how melodramatic Doris could be, and deciding not to be too concerned until she knew who the girl was talking about.

'Vicar Roche, of course!' Doris almost squealed. 'Dead as a dodo and twice as ugly, I daresay, since he had a blooming good start on that! It was a massive stroke, and he never recovered once they got him to hospital, so the good Lord didn't look after him too well for all his preaching, did he?'

Sara hardly heard her mother chiding Doris for being so blasphemous, because Doris's words were drumming into her head. Her fingers seemed to lose control and the glass vase she was holding slid out of her fingers. It crashed to the floor, breaking into smithereens. Ellen came through to the conservatory at once.

'What's happened in here? I thought you'd smashed a window pane or something!'

'Sorry, it was only a vase,' Sara gasped jerkily. 'Leave it to me, Mum. I'll get a dustpan and brush and sweep it up.'

Her mother tut-tutted at her carelessness and went back to explaining to Doris which rooms needed preparing as they went upstairs together.

Sara's hands were shaking as she rushed to the cupboard in the kitchen to fetch the dustpan and brush. She knelt down to her task in the conservatory, gingerly avoiding any splinters of glass. It was crazy to think that what Doris said would have any effect on her life. Hadn't Leah said for ages that that old buffoon Roche would kill himself in the end with all his ranting and bullying? And hadn't the self-important way he'd gone about organising everybody at the social event proved her right?

But that household had already been in deep mourning over the son who had been killed during the war. Rumours had gone around the town that Mrs Roche had almost gone into a decline, and her husband and daughter had had to watch her very carefully, for fear she would do some harm to herself in her grief. How much of that was true, Sara didn't know, but how would the two women be now, without that rock of a husband at their sides? And how much more limpet-like would Miriam cling on to Robbie, expecting him to help, to be their strength? She would never let him go now, and he would never be so heartless as to desert her.

'Haven't you finished yet, Sara?' she heard her mother's voice say from the kitchen. 'For heaven's sake, girl, there's work to be done.'

Sara moved at once, not wanting her mother to see just how affected she had been by the news of Vicar Roche's death. Perhaps she was making mountains out of molehills, she thought desperately, while knowing in her heart that she was not. She might not have old Leah's uncanny way of 'knowing' things before they happened, but she had a horribly strong intuition over this.

The news spread quickly through the town, and there was plenty of speculation over how the poor widow would cope. She had always been overshadowed by her husband, often bullied, some said, but there were women who didn't object to such a situation and meekly accepted it, and Mrs

Roche had always seemed to be one of them.

As Sara took the solicitors' business letters to the post box a few days later she came face to face with Miriam in the street. The girl looked less pasty than usual. Her face was puffy and her eyes were red-rimmed. Sara couldn't help pitying her at that moment. She had never lost a parent herself, and Miriam had now lost her brother and her father. There was a brief, awkward silence between them as if neither knew what to say, and then Sara put her hand on the other girl's arm.

'I'm sorry to hear about your father. It was an awful thing to happen, and please tell your mother my family are thinking of you.'

Miriam shook off Sara's hand. 'We don't want your sympathy. Me and Mum are all right, and we've got Robbie to look after us now.'

Even now, thought Sara, she couldn't resist that little sly dig. But she couldn't blame her. Despite the brittle voice, there was stark misery in Miriam's eyes, and Sara knew it must be a terrible time for her and her mother. She gave a small nod and stood aside to let Miriam pass.

'What did you expect, my dear?' Lionel Potter asked her, when she returned to the office. 'It's common knowledge that you and she aren't the best of friends, and the reason why, and I'm sure she sees you as a threat to her happiness every time she sees you.'

It was no wonder he was so good with his clients. He could pin-point exactly what their problems were, but she didn't want him pin-pointing hers quite so clearly.

'I can't do anything about that, can I? Besides, from what she said, maybe I won't be such a threat from now on, and I don't want to talk about it any more if you don't mind.'

'Well, any time you do, Sara, you only have to ask.'

She knew he was a kind and tactful boss, and she was lucky to have him. But she couldn't bear to pour out all her feelings and frustrations, because if she did, it would all come out. And no matter what tales he heard from his clients, he wasn't involved personally with them.

She hoped she would hear something from Robbie, one way or another. It was inconceivable that he wouldn't get in touch with her after what had happened. She couldn't go down to his shop or studio though. In the circumstances it would be awful to find Miriam there. The last time she had seen Robbie, on the night of the social, he had assured her that they only had to wait long enough for him to find the right moment to tell Miriam, and then the way would be clear for them.

Even before Vicar Roche's death, Sara had been having misgivings about how it was going to happen. She knew Robbie loved her, and she trusted him, but she also knew him well enough to know he wouldn't let Miriam down cruelly. And if and when he did so, could they really pick up where they had left off, brazenly courting in the town where Miriam would still be bruised and bitter? It would be an impossible situation for them all.

But now this had happened, and Sara knew

that everything had changed. It was as though Vicar Roche himself had set the seal on the future of three people by his sudden death. Was it wicked to think so? Was it blasphemy? Sara didn't know and she didn't care. The Roche women were mourning their loss now, and she mourned hers just as keenly. And that was probably blasphemous too.

There was little time to ponder on such things after Doris sprained her wrist and was only of minimal help to Ellen during the following week when the Boskellys had their late visitors. To their surprise they had an even later booking for the next week too, and Sara was more than willing to do her share of the chores before and after work, since keeping busy was always the best way to ward off anxieties. The day the first family left on the following Saturday, it would be Vicar Roche's funeral, and according to Doris, it was to be a big affair as befitted his status in the town.

'Me and my gran are going to see him off,' she announced excitedly. 'I like a funeral, and it'll be interesting to see who turns out for the old blighter, begging his celestial pardon,' she finished with a giggle.

'How can you like a funeral?' Sara asked her with a shudder. 'They're always sad and miserable with everybody crying.'

Doris shrugged. 'I used to do a bit of cleaning for Mrs Roche, though I was always glad when he wasn't there, and I expect she'll be glad to see me. I daresay they'll have quite a bunfight at the house afterwards as well.'

She eyed Sara thoughtfully. 'You won't be going then?'

'No,' Sara said shortly.

Why would she? Miriam wouldn't want her there, and she couldn't bear to see Robbie in attendance, comforting Miriam and her mother as he surely would be. She blessed the latest booking, which meant that there would be plenty of work to do at the guesthouse all day, changing bedding and cleaning the rooms and helping her mother prepare the menus.

She still hadn't seen Robbie, and she wondered if he was avoiding having anything to do with her until after the funeral. Though quite what difference that would make, Sara couldn't think. It wouldn't have hurt him to send her a brief message of some sort. There was a telephone at the guesthouse, or he could have sent her a note, if he didn't think it wise to come calling on her. But there was nothing, and as the days went on, Sara began to feel a gnawing hollow where her stomach used to be.

It would soon be her birthday, and she wondered if he would even remember it, or if he was so concerned with the Roche family now that it would go unheeded. The thought depressed her even more, seeing it as a dire omen that if the day came and went with no word, she may as well give up hope that anything was going to change.

'I wish you'd perk up a little, Sara,' her mother told her sharply when she was listlessly setting the tables for the next morning's breakfast. 'The guests will start wondering what's wrong with you.'

'I'm sorry, Mum,' she said with a sigh. 'Everything seems a bit of an effort right now.'

'Then perhaps you should see Dr Melrose. You've been through a lot these past months, and long before that too, so perhaps you need a tonic. You know what Leah would say, don't you?' she said, trying to jolly her daughter.

'Oh, I know! She'd say a good dose of castor oil would see me right. But I don't think so, thank you all the same!'

Ellen put her arm around her daughter. 'Why don't you see him anyway, darling? Your father and I have become quite concerned about you lately. It will make us feel easier once we know there's nothing wrong.'

What would her respected mother have thought, Sara wondered suddenly, if the worst had happened after that night when she and Robbie had made glorious love in his studio? But the worst for whom? For the town, of course. For the scandal it would have provoked, labelling her forever as the scarlet woman they had all suspected her of being.

But not for her, nor for Robbie, if what had begun as an act of pure love and need, had resulted in a child of their own. It would have been proof for ever that theirs was a love that could stand any test. Although, even now, she couldn't be so sure what his reaction would have been.

'Sara?' she heard her mother say anxiously, and she blinked the thoughts away, knowing that if it had happened, she could never have stayed here where she belonged, because what should have been a joyous event between two married people, would, under the circumstances, only have brought more shame to her family. The prodigal daughter would have been an outcast once more.

'I may go and see the doctor if it will put your mind at rest,' she promised her mother. 'Perhaps I do need a tonic.'

'Good. And I'm making a high tea for your birthday, so you'd better feel well enough not to pick at it, or I'll want to know the reason why.'

Ellen didn't say as much, but she already knew the reason for Sara's low spirits – or had made a shrewd enough guess. Sara had overheard her parents talking quietly on the evening that Vicar Roche died.

'You know what's wrong with Sara, don't you, Frank? It's all this business with Robbie. You could see by the way they were dancing at the social that there's still something between them, and the Roche girl saw it too.'

'Maybe so, but it's not something that we can have a hand in, Ellen,' her husband said sharply. 'This is one time when they have to sort out their problems by themselves.'

'But you were aware of it too, weren't you?' Ellen persisted. 'Would you have Sara being unhappy for the rest of her life because of what might have been?'

'I think she started that particular ball rolling when she went chasing after the American, and I also think there's nothing we can do about it now.'

'But what if Vicar Roche's death will make Robbie do the decent thing by Miriam and stand by her – even if he still loves somebody else? What kind of a marriage would that be?'

Ellen had shivered, secure in her own long-lasting marriage, and not wanting to imagine a loveless one. She felt Frank's arms go around her for a moment.

'It's no good us speculating on that, my love. Only time will tell what will come of it all.'

Sara had crept into her own bedroom after hearing that little conversation, chilled at her mother's comment about what kind of marriage a loveless one would be. Until that moment, she hadn't really connected the word marriage with Robbie and Miriam. She had still been living in dreams, but her mother had unwittingly put the thought into her head, and now she couldn't get it out.

Sara wasn't the only one who was finding the whole situation less than easy to deal with. Robbie faced up to the fact that the Roche women had none too subtly shifted the weight of being the man of the house on to his shoulders. He was as sorry for them as anyone would be in their circumstances, but he didn't want to wear a dead man's mantle. He didn't want to do the errands they asked him to, helping to sort out the mechanics of death, while faced with Mrs Roche's blotchy, tear-stained face, and Miriam's doe-like, appealing eyes.

In fact, he didn't want to be here at all in this house of gloom and misery. And he certainly wasn't looking forward to the funeral, when he would be expected to hold up the two weeping women, since it would seem to set the seal on his future role in the family. He could only hope that the Roche relatives from Dorset who were supposed to come and stay for a week or two would turn up as promised this evening, the night before the funeral. He had never met them, but if they were anything like the rest of the bunch, he wondered how he was ever going to get through the evening, let alone tomorrow.

It didn't help to know that he had brought all this on himself by getting involved with Miriam in the first place ... which he would never have done if Sara hadn't gone away ... but it would be madness to let his thoughts go there for more than a moment.

He arrived at the Roche house that evening to find several cars outside. The relatives were far from penniless. There were Mrs Roche's two sisters and their large, brawny husbands who Miriam had told him were builders. There was also a ruddy-faced young man who was introduced as Miriam's cousin Zach. He wasn't a blood relation for he had been adopted at birth by one of the couples, who couldn't have children of their own. Although Mrs Roche had always kept in touch with her sisters, none of them had turned up after Brian's death, and Robbie had learned that it was because both the outspoken builders had had a blistering row with Vicar Roche, a situation that Robbie could well understand.

The whole town knew it had never taken much to ruffle those particular feathers, and Miriam had told him that Vicar Roche had informed his brothers-in-law they would never be welcome in his house again while he was alive, and the families had taken him at his word. But now everything had changed, and despite the circumstances, it was clear that Mrs Roche was overjoyed to see her family again.

'Our Miriam tells me you're an artist,' Zach said to Robbie a while later, when the older members were deep in conversation and reminiscences.

The young man looked Robbie up and down in a way that couldn't be construed as anything less than insulting, and spoke again before Robbie could answer. 'Bit of a poncey job for a chap, isn't it?'

'I don't suppose Michelangelo thought so, if the name means anything to you,' Robbie said, unable to resist the barb.

'Don't know and don't care,' Zach said casually. 'I'm in the building trade like my old man and my uncle, and if this Michael chap's got nothing to do with sand and cement, I'm not interested. I must say our Miriam's turned out a fine-looking girl. It's a few years since I saw her, but I took quite a shine to her even before she filled out in all the right places, if you know what I mean.'

'Did you now? Maybe I've got a rival then,' Robbie said, ignoring the coarse remark. He wasn't sure where this conversation was leading, but couldn't let it go.

Zach laughed. 'I doubt that you'd be any rival to me, mate. Got a bad leg that kept you out of the war, haven't you? A lot of chaps had fancy excuses that kept them from fighting for king and country, and I daresay some of them were genuine. I was in the infantry myself.'

Miriam sidled over to them just as Robbie was

about to explode with anger at the young man's snide remarks. He was surprised by the unexpected sparkle in her eyes after the previous dark days, and she didn't seem averse to the outspoken kind of talk that was echoed by all three men, and which was certainly jollying her mother along.

In fact, Mrs Roche was more animated than Robbie had seen her in ages, and nothing like the downtrodden wife she usually appeared as she scuttled about the town. They were all in a cheerful and robust mood, and although it seemed strange to Robbie to behave that way on the eve of a funeral, it was fairly obvious that there had been no love lost between the rest of the family and Vicar Roche.

'Now then, what are you two boys talking about?' Miriam said archly, linking her arms through both of theirs.

'Nothing much, kid. I was just telling Robbie here that you're a sight for sore eyes now,' Zach said. 'So what time are we planting the old boy tomorrow?'

He was unbelievable, but so was Miriam's reaction. Instead of going red-faced and horrified as anybody with any sense of decency might have expected, she burst out laughing and hugged Zach's arm even tighter.

'You'd better not let my mum hear you say such things, although she might well have a bit of a chuckle too,' she giggled. 'We've got to be dignified tomorrow, Zach, and don't you forget it. I'm really, really glad you're here. You could always make me laugh, and there hasn't been much laughter around here lately.'

If that was a dig at Robbie, as well as the initial gloom following her father's death, he didn't heed it. He was far more interested in the way Miriam had become more animated since Zach's arrival, and the unexpected fact that he had once taken a shine to her.

'How long are you planning on staying in St Ives?' he said casually.

'You could have been nicer to Zach, Robbie,' Miriam complained, when she saw him out of the house that evening. 'You seemed to be looking down on him all evening, just because he's got rough hands from the building work and doesn't know the things you know.'

'I didn't know that being nice to him was part of my role, but he could certainly put a smile on your face.'

She beamed. 'Were you jealous?'

'I was just glad to see you looking a bit more cheerful,' he hedged.

God knew he hadn't been jealous. Relieved, glad, hopeful, exhilarated ... any of those adjectives would have described his feelings far better.

'If he has the means to make you smile, that's got to be a good thing,' he added when she frowned.

'I'd forgotten how he could always make me smile. Mum was always fond of him too, so I hope he and Auntie Gert will stay for a while even if the others have to go back.'

'Doesn't he have a job to go to?'

'He works with my uncles and Mum says they've always been indulgent towards him. There's been plenty of rebuilding work for them after the war, but they've always treated Zach as a bit of a pet, since he's the only kid they've got between them. Zach always said saucily we were never much of a family for breeding,' she said with a giggle.

Robbie smiled back. She surprised him with everything she said. Even if she hadn't seen Zach for some time, he seemed to have quite an influence on her thinking, and that suited Robbie very well. It was obvious that the cousins enjoyed one another's company, and it would be an odd quirk of fate if Vicar Roche's death turned out to be a mixed blessing as far as Robbie was concerned – and after the ups and downs in his life recently, he wasn't apologising to the Almighty or anybody else for thinking that way.

'I'll be at the funeral tomorrow, of course,' he told Miriam as they said goodnight. 'But after that I think I should stay discreetly in the background while your family's here. You'll all have plenty to talk about and I'll just be in the way. So of course I shall quite understand if I don't see you in the evenings for a while.'

'Well, if you think that's best,' Miriam said vaguely. 'I'll have to go back to work soon, I suppose, but I shall try to wangle a bit more time off while Zach's here. We're not so busy at this time of the year. Maybe I can say Mum's poorly. They're used to hearing that!'

'Good idea,' Robbie said, not missing the fact that she wanted to see more of Zach than the aunts and uncles.

He almost started whistling as he went home, but considering he'd just come from a house in mourning, however bizarre their type of mourning seemed to him, it would hardly have been respectful to do so.

Chapter 17

Sara was thankful that the Saturday of Vicar Roche's funeral was a busy one at the guest-house. She didn't want to think about it at all, remembering the trauma of Leah's funeral for those who loved her and knew her best. It would be the same for Miriam and her mother, however hateful the man had sometimes been in life. He was still a father and husband, and they would be full of grief and remorse on this day. And Robbie would be there to help them get through it. No, she didn't want to think about it for one second, thank you very much.

Unfortunately, when Doris came toiling back up the hill late that afternoon, she was bursting with importance and information about how it had all gone.

'It was a real scream,' she said excitedly. 'You know how heavy the old blighter had got, and Mrs Roche's brothers-in-law were two of the coffin bearers. Well, either they didn't have hold of it properly, or they didn't want to be doing the job at all. Everybody knows they didn't get on, and just as they got the coffin to the graveside it seemed to slip sideways and wobble for a minute, and they couldn't hold it. After a minute when everybody was holding their breath, it toppled over and went straight down into the open grave. It was a wonder the old boy didn't end up being buried head first, and there was such an uproar as people crowded around to see if it had burst open. That cousin of Miriam's couldn't stop laughing, which was terrible, really, except that young Miriam was laughing as well, and everybody could see the two of them, clinging on to one another and scandalising the rest of us. Robbie Killaine wouldn't even look at them. He just stood behind Mrs Roche and her sisters, looking like thunder, but I swear that even Mrs Roche was finding it hard to keep a straight face while the new young vicar tried to keep the whole thing as dignified as possible while he did the ashes to ashes thing. Which was pretty difficult when Vicar Roche's coffin was stuck where it had fallen, sort of tilted on its side six feet below!'

Never having had much respect for vicars in general, by now Doris was chortling with the memory and gasping for breath when she finally finished the tale, and Sara and her mother were open-mouthed. Ellen spoke first, clearly horrified at the picture Doris was painting.

'Good heavens, Doris, it was a terrible thing to happen, and poor Mrs Roche must have been beside herself. We all know the man wasn't a kindly soul, but nobody deserves such a farcical happening at their funeral.'

Doris snorted, wiping her eyes now. 'I think Mrs Roche might secretly be thinking it served him right for the way he treated her. Don't go wasting your pity on neither of them, Mrs Boskelly, and as for that young Miriam, well, she and that cousin of hers probably only did what everybody else didn't have the nerve to do.'

'What happened afterwards?' Sara said in a strangled voice, unable to get the image of Vicar Roche's coffin toppling sideways into the open grave and being stuck there out of her head. Supposing the coffin lid really had come off, leaving them all looking down at his dead white face glaring up at them all...? Would his expression have been outraged at landing sideways, six feet below...? The urge to giggle almost overwhelmed her at that moment, but she stifled it immediately, seeing how genuinely affected her mother was at the picture of it all.

Doris was only slightly more sober. 'Some of us went back to the house for the bunfight. By then, everybody was in quite a jolly mood and it ended up as more of an afternoon tea party than anything else. Those who were still offended by it stayed away.'

What about Robbie? Did he stay away?

Sara dearly wanted to ask the question, but she didn't dare. In any case, Doris answered it for her.

'I don't think the Killaine boy thought it was so funny, and he only stayed at the house for a short time. I daresay he was thinking back to the time when the brother was killed, which was when he – uh – got to know Miriam. That's how people should behave when somebody dies, all miserable and gloomy and clinging to each other for support, and nobody was clinging to him, if you get my meaning. Still, it was certainly different,' she added, brightening up again. 'It was the best funeral I've been to in ages.'

Ellen was more concerned with the effect all this

would have had on Mrs Roche. Although she didn't know the woman well, the whole town knew of her circumstances with her bombastic husband. But nobody knew what really went on behind the closed doors of a marriage, and despite everything, the woman was going to miss her husband. At the funeral, and afterwards, she would have been buoyed up by her family and by the numbers of people around her, but inevitably the reality of it all was going to hit her at some time, and then she would remember how perfectly ghastly the whole occasion had been.

'I think she'll do very well,' Doris said cannily. 'Her sisters were saying she should pack up and go back to Dorset and live with them. They were all born there, apparently, but I daresay it's far too soon to make any decision like that.'

So if Miriam's mother went back to Dorset would she go with her?

Sara knew she hadn't said the words aloud, but they were hammering so loudly in her mind that she almost thought she had. She found herself willing it to happen, solving everything...

'Well, this has all been very interesting, but there's work to do and we'd better get on with it,' Ellen said now, just as if she could read everything that was in her daughter's mind right then. 'Sara, your father has to go to the station in half an hour to collect our new visitors. He's still in his workshop, so would you go and remind him, please?'

It was a respite, whether her mother intended it or not. In any case, Sara had heard quite enough about the antics at Vicar Roche's funeral and bunfight, and she gratefully fled outside to her father's workshop where he was busy mending a picture frame.

She watched his deft fingers for a few moments as he carefully glued the edges of the wood together and wiped them clean. If only everything could be so easily fixed, she couldn't help thinking.

'I'm to remind you about collecting the guests from the station,' she said.

'I haven't forgotten,' Frank told her, his mind still on his handiwork. When she still stood there, he glanced up and looked at her properly. 'Your mother's been saying you seem peaky, but right now you look very flushed, Sara. Are you feeling all right?'

She gave an awkward laugh. She hadn't been going to say anything, and he'd hear it all soon enough, but he was waiting for an answer now, and she couldn't resist it.

'Doris has just told us about Vicar Roche's funeral, and how it all ended up more like a pantomime.'

Frank paused, his eyebrows climbing in surprise.

'That's hardly the way I'd describe a funeral!'

It was impossible for Sara to smother that giggle now. It might be irreverent, but she just couldn't help it any longer. Doris's descriptions had been so hilariously visual, and she repeated them to her father with her voice rising to near-hysteria by the end of it, and Frank's mouth was twitching, despite himself.

'Well, if that's not the funniest thing I've heard

yet. I doubt that most of the family thought so, though, and when the shock has settled, I daresay they'll be really upset by it all. Vicar Roche was such a serious and solemn man.'

He was trying to be serious and solemn too, but the images were too much for him, and he let out a huge guffaw that had Sara laughing out loud, and made her remind him again of his errand.

'You're right, and I'd better leave all this for now and get off to the railway station,' he said finally. 'Visitors expect a cheerful and welcoming face, but I'm not sure how they'd react if they knew the reason why!'

She left him to it, thinking how wonderful it was for them to be sharing laughter again, the way it always used to be. Even though the laughter was at poor Vicar Roche's expense, he wasn't aware of it, and nobody in their right minds could really think of him as anything but a pompous jackass, so what did it matter! Some might even say he got what he deserved for delivering such dire and gloomy sermons that bored everybody silly. At least he had finally done something to cheer everybody up!

She was humming as she went back into the house, realising how long it was since she had done such a thing. She was happy, she thought cautiously, and it had nothing to do with old Rochey's misfortune. She was happy because she was home where she belonged and she knew that Robbie still loved her, and she knew instinctively, with all her Cornish intuition, that things would somehow come right for them.

Doris was still gossiping with her mother. Sara

wondered if the woman ever stopped. Her day would surely be ruined if there wasn't somebody she could tear to pieces, or add her own juicy bit of scandal to the tale. Sara avoided the kitchen, and was halfway up the stairs to her own room when her attention was caught by Doris's voice. Her hand froze on the banister.

'My guess is that the Killaine boy has had his nose put right out of joint since the cousin's turned up with the rest of the family. Young Miriam's not the best catch in the world, as we know, but it was a fair bet that the two of them would make a go of it. It pains me to say it, Mrs Boskelly, but I don't think your Sara coming back has made a ha'pence of difference there, and I reckon Miriam's playing the same game as Sara did back then. 'Twould be a real bit of bad luck if the Killaine boy got turned down by another little maid who saw something better. People would come all over sorry for him again, just like they did before.'

Her voice trailed off as though she finally realised who she was talking to, and Ellen snapped at her.

'I think I've heard quite enough about that, thank you, Doris, and I'll thank you not to repeat such things, not in my hearing, nor anybody else's.'

Sara had heard quite enough too. She felt shock ripple through her as she fled upstairs to her bedroom and shut the door behind her. She leaned against it for a moment, feeling her heart beat much too fast. Feeling as if she had been running a long, long way, and still hadn't got her breathing under control. But what had she expected? If Miriam had been flaunting herself about with her cousin, there was bound to be gossip. In this town there was always gossip. She tried to remember that it was to hers and Robbie's advantage if Miriam took a fancy to her cousin. It had to be, didn't it?

What she hadn't bargained for was the amount of sympathy and renewed gossip Robbie might have to suffer if the town saw what it wanted to see – that just as Doris had so charmingly put it, he was turned down by another little maid who had seen something better. Robbie was a proud man, and Sara knew he still loved her as much as she loved him, but could he face the fact that the town would think him weak enough to finally settle for the first girl who had left him for somebody else, if the second one did the same?

She shook herself angrily, knowing she was letting her imagination run away with her. Nothing of the sort had happened yet, and maybe it never would. Maybe Miriam and her cousin were simply old friends, and not as the Americans called it 'kissing cousins'. All the same, she thought desperately, that was exactly what she was hoping the two of them would become. What she wanted more than anything, was that Miriam's mother would decide to leave Cornwall for good, go back to Dorset to live with her family, and that Miriam would go with her.

The old saying, 'Be careful what you wish for', came into her mind then, but there was no need to be careful about this! It was her dearest wish. She didn't wish Miriam any harm ... she just wished she would go away.

A tap on her door made her jump and she moved away quickly and opened it. Ellen stood there, an anxious look on her face.

'I don't know if you heard all that Doris was saying just now, Sara, but if you did, you're to take no notice of it. I've given her a stern talking-to.'

'I heard a bit of it,' Sara muttered, 'and it's Robbie I'm sorry for. If he hears any more gossip I'm not sure how he'll take it.'

'The same as you, if he's got any sense. But I'm sure the Roche girl is only being pleasant to a family member. When their visitors have left and she and her mother are on their own again, it'll all be forgotten. Put it all out of your mind, Sara, and don't forget I suggested you should see the doctor about getting a tonic. You still don't look yourself.'

'I'm just fine, Mum, and I'm not going to bother the doctor, so please don't fuss. Look, now that Doris's here, if you don't need me any more I'd like to go out for a while.'

'All right, darling. She's quite happy to stay and earn a bit extra, so take the rest of the day off.' Ellen reached out and patted her daughter's arm. 'It will all come out right in the end, you know. Things have a habit of sorting themselves out.'

Well, not by Miriam and her mother staying put, Sara thought grimly. But nobody knew that Sara and Robbie were sweethearts again – not only sweethearts but secret lovers too. Just thinking of the word and all it meant sent a sharp thrill through her veins. He was her lover ... he was hers, in a way that Miriam Roche had never been, and could never be. They had been intimate, as old Leah would have put it, in a hushed and mysterious voice, as if the very act of making love was something mystical. And so it was, thought Sara, as she left the guesthouse and cycled in the direction of the harbour in the still balmy November sunshine. If such intimacy could produce new life, then of course it was something mystical. It was something that would hopefully happen between herself and Robbie, when the time was right. A child of their own would be proof for all to see that their love was strong, and that they were meant to be together as they had always been.

But dreaming of such a blissful future wouldn't change anything that was happening now, and nor was it wise to dream when there were still the Saturday afternoon crowds milling about. She concentrated on the road as she narrowly avoided two small boys carrying fishing nets and jam jars of minnows.

Robbie's pictures were propped up outside his shop as usual, and their glorious colours were attracting a few late holiday-makers. Sara dearly wanted to go inside and talk to him, but these were his business hours, and what they had to discuss couldn't be said casually with people listening. In any case she could leave it until later, now that her mother had given her the rest of the day to herself.

She cycled out of the town towards the open moors and farmland. Without being conscious of it, she was imagining Miriam's reaction if her mother did decide to leave Cornwall. Remembering Miriam from their schooldays, she had never thought her a particularly sensitive person. Skin like a rhinoceros was how she had often been described by her fellow pupils. Sara couldn't imagine her having the same gut-wrenching feelings at leaving Cornwall that she herself had experienced when she had first set foot on the ship for America.

People assumed it had been so easy to leave everything that she truly loved because of her passion for Chesney Willand. But it hadn't been easy. It had been the most difficult thing in the world to turn her back on her home and her parents, and on Robbie. The memories of home had never been more acute than when the ship had taken her ever farther away from them. The beautiful bays of St Ives; the spectacular coastlines with waves foaming and crashing against the cliffs; the gaunt sentinels of the old tin mine chimneys on the moors; the clear light of the town that was such a magnet for artists and potters and craftsmen of all descriptions. The colourful fishing-boats bobbing in the harbour were a mark of home too, and so different from the crowded ship she had been on, along with all those other eager, hopeful and excited GI brides and girlfriends. She had been swept along with their excitement, only to find that everything had gone so stunningly wrong when she discovered Chesney's lies.

She felt a small sob in her throat now. She had wanted to put him out of her life for ever, and then he had turned up here with the group of returning Americans. She didn't know what he expected of her, but she had felt nothing but contempt for him then, and even that had seemed wrong. If the love she thought she had for him had been so powerful, so overwhelming that she could cross an ocean to be with him, how shallow did it really make her if she had finally felt nothing for him?

She had been cycling furiously with her head down until she realised she had reached Pennywell Farm. If Hilly wasn't at home, she thought desperately, she didn't know what she was going to do. She had to talk to somebody, and if it couldn't be Robbie, then Hilly was the one to whom she could always unburden her heart.

'My goodness, Sara, you'll do yourself and my chicks an injury, tearing about like that,' she heard Hilly's mother say in her placidly comfortable voice as she slewed to a stop in the farmyard. The chickens that Mrs Weeks was feeding scattered and squawked as the dust flew, and Sara gave an embarrassed laugh.

'Sorry, Mrs Weeks, I wasn't thinking. Is Hilly about?'

Please let her be here.

'She's doing something over in the fields with her dad, but I daresay she'll be glad enough to come back now that you've turned up.'

'Thanks. I'll leave my bike here then and go and find her.'

She didn't stop to discuss whether or not Mrs Weeks would prefer that Hilly went on working. Whatever Hilly's father needed her to do, there were times when a friend's need was the greater, she thought keenly, and this was one of those times.

Hilly looked up from her task with a sigh of relief as she saw Sara striding across the fields towards her. She was glad to finish. Farming could be back-aching work, and she had to be refreshed for the flicks with Dave tonight. She frowned a little, because much as she had liked Dave at first, he was getting to be a bit of a pest lately. A bit of an octopus ... all hands where she didn't want his hands to be, and she was getting fed up with fending him off. Besides, she missed going to the flicks with Sara, and she gave her an extra big smile when the two finally caught up.

'What's up?' she said cheerfully. 'I don't usually see you out here on a Saturday afternoon, but I'm glad you came. You're such a woman of the world, so you can tell me what to do about Dave!'

She hadn't meant it as anything more than a teasing remark, but to her absolute horror, Sara simply looked at her and burst into tears.

'Cripes, Sara, what have I said? You know I didn't mean anything by it. I just meant that, well, you've had two chaps, and I'm still getting used to having one around, and I'm not too sure I'm as keen on him as I thought I was, that's all.'

'Well, if you want to know if there's a painless way of getting rid of him, you've come to the wrong place, haven't you?' Sara found herself lashing out. 'I do things the cruel way, remember? I just leave a note and disappear!'

The tears grew noisier and she couldn't seem to stop them. Maybe her mother was right after all, she thought desperately. Maybe she did need to see a doctor – a head doctor – or a heart one. She felt Hilly's arms go around her, holding her tight.

'Forget I said anything about Dave and tell me what's wrong. Something's definitely up, so you'd better come out with it before you explode.'

'I don't know how to start,' Sara sobbed. 'It's all so crazy, really, and it all began with Vicar Roche's funeral.'

Hilly released her and grinned. 'I've heard of some crazy reasons to start a person crying, but that's not one of them. What in heaven's name does Vicar Roche's funeral have to do with the state you're in? You didn't go to it, did you? I know you can get over-emotional about stuff, but not over that old goat, surely!'

Sara snapped back. 'No, I didn't go to it, and I didn't give a fig about him, but I never expected his death to put a sort of question mark over things, either.'

Hilly sighed. She sat down on the bone-dry grass, and folded her arms.

'I'm not moving from this spot until you tell me why you've come. If you're just going to go round and round in circles I'm not even going to listen.'

'Have you ever been to a funeral?'

'For crying out loud, Sara!'

Sara sat down heavily beside her. 'Sorry, but it does have a relevance, honestly. If it hadn't been for Doris coming to the guesthouse today and telling us all about it, I'd never have thought about the significance of it all.'

Hilly compressed her lips, folding her arms

even tighter as she waited, and then it all came tumbling out. The more Sara told it, the more ludicrous it became, until in the end the two of them were rolling about on the grass.

'It's just what he deserved,' Hilly croaked, when she could finally speak. 'I know it's wrong to speak ill of the dead, but he bored everybody so much when he was alive, it serves him right to give us something to laugh about now he's six feet under. Or one foot one way, and five feet the other way, depending on how you look at it,' she added, going off into shrieks of laughter again.

'We really shouldn't laugh,' Sara gasped. 'And anyway, that's not the only thing I came to tell you. It's what happened afterwards. What Doris said, really.'

'What about?' Hilly said, sitting up.

'About the possibility of Miriam and her mother going to live in Dorset with their family for one thing, and about Miriam spending so much time with that boy cousin called Zach and shutting Robbie out.'

'Well, what's wrong with that? I thought you'd be celebrating if it happens! It'll leave the way clear for you and Robbie, and that is what you want, I suppose.'

She suddenly grasped the fact that Sara was looking more downcast than she should have been about the thought of Miriam going away, and she grabbed Sara's arm and gripped it hard, her eyes flashing angrily.

'You're not telling me that after all you've put him through, you've changed your mind about him again, are you? You're not still hankering after that Yank now that you've seen him again, are you, Sara? You couldn't be that cruel to Robbie.'

Sara shook her off. 'For heaven's sake, of course I'm not still hankering after Chesney. That was all over long ago, and I never want to see him again. And of course I still love Robbie. I never stopped loving him.'

'Just enough to make you leave him with a note and go chasing somebody more glamorous,' Hilly put in, unable to resist the barb.

Sara scrambled to her feet. 'If you're not going to listen to what I'm saying, I might as well not have come. I thought you were my friend.'

Hilly jumped up too. 'I am your friend. I just don't know where all this is leading, that's all. And what does dopey Doris have to do with it?'

Sara's shoulders slumped. 'I overheard her talking to Mum. She implied that it would be like a slap in the face for Robbie to have two girls walking out on him, and even more so to take the first one back. That's me, in case you didn't know! If she can think like that, what will the rest of the town think?'

'Isn't it more important to worry about what Robbie will think?'

'Well, of course it is, and that's what I meant. But Robbie would have to face more gossip, just as he did the first time, and I don't know if he could stand it. Not everybody will see us as Romeo and Juliet.'

'God, I hope not. You know what happened to them,' Hilly said dryly.

She linked her arm through Sara's, and hugged

it to her. 'Honestly, love, I think you're making too much of all this. So Doris had a juicy bit of gossip that she couldn't resist passing on, but you can't do anything about it except wait and see what happens. We both know Robbie would be far better off without that dumb-bell anyway. It's obvious you and he are meant to be together, and I don't think a bit of town gossip is going to prevent it.'

By the time she cycled back to St Ives later, Sara thought over all that Hilly had said. She was always the practical one, the one with the common sense, the one who didn't jump into things recklessly the way Sara did. The one who probably hadn't found the love of her life yet with this Dave of hers, and despite what she had said, the one who would cheerfully tell him to get lost if and when she felt the time was right. It may not be the most tactful way of going about things, but at least you always knew where you stood with Hilly.

She slowed down as she reached the harbour and saw that Robbie's shop was empty now. She hesitated, but then propped up her bike and went purposefully inside. The look in his eyes when he saw her made her heart turn over, but this wasn't the time or place for all that she wanted to say.

'I have to talk to you, Robbie,' she said abruptly. 'But I don't want to risk being interrupted. I'd like to come back later this evening if that's all right – unless you've got other plans, of course.'

He might have. He might be seeing Miriam. She only had Doris's word about the involvement with the cousin, and it might all be idle gossip. She felt her heart begin to beat uncomfortably fast. Maybe none of it was true. Maybe there had never been any question of the Roche family asking Miriam and her mother to move to Dorset with them. In any case, they may not want to go. Even if her mother did, why would Miriam, when she had everything she wanted here? A nauseating sense of panic swept over her.

'Are you all right?' she heard Robbie say, as she seemed to sway.

'Yes,' she said faintly. 'I've been over to Pennywell Farm to see Hilly, and it's a long time since I've eaten anything. I just felt a bit dizzy, that's all.'

'Go home and have some food,' he told her. 'I don't have any other plans this evening, so come back whenever it suits you.'

It wasn't particularly welcoming, but it was the best she could hope for. She didn't know what she was going to say to him, anyway. She just knew she had to be with him.

Chapter 18

'You're going out again tonight?' Ellen asked her.

'I hope you don't mind, Mum. I've finished clearing the supper tables, and there's nothing else I have to do without getting in Doris's way, is there?'

Ellen looked at her daughter, knowing she had been fidgeting about all evening. There was something amiss, though she didn't know what it was, and she wisely decided not to ask. If she still thought Sara should see the doctor for a tonic, she knew better than to press that too.

'Well, please don't be too late,' she said instead.

Since Sara didn't really know what she was going to say to Robbie, nor what his mood was going to be, she thought she might well be back quite soon. She needed to talk to him, but how sensitive he was going to be about the present situation with Miriam was something she would have to find out, and she knew she would have to tread carefully.

Saturday evening was quite busy in the town. Unlike the enforced darkness of the war years, there was a necklace of lights along the harbour now, giving a subtle and romantic element to the curving of the shore and the gently nudging fishing-boats and colourful tripping boats. Always loath to end the day by spending time indoors, late holiday-makers took advantage of the long balmy evenings. The locals usually went to the cinema or the dance halls or the waterfront pubs, or just strolled about meeting friends and having a yarn.

Sara propped up her bike in the small side street at the back of Robbie's studio and knocked on the door tentatively. He must have been watching out for her from the flat upstairs because he answered the door almost immediately. Or perhaps he had been watching for any sign of Miriam and her cousin. She wondered just how suspicious and annoyed he had become over their apparent closeness, yet she couldn't find it in her heart to be thrilled about it at that moment. The feeling wouldn't last, of course. She knew herself too well for that, but she also knew how it felt to realise that the person you loved had found somebody else.

How much Robbie had really loved Miriam was something only Robbie knew. He had given her sympathy when her brother died, and he had been a rock for her to lean on. But when had that turned into love? Sara swallowed hard as he opened the studio door and she saw his uncompromising face. This was not the face of a lover, she thought fleetingly.

'Come on up to the flat where we can be more comfortable to talk,' he said abruptly. 'Would you like something to drink?'

She felt her heart sink as she followed him up the stairs. He was so formal, almost as if she was no more than a business acquaintance or a customer come to view his paintings. Although, if she had been a customer, there would have been smiles, and for her right now, there were none.

'A drink would be lovely,' she said, her voice wooden, her hands clammy as she realised there was nothing of her sweetheart about him now. He was edgy, just as she was. How could she possibly ask him what she desperately wanted to know? What was the future going to be for them, if Miriam skipped off to Dorset to live without giving him a second thought? She could hardly be so crass as to blurt it right out, but Doris's careless words about the effect on him if he was left by another girl kept haunting her. Robbie had a strong backbone, but he was a recognised figure in a town that loved a bit of gossip, and the legacy of the war years could still produce plenty of it. He'd had to deal with it once, but could he do it again?

'Lemonade, cider, or tea?' Robbie went on when they reached the flat.

She felt like exploding. 'For heaven's sake, Robbie, don't treat me like this!'

'Like what? You've come to talk and it's polite to offer a visitor a drink, so what's your poison, my lady?' he added, trying to make light of it now that he realised she was becoming upset.

'I'll have cider, then,' she said recklessly, knowing the heady stuff could make her senses swim, and not caring. If it helped to loosen her tongue with all that she had to say, so much the better.

'All right, so will I.' He poured them each a glass of the golden liquid. 'Then we'll sit by the window and watch the world go by like Darby and Joan,' he said with a tight smile.

It was hardly Romeo and Juliet, the way she

and Hilly had referred to them earlier, but maybe it was so that he could still keep an eye on the two people he was most interested in seeing. For the life of her, she couldn't get them out of her head now. She hadn't even seen the cousin, but obviously Robbie had. She took a gulp of her drink and spoke without thinking.

'So I suppose Vicar Roche's funeral was a bit of an ordeal for you?'

She looked down into her glass, wondering why she had said such an idiotic thing. Funerals were an ordeal for those who were most closely involved, and Robbie wasn't really that. He might have expected to be the one to support Miriam if she hadn't had close family of her own, and if the cousin hadn't taken over the role of chief protector. But Sara wasn't supposed to know that yet. She only had Doris's word for it, and the woman was a well-known gossip. What she wasn't sure about, she invented. She may even have elaborated about the events at the graveside, Sara thought indignantly, and it had been all too easy to believe her.

Robbie gave a harsh laugh. 'Don't pretend you haven't heard about the farce in the churchyard, Sara. I imagine it's all around the town already. I'm expecting banners to be waving from every street corner soon, detailing all that went on.'

She looked at him warily. 'Well, I did hear something,' she said cautiously. 'We've got new visitors today, so Doris is at the guesthouse helping out. She was at the funeral and at the house afterwards, but I'm sure you know that. I don't know why some people find it enjoyable to go to other people's funerals, even strangers. There's time enough for that when it's somebody close to you.'

She stopped talking as he glared at her. She could hear the anger in his voice now. 'So you know how Miriam's uncles dropped the old boy in it,' he said crudely. 'The new vicar, poor devil, looked as if he was going to throw a bloody fit when a few of them started laughing. I'm not particularly religious, but there's a time and place for laughter, and that wasn't it.'

'I'm sorry, Robbie.'

'What the hell are you sorry for? It had nothing to do with you, did it?'

'Of course not, but it must have been awful for Miriam and her family.'

She was testing him now, willing him to say something, even hoping they could both smile over it all, because she couldn't come straight out with it and ask who were the worst offenders, even if she damn well knew who they were...

'What else did that old gasbag Doris tell you, as if I didn't know?' he taunted.

Her temper boiled over. 'Well, all right. I can see that you want me to rub it in for some crazy reason of your own. She said that Miriam's cousin was the one who started laughing, and that Miriam joined in. Is that what you want me to say?'

'That's exactly what happened, so why pretend you didn't know?'

'I wasn't aware that I was doing anything of the sort! Why are you getting at me like this? I came to offer my sympathy. I'm not your enemy, Robbie!'

He didn't say anything for a minute, and then he reached out and squeezed her arm for the briefest moment. It was such a small contact, when what she wanted most of all was to be swept into his arms and to be told that he loved her and would love her for ever – but it was clear that he was in no mood for anything romantic.

'You'll never be my enemy, but right now I've got a lot of things on my mind, Sara, and you'll have to accept that.'

It was far too vague an explanation. Her nerves were brittle by now, and she snapped out at him again. 'What things? Like wondering how you'll cope without Miriam if she and her mother go off to Dorset to live? Oh yes, Doris told me the rumours about that as well. Funny, but in my tiny brain I thought it might have solved everything for us, but perhaps I was all wrong about that, just as I was wrong about a lot of things! Such as thinking that you had really forgiven me, and still loved me,' she finished, choking back a sob.

This was all going wrong. She hadn't meant to burst out with it all like that. She had intended to feel her way slowly, but as usual her heart had ruled her head, and the words just kept rushing out.

'I'm not sure what you want me to say, Sara, but whatever happens between us, it'll have to wait. Now is not the time,' he said angrily.

'You're not denying it then! At least give me that!'

He was no longer listening. She saw him lean forward as his attention was caught by a noisy fracas along the harbour. A group of young people had emerged from one of the waterfront pubs and a fight had broken out. It was the unspoken signal for cheering and hollering and egging them on from bystanders, whether they were involved or not. People were gathering, some to enjoy the entertainment and some to try to disperse the troublemakers. The wail of a police siren could be heard somewhere in the distance.

On the fringes of the group were a few people Sara recognised, and she hoped Hilly and Dave weren't going to be around to get caught up in it, although it was too early for the cinema to spill out its clients. But when Robbie gave a barely-smothered oath, it was obvious that he had seen somebody that he knew

Sara stood up behind him, in time to see Miriam waving up at the flat. She was clinging on to a muscly chap with a rugged, arrogant air about him. The instant Sara appeared, Miriam caught sight of her, and her expression changed at once. She looked murderous as she muttered something to her companion, grabbing his arm and pulling him away. The next minute they had left all the harbourside excitement and were storming towards the studio.

'I take it that's the cousin,' Sara said unnecessarily.

'It is,' Robbie said. 'Get ready for the onslaught.'

She felt that she had to say something, and there was only one thing she could think of to say. 'She doesn't exactly look like the grieving daughter, does she?'

Robbie gave a snort of derision. 'Why would she, with that gorilla to goad her along in what he calls cheering her up?'

They soon heard banging on the studio door. Since Sara's arrival it wasn't locked, and it didn't take a minute for Miriam to open it and come raging upstairs to the flat, with her cousin close behind her.

'Well, this is a cosy little set-up, isn't it?' she snapped at once.

'Sara, meet Zach,' Robbie said, oozing with sarcasm.

Zach grinned at Sara, looking her over in a way that was uncomfortably reminiscent of the brasher GIs who had invaded the town during the war.

'So this is the other one, is it?' he said in a drawling voice. 'You've got good taste in women, my man, I'll say that for you.'

'Shut up, Zach,' Miriam snapped again. 'What's she doing here?' she demanded, glaring at Robbie, her eyes not missing the two half-drunk glasses of cider on the table between them.

Robbie sat back and folded his arms. 'I could ask you what he's doing here, since he wasn't invited.'

'And she was, I suppose.'

For all Zach's gorilla-like charm – and Sara couldn't argue with Robbie about his description – she suddenly realised that Robbie was rather enjoying the situation. The anger that had been consuming him earlier seemed to have disappeared, and he looked back at the two people standing over him with a superior smile.

'She was, as a matter of fact.'

Miriam's eyes narrowed. 'And how many times

has she been here without my knowing it? Have you been carrying on with her all the time I'm supposed to be your girl?'

'Don't be stupid, Miriam,' Sara couldn't help lashing out. 'I only came here tonight to talk to Robbie, that's all. We have not been carrying on, as you so charmingly put it.'

Zach looked as if he was hugely enjoying himself as he gave a guttural laugh. 'Oh, come on, Miriam, love. Don't get your knickers in a twist just because your chap likes a bit on the side. It's probably harmless, and I doubt that he's man enough to cope with two bits of stuff anyway. Besides, he can have you all to himself again when I've gone back home.'

Sara caught her breath in a fury. She didn't know which made her madder: the insult to herself, or the insult to Robbie. But the thing that sent her heart really plummeting was his last remark, which seemed to imply that Miriam and her mother weren't going to move to Dorset after all.

Then she had no more time to think about anything, as Robbie seemed to hurl himself away from the window seat, his fist ramming straight into Zach's gut. The other man was much bigger and stronger, but Robbie's fist had caught him completely off guard and winded him. He staggered back and fell to the floor, doubling up in pain and fury.

'You stupid bugger,' he bellowed. 'What did you do that for? We were only larking about.'

Miriam was screaming and kneeling on the floor beside Zach as he tried to scramble up,

brushing her aside irritably. Sara was terrified, wondering what Zach might do next, even though Robbie towered over him now, resolute and in control, his fists still clenched at his sides.

'Nobody asked you to come here with your bloody taunts, so get the hell out of my flat and don't come back.'

'There was no need for that, Robbie,' Miriam screamed, still clutching her cousin. 'If Zach's going, I'm going too.'

'Well, I'm not stopping you,' Robbie said coldly.

Sara felt as if she had been holding her breath all this time, and even more so at his words. Her eyes seemed to clash with Miriam's at that moment, and then the other girl's eyes narrowed. In an instant she had left Zach still sprawled out on the floor and put her arms around Robbie's neck.

'Robbie, he didn't mean anything,' she said in a pleading voice. 'You know how we've all been at sixes and sevens since my dad died. It's been horrible for Mum and me, really it has, and if we seem a bit callous, it's only to take our minds off it all. I can't bear to think of what happened at the churchyard so I try to hide it as best I can, and so does Zach, I'm sure.'

Behind Robbie's head, her eyes met Sara's again. They were swimming with ready tears now. They were no more than crocodile tears, Sara thought furiously, not believing a word of her sob story. But men were always more gullible than women when it came to tears, and Robbie was no exception as Miriam continued to cling to him. Zach got up cautiously, looking at Robbie with a flicker of respect in his eyes now, and he spoke grudgingly.

'Look, mate, perhaps I did speak out of turn, but you must admit it gave our Miriam a nasty shock to see you all cosy up here with your old flame. You couldn't blame her for getting uppity, and what kind of a cousin would I be if I didn't defend her? No hard feelings, eh? Except for the ones in my gut, of course. You pack quite a punch for a painter.'

Robbie ignored the fact that he couldn't see the insult in his words, and tried vainly to remove Miriam's arms from his neck.

'I think we should forget it. And Miriam, this is a small town, so if you think I'm going to ignore Sara in future, then you'll have to think again.'

'All right,' she said, too meekly to be sincere. 'Then we're all right again?'

'We're all right.'

She was still holding on to him, and before he knew what she was going to do, she pressed her lips to his, and then she let him go and twisted around.

'That's just a reminder of where your loyalties lie, then.'

Minutes later they had clattered back down the stairs and out of the studio, and Sara and Robbie were alone. As if by one accord, they kept well away from the window, but whatever Sara had hoped to achieve that night, she knew it had all gone wrong. Miriam's last words had been a warning, a reminder that even if he hadn't made certain promises to her, Robbie had been acknowledged as her young man for a long time now, and he had better remember it.

'I'm sorry,' she said in a low voice.

'What have you got to be sorry for? It's my knuckles that are smarting, not yours,' Robbie said, in an attempt to lighten the atmosphere.

'If I hadn't come here tonight, none of this would have happened, and she's right, isn't she? You do owe her something, Robbie. I doubt that she'd do to you what I did.'

No, Miriam was more of a clinging vine, thought Sara, but she didn't think it the best time to say so. She got up clumsily.

'I think I'd better go, and perhaps we should wait and see what happens before we think of doing anything rash.'

'I hope you're not thinking of leaving town again, just because you think it's the right thing to do,' he said harshly.

She hadn't thought of any such thing. Until now. Until he had put the possibility into her head. But with absolute certainty, she knew that never in this world would she be able to stay in St Ives if Robbie and Miriam became engaged ... and got married ... and had the babies that should be hers ... but Robbie was an honourable man who just might do what he considered the right thing...

She smothered a sob and turned to go back down the stairs, when Robbie caught her arm.

'Wait. I've got something for you. I was going to post it, but on second thoughts it's probably better that I don't. You might think it's a Dear John letter. That's what the Yanks call them, isn't it? Only in this case it would be a Dear Sara, of course.'

She realised he was as agitated as she was by this whole evening. He left her to go into his bedroom and he was gone for a frustrating few minutes. Sara couldn't help wondering how many times Miriam had been here with him, in this cosy room overlooking the harbour. How many times had they sat close together, laughing and joking, and kissing...? She caught her breath between her teeth, trying to push the unwelcome images out of her mind.

She turned to the window again. Miriam and Zach were walking some distance away from the flat now. Zach had his arm around his cousin, leaning down towards her. As she watched, Miriam put her head on his shoulder, and slid her own arm around his back. So much for her so-called undying love for Robbie, Sara thought indignantly. It was so tempting to point it out to Robbie, but by the time he returned, the other two had disappeared. He handed her a large envelope, and when she went to open it, he stopped her.

'No, don't open it now. Open it on Tuesday.'

'Tuesday's my birthday.'

'I know. Open it then and not before.'

She felt her face flush. It was obviously a birthday card. He hadn't forgotten, and she was dying with curiosity to know what he had written on it, and she prayed that it contained the same sweet coded message as always.

'I'd better go now then,' she said hesitantly. 'But Robbie – we are all right, aren't we? No matter what?' Unconsciously she echoed Miriam's own words.

He put his arms around her and held her close against his heart, and she breathed in the dear and familiar mixture of paint and chalk and chemicals and his own personal scent. He planted a brief kiss on her lips.

'No matter what,' he said roughly. 'Now go.'

She cycled home with the birthday card, feeling as though it was practically burning a hole in the basket of her bike. She had picked up a large stone to cover it, afraid that the wind might catch it and blow it away, to be lost for ever in the dancing waves of the harbour. And that would be a tragedy.

As soon as she reached home, she put her bike away and called out goodnight to her parents, saying she was going to have an early night. And once in her bedroom, she didn't waste a minute before she tore open the envelope that Robbie had given her. And then she stared at it in disbelief and laughter.

Inside the large envelope was another one with her name on it, and above it in bold capital letters he had written:

I TOLD YOU TO WAIT UNTIL TUESDAY.

She was still tempted ... oh God, she was tempted ... but reluctantly, still smiling because he knew her so well, she did as she was told, and put it under her pillow. Ten minutes later she knew this was a bad idea. She was too conscious of its presence, and too likely to crease it, so she got out of bed and padded across to her wardrobe. Even if it was out of sight, it was never going to be out of mind, but at least she wouldn't be tempted every moment to tear open the envelope.

At the back of her wardrobe sat an old box of soft toys and mementoes from her childhood. They had once had pride of place on her chest of drawers, but since coming home from America they had been relegated to her wardrobe. She hadn't looked at them since then, and this wasn't a good time to wallow in nostalgia. It wasn't what she had intended doing, anyway. She was just going to thrust Robbie's card to the bottom of the box, beneath the old photos and school reports, the soft toys and other paraphernalia. But as she reached down, her fingers brushed against something soft and furry. She resisted the stupid urge to scream, in case it was something alive, because of course it wouldn't be something alive. It was something precious that had been hers since she was thirteen years old.

In the soft glow from her bedside lamp, Sara pulled out the small teddy bear, staring at it with blurry eyes. And once again she was transported back to that time at the fair in Penzance when Robbie had won it and laughingly handed it to her. All these years later she could still remember that day as if it was yesterday.

'You can't throw darts for toffee,' she had yelled at him, when he had missed the dartboard a few times. 'Can't dance, can't run, can't throw!'

Was it cruel, referring to his lame leg in that way? She had never thought so, and neither did he. It was simply a fact of life that never bothered either of them.

'Yes, I can! I'll win you a teddy bear, and you can name it after me,' he'd yelled back above the noise of the crowd.

'No, I won't. I'll call it Darling, after the people in that book we're reading at school. The one about the crocodile and the boy who never grew up.'

'You mean Peter Pan,*' he had said.*

'So is it all right if I call my teddy bear Darling?' Sara had asked daringly, not knowing why it should be so significant, but important that he agreed.

Oh yes, she remembered. She remembered falling in love at that moment, and being so very sure, with all her thirteen-year-old girl/woman certainty, that he had fallen in love with her too. She hugged the teddy bear to her chest, feeling the warmth of the fur through her thin nightgown. And wishing so hard that it was Robbie she held close to her heart.

She pushed the birthday card into the box before she changed her mind, and got back into bed, still clutching the teddy bear as she turned out her light.

'Good night, Darling,' she whispered.

It wasn't to an inanimate bit of fur that she was saying the words, but for now it would have to do.

At one minute past midnight on the morning of November the 18th, Sara was careful not to risk disturbing her parents sleeping in the next room as she tore open Robbie's envelope.

Then she caught her breath, for this was no ordinary birthday card. It was beautiful and thoughtful and so sweet ... and her eyes prickled so much she could hardly take it in. This was no card that had been bought from a newsagent. This was a card that was very personal.

She remembered instantly how Robbie had painted her on the night of the storm. She had been gazing out to sea, with only her back view superimposed against the wild pewter grey of sea and sky. Her green dress had clung to her; her hair was a dark tangle of sodden strands, but the painting had been vivid and alive and told its own story.

This birthday card was a smaller version of that painting, but the raging storm of the original had been softened and muted. The sea and sky were still grey in order to show the relief of the solitary figure, but they were quieter now, with a hint of blue mixed in with the grey. The girl in the foreground still posed with her back to the shore, and the green dress still clung to her seductively, but the hair was now a glorious coppery sheen, falling to her shoulders. Even though her face wasn't seen, it was obvious to anybody who cared to look, that this girl was loved.

Sara's mouth trembled, knowing exactly why he had done this. It said all the words he couldn't say while the barrier of Miriam Roche was still between them.

She opened the card. There were no effusive words of love inside. There was only Robbie's initial in the centre, and several more small groups of initials at intervals all around the border of the card. Sara found herself laughing and crying at the same time as she traced them all. ILY; J t'A; ILD; TQ; M a'K...

They all meant the same thing – I love you – whether it was in English, French, German, Spanish or Cornish. It was the sweet silly code they had always used on their birthday cards to each other, and it lifted her spirits beyond words to know that Robbie hadn't forgotten.

Chapter 19

Unknown to Sara, Ellen had invited Hilly to have high tea with them on the evening of Sara's birthday. The last of the late season's visitors had finally left, and there were unlikely to be any more until next year.

Sara had had cards and gifts from her parents, from Doris and from her bosses at work, and the cards were displayed in the family sitting room. She had put the one from Robbie inside an old photo frame, so that nobody but herself knew what it said inside. It merely looked like a picture in a picture frame when she showed it to her parents who admired it and thought it very unusual. If they thought anything more about her having a card from Robbie, they kept it to themselves, and once they had seen it, it was placed on Sara's bedside table.

Hilly turned up, flush-faced from the cycle ride from the farm. She found Sara getting changed in her bedroom and ceremoniously handed over a card and package as she sat down heavily on Sara's bed to recover.

'I thought you'd like the sentiments,' she announced as Sara tore open the wrapping paper.

Perry Como's face smiled up at her from the record sleeve. The title of the song was 'Till the End of Time', one of their current favourites.

'It's smashing. Thanks, Hilly,' Sara said, her

breath catching slightly, because whenever the words of the song ran through her head, it was always with Robbie in mind. 'We'll play it up here after dinner.'

Hilly was no longer watching her reaction. Her attention was caught by the picture frame on the bedside table.

'Hey, that's you! Did Robbie do it?' she said, trying not to sound too surprised, and knowing that of course it was his work.

Sara smiled, unable to keep the joy out of her voice. 'Don't get excited. It's not a present, just a specially-made birthday card, and I put it in the frame because I wanted to keep it from getting creased.'

'And to keep other people from seeing what he'd written inside, I bet,' Hilly said shrewdly.

'That too,' Sara said. 'So let's go downstairs and eat. I'm starving.'

She gave one last glance at the picture frame. As an object it had assumed more importance now that it was behind glass, but, however it was packaged, nothing could have made it more precious to her. Robbie had taken the trouble to do this for her, and that meant everything. If she hadn't ruined everything by her foolishness, she might have expected something very different by the time her twenty-third birthday came around.

By now, they might have been engaged, and Robbie would have been sharing this birthday meal with her. But she wasn't going to dwell on such things now. That was foolish. She could just hope that the future wasn't as black as it had once seemed.

The two girls went downstairs to where Ellen was setting the table with a ham salad, followed by apple pie and condensed milk, and a birthday cake for later. Sara put on a bright smile as she asked what Dave was doing tonight.

'Don't know, don't care,' Hilly said breezily. 'I told him it was all over between us, and I can't say he seemed unduly worried. Which was a bit blooming galling, now I come to think of it. I mean, he could have looked a bit upset about it, couldn't he?'

Sara was still laughing at her nonsense when they joined her parents.

'You've got a nerve, haven't you? You didn't want him, but you wanted him to grovel a bit.'

'Something like that,' Hilly grinned.

They shared an agreeable evening with Sara's parents, and even though Sara made tentative noises about helping with the washing-up after the meal was over, Ellen would have none of it.

'I'm sure you don't want to spend any more time with us two old fogies, either,' she said good-naturedly, 'so I won't suggest a game of Scrabble, since I daresay you two girls have got more important things to gossip about.'

They escaped cheerfully, and decamped to Sara's bedroom again. Once there, they kicked off their shoes and Sara put the Perry Como record on her portable gramophone machine. They lay on their backs on Sara's bed, lost in their own thoughts, as Perry's smooth, melodic tones drifted out into the room.

The song echoed Sara's thoughts about Robbie perfectly. Till the end of time was how long she would love him, and it had been the worst mistake of her life to do what she had. How could she ever have thought that what she felt for Chesney was anything more than lust? But she flinched as the ugly word entered her head, because she knew it had been nothing like lust. She had loved him with a young girl's innocence, and in the heady excitement of having a glamorous, sweet-talking GI paying court to her, she had believed he loved her too. It was only later that she had learned how deceitful he had been, and how much he had hurt her and everybody else she knew. But she had been the one to do that, she thought bitterly. She had been the one to hurt those she truly loved.

'What's up?' Hilly said, feeling her flinch beside her. 'You haven't gone off Perry, have you?'

'No, of course not,' Sara said, her eyes damp. 'He's gorgeous. It's just the song. I love it, but it reminds me how stupid I was. You know when.'

Hilly leaned up on one elbow and stared down at Sara.

'Well, we all know that, but you should be over it by now, Sara. You faced up to your Yank when he came back and told him just what you thought of his lies. We all know that what he did was wrong, but for God's sake, you can't go on punishing yourself for ever for being taken in by him.'

'You weren't, though, were you? You never thought much of him.'

'That's because I've always been more cynical than you, Sara.'

She lay down again as the record ended, and Sara got off the bed and wound the handle before she replaced the needle to play it again. She wasn't going to spoil Hilly's present by allowing the words to upset her.

'I can't argue with that,' she said. 'Anyway, what about you? Are you sure poor old Dave wasn't devastated when you threw him over?'

'If he was, he didn't show it.' She gave a sigh. 'No, I don't think I've found my one and only yet, Sara. But you haven't told me how come Robbie sent you that card, so stop holding out on me.'

'He didn't send it. I went to see him on Saturday night. We needed to get a few things straight between us.'

'Crikey. Wasn't he seeing the delightful Miriam on Saturday night?'

Sara shrugged. 'She's still too busy with that cousin of hers. I think there might be something going on there, if you ask me.'

'You mean you hope there is.'

Sara told her all that had happened on Saturday night, including the moment when she had seen Miriam put her head on Zach's shoulder, and the way her arm had gone around his waist.

'Well, there might be something in it,' Hilly said dubiously. 'Or it could just have been done in the hope that Robbie was watching, to make him jealous.'

'Well, thanks for spoiling it,' Sara said crossly.

'I didn't mean to. I'm just being realistic. You've been back a while now, and he hasn't finished with her yet, has he? He must have had plenty of opportunities, so are you sure he's ever going to?'

Sara obviously hadn't wound up the gramophone enough, because it suddenly slowed, and Perry's smooth tones descended into growls before they stopped completely.

'You'd better lift the needle off the record before it scratches it,' Hilly went on matter-of-factly, just as if she hadn't shattered Sara's hopes with those words.

Sara did as she was told, and replaced the record in its sleeve, her hands trembling a little. Even though she hadn't seen anything of Robbie, it had been a good birthday so far...

'I feel like some fresh air. Do you fancy a walk?' she said abruptly.

'Not particularly. It's getting late, but if you want to go out let's cycle down to the town and park our bikes, then I can go on home later.'

There wasn't anything open on a Tuesday night except the pubs, and by now it was definitely looking late in the season. It was only Saturday nights when the place seemed to come alive now. A couple of their guests who had come for a winter break just before Christmas one year, had said it seemed as if Cornwall simply closed for the winter. It wasn't true, but it must seem that way if you came from the bright lights of a city like London. Sara knew she was in danger of becoming morose, and she couldn't seem to shake herself out of it.

'What's wrong with you now?' Hilly said. 'You've hardly said two words since we got here. It's your birthday, remember?'

They had cycled down to the town and parked their bikes along Smeaton's Pier and were gazing out at the darkened water. The sky was overcast so there wasn't even any moonlight to lighten it.

Sara sighed. 'It's what you said before, and I know you're right. Robbie's had every chance of ditching Miriam since I came home, and he hasn't done it, so what's that telling me?'

'It should be telling you he's a decent chap who doesn't want to hurt her feelings, but I'm darned sure he'll do it eventually. I can't imagine him tying himself to her for life, can you?'

'Not unless he loves her.'

She didn't know why she was torturing herself like this, when she knew very well that Robbie loved *her*. It was as though there was some devil inside her, forcing her to bring her fears out into the open every now and then.

'That's plain daft,' Hilly said shortly. 'You know he's mad about you and always has been. He painted that birthday card for you, didn't he? And I bet he said something all lovey-dovey inside it too.'

'You'll never know,' Sara murmured, remembering. 'But people can love more than one person at the same time, can't they?'

'Not enough to marry them, idiot! I can't see Robbie being a bigamist, even if it would have suited the other one to have several wives and girlfriends on the go. For God's sake, cheer up, Sara. Have you had your invitation yet?'

'What invitation?' Her attention had been caught now.

'Well, if you don't know, then you haven't,' Hilly said uneasily. 'I'm sure you'll get it, though, and mine only came today.'

'I don't know what you're talking about, so

you'd better tell me.'

'Our old school is having a reunion for all the pupils of the past five years. They're holding it at the school at the beginning of December, as a sort of pre-Christmas celebration. You're bound to get yours any day.'

'Unless they think I'm too much in disgrace to bother sending me one! I wouldn't want to go to it, anyway!'

'Why ever not? It'll be a laugh to see some of the spotty twerps that some of the boys were – and to remember those who won't be there because of the war, of course,' she added more soberly.

'Like Miriam Roche's brother,' Sara stated.

'Well, yes, him and a few others. Oh, come on, Sara, hold your head up high, and don't let them think you're hiding away!'

'I'll think about it. I've got to get an invitation first.'

By the time they parted company that evening, Sara was feeling really agitated. Some birthday this was turning out to be. Supposing she really had been left off the invitation list because of her bad behaviour? How shaming would that be if her parents got to hear about the school reunion, which they surely would? Her thoughts went around and around. While she desperately wanted to be included, at the same time she didn't want to go; thinking of who would be there – and who wouldn't, because Brian Roche wasn't the only St Ives boy to be killed during the war. Thinking about Robbie.

She was also wishing more than anything that

Leah was still around, so she could ask her opinion and listen to her advice. She could always ask Leah the things she could never ask her mother, which was sad in a way, but probably not so unusual.

She went to bed that night hugging the teddy bear Robbie had won for her. In the small amount of light from her window, she could also make out the shine on the glass photo frame, knowing that inside it was the painting Robbie had done for her, and the coded initials on the inside of the card. She had captured them inside the photo frame for all time, and nobody could take that away from her.

There was no invitation in the post the next morning, and she tried to hide her acute disappointment as she left home to go to work.

But a school reunion wasn't the most important date that was on many people's minds. London would be full of excitement for the imminent wedding of Princess Elizabeth, and even as removed from the capital as they were in the far south-west, there was plenty of gossip over what the princess was going to wear, how many bridesmaids there would be, and how handsome her bridegroom was.

'I suppose it's all you young girls are thinking about now,' Lionel Potter said to her agreeably, when she seemed to be staring at the current piece of pre-wedding news in the newspaper for far too long. 'A royal wedding might seem like a fairy-tale to ordinary mortals like us, but I wouldn't be too envious of them, Sara, living in a goldfish bowl as they do.'

'I'm not envious of them at all,' she said spiritedly, not having thought of any such thing.

No, the thing that was becoming more and more depressing to her now, was the thought that Robbie and Miriam would also have had invitations to the school reunion by now, and would naturally be going to it together. Even if hers eventually arrived – like an afterthought, no doubt – how could she stand seeing Miriam flaunting her relationship with Robbie? It would be far more sensible to stay away. With all her old classmates knowing exactly what had happened, holding her head up high, as Hilly had suggested, would be impossible.

'Whatever it is, it can't be that bad, Sara,' she heard Mr Potter say gently, and she realised her shoulders had drooped. She put on a determined smile.

'It's just a goose walking over my grave. Sorry. I'll cheer up, I promise!'

He patted her arm as he went back upstairs, and she tried hard to concentrate on her work. She didn't want to go to any damn school reunion, anyway, she thought fiercely. She didn't want people staring at her and whispering about her and speculating about her. She didn't want to be ostracised, either ... and that was the thing that was gnawing away at her now. She would obviously refuse to go, but at least she could have been asked!

She tried to put it out of her mind, wishing that Hilly had never said anything about it. But of course, she'd had to do so. She'd expect the two of them to go together, especially since there was no chance of Sara going with Robbie. She hardened her heart towards him. If he'd had enough backbone to tell Miriam what he should have done in the beginning, they wouldn't be in this position now. He should never have let Sara believe there was still a chance for them, and she should never have let him make love to her ... 'letting him have his way', as the stern-faced agony aunts in the magazines advised you never to do.

What they never told you was that it wasn't just letting him have his way. At least not between herself and Robbie. It was not nearly as sordid as the words implied. She had wanted it as much as he did, had gloried in it as much as he had, felt closer to him in those moments than to any other human being ... and she knew he had felt exactly the same. Nothing could take that away.

So why hadn't he told Miriam yet that it was Sara he loved, she thought angrily, becoming more and more resentful of him? He owed it to both of them, and he was just sitting on the fence. No, she damn well wouldn't go to this reunion to have to face the two of them, with Miriam simpering and smirking and clinging on to him like a limpet.

On the day of the royal wedding, the invitation finally came in the post. She knew immediately who it was from. Even after six years, Sara could recognise the headmaster's bold handwriting on the envelope, bringing back an instant sense of school bags and wet daps and chalk and exercise books. Sara stuffed it into her pocket before her mother could ask who it was from, and cycled to work. Of course, it could just be a note to say she had been excluded from the reunion, she thought, still torturing herself ... but she knew it wouldn't be that because she could feel that there was a card inside the envelope.

She stopped pedalling when she was down by the harbour and tore it open, unable to resist seeing it a moment longer. It was just as Hilly had said:

SCHOOL REUNION

In the school hall on Saturday December 6th
Come and remember your schooldays
from 7.30 pm
Soft drinks will be provided, but we invite
parents to supply provisions to make this a
memorable occasion for the pupils.
Please contact Miss Jellison.

Sara found her mouth twitching. It was such typically formal wording, and Sara couldn't imagine their old stiff-necked headmaster allowing dancing or too much frivolity. And Miss Jellison, their soft-voiced domestic science teacher, would be twittering around as usual, and getting in a real state about it all.

She was about to thrust the card back into the envelope when she realised there was a folded piece of paper inside that she hadn't noticed. She drew it out, and her eyes widened as she read the words on the brief note.

'Please do come, Sara. I know things haven't been easy for you recently, but it would be so nice to see you and all my girls again. Affectionately, Marie Jellison.'

Good Lord! Sara felt her face flushing. At one time she had had a schoolgirl crush on the domestic science teacher, even though she'd also felt rather sorry for her. She was such a fusspot, yet so caring about the girls in her classes, and so keen to teach them what she grandly called 'the rudiments of housewifery'. She should have been married with a brood of children of her own instead of teaching a pile of unruly girls.

Sara remembered how she and Hilly had invented some tragic story about her having been disappointed in love. And now she was writing to Sara almost as if they were contemporaries. It was weird, and yet very sweet too. It was offering the hand of friendship when Sara wasn't at all sure that there would be too many of those at this school reunion.

She was still leaning on her bicycle, the card and the note in her hand when she heard Miriam's voice.

'I see you got an invitation then. I don't suppose you'll want to show your face, will you?' she taunted.

'Why wouldn't I? I've as much right to be there as anybody!'

Miriam laughed. 'Oh well, you always did have some nerve, didn't you?'

She certainly didn't seem to be still in mourning for her father, Sara thought fleetingly, and she couldn't resist asking her the question that was uppermost on her mind.

'I heard you might be moving to Dorset. Is that right?'

Miriam's eyes flashed. 'It would suit you if I did, wouldn't it? Anyway, that's between me and my family, not for the likes of you to gossip about.'

'I'll see you at the reunion then,' Sara called out as Miriam swished on her way. She didn't know why she said it, since she hadn't really intended doing any such thing, but if Miriam didn't want her to be there, it gave her every incentive to do just that.

Hilly would thoroughly approve. Even if Sara's return had been a nine-day wonder, which Sara wasn't so sure about, it was still one thing to see some of her old school-friends in the town occasionally, but it was quite another having to see them *en masse*. But it was a bit late to start getting cold feet now, she had made up her mind and that was that.

Besides, what was one little bit of small-town gossip, compared with the important national event that was taking place in London today? It wasn't every day that a princess got married. Sara wondered if she had the same collywobbles as every other girl on her wedding day. It probably wasn't seemly to wonder about the wedding-night, but whether you were a princess or a laundry-maid, it must give you the same kind of jittery, nervous anticipation.

She found it hard to sleep that night. Her mind was a jumble of thoughts and images, imagining how she would feel if it was her own wedding-day tomorrow. Imagining that it would be Robbie waiting for her at the altar in a small local church, instead of the pomp and ceremony that had awaited Princess Elizabeth and her prince in the grandeur of Westminster Abbey. Sara's parents would be no less proud than the king and queen. Her own nerves would surely be a match for those of the princess's and that of her one bridesmaid – Hilly, of course – instead of the retinue of bridesmaids and page-boys the princess was reported to have had. And a fabulous wedding-gown created by Norman Hartnell, no less...

Sara gave a wry smile in the darkness of her bedroom. She didn't envy them all their excesses. She only envied the fact that the princess was marrying the man she loved, while her own future with Robbie seemed as remote as ever.

She tossed restlessly in her bed, suddenly realising that she was sweating profusely. Or would that be glowing, according to all the rules of etiquette the magazines would have you believe that ladies did? 'Horses sweat, gentlemen perspired, ladies glowed'... No, she was definitely sweating. If she had any concept of what a Turkish Bath felt like, she would swear that her bed resembled it now, the bedclothes becoming more sodden by the minute.

Perhaps she had been asleep for a while after all, dreaming enviously of how princes and princesses must live their lives, and the glamorous way in which they were married. But by now, her throat was ragged and sore and her head began to feel as though a dozen saws were trying to get out of it.

The lovely gentle images of herself taking on the role of a princess, and floating down the aisle of a church to where an adoring future husband awaited her were turning into nightmarish flashes of angry blacks and reds and greys with no shape or meaning whatsoever. Her limbs ached, and her whole body felt as if it was on fire.

In a sudden fit of terror about what was happening to her, Sara staggered out of bed and clawed her way along the corridor to her parents' room. It was very late by now and her parents must have been in bed for some time, because the guesthouse was all in darkness. It was an effort even to drag her feet along the few yards until she reached the other bedroom, and she called out hoarsely as she rapped on her parents' door. Even that seemed to take all her remaining strength, and before her mother could reach her she had collapsed on the floor.

Dr Melrose was never too keen on being called out in the middle of the night, and only did it if he felt it was absolutely necessary. Too many anxious mothers fretted over a simple bout of croup in their infants when a soothing cuddle and a dose of boiled sugar water would usually put them right. But Ellen Boskelly wasn't one of those anxious mothers. She was a sensible woman, and she had sounded so frantic on the telephone that he made this call an exception. And she had been right to call him out. Her daughter was definitely poorly, but it was nothing that couldn't be put right.

'It's a simple case of influenza,' he told Ellen, when he finally straightened up from examining

Sara. 'She needs to stay in bed for a few days, maybe a week, and to drink plenty of fluids. Give her lots of warm sponge baths until her temperature goes down, and replace her bedding regularly to make her as comfortable as possible. She can take aspirins to relieve the discomfort, but other than that it will just run its course. She's a strong young woman and she'll soon get over this with the care that I'm sure you will give her, Mrs Boskelly.'

He continued to address Ellen as if Sara didn't exist, and at any other time she might have complained forcefully about being invisible. As it was, the words floated about her as if they were on strings. The doctor might call this a simple case of influenza, but she felt as though she was about to expire, and all she wanted was for everybody to get out of her bedroom where her father had carried her, and to be left alone to get on with the act of dying.

She fully expected to see a white light coming for her from out of the ether, or was it supposed to be out of a long tunnel? And for the angels to start warbling over her head, of course, as they led her to the pearly gates. Leah would be one of them, no matter how fat and hefty she might look, brandishing her angel's harp. The thought was so bizarre that for a moment Sara felt like laughing out loud, and would probably have done so if it hadn't hurt her throat so much.

'Call me again if you're worried, but I don't think there's any need,' came the doctor's parting words as her father escorted him out of the house.

Sara spoke raggedly, trying to summon up the tiniest bit of anger about what was happening. 'How can I have the 'flu, Mum? I hardly ever get a cold!'

'I don't know, love,' Ellen said sympathetically. 'But we can be thankful it's nothing worse, and you're to do exactly as the doctor says. I'll telephone your work tomorrow and let them know, and meanwhile I'll help you to sit up while I fetch some clean sheets, and then I'll make you a warm milky drink to help you sleep.'

Sara thought she would probably never sleep again. She felt so exhausted and yet so on fire, as if every nerve was alive. Through it all, she also felt as though she was acting out some melodrama, and that she had to record every second of it for the main performance. Miss Marie Jellison, her domestic science teacher, had always said she had a touch of the dramatics about her.

Now why should her name have popped into her mind at that moment? There was something she should remember about Miss Marie Jellison, but for the life of her she couldn't think what it was. Something about schooldays, perhaps. Didn't they say that when you were dying, all of your past life flashed in front of your eyes? She felt a brief stab of anger, because there was surely something far more interesting in her past life than domestic science lessons!

It was all too much of a bother to try to sort it out while her head was bursting, and she gave up worrying about anything as she waited for her bedding to be changed. Half an hour later, when she was safely back in bed in clean, dry sheets, sponged down, and having drunk the warm milk and taken an aspirin, she drifted off into an uneasy sleep, and this time it was peopled with imaginary princes and princesses dressed in beautiful clothes and fabulous jewels, and making vows of undying love to one another.

Chapter 20

Three days later, Sara awoke with her head clear and her throat feeling less like a jagged saw. The last days and nights were a blur of people coming and going, of muddled dreams that began and had no ending, of a framed picture beside her bed of a girl who seemed vaguely familiar looking out to sea. Somehow she knew the picture was important, but she couldn't remember why.

She had been aware of her mother continually nursing her, and her father talking softly to her as he had done when she was a child, and sometimes reading to her until she fell asleep. She had been conscious of Doris's frightened face from time to time, and of Hilly turning up and looking down at her with tears in her eyes. If practical Hilly could get so upset, then she thought she must definitely be dying, only nobody had bothered to tell her.

But now she decided that she wasn't going to die after all. She struggled up in bed, realising she was still weaker than she thought, but thankful to look around her bedroom and see that everything was in its rightful place again, and not swimming about as if it was on a raging sea.

As her memory rushed back, she knew instantly that the picture in the photo frame was the one that Robbie had painted, and inside the card were his coded words of love. But she had let

Robbie down so badly.

But since then he and Sara had made love, and she was never going to let him go again, she thought fiercely. Everything rushed back at her so quickly it was like a shock of cold water on her brain. She was still musing over how she could possibly have forgotten it at all when her mother came into her room.

'Thank goodness you look better at last, my love. Let's hope you feel like eating something today to build up your strength.'

To her own horror, Sara burst into tears. It was weak and it was stupid, but she just couldn't help it. When you thought you were dying, and then you knew you weren't, it all took a bit of getting used to. And this wasn't the way to greet her mother's words.

'I'm all right, Mum,' she gasped through her sobs. 'I'm just so glad I'm still here. I know it's daft, but for a time I was almost sure I could see Leah and Aunt Dottie waiting for me on the end of my bed.'

Ellen knew better than to scoff. 'If you did, I'm sure it would have been only to tell you it would be a long time before you were ready to join them yet, darling. Now then, I'll fetch you some breakfast, and I'm sure you'll want to look at the newspapers with all the photos of the royal wedding. We've saved them all for you.'

For a moment Sara couldn't think what she was talking about. But of course, that was the reason for the images of princes and princesses that wouldn't seem to go away through her delirium. The royal wedding. It was all over now, and she had slept through it all. Not that they would have noticed, she thought, with a glimmer of humour. Why would posh London folk care a jot about a girl they didn't know in a remote part of Cornwall?

'I'll look at them later, Mum,' she said weakly. Did she even care? She *had* cared, she remembered. She had thought it so glamorous that Princess Elizabeth was marrying her prince. Yes, she would look at the newspapers later.

It was mid-afternoon before she felt anything like alert enough to do so. Before then, the words had jazzed in front of her eyes and the newspaper photos were too busy and crowded with people. But finally, all her senses seemed to be returning, and she sat up in bed with the newspapers spread out on her lap, and read the enthusiastic and gushing reports of that momentous day that she had lost. She even remembered how Lionel Potter had said it was good for the country to have something positive to celebrate, now that the euphoria after the end of the war was over. Royal families from times past, according to him, could always be relied on to marry off one of their offspring at such times. That was why they always bred so many of them.

Sara had laughed at the time, calling him privately a cynical old goat. But there may be something in it, she admitted. Her boss hadn't been so cynical while she was ill, though, sending her a bunch of flowers and a card to wish her well, and telling her not to worry about work until she was fully fit again.

Hilly turned up as she was still staring at the

newspaper accounts.

'I saw Robbie earlier,' she announced. 'He seemed a bit put out that you hadn't spoken to him after he sent you a birthday card, but he didn't know you'd been ill until I told him. He said he'd come and see you later today.'

The sun suddenly burst out in all its glory. Well, not literally, but it seemed that way to Sara. She wasn't even aware that she'd been holding off thoughts of Robbie until now. He hadn't sent any messages or come to see her ... but now she knew the reason why, and that made all the difference.

'So what do you think of all the pomp and circumstance then?' Hilly went on, not realising how Sara's mind was jumping about like quicksilver now. 'All right for some, isn't it? She did look lovely, though.'

Sara tried to concentrate, seeing Hilly turn the pages of the newspapers now. Yes, the bride had looked beautiful; the bridegroom had looked handsome; and everyone else had looked lovely too. The accounts told of the bride and her father, King George, being driven to Westminster Abbey in the Irish State Coach escorted by the Household Cavalry in their scarlet tunics. The crowd was fifty deep all along the Mall and Whitehall, and many had camped out overnight to be at the front so that they could watch the procession. There were two and a half thousand people in the congregation, and after the honeymoon at Broadlands in Hampshire, the couple were going to live in Clarence House in London.

It was almost too much information for ordinary folk to take in. The names of the places meant nothing to Sara or Hilly, but they seemed to underline how romantic and glittering the whole occasion must have been.

'I'd still be just as happy marrying a chap in a country church,' Hilly commented. 'If I had one, that is.'

'You've not made it up with Dave then?' Sara murmured, forcing herself to remember things that had happened before her illness.

'I'm not going to. I told you that. But how about you and Robbie? Do you think he's done the decent thing yet and told Miriam to get lost?'

'I'm not sure he'd think that was the decent thing. That's the trouble.'

'Well, he wouldn't marry her when he's in love with you, would he?'

Sara moved restlessly in the bed. The weight of the newspapers was suddenly bearing down on her, and as she shifted her legs they slid to the floor. It saved her from answering an impossible question.

'Sorry about that, Hilly. Would you take them back downstairs and give them to Mum when you go?'

'In other words, you've talked for long enough. Don't worry, I can take a hint.' She smiled to take the sting out of her words, and bent to do as she was asked. 'I'll come and see you again, Sara, and you be sure to get well in plenty of time for the school reunion.'

Sara's memory jolted again. So that was why one of her weird dreams had involved Miss Marie Jellison and the domestic science lessons. Miss Marie Jellison had sent her a note, saying she hoped Sara would be at the reunion.

'I'm definitely going to be well in time for that,' she said, with more spirit than she had shown so far.

'That's my girl,' Hilly said with a grin. 'I always knew you would!'

Until now, Sara hadn't given a thought to how she must look. She was grateful for the many times her mother had sponged her down, and she was aware that her hair had been tied back in a ribbon to keep the weight of it away from her sweating body. But Hilly said Robbie was coming to see her, so for the first time, she put her feet to the ground and took some tentative steps, realising how weak she really felt. Her legs looked like pins, she thought with a little shock, even in those few days of inactivity. She tottered across to her dressing-table mirror, sank down on the stool in front of it and stared at the image in front of her in horror.

She was so pale it seemed as if her skin was almost transparent, and when she dragged the ribbon out of her hair it hung about her shoulders in rats' tails. She burst into tears, and was still sitting there, full of abject self-pity, when she heard her mother's voice at her door.

'Good heavens, girl, what are you doing out of bed?'

'I look like a freak,' Sara gulped. 'I look terrible!'

'Don't be so silly. You've had the 'flu, and you haven't eaten anything for days, so how do you expect to look? Anyway, Robbie's here to see you.'

'Oh, send him away!' Sara almost shrieked. 'Don't let him see me like this!'

She wanted to see him, of course she did, but not looking like something out of a horror story. It was too late. As she twisted around to get back into bed, she saw him hovering at her bedroom door, but Ellen spoke to him quickly.

'You heard the lady, Robbie, and she's obviously feeling a little better to make such a fuss. I think you should go downstairs and chat with Sara's father for a while, while Sara and I do a few repair jobs on her appearance.'

There was a smile in her voice now, though, as well as relief. If Sara was feeling so flummoxed at seeing Robbie in her present state, it could only mean that she was on the mend.

A while later, in a fresh nightdress and with her hair brushed as well as it could be, considering the amount of knots in it, Sara was sitting in bed, propped up on two pillows, and her mother was calling down to Robbie that the patient was well enough to receive a visitor. It sounded grand and ridiculous at the same time.

'I'll leave your door open, and I'll be within earshot if you need me,' Ellen said as she ushered Robbie inside.

'Does she think you're going to ravish me in my state of health?' Sara muttered when he sat down on the chair next to her bed.

'Well, I might,' he said with a grin.

'Oh yes? And does she think any man would even want to when I look such a scarecrow?'

'Shut up, you idiot,' Robbie said roughly. 'You look beautiful.'

'Oh, I'm sure I do!'
'You always look beautiful to me.'
'No I don't!'
'And to anyone else with eyes to see. You should know that.'
She was momentarily dumb. The quick-fire exchange of words fizzled out in embarrassment. He had sent her the lovely birthday card with all the sentiments she longed to have from him in their special codes, and now she couldn't think of a thing to say. She should thank him, but the spectre of Miriam Roche was still between them, and she was acutely aware of how vulnerable she must look. How vulnerable she still felt, in every sense.
'Are you all right, Sara?' she heard her mother call out in the silence.
'Yes, of course, Mum,' she called back.
She suppressed a giggle and gathered back her breath. 'What did she think the silence meant, I wonder? Either that you were kissing me, which I don't advise in case I'm still full of germs, or that you've strangled me. What do you think?'
'I think you think too much. Anyway, I've got something to tell you.'
'Thanks so much for my birthday card, Robbie,' she interrupted, in case he was about to say something she desperately didn't want to hear, such as not being able to let Miriam down after all. 'It was lovely. I've framed it, see?'
'I saw.'
'It was far too nice a picture not to have it framed, and Mum and Dad really admired it. And Hilly, of course.'

'For God's sake, Sara, will you listen? I've told her.'

Her mind went a total blank for a few seconds.

'Told her?' she said weakly.

He seized both her hands in his, and came very close to her, regardless of any thought of germs or anything else but that this was the girl he loved and had always loved, and would love until his dying day. His voice was strong now.

'I told Miriam that there was no future for her and me. I told her that it was you that I loved and always would, and that it would be hurting her even more to go on pretending. I was as tactful as it was possible to be, knowing that it was a hellish thing to do to someone, but she deserved to know the truth, and now she does.'

For the second time that day, Sara was struck dumb. This was everything she wanted, but now all she could think about was what Miriam's reaction must have been, and how awful it must have been for her. She wasn't so much of a pig that she couldn't imagine how the other girl must have felt. Her mouth was dry when she finally answered.

'What did she say?' she whispered.

Robbie's grip on her hands loosened, and he gave a strange laugh.

'That was the weirdest thing. I don't really know what I expected, tears or tantrums, scratching my face, cursing me, hitting me, Lord knows. But there wasn't any of that. She didn't say anything at all. She just stood and looked at me. She must have known it was coming, though. She's not stupid.'

'She must have said something,' Sara persisted when he stopped abruptly.

'Oh yes, eventually she said she couldn't bear to go to the school reunion seeing you and me there together, so until that was over, we had to go on pretending.'

'What?' Sara said. 'But that's pointless, isn't it?'

Robbie shrugged, watching her warily now. 'Of course it is, but she said I owed her that much. If I didn't agree, she would make the biggest scene there ever was in front of everybody. She would tell everyone that we'd been practically engaged and then I just threw her over when you came back. But after the reunion, she said she didn't care what happened to you and me. In fact, to put it in her words, she said the two of us could go to hell as far as she was concerned. Nice words, coming from a vicar's daughter!'

Sara's eyes were wide as she listened to him. His voice was getting more bitter by the moment. She had always known what a vicious little cow Miriam could be, but she hadn't bargained on anything like this. She couldn't fathom what Robbie had felt when he heard Miriam's terms, either. She knew he wouldn't want to go on pretending at the reunion that he and Miriam were still close, when they weren't. He'd been trying to do the honourable thing, and he'd want the break to be clean, not to continue with more deceit. She couldn't think of their future for the moment, only what it must have cost him to agree to all of this.

'Oh God, Robbie, I've made such a mess of things, haven't I? It's all my fault, and if I hadn't made such a stupid mistake over Chesney, none of this would have happened.'

Her eyes filled with weak tears. She loved him so, and now he had to go on paying court to Miriam for this one last time, for everyone at the school reunion to see. Miriam was exacting her own style of revenge.

'Don't say such things. We have to forget what happened in the past. I know I've got to go through with this, but when it's over we'll be free to start all over again. You will still be my girl, won't you, Sara?'

For the first time, he sounded hesitant, wondering if what Miriam demanded was all too much for Sara to cope with. He could have refused her terms, but he also knew just how vindictive she could be, and then there would be even more scandal laid at Sara's door, and Miriam would emerge as the innocent victim in it all.

'I've always been your girl,' Sara replied unsteadily, 'and I always will be. Wind up my gramophone and play the record Hilly bought me for my birthday. Just play it, Robbie.'

He didn't follow her logic, but he did as she asked, and Perry Como's smooth, melodious voice drifted out into the room. 'Till the end of time', he sang, and between them no more words were needed.

Robbie could see she was becoming exhausted, both from her illness and her wavering emotions. When the record ended, he kissed her goodbye and said he would come and see her again tomorrow. While she was still incapacitated, there was no reason why they couldn't be together. Just not in public.

Sara lay back on her pillows with her eyes closed for a long while after he had gone, a mixture of emotions running through her. She had to admit that at least it was a result of sorts, and if it was going to be something of an ordeal at the reunion to see Robbie and Miriam laughing and being together, it was no more than she had already anticipated. But now she knew it was all going to be a pretence, and that he really belonged to her, and once that particular evening was over, everyone else would know it too.

All the same, it was Miriam's triumph. She was manipulating Robbie and Sara, and that was what really stuck in her gullet. She knew she had to try to get over this resentment. If Robbie could do it, then so must she. If only she didn't feel so weak and weepy, when she should be feeling so elated...

She didn't know her father had come into her room until she heard him speak sharply. 'Robbie didn't say anything to upset you, did he, my love? If so, it might be a good idea if he doesn't come here again.'

She stared at him mutely, and then the words flooded out incoherently.

'No, he didn't upset me, Daddy! Everything's all right between us, but he was far too nice not to let Miriam Roche down gently. He's already told her it's me he loves, and it's all right, or at least it will be after the school reunion. Please don't ask me any more, but it's all going to be all right, really it is.'

She had to keep on repeating the words to make him see that she was all right about it too... Well, as all right as she was ever going to be.

'If you're sure, then,' Frank said dubiously, not understanding her reference to any school reunion.

Sara remembered at once that she hadn't told her parents about it. The invitation had come on the day of the royal wedding, which seemed like part of another time now, and she had stuffed it in her coat pocket and forgotten it when the attack of influenza had struck her so suddenly.

'There's an invitation in my coat pocket, Dad,' she said. 'Show it to Mum too. I thought I wouldn't go at first, but now I will.'

He found it and read it, and nodded his approval. 'Of course you must go, so you just get plenty of rest so that you're completely well in time. It's always good to have something to look forward to, Sara.'

He kissed her forehead lightly and took the invitation downstairs to show Ellen, and Sara gave a small smile. He would never know the special reason why it was good – and scary – to have this particular something to look forward to, she thought. She was suddenly very tired. This was the first day she had felt anything like lucid, and there had been visitors to talk to, and a lot of things to take in. Right now all she wanted to do was sleep, and there was nothing to stop her.

Halfway between waking and sleeping, she thought again that she could see Leah and Aunt Dottie smiling at her approvingly at the end of her bed. There was nothing in the least spooky or unexpected about it now, and she smiled back at them, calmer in her mind than she had felt in a very long time.

Predictably, Hilly thought Miriam's plan was horrendous and spiteful. She came to see Sara again the next day, by which time Sara was dressed and had come downstairs, if a little shakily. They were sitting in the conservatory, drinking cocoa and eating slices of Ellen's fruit cake, which was intended to build Sara up, as she put it.

'I don't know how he could have agreed to it,' Hilly said angrily.

'Well, how could he have refused and risked Miriam telling everybody we'd been carrying on behind her back ever since I came home?'

'And have you? Been carrying on? You know what I mean.'

Sara's pale face flushed. 'I didn't mean to use those words.'

'No, but have you?'

'Of course not. Not in the way you mean it, anyway.'

'What other way is there to mean it?' Hilly almost squeaked. 'You said you'd done it once, but how many times, Sara? You'll have to tell me now!'

'I don't have to tell you anything, and stop badgering me. You're making my head ache all over again.'

She realised that Hilly's face was almost childishly eager, longing to know how often Sara had done this wonderful and mysterious thing that they were never told about properly in biology class at school. It was always glossed over, with particular reference to rabbits, and the general remark that all mammals 'made connection' and reproduced in the same way. It was enough to get the boys sniggering, and the girls red-faced and longing to know more. It was obvious now that Sara knew far more than Hilly did, and Hilly clearly hadn't been infatuated enough with Dave to have taken the final step.

Sara relented slightly. 'I'm not saying how many times. I told you before that it happened, that's all, not that it's any of your business.'

Hilly's voice was a mixture of impatience and curiosity now. 'You never said much! You never said if it hurt, or if it was wonderful, or embarrassing, or if you had to take your clothes off.'

Sara just managed not to laugh out loud. For a farmer's daughter who knew all about the rudiments of animals mating and giving birth, Hilly was incredibly naive about the business of people making love. And so she should be, Sara thought more soberly. It wasn't a subject to be taken lightly.

'I don't think I should say any more, not even to my best friend,' she said more gently. 'It's something very private that happens between two people. I will say that it's not at all embarrassing when it's with someone you love.'

'Oh, well, I suppose that's all right then,' Hilly said, and Sara knew she was the embarrassed one now. It had been instilled in them since childhood that it was wrong for a girl to give in to a boy before they were married, but she hoped she had somehow managed to put enough dignity into it for Hilly to be satisfied.

'So what are you wearing to the reunion?' she asked, quickly changing the subject before the sweet memories crowded in on her.

'Dunno,' Hilly said. 'Something other than my dungarees, I suppose.'

Sara burst out laughing now. She was feeling better by the minute, and she realised she had unconsciously been doing something Leah had taught her. If you had something nasty ahead of you, then you should project your thoughts beyond it towards something nicer. It was something she always did when she had to visit the dentist. The reunion itself might not turn out to be the most comfortable event, but after that ... after that, she and Robbie would be free of Miriam for ever.

She spoke determinedly now. 'You've got to dress up for the occasion, Hilly, and you need to look more like a young lady than a farm labourer! You may have ditched Dave, but for all you know, the man of your dreams might be there.'

Hilly snorted in a most unladylike way. 'Well, remembering some of the twerps in our old class, pigs might fly.'

'You will dress up, though, won't you? I will if you will. We'll both show the rest of them that we can hold our heads up high, like you're always telling me. Don't forget I'll need your support, Hilly.'

She was rewarded by an embarrassed hug. 'We'll support each other, kid.'

It was something to think about, and to keep her

determined as the days went on and her health improved. It would be the two of them against the rest of the world. She would have to ignore the fact that Miriam would be fawning all over Robbie, because she would know it was all a front. It was only for Miriam's need to save face. It was Miriam's final triumph, but it wouldn't mean a thing, and soon everyone else would know it too.

Robbie came to see her several times more before the day arrived, and if he was nervous or angry about what he had to do, he never revealed it, and they simply didn't discuss it. They spoke of other things, of things they had done in the long-ago, memories of childhood and growing up together, and how good life was going to be in the future. It was as if it was tacitly accepted that there was no longer any need to go over that terrible in-between time, when Sara had done the almost unforgivable and gone chasing her Yank, and he had turned to someone else. There was no need to go over what was now going to be inevitable at the reunion.

Whatever Sara's parents thought about the fact that he was here so often now, but that according to Doris he had still been seen in the town with Miriam and that cousin of hers, they kept it to themselves, knowing that Sara's mood was still fragile. Their daughter had had enough to contend with recently, and they could only hope that Robbie Killaine was as honourable a man as they had always thought him to be, and that he wasn't going to hurt Sara all over again.

Chapter 21

Lionel Potter telephoned the guesthouse to let Sara know that she wasn't to come back to work until she was fully fit. Influenza could be nasty, and it was arranged that she would start again on the Monday after the school reunion. She was relieved at his consideration. She didn't intend to remain a recluse, but she didn't fancy bumping into Miriam while on her way to or from work, knowing what she did about her arrangement with Robbie.

It was an odd little secret the three of them shared now, she thought in annoyance. She didn't even know if she was supposed to know about it, but if Miriam had any sense at all, she must know that Robbie would have told her. It was something far too momentous to keep to himself, especially as Sara was just as personally involved.

She had told him not to come and see her too often before the reunion, or her parents might start to think it was suspicious, since she hadn't told them anything more. How could she? Doris had been so sure to tell them he was still being seen in the town with Miriam, and Sara still couldn't think how anyone could be so devious as to have thought up this stupid plan. The more she thought about it, the more angry and resentful she became, and she knew it was best to keep as far away as possible from any chance of bumping into the other girl in the next week or so.

Hilly thought it was outrageous and made no bones about saying so.

'You haven't told anybody, have you?' Sara said sharply.

'What do you take me for? Of course I haven't told anybody. I don't know how you're going to feel on the night, though, seeing them both together. It will be so humiliating for you.'

'I'll get through it because I'll know it's all for show.'

She hoped she sounded more confident than she felt, because it was still going to be an ordeal, especially with her old classmates watching her and wondering how she was feeling. They all knew how close she and Robbie had once been, and it didn't need much imagination to know that she would feel like something under a microscope. She had already felt like that when she first came home to Cornwall, but it had gradually all died down. She had got through that, and she would get through this.

'Anyway, let me show you the dress I'm going to wear,' she said, determinedly changing the subject. 'I bought it in America, and you haven't seen it before. It's a bit loose in places and I'll have to pull it in at the waist with a belt. I hardly ate a thing for a week while I was ill, and I lost a bit of weight.'

She pulled out the emerald green dress from her wardrobe to show Hilly. She hadn't worn it since coming home, because it had a bit of glitter around the neckline and sleeves, and she'd thought people might consider it was too flash. It was just what she needed to give her confidence at the reunion, though. It was going to be perfect, she thought defiantly, and Robbie always said that with her dramatic colouring she looked wonderful in green.

'Wow!' Hilly said. 'Are you sure St Ives is ready for this?'

'I don't really care. All I know is it will give me confidence.'

'Mum's making me a new dress,' Hilly said, 'it's nice, but it's hardly going to compare with this!'

'We're not in competition, Hilly, and you don't need anything to boost your confidence,' she said, knowing it was true. Even though Hilly never did much with her life, and was perfectly content to live and work on the farm, she had oozed confidence ever since she had known her.

Sara had once felt like that, sure of where her life was going – until Chesney Willand came along and put a spanner in the works. But she couldn't put all the blame on him. She had been the one to spoil things between herself and Robbie, and ever since then she sometimes thought herself a mass of indecisions and confusion. But that was all going to be over soon, and she mentally crossed her fingers as she hung the emerald dress back in the wardrobe.

'We'll be the belles of the ball – except that I'm sure there won't be any dancing. The headmaster's far too stuffy to allow pupils to dance together, even though most of us are adults now! What do you think we're expected to do all evening? Sit and make small talk with schoolteachers, or make fun of all the boring dopes who were in our class?'

'Something like that,' Hilly said with a grin.

The day arrived all too soon. By then, Sara was a bag of nerves. She was almost on the point of changing her mind about going at all, except that if she didn't turn up, Miriam would definitely have won. It was the only thing that kept her going. She wondered how many other pupils she had known would turn up as couples – and how many names would be missing, because of the war. Would they read out all the names of those lost in action, she wondered – and if they did, how upsetting and depressing would that be! But knowing their sombre headmaster, she could almost guarantee it.

Hilly's dad was going to drive her to Sara's house after tea. She would change into her new dress there so that she wouldn't mess it up by cycling all that way from the farm and getting herself into a state before the evening began. Then Frank would drive the two girls into town when they were ready, and they would make their own way back to the guesthouse where Hilly was going to stay the night.

'It's a bit like being royalty, isn't it?' Hilly giggled. 'Being chauffeur-driven all over the place, I mean.'

'If you say so.'

'Oh, for goodness' sake, cheer up, Sara. This is a big night for you.'

'I know, but I can't help the nasty feeling that Miriam's got another little surprise tucked up her sleeve. Think about it logically, Hilly. She's going to swan about tonight with Robbie, making sure everybody knows they're practically engaged or something, and then what happens? Is she going to stage some big dramatic scene in front of everybody to say that it's all off between them? I don't like it. Something stinks about the whole thing.'

'Well, it's a bit late to start analysing it now. The time for that is long gone, and we should start getting ready unless you're going to sit here brooding all night.'

Sara knew she was right. Whatever was going to happen would happen. She gave up worrying and slid the lovely emerald dress over her head, feeling the sensuous folds of the material caress her skin. As caressing as a lover's touch, she found herself thinking, and her heart gave a giant leap, because very soon now, that was exactly what Robbie would be once more. Her lover, for all the world to know. Well, not quite, she thought with a secret smile. Her sweetheart, she amended...

She turned to look at Hilly, and gasped. Hilly was transformed from the usual tomboy farm girl to a curvaceous young lady in a rose pink dress, her dark hair loose about her shoulders.

'Good Lord, Hilly, there's a girl in there after all!'

'Oh, shut up and don't be so daft,' Hilly said, nearly as pink as her dress.

'I mean it. You look lovely. Look at yourself in the mirror if you don't believe me. Dave will know just what he's missing once he gets a good look at you.'

They stood side by side, looking at their reflections in the dressing-table mirror and unconsciously preening themselves. Hilly seemed to have blossomed in minutes, and Sara could only hope that in the beautiful emerald dress she too would appear more confident than she felt, and that the butterflies in her stomach would eventually disappear. This was a far more important evening than anyone else there would know. Except the three people concerned.

'Nobody could hold a candle to you,' Hilly said generously, 'and if Miriam doesn't see it, she must be blind as well as daft.'

'You don't think I've gone too far, do you? I don't want to flaunt myself.'

'Well, you should. What have you got to lose – and what have you got to hide, anyway? You look like a film star, Sara, and you know it.'

'Yes, but I wasn't actually going to say so myself,' she said with mock modesty before they both dissolved into nervous laughter.

'I actually feel a bit awkward about wearing make-up tonight,' she went on, 'even though I'm perfectly entitled to at my age. It's just the thought of the headmaster and Miss Jellison and all the other teachers looking down their noses and disapproving.'

'Yes, but we're their equals now,' Hilly said solemnly. 'We're not the silly little dumb-bells in school any more, but Young Ladies of Fashion!'

This started them giggling helplessly again until they heard Frank calling out to ask if they were ready.

There were banners outside the hall announcing the school reunion, and a lot of people were already arriving. Several teachers were on the door as a welcome committee, and also to take the various offerings of refreshments that parents had provided. Sara handed over her mother's best chocolate sponge cake to a twittering Miss Jellison as she was ushered inside.

'Sara, my dear,' the teacher exclaimed, red-faced and beaming with delight. 'I'm so pleased you came. We must have a little chat later.'

'What the dickens have we got to chat about?' Sara whispered to Hilly as they took their coats to the cloakroom, where a dozen other girls were chattering like magpies as they fixed their hair and touched up their lipstick. They greeted one another like long-lost sisters and complimented one another on their appearance and asked how they were doing, just as if they didn't live in the same town or nearby villages and most of them had known one another since childhood.

It was surreal, Sara thought later. She had once had everything in common with some of these girls, and now there was no point of contact at all. She had done what none of them had done, she realised. She had caused a scandal in the town by running off the way she had, and then invited more whispered speculation by coming back to face the music. There was definitely a certain restraint between her and some of these girls. Maybe even now, some of them wondered what had been behind her sudden disappearance – and what had kept her away for so long before she had decided to come back.

'Head up high, Sara,' Hilly murmured when they had joined the hordes of excited ex-pupils sitting at the small tables crowded into every space in the room. 'He's not here yet, and neither is she.'

Sara didn't need to ask who she meant. She was on tenterhooks, wondering if they would arrive together. It was probably all in her imagination, but she had the feeling that everyone else was watching to see her reaction if they did.

She chatted with Miss Jellison as requested, though for the life of her she couldn't remember a word of what they had said. All the teachers circulated around the room, chatting to the former pupils, asking questions and answering them, and all the time she smiled and kept her head up high, determined not to let a single soul guess how difficult this was for her.

It was strange how most of the boys and girls automatically separated themselves into two groups, even now that they were no longer children. Some of them were linked together. There were a few who had actually got married since leaving school and others who were courting or engaged. One or two had brought their new fiancés with them, even though they weren't strictly ex-pupils, but this had apparently been allowed.

While she was wondering if Robbie was ever going to arrive, or if Miriam was planning a grand entrance with him, Hilly nudged Sara's arm, almost spilling the beaker of lemonade she held in her hand.

'Is that Leslie Pollard?' she hissed. 'He's looking this way. Don't look!'

'How can I answer if I don't look?' Sara said crossly. She looked across the room through the maze of people, and saw the tall, dark-haired young man Hilly was referring to. 'That can't be him. He looks half-decent now, and nothing like the string bean we always called him.'

'It is him. I'm sure of it. And he's coming over,' Hilly squeaked. 'I'm sure he's seen you.'

Sara turned away to talk to someone else, not in the least interested in whether Leslie Pollard had seen her or not. Minutes later, she saw Robbie enter the room and felt her heart stop. He was on his own – but not for long. Almost immediately as he caught her eye and nodded imperceptibly, Miriam was by his side, hugging his arm, and grinning like the Cheshire cat.

She couldn't bear to see them like this, especially knowing it was such a farce. Miriam knew he didn't love her, but she was going to spin out this evening as long as possible for some stupid reason of her own. Sara looked around to see where Hilly had got to, and saw her and the once lanky Leslie Pollard, who had filled out nicely now, sitting together and making very animated conversation indeed. Dave was clearly very definitely out of the picture now, and Sara had never felt quite so alone as she did at that moment.

Miriam deliberately walked over to Sara, her eyes flashing as she took in the glamorous dress Sara wore, while Robbie greeted other friends.

'Dressed up to the nines, I see. You'd better make the most of this evening, because I'm darned sure I'm going to,' she murmured so that only Sara could hear.

'What's that supposed to mean?'

'You'll see.'

She waltzed off to catch hold of Robbie's arm again, chattering far too animatedly for a recently bereaved daughter, and Sara knew she was up to something. She wouldn't trust her one inch, and she prayed that she wasn't going to mortify Robbie tonight. She fought her way through the crowds to join Hilly.

'Leslie's gone to fetch me a drink and something to eat from the buffet table,' Hilly said in a slightly bemused tone. 'He's asked me out to the flicks next Saturday, Sara, and he's so *nice*. What do you think?'

Until now, Sara hadn't been thinking of anything else but the unpredictable way this evening might turn out. Looking at the other girl's sparkling eyes and parted lips now, though, it was obvious what Hilly thought about the invitation. In an instant, even if Hilly didn't yet know it herself, Sara knew that Hilly was in love.

'I think you should say yes,' she replied with a smile.

'So do I,' Hilly said.

Some time later, when most of the guests had eaten and drunk their fill, the headmaster called for quiet, and out of long obedience, the buzz of conversation dutifully died down as he spoke loudly into the microphone.

'On behalf of all the staff and myself, it's my great pleasure to welcome you all to this school reunion,' he began in his usual pompous manner. 'It's a great credit to all of us to see how well our former pupils have turned out, and I know I can say, with a happy heart, that we are proud of you all. We sincerely hope you are all enjoying this opportunity of reacquainting yourselves with old friends. But inevitably, there are some absences among us, due to circumstances far beyond our control, and with your indulgence I should like all of us to listen to the names of those young people who were cut off in their greenstick years and who fell in the service of their country. Then I would ask you all to spend a few moments reflecting on our past friends. I will now read the roll call of those whom we honour.'

'Good Lord, did he have to be quite so pompous about it all!' Sara hissed to Hilly. 'He never could say anything without making a speech of it, could he?'

She realised that Hilly was hardly listening. Hilly was too busy studying the back of Leslie Pollard's neck and the way his dark hair curled into it. She was definitely smitten, thought Sara, and turned back to give the headmaster all her attention. As she did so, she couldn't help noticing out of the corner of her eye, that Miriam was sidling somewhat closer to where the headmaster was standing. She couldn't see Robbie anywhere, and her heart missed an uneasy beat.

But the roll call was being given now, and despite the earlier excitement of the occasion, there were tears and sniffles among a number of the pupils, as the name of a friend or a brother was read out so solemnly. She wasn't callous, but if the headmaster had wanted to dampen the spirit of this evening he could hardly have done it more effectively. And then, when the roll call was over, and the several moments of reflection were done, the headmaster spoke again.

'On a happier note, we should also remember several of our older girls who became GI brides and went to America to start a new life over there. As my deputy head now, Miss Jellison keeps in touch with them, and the girls you will remember as June Rhodes, Molly Grey and Sarah Trewin are all happy and well.'

Sara's breath had caught when she heard the name of Sarah Trewin, thinking for one terrible, heart-clenching instant that it was going to be a reference to herself. How dreadful and humiliating would that have been – but she should have known that Miss Jellison would never be so cruel.

She felt someone briefly squeeze her hand and saw Robbie move slightly away from her. She hadn't even been aware that he was near, and she was starting to feel very light-headed and claustrophobic, as if the room was closing in on her. It must be the remnants of the 'flu, she thought, desperately hoping she wasn't going to disgrace herself and pass out. She realised that Miss Jellison was speaking now, and she forced herself to listen.

'Some of our pupils have gone on to make names for themselves in various fields.' She ignored the slight titter at her choice of word and plunged on. 'Among them is Robbie Killaine, of course, and I understand that he has just been invited to hold an exhibition of his paintings in a large art gallery.'

There was general applause at this, and a gasp from Sara. Robbie had said nothing about this to her, but it would certainly be a huge feather in his cap. This was one very agreeable surprise – and from the glare on Miriam's face, she was pretty sure that she hadn't known about it, either.

Miss Jellison went on speaking. 'We have invited a few of the pupils to tell us what they have been doing in these intervening years, and of their achievements too, and I will now hand the floor over to them.'

Several girls and a couple of boys spoke of what they had been doing. Since none of them was used to a microphone the voices carried a variety of squeaks or booms. Everyone listened politely at first, and then the attention wandered and there was a certain amount of muttering as people preferred to talk among themselves.

'What's she going to do now?' Hilly suddenly hissed in Sara's ear.

Her heart thumped as she saw Miriam take the microphone out of Miss Jellison's hand. Her cousin Zach had also appeared now; presumably he had been waiting until the appropriate time to arrive. Sara had a horrible sinking feeling in her stomach and wished she could find somewhere to run and hide. But that wouldn't be the answer, and nor could she show herself up by pushing through these crowds. In any case, even if she felt like a rabbit caught in the headlights, she knew she was compelled to wait and hear what bombshell Miriam was about to drop.

'You all knew my brother Brian who was killed

during the war,' Miriam began, her voice scratchy, 'so I won't go on about how awful that was for my family, except to say that I probably couldn't have coped with it until my dear friend Robbie Killaine came to my support and got me through those terrible days.'

It felt to Sara now as if she had been holding her breath for ever as everyone glanced Robbie's way, nodding approvingly, but she could see how tight-lipped and unsmiling he was.

'But now my dad's died as well, and it's been very hard for my mum lately. Luckily we have a very caring family, not here but in Dorset, where all our menfolk are builders. My special help has been my cousin Zach here, who has been wonderful to me, and everything a friend in need should be.'

She looked directly at Robbie as she spoke, and Sara couldn't miss the flash of triumph in her eyes now.

'Anyway, Mum and I have decided to move to Dorset to live with our family. It's all been arranged, and we'll be leaving next week so that we can settle in before Christmas. There's no easy way to say this, and I'm sorry to let you down, Robbie, but this means that our friendship has come to an end. It was fun while it lasted, but it was never really going anywhere, and I'm sure you will find other compensations when I'm gone. And since Zach and I are getting on so well, I am probably going to end up as a Dorset builder's wife.'

There were gasps all around at her pointed remarks, and she and the grinning Zach moved closer together, while Miss Jellison grabbed the microphone from Miriam's hand before she could say anything more. Even to the mild-mannered teacher, there was no mistaking the malice in Miriam's voice.

Miss Jellison spoke in tones of desperation, trying to hide her shock at the girl's effrontery.

'Thank you, Miriam, and I'm sure we all wish you well in the future. This brings us to the end of our pupils' announcements, boys and girls. There's still plenty of food and drink on the buffet table, so please come and help yourselves and enjoy the rest of the evening.'

Miriam was suddenly surrounded by ex-pupils who wanted to know all about this brawny cousin whom she was presumably going to marry.

'Sara–' Hilly began, but when she looked around she couldn't see any sign of her friend, and it was Robbie who suddenly appeared beside her.

'I'll find her,' he said roughly. 'This is for us to sort out now.'

Somehow he knew where she would be. Even if the December night was chilly, he knew she would have gone outside. She would need to get her breath back after Miriam's spiteful words in front of everybody, and so did he. She would have needed to get away from those prying eyes. She wouldn't even have stopped to fetch her coat, and his instinct guided him at once to where he saw a flash of green by the harbour wall.

'Sara, darling,' he said softly.

She was standing very still in a pose he

remembered so well. So perfect and so motionless, as if she wasn't going through a torment of emotions inside. She had always had the capacity to keep her feelings to herself when needed, but whatever she was feeling now, he felt it too. Her arms were ramrod stiff at her sides, and after a smothered exclamation he wrapped his own arms tightly around her. It wasn't only to keep out the chill, but to show her that he was a part of her, as she was of him.

She leaned her head back against him, and he could smell the fragrant scent of her hair. He could feel the rapid beat of her heart, matching his so exactly.

'How could she do such a thing?' she said in a choking voice. 'How could she announce before everybody that she thought so little of you? She was supposed to love you, Robbie, but this wasn't love. This was hate and spite. The only thing that surprises me is that she didn't bring me into it! But she didn't need to, did she? If people see us together after this, they'll know, and she's probably spreading that little bit of poison right now, dragging my name through the mud again.'

'If people see us together? Is there any doubt?' he said angrily, ignoring everything else.

He twisted her around in his arms so that they were facing one another, so close that their heartbeats merged into one.

'You know how much I love you, Sara, and how much I've always loved you. And by the way, in case I haven't managed to tell you yet, you look absolutely stunning in that green dress, and no matter what else has happened in the past, you're the only one I want to share the rest of my life with. Nothing else matters. Not the storm in a teacup that she started back there, which will soon be forgotten, nor how famous I might become with my paintings.'

She stared up into his face in the moonlight, realising that he was trying to tease her now. And he would become famous, especially with an exhibition in a large art gallery, she thought with a flash of old Leah's intuition, and she felt an enormous stab of pride and excitement for him.

'So you'd better tell me that you love me too, or I shall probably throw myself off a cliff and you'll never know just how famous I could be,' he went on, still teasing, but with just a touch of anxiety in his voice. Knowing him so well, she could recognise every nuance in his voice and she had to reassure him.

'Of course I love you!' she said all in a rush. 'I love you so much it hurts, and don't you think I want the world to know it too?'

He stopped her with a kiss full of all the passion that had been repressed for so long and, locked in his arms, it was a while before either of them felt able to speak sensibly again.

'We'll have to go back to the reunion,' Sara whispered eventually. 'Hilly's coming home with me for the night, and I can't leave her there on her own.'

Although, with any luck, Hilly wasn't going to be alone for much longer, judging by the adoring looks Leslie Pollard had been giving her. What a night this was turning out to be after all.

Robbie kissed her one more time, and his

shoulders straightened.

'Of course we must go back. We've got nothing to hide any more, and the sooner everybody knows it, the better. This is how it was always meant to be, Sara.'

They walked back towards the hall slowly, still holding one another, their heads and hearts full of wonderful plans that at one time had seemed impossible. They were both reluctant to go inside the hall again, not wanting to break the spell that this evening had finally brought, but nothing really mattered any more save the deliriously happy knowledge that they were together at last, and that this was going to be for always.